THE
ATHEIST

MIKE
ROBINSON

THE ATHEIST

A Muse Harbor Publishing Book
PUBLISHING HISTORY
Muse Harbor Publishing paperback edition published June 2016

Published by Muse Harbor Publishing, LLC
Los Angeles, California
Santa Barbara, California

ISBN 978-1-61264-283-3

Visit Muse Harbor Publishing at
www.museharbor.com

⚸

$\mathcal{Y}$

*H*E HAS LOST SOMETHING—*that is his first thought. A weight has been shed, but he does not know its origin, nor does he feel compelled to move, imagining in his newfound lightness he might be unable to control the length and speed of his movement, much as sliding on ice. His vision is hazy, but within the haze he discovers a sphere of clarity expanding and burning away whatever had blinded him. Does he have eyes? Somehow he recognizes these are not the eyes to which he is accustomed. They are grander. They are telescopic, microscopic, periscopic. They plumb dimensions yet unseen. They are privy to a singular, lighted architecture supporting all things, animating all forms.*

He knows this place. He knows the haunted and sterile white walls, the bustling movement of deft figures masked and gowned, and the constant shifting interplay of life and death. This place, he realizes while moving cautiously down the hallway, this place is still where gods are daily embraced and daily abandoned. He can see their reactions, the waiting people and the visitors, the doctors and the nurses, all their emotive outpouring rippling like water across the liquid tissue of whatever realm he now walks.

He sees his own visage before him, almost a reflection,

except he is burned and gray, almost shriveled. That is me. But it is not. He observes the frantic shadow-party as the doctors work to give him color once more. But he knows color now, color far more vibrant than any produced by the crudeness of rods and cones. Don't fret too much, he thinks to the people around his body, and he sees the ripple of his thought, a creasing wave in space.

Don't work yourselves to death.

The colors are growing brighter, their luminosity an audible thing, a choir of hue and shade. Within his mind— if he can call it a mind—float fragments of the person he is, or was. They pop to the surface now and again to remind him that this is impossible, that if all this truly is, then he must be merely an extension of that lump of ashen flesh lying beneath him. He is still salvageable. Fret, dammit, he thinks. Bring me back.

Bring me back.

A grander sensation, an expansive contentment, a far greater mind, rears up behind his old self like a sun dwarfing one of its planetary kin, revealing a tiny dark mole in contrast to its brilliantly radiant surface. This Other Mind, the one he is just now recognizing, just now sliding into, is a far more powerful entity. He senses that it is enormously generative, creative. Rather than take, it gives. Rather than cower, it commands. Whatever he imagines arises within this new mind—he sees his son, he sees others, including his mother. He sees Johnny. Whether he is summoning them or moving into their presence he does not know. He realizes it makes little difference. That there is no difference. Mind and matter are conjoined. Bodies of life are bodies of water, just as objects of matter are those of mind. They flow endlessly as churning, unrestrained currents.

He takes in the panorama of his own totality, from birth to this moment, if it is indeed a moment. He can see the shadow between every illuminated minute and day and hour and week and month and year. The cosmology of himself. Still more he lightens, his physical self like a garment released from his frame.

The colors throb, all hastening toward some crescendo uncontainable by these walls.

INTERVIEWER: You've been away for quite a while.

ARTHUR MOORE: I have.

INTERVIEWER: Much has happened to you lately, it seems.

MOORE: I certainly can't argue with that.

INTERVIEWER: We're glad to have you with us. And I don't just mean here.

MOORE: Thank you.

INTERVIEWER: Dare we use the term "resurrection"?

MOORE [*smiles*]: You can use any term you'd like.

INTERVIEWER: Is there any particular reason you agreed to be with us today?

MOORE: It's as good a time as any. Well—[*interrupted*]

INTERVIEWER: I'm sorry, I cut you off.

MOORE: I was going to say that now might be a better time than any other.

INTERVIEWER: And why is that…?

ANSWERS

I

"YOU'RE GOING TO GET CRUSHED TONIGHT."
With a fabricated smile the host extended his hand and they
shook. The two men stood alone in the cramped hallway
connecting the fitting rooms and offices.

"Crushed, huh?"

The host tittered with a juvenile expectancy. "You've
gone a little soft in the last few years."

Arthur Moore didn't respond.

"Listen," said the host, palming his gelled-back hair to
ensure its ideal sculpture. "You want folks to pay attention,
you've gotta speak up. Come at me like a maniac, man. I can
take it. Loudest man wins in this ballgame."

"What does that prove?"

"Nothing. But nothing is solved on TV. You ought to
know that by now. We never solve anything here. Ideally we
leave solutions to the viewers."

How's that gone so far?

"See you on the front lines, doctor."

The host turned and left, hands continually mining his
richly packed hair. It took serious effort for Arthur not to
run over and give him a noogie.

The circus of words, he thought, tossing a pill into his
mouth that he swallowed at the drinking fountain.

The media. This cerebral coliseum. There had scarcely been pleasantries, hardly any humanity exchanged, and yet they were here to debate the existence of God? He was going to field questions from a disparate viewpoint about morality and existence from a man whose best advice was to out-bark others?

For a long time Arthur had suspected that he was little more than the butt of a damn joke, and always had been. He found himself increasingly resenting each show, and wondered why he continued to bother. He tried to imagine the end of the day, tried to visualize it the way he used to as a student. At some point each day had to end; not far in the immediate future he sat at home reading with a second glass of wine in his hand, his shoes off and the world beyond reduced to a dark, wild hush. The television off. The radio off. The computer off. Nothing but a playful dance of booze and literature in his brain.

Maybe Jim'll be there, too.

A young man ushered him to his seat on the set. The soundstage flooded with light, blotting out the faces of those maneuvering cameras and microphones into position. So garish and phony, he thought. The weight of his makeup heightened his self-consciousness.

He sat alone facing the lights, the host's chair empty. Arthur lowered his head, deep in thought, until they gave the one-minute countdown to air. A lightness grew in him, tingly, easy. The pill's effects, just in time. He looked up, steeled himself.

The host emerged and briskly passed Arthur, buttoning his suit, maintaining the smile that had grown a tooth or two for the camera.

The host said, "Let's roll, already."

A noise outside.

Arthur muted the image of himself on the television and listened. Like an absurd mime performance the show continued silently, underscored by the rolling news ticker. He rose from his bed and, from the open window, peered down at the U-shaped driveway and what he could see of the porch.

Dusk had settled. The stately colonial homes of the Kingsmill Country Club brooded in tangled shadow. Chickadees put in their final canorous two cents, leaving the nighttime score primarily to the barred owls and the gentle rippling babble of the James River, across which winked the glow of residential lights.

Nothing down there, nothing at least he could see.

Even so, Arthur felt vulnerable in his own house. The feeling was not particularly new, although it had grown stronger in the last decade, alongside his celebrity.

He heard another noise somewhere outside. A kind of fumbling sound, like a trashcan being knocked over.

This time, he thought. *This time they've come, pitchforks and torches and all.*

Just shut up.

He donned a bathrobe over his undershirt and pulled on a pair of pajama pants. He grabbed the baseball bat from its designated corner near the bed and a flashlight from the top drawer and made his way toward the stairs.

Something heavy struck the door. Rattled it. He paused midway down the staircase, his bat raised. Breathing came hard, rasping in his lungs. A kind of emotional emphysema threatened him, a panicky squeeze in his chest. He felt dizzy.

Arthur waited. He heard a quickening patter of footsteps, the flutter of excited voices fading in the dark. He stepped down, flipped on the porch light and opened the door.

Blood. Splashed across his porch, dripping from the railing and pooling across the wood in bright red patches.

His world became a dizzying smear of red and black, of terrible and inconceivable chaos…until he noticed the paint can lying empty, at the end of a paint trail that oozed down the front porch steps.

Arthur tightened his grip on the bat, still breathing hard. He knew enough to expect this shit. After all, in the past several years charred copies of his books had arrived by mail in anonymous brown envelopes. And while attending public events, he'd occasionally been hit with pies or withered fruit by his angry detractors. Someone once even scratched a giant cross in the paint on the hood of his car, and he'd received a couple of death threats that the police had taken seriously enough. He knew these backlashes could come from anywhere, from any group or individual. Arthur had seen esteemed and even learned men regress to their schoolyard selves. Had caught from usually calm and settled housewives certain looks most often reserved for warts and boils. But intimidation was a throbbing weakness, dammit, inspiring his enemies to behave even more provocatively.

Gotta keep the sword in the scabbard. He drew a deep breath and slowly lowered his bat. For a long while Arthur stared at the paint can and the shadowed world beyond. Eventually he wandered back inside and retrieved a couple rags. He knelt down but didn't begin cleaning right away. Instead he lifted his gaze to the crescent moon burning spectral in the sky.

Wendy, I need you.

The sound of an approaching engine pulled him from his reverie. Headlights rolled down West Landing, the only road that passed by his house. The car slowed and Arthur tensed. What now? He picked up his bat again, standing ready until he recognized the vehicle as it pulled into the driveway.

The headlights blinked off and Jim climbed out carrying a duffel bag, wearing the Red Sox cap Arthur had bought for him on his fourteenth birthday. The intervening decade had visibly thinned the fabric, and the bill was as curved as a horseshoe.

"Dad?"

Jim stared quizzically up at Arthur standing in his bathrobe on his paint-drenched porch, until Arthur snorted and shook his head.

Jim smiled wanly. "I'll help you clean."

JIM FETCHED THE HOSE from the side yard while Arthur retrieved old towels from inside the house. They scrubbed and sopped in silence, until a nearby rustling called Arthur's attention to a deer visiting from the woods. It sniffed and sampled the grass along the fringe of the estate. Arthur envied the animal's calmness.

"I came to pick up my books," Jim finally said, as they kneeled in drying paint.

"I take it you haven't read *Unholy Ghost* yet?"

"Not yet no. Saw your interview today though."

"What were you doing home?"

"David's still sick."

"That's not really a reason to stay home."

"Hey," Jim said with a wry smile. "In sickness and in health."

"You aren't married."

Shut up.

Jim continued to rinse his hands and said nothing.

"He's been sick for a while, right?"

"Kind of. He's been out of it for a while. I mean, we haven't even had—"

Arthur held up his hand. "Right, right, I got it." His gaze strayed from Jim's. His pocket vibrated and, thankful for the interruption, he took the call.

"Hello?"

"Art!" Linda said, her voice brimming with untold good news. Linda's greetings were often squeals of excitement, sometimes to the point that Arthur thought them blatantly forced. Depending on his mood, she could elevate or irritate. But her voice lifted him now, so much that he didn't even think to mention the paint-splattered porch.

With a reassuring wave to Jim that he would be only a moment, Arthur meandered into the house.

He'd spent three months on Millionaire-Matches.com before the site delivered to his inbox an email proclaiming, "Potential Dates In Your Area!" with a bob-cut blonde named Linda Renworth popping up first in the smiling photos. She'd looked pleasant—a tad portly, but it added to her cute charm—and upbeat, though not without some sadness haunting her eyes. That appealed to Arthur, who understood that he needed a tinge of melancholy in the women he dated, as long as they could contain it.

The day after he received the email, he and Linda met for coffee. Their romance had proceeded tenuously from there. It seemed like so long ago now—not necessarily in a bad way, just surreal. But maybe that was normal for someone who hadn't played the dating game in quite a while.

"My friend gave me two tickets to a play in Charlottes-ville, on Wednesday night," Linda said. "Wanna go? I know it's a little last minute."

"That should be okay." Arthur tried to mentally conjure next week's calendar, but drew a blank. Surely he had things going on—they just weren't popping up. Perhaps even more distressingly, nearly all of last week also seemed a blur.

"Great," Linda said. "I know nothing about the play. But my friend says Randolph Garter is in it."

"Who's that?"

"Oh, I don't know." Linda chuckled. "I was hoping you did."

Phone call over, Arthur returned to the porch. Jim stood alone on the wet wood, tying off a garbage bag that bulged with paint-soaked towels. A pang of guilt shot through Arthur.

Jim's wry smile flashed. "You're welcome."

IN HIS OLD ROOM, now devoid of almost all traces of his former occupancy, Jim knelt and tugged at the few stray books on the center shelf of a lonely, half-bare bookcase. He picked out his copy of *Faith and the Future*, gazing at the cover photo of his father looking intensely out at the prospective reader, as if daring the reader to enter the realm of its pages. Arthur's arms were folded in the photo. His creased, middle-aged face hinted at an archaic wisdom hidden deep in the green corridors of his eyes. The lips were stern and tight, his remaining ashen hair combed and pressed hard against his scalp. "Still a handsome ol' guy," Jim had reminded his father over the years. Arthur had appreciated the sentiment enough not to inquire why the adjective "ol'" had been tossed in.

"Sorry I didn't take this with me," Jim said, glancing over his shoulder. "I thought I'd gotten all your books."

"Well, I for one was offended you left that behind."

Jim eyed him, unsure if his father was joking. Arthur's humor was rarely given to punch lines, however. His "jokes," if indeed they were jokes, tended to dissolve into self-deprecating sarcasm, at best inspiring a chuckle or a patronizing head shake. Rarely did they spark openhearted laughter.

"Would you like anything?" Arthur asked from the doorway. "A drink? I opened a nice Cabernet not long ago."

Jim shoved a few more books inside his bag and zipped it up. "Dad, I'm driving."

"One glass won't do you in."

"No, thanks." He squeezed hurriedly past his father, ignoring the flash of hopefulness in his eyes.

Arthur's arm tensed, the result of a sudden urge to bar Jim from leaving. He stayed the impulse however, and instead followed Jim downstairs—past the plush study with its walls lined with books, past the wine cellar, through the enormous kitchen and marble foyer—all the way back to the front door.

"One drink?" Arthur offered again.

"I'd better get home," Jim said. "See how David's doing."

Home, Arthur thought. When, he wondered, had home become somewhere other than here in his son's mind? Outside on the porch, small spatters of paint still clung to the railings.

"Tell David to get better," Arthur said, and realized with a wave of relief that he meant it. He waited on the porch while Jim carefully descended the steps, expression shadowed in darkness.

"And say hi to Mom," Arthur added.

"Okay. When I get a chance. Oh, I forgot to tell you— she and Dan are traveling through Greece this month. I think they'll be back in a week or so."

Arthur pursed his lips. "I take it she hasn't tired of the California sun?"

"Given she grew up a Floridian, I doubt it."

Arthur nodded. "We still need to catch an Orioles game before the season ends."

"We haven't been in, what—?"

"Three years. We're long overdue."

Jim grinned. "Sure, I'd like that. Are we still on for the Fourth of July?"

"Absolutely."

Slinging his duffel bag over his shoulder, Jim turned and walked to his car at the end of the night-shrouded driveway. Arthur recalled all the previous times he'd watched his son strolling off just like that, his thumbs tucked beneath the straps of his backpack on his first day of elementary school, then junior high and still later his first day of high school. Arthur raised his hand, about to call out to one of the apparitions in his own mind, but something stopped him.

He waited as the car circled the brick-paved driveway. He cast a meager wave at the diminishing taillights, waiting until Jim had disappeared from sight. Calm now, he surveyed the woods and the nearby dark golf course. No one else was around, at least that he could see.

ARTHUR TURNED and went back inside the house.

In the bedroom he snapped on the television and listened to its incoherent mutter. The tail end of the nightly news, a recitation of humanity's worst impulses. As he readied for bed he heard the anchor mention Benjamin Holden. He stopped. He knew that name. Or at least he thought he did. It was a Ben Holden who not long ago sent him that letter, a single page of rambling madness that angrily described God's justice and mercy—with a promise that Arthur would be among his fallen when the time arrived. Arthur hadn't been sure if the pronoun "his" had referred to God or to Holden, but either way he'd felt the chill of fear when he'd read the letter.

Arthur sat on the bed and watched.

"In a predawn raid by Federal agents at an undisclosed midtown apartment," continued the plastic-eyed anchorman, "Agents found at Holden's apartment maps of past and intended crime scenes, militia paraphernalia and a cache of illegal weaponry and ammunition.

"Holden is suspected of leading a group that calls itself the Judges of God, believed to be responsible for the seven recent random murders between Boston and Philadelphia. Authorities have yet to release the identity of the latest shooting victim, a middle-aged Caucasian male who was killed in Burton Park. The victim's wife, who was with him at the time, was not injured in the attack."

Arthur stared at the TV and wondered about the wife, why the killer's crosshairs might not have found her. Darken the rest of her years, maybe. Stain her mind, perhaps. Recalling the way he'd felt when he'd seen the red paint on his own front porch, he could only imagine her visceral reaction to the spray of her husband's blood across her face. Out, out, damn spot—never out. That kind of thing could poison her dreams, taking aim below the skin at her very soul. It might even abolish her God, assuming she had one.

Arthur stared, more than listened, at the remainder of the report and all those that followed—congressional budget politics, wildfires lashing Southern California, new cancer treatments awaiting FDA approval—but none held the power to draw him out of his own vague sense of dread. He shut off the television, then the light, but for hours his restless mind continued to hum.

Shadows slowly fill the woods, and he knows he ought to return home. But this is magic hour; the late afternoon breezes are soft, warmed by the sunlight. Pollen drifts lazily through the air and the underbrush hisses and whispers with

small, unseen creatures. His childish brain fills with silly
notions of the pine trees behind him making faces at him, the
faces instantly vanishing when he turns. But he doesn't care.
He allows his imagination ultimate freedom, unleashing his
thoughts to bounce and zing and ricochet off every trunk and
every rock and swallow the clouds and mine every crevice.

"Arthur?"

A voice he knows.

"Arthur, up here."

He turns and sees his brother squatting on a thick tree
branch above him, draped in leaves and clad in a camouflage
outfit given to him for his birthday. Johnny holds a BB gun in
his small hands.

"Johnny, what the hell you doing up there?"

Arthur steels himself the moment he utters "hell," hoping
he hasn't said it loud enough to reach his mother's ears.

"What am I doin' up here?" Johnny says. "What the hell
you doin' down there? Can't see crap from down there."

They can curse freely in the woods. Never at home or at
school. In the woods, they have no rules.

"I'm hunting, that's what I'm doin'," says Johnny.

"Mom's not gonna like you bein' up there."

"Well she don't have to know and you don't have to tell
her if you wanna keep your teeth."

John never hunts, Arthur thinks. We never hunt. What's
going on?

"What're you huntin'?" Arthur asks.

Johnny shrugs. "Anything that comes by, I guess."

A pause. Somewhere nearby in the tall green sea, a dove
coos.

"You wanna come up here?" Johnny says with sarcasm, as
though not expecting his brother to brave such heights.

He shakes his head. "Nah."

"Suit yourself."

Arthur stands upon a rock, one placed beneath the tree by Johnny as an initial stepping stone to begin the climb. His brother remains perched above him like some kind of human owl. Suddenly, Johnny's branch crackles, trembles. He flinches, dropping his gun, clutches at the precarious platform. Before either boy can speak, the branch splinters. Arthur watches his brother fall with horrible, cartoonish speed toward him. Arthur does nothing but jump off the rock, which Johnny's head strikes with a ghastly snap and a spatter of blood. Instantly Johnny's young body begins to deteriorate, the innocent skin peeling back and shriveling into the encrusted and tortured kerfs of ancient molds. The eyes grow sunken and black, the mouth fixed in a soundless grimace. Arthur finds his voice and shouts as he runs back through the woods, only to find he has lost the pathway to his house. Around him, the forest remains deathly still, the silence absolute.

Arthur awoke, grasping only fibers of the dream.

Five thirty in the morning. He did not return to sleep.

Arthur had spent his entire life on or near the East Coast, but had never tired of the thunderstorms. From his back porch he could see the rippled gray clouds amassed in the sky, large and looming yet as simple and surreal as charcoal smudges on a canvas. Lightning touched down in the distance, while thunder moved in guttural waves through the forests. Arthur sensed something raw and real about these storms that opened passages deep in the human subconscious. He understood perfectly how Zeus had become the head honcho of Mount Olympus, how lightning had become God's popular method of choice for condemnation. This energy represented something far bigger than anyone could imagine, so close that its presence consumed the human senses.

Nature marking her territory, he thought, coffee in hand, absently watching the clouds gather. In a truly absurd, Faustian urge, he sometimes wished to soar into the sky, to rip out the heart of the storm and discover what it truly was.

He thought again about Benjamin Holden and the Judges of God, and he thought about evil, a word, a notion, an idea that generated much perplexing conflict throughout his speaking, writing and interviewing career. Religious personas claimed that evil more or less indicated the absence of God. Evil, according to Christian theology, had been more prevalent in the world than good ever since man fell from paradise as a result of forsaking God's commands. And without a divine booster seat, the world would inevitably become a smoldering Auschwitz hellscape.

Arthur had debated many religious pundits and philosophers about the nature of evil. Some had been worthy opponents, most of them not. From Arthur's perspective, all elements of a person, all facets of "the human condition," could be traced to an empirical cause—physical or environmental, or a complex entwining of both. There was no "predisposition to sin" antedating the neuroanatomy developed in the womb, no spiritual taint that smelled of half-eaten forbidden fruit. A full grasp and a possible vanquish of "evil" could only be accomplished through sound reasoning, psychological understanding and scientific and cultural progress.

Except no one could predict the patterns of people like Holden. Like bad weather, such people stewed and gathered over time, then struck unpredictably with sheer force and fury. Dreadful as it was to admit, even to himself, there was a certain grotesque poetry in irredeemably evil acts. Evil, that sadistic delight in causing harm for harm's sake, whatever the warped rationalization, was arguably the only primitive or intrinsic behavior exclusive to human beings. Other creatures loved. Other creatures mated or strategized, or grew tired or bored or depressed and frustrated or aggressive and even jealous. But no other creature could so meticulously fashion out of nature's fire such a singular blade of sick intention.

Arthur's mind accelerated. He wondered if perhaps another book had been seeded, one that addressed formally and definitively this "evil" business, until a burst of ripples in the nearby pond distracted him.

The good-sized body of water—indeed, there'd been some playful debate on whether to classify it a lake or a pond—stretched along the second-hole fairway of the golf course, mere yards from Arthur's back porch. In the years he had lived in Kingsmill Estates, the lake-pond had delivered consistent, almost daily entertainment, prompting Arthur to tell his guests it was something of an outdoor television minus the commercials, a claim usually followed by his admittedly silly line, "It's the highest of the high-definition screens." Whether attracting golfers scouring for their lost balls, birds scouring for brunch or a turtle inching along the marshy fringe, the pond was a good place to watch for random and unscheduled theatre. Arthur had once seen a desperate golfer strip his clothes, pluck from his bag a snorkel and a mask and swim buck naked for his ball. The man retrieved one—whether or not the ball was truly his, Arthur could never know.

Again he saw movement in the pond. Coffee cup in hand, Arthur strolled down the back deck steps and approached the body of water. A massive dorsal and caudal fin gently breached the surface. As he trod closer, more fish rose and seemed, briefly, to regard Arthur with eyes both spastic and suspicious. Then the largest of them disappeared below the murk.

Moby, the Big Fish, he thought. Arthur hadn't seen the beast—the length of which he estimated to be four feet—for quite some time, and in that interim he'd been afraid that The Recurring Fisherman had made off with it.

Arthur did not know the man's name, but sometimes he spied The Recurring Fisherman dressed in a gray parka and a nondescript ball cap, standing at the edge of the water with a rod and line. Of course fishing was illegal in the pond, but apparently no one had ever complained or chastised the man. The Fisherman would appear every so often, presumably early in the morning to avoid detection.

Arthur watched as the ripples smoothed into the clean dark surface of the water. Thunder erupted not far away. Arthur felt the first tenuous drops of rain and made his way back inside.

The phone rang. He expected the call would be from his manager but answered anyway, despite his sudden urge to walk outside again and experience the downpour.

"Te-eh-eh-dy," said Jeffrey Howes, elongating the name in a nasal whine. Theodore was his middle name. Jeff knew he hated the nickname, but Arthur had long ago given up asking Jeff to refrain from its use.

"Hey, Jeff," Arthur said.

"Did you get my email? Remember the Williamsburg book fair's the weekend of July twenty-ninth. You're scheduled for a two-hour slot, both days. An hour longer than anyone else booked at that booth."

"I coordinated the time slots, remember?" Arthur said. "It's my group. You had nothing to do with the schedule."

"Simply keeping you on the ball," said Jeff. "Lately you've been rolling a little out of bounds. I'm just doing all I can to ensure you do what you need to do."

What I need to do, Arthur's brain echoed.

"How's your new honey, by the way?" Jeff asked.

Arthur shifted his weight. Odd for Jeff to so abruptly segue to the personal stuff. "Um, she's alright."

"I gonna get to meet her?"

Why, so you can steal her? Jeff had never done such a thing, of course, but he was the type less interested in actually meeting someone's date than sizing her up and using her to practice flirting—all in the name of friendly fun.

"Someday," Arthur said.

"How about a foursome?" Jeff sighed in pleasant reflection. "I mean, like dinner. You have to meet this woman I'm seeing now. It'll be a time."

"I should go, Jeff," Arthur said.

"She's hot. Like smoking hot."

"Jeff?"

"Oh, okay." He sounded almost offended. "I'll see you soon, Teddy."

"My guest this morning is Doctor Arthur Moore," said the radio host. "He is the author of *The Unholy Ghost*, which recently hit store shelves, and *Faith & the Future*, which debuted on the *New York Times* Best Sellers list several years ago. Thank you for coming."

"Thank you for having me."

Arthur suddenly felt boxed in, trapped in this tiny dark studio starlit with hundreds of buttons and switches and dials, the microphone pressed imposingly at his mouth, the host so near that his sweat-filtered cologne filled Arthur's sinuses.

A rapid catalogue of his life in media lit up his mind's eye. As a younger personality, a younger author, Arthur had been giddy with the sporadic, sometimes charitable opportunities for exposure. Each panel, interview, debate, no matter the station or channel, had opened in him a previously unknown sense, thrown light on some unexplored corner of his being. Now however, these experiences had fallen to selfsame drabness. The staleness had also worsened. Similarities in format, procedure and content had compelled Arthur to privately remark that all such outlets were the same beast wearing different masks, whether casual or confrontational, liberal or conservative, whether the promos countenanced "the hard line"—usually in featuring its grim-faced, no-bullshit host—or more genial fluff.

The experience—once so titillating, so adrenal—had lately become a foamy, unremarkable routine.

"So, Doctor Moore," said the host. "Tell us what's new."

"They just came out with a new iPhone, didn't they?" Arthur said into the mic.

The host furrowed his brow, as if processing the comment, then said, "I meant what's new with *you*."

"Ah," Arthur said. "Nothing overly exciting, I'm afraid."

This host, himself an unremarkable personality and intellect, swiveled steadily back and forth in his chair, as if needing to dart at earliest convenience to the bathroom. "Okay, I'm sure you've seen the news lately of the debate over the installment of 'intelligent design' into school curriculums."

"Sure," Arthur said. "Though that's been news since the 1920's."

"Sure, sure. But I noticed you haven't been very outspoken about the subject, as other people of your kind have been in the last few years."

People of my kind, his brain echoed.

"I notice you didn't mention the debate in the last book of yours that came out," the host added.

"Well, this asinine country leaves no shortage of things

to get your blood pressure up, so I suppose I'm just picking my battles as I get older."

The host cleared his throat. His incessant swiveling ceased.

They can deal with it. Fuck them. Let it go. What can they do?

"Though I also believe," he pressed on, "that reason will ultimately prevail. We just have to be patient. It took more than a millennium for the last renaissance to occur, after all."

"Alright," the host said, smirking. "You and I of course have very different ideas of what constitutes a renaissance and how religion plays into that. In your new book, *The Unholy Ghost*, you talk about how religion is, quote, 'eroding our capacity for primal wonder, one of the very early building blocks of the modern human.'"

Arthur nodded.

"Can you elaborate more on this idea?"

Arthur had elaborated on this idea many times. Too many times. The argument had been branded into his brain. Repeating it now, listening to his own voice, he realized the words carried none of their initial passion. And if his words carried little passion, what effect could they have on somebody listening to a car radio or sitting in a cubicle fifty miles away? Of all people he thought of C.S. Lewis, who'd remarked that nothing drained the life from a belief more than constantly defending or speaking on it.

Arthur shifted in his seat. "I believe religion has facilitated the death of spirituality in this country. And I of course use the term *spirituality*, you know, very loosely."

"How do you mean spirituality in this case? And how has religion destroyed it?"

"In this case I use spirituality as an umbrella term for awe, appreciation and wonder at the universe. Theological doctrines generally don't take into account the vastness of the cosmos and our smallness within it. As Thomas Paine and others have consistently pointed out, such doctrines are very Earth-centric. In this sense, religion has restricted people's spiritual beliefs to a rather myopic perspective, a micro-verse that involves Earth, us, God and maybe the stars as an afterthought," Arthur smiled, and continued, "put up there to look nice, perhaps, like Christmas decorations. Religion stunts our appreciation for the preciousness of life and slows the process of discovering our true place in the universe. Though whether such a thing is even discoverable is of course up for debate."

"So what you're saying is—?"

"What I'm saying is, in addition to being divisive, religion renders us intellectually and emotionally lazy. It hands us the big questions on a silver platter, already cooked and neat so we don't have to wonder or think too much, so we have room in our heads to wonder instead who's dating who in Hollywood and what kinds of accessories one might want in the next cell phone upgrade. There is a strange dichotomy occurring in America. We're becoming more religious at the same time we're becoming more materialistic. Shouldn't these two impulses contradict one another? Didn't Jesus himself tell us that we can't serve both God and money?

"The tragedy is that, for many, the riddle of God has been solved, reduced to a weekly chore that gets us up earlier than one might normally like on a Sunday morning. Our focus on divinity is relegated to a few hours a week, maybe another one or two around the holidays. Assuming the journey for answers is over, we're content with the bench, the pew, the confessional, the Bible, the Koran, the Torah—take your pick. Religious folks have their answers, so when they see scientists still *looking* for answers, they feel

threatened, and they willfully ignore whatever new information science may bring back. It's mind-boggling to me."
Arthur shook his head, envisioning a post-show glass of
wine in his hand, at his lips. "Carl Sagan said he found it
far more spiritually gratifying to know we're the offspring
of stars than a failed clay experiment by some belligerent
creator. And I agree."

II

JIM BESIDE HIM, THEY MADE THEIR WAY
through the crowds and up a hill among the patchwork of
family picnic blankets. Muskets popped and snapped. Audible shouts and military commands rose with the gun smoke
that bit the summery air. Far below their vantage point,
arrayed across the green battlefield, tattered Revolutionar-
ies and Redcoats felled one another with great flourish and
fanfare. Drums and flutes echoed across the fringes of Colonial Williamsburg. Hundreds of people watched from the
nearby slopes, their shadows plied beneath the setting sun.

"I think we missed most of it," Jim said. "Looks like
Cornwallis is just about toast."

They found an empty spot and spread their blanket, then
unpacked chips, crackers and cheese, grapes and a bottle of
chardonnay from a canvas bag that Arthur had lugged from
the car.

"Thanks for this." Jim said, pouring them both cups of
wine.

"For what?"

"All this. For coming out."

Arthur took his cup of chardonnay. "Oh, of course.
Thank you." He sipped the wine. "I'm sorry David couldn't

make it."

"Me too."

Two loud canon blasts reverberated across the field. A young boy sitting next to them buried his face in his father's coat. His mother began scolding his older sisters, who were making fun of his fear.

"How's the new piece coming along?" Arthur asked Jim.

"Coming along pretty nicely," Jim said. "I should have something to show you soon. I definitely want to include this piece in my portfolio. I think you'll like it."

"I'm sure I will."

Because I'll smile and nod at everything, Arthur thought bleakly. *What does Mr. Science know about art?* He worried sometimes that Jim viewed him as one of those parents who indiscriminately loved anything his child placed in front of him. In fact Arthur genuinely enjoyed seeing Jim's new canvases, even when he had trouble understanding them.

He watched the smoke-shrouded battlefield below, the soldiers crumbling in artful death. The final reenactment was near its end. Beyond it all the sun bled fire across the horizon, casting a luminescent accent upon the forest.

Arthur noticed that Jim's attention had turned to his cell phone. His thumbs flew over the keypad.

"You just missed the fireworks," Arthur teased.

"Right, right."

"You don't do that while you drive, do you?"

"No, Dad."

"Good." Arthur envisioned near-future gizmos that would tap into and distract every one of a person's five senses, that would shut out reality once and for all, while leaving the mind to submerse itself in a warm bath of endless triviality. He wondered if he was getting old. Or was he simply afraid of technology destroying what little remained of humanity?

Arthur picked at the bread and grapes on their picnic plate, trying to focus on either the battlefield or the surrounding families. Jim's image remained fixed in the corner of his eye, still hunched over that damn phone.

Calm down.

About a half hour after sundown the fireworks began. Magnificent spectacles of showering light and color, their miniature big bangs bellowed their inceptions in thunderous futility at the vast skies.

A strange, emotional tension gripped Arthur. He felt simultaneously heightened and lowered. Half of him grew light and tingling, ready to rise up and drift off toward the sky to join those colorful particles in their dance across the dark. The other half sat heavily rooted to the earth, ensnared in a web of beautiful decay.

He had a vision just then of the falling, crumbling Twin Towers entombing thousands, of the massive smoky blackberries pluming over Manhattan and cloaking the island in its own private enactment of the Book of Revelation. The red, white and blue above him summoned memories of the countless flags that had fluttered across screens and streets. The hues of the patriot.

And like a monolith forming itself out of the heavy clay of his mind rose a single word:

Johnny.

His brother, John Moore, had joined countless others in the fallen twisted sepulcher of the South Tower. For untold weeks dark fantasies had visited Arthur. He'd had notions of beheading the perpetrators himself, of personally disemboweling them. He had almost let slip on-air that the Middle East was due for another Biblical cleansing, one far greater than the flood survived by Noah—mercifully, last-minute conscience had snagged his tongue. Yet he'd been unapologetic in his support for the Afghanistan invasion and even, at the outset, for the war in Iraq, which drew lines between him and his other more liberal peers.

"I reacted out of emotion," Arthur said, years later. "Iraq was a mistake. It was a rich family's score settling we were duped into supporting."

Over the ensuing years, as his political criticisms became ever more heated, and as he increasingly took on God—that ultimate patriot, yes—Arthur had been denounced as "un-American" by several figures on the right. He knew that trend would likely persist as long as he breathed and spoke. But to him there existed an America beyond the buildings and the plains and the people: tipping neither left nor right, it was an ideal of pure freedom. It was speech itself, action itself: all sanctioned by that apolitical, indifferent light. Even a sign as hopelessly crass as "America Sucks" was patriotic in its uninhibited creation and expression. Thus he cared little about what they said about him. His patriotism was for himself and not for them, and it was most poignantly and privately expressed on these kinds of nights, made all the more special because this place, this soil, had borne witness to the tumultuous labor and delivery of the nation now being celebrated.

Linda took two practice swings, then readied herself at the second-hole tee. Head down and determined, she stood transfixed for what seemed a long face-off with that little uncooperative ball. Nothing challenged her focus. Her hazel eyes did not blink; her portly frame steeled itself. Even the breeze dared not tussle her yellow-gray bob cut.

With a resigned sigh she at last began her rickety back-swing. In a metallic flash she struck the ball, slicing it into the woods where, with a snap and a delicate crunch, it rolled to rest.

"Were you attempting some symbiotic *kumbaya* there?" Arthur offered a sympathetic smile as he teed up.

"No," Linda sighed and shook her head. "I like to clear my head before I hit. Concentrate. It doesn't really seem to help though."

Perhaps to compensate for the time Linda had lingered, Arthur launched into his own ball without a practice swing, skimming it across the grass. The ball bounced up the middle of the fairway before veering into the rough.

"Grounder to first," Arthur said. "Classic worm burner."

The afternoon light was already beginning to fade. Much of the gilded sparkle of the course gradually withdrew into the encroaching dusk. Given his home's proximity to the second hole, Arthur considered these the best hours to hit the links, since no foursome would be starting a round so late. He'd never enjoyed played alone—advantageous as it might be to leave no eyewitnesses to one's flubbed shots or fudged scores. Fortunately for Arthur, Linda was an even less accomplished golfer than he was.

"Ah, well," Arthur added with aplomb. "You know the saying. The worst game of golf beats the best day of work."

"That reminds me," Linda said, "How's the new book coming?" They headed down the fairway, each carrying only the four agreed-upon clubs since Linda had none of her own. "Hit your page quota for today?"

Arthur shrugged. The paint-can incident had shaken him more than he cared to admit, though he mentioned nothing of his nagging fears to Linda. He wasn't tired of working—at least he didn't think he was—so much as unwilling. Writing seemed like an endless chore these days, like taking a pickaxe to hard soil and digging out a tunnel clot by clot, with no clear destination. A decade ago this sort of vandalism—such a pathetic attempt at retaliation—

would have had the opposite effect on him. He'd have been galvanized to write page after page.

Musing on the paint-can incident had also, somewhat perversely, piqued his interest in beginning the project on evil that the Judges of God had inspired, and which gratified him with its morbidity. And as any writer knew, the biggest threat to an in-progress book was the sudden, relentless seduction of a new idea.

"I'm slogging through it," Arthur said. "But I've actually got another idea in mind."

As they veered into the darkening woods, he said, "Have you ever heard of the Judges of God?"

"Those psychos with rifles?" Linda said, frowning.

"Yes. They're cultish Christian extremists, or something along those lines. They claim an affinity with Christianity, but they appear to live in their own little bubble of absurd fantasy and paranoia."

"Then they have nothing to do with Christianity," Linda said.

"Not really," Arthur agreed. "But I'm thinking of writing about them. Profiling them against a larger theme of how we approach and consider evil."

"That sounds a little...grim." Linda raised her five iron and chopped away at the gnarled twigs in her path. "Why write something like that?"

"I suppose it's the same voyeuristic fascination that drove Capote to write *In Cold Blood*," Arthur said. "You wouldn't be the least bit curious about knowing what makes these guys tick?"

"No, they're monsters."

Simplification, Arthur thought. *The supreme tool of the faithful.*

Yet he also knew his evaluation wasn't entirely fair. Though a self-professed Christian and a lifelong Presbyterian, Linda was hardly the same ilk as what Arthur termed "the faithful." To him, that word connoted laser-show tent revivals and evangelical megachurches into which thousands crowded, sobbing and reaching skyward for salvation. As Linda had once described it for him, her own faith seemed like a thoughtless routine—a punch-in, punch-out churchgoing obligation—instead of an anchoring value that added real meaning to her life.

"I don't see my ball anywhere," Linda said. "The proverbial needle in a haystack, if you ask me. And it's getting late."

Arthur pointed off to their left. "There it is. Why don't we play one more hole?"

Linda took two arching steps, bent down and brushed aside some dry leaves. Suddenly she cried out. Arthur dropped his clubs and reached for her, intending to break her fall, but she didn't stumble. Instead she waved her hand violently back and forth, as if she'd been burned.

"I think something bit me."

Arthur glanced toward her ball and noticed a startlingly large spider scampering across the nearby twigs.

"Wow, that was a pretty big spider," he said. "I didn't get a good look at it. Did you?"

"No," Linda said curtly, "I was too busy being bitten."

"Let me see."

She presented her hand. An area of skin around the joint between her thumb and forefinger had already plumped up and turned noticeably darker.

"That looks painful," Arthur said. "We should probably get you to the pharmacy."

Linda nodded solemnly.

ARTHUR WASN'T SURE WHY he was driving so fast. Spider bites usually weren't that serious. But Linda's overreaction distressed him. The sooner she felt better, the sooner he'd relax.

He pulled his BMW into the Save-Lots pharmacy on Gramercy Street. Linda bustled out of the car, forcing him to trot to match her pace. He suspected she blamed him for the spider bite, although he wasn't certain why. Simply because he'd suggested they play golf? Or was she irritated by his incessant need to control every situation? Was she angry that he'd insisted they come to the pharmacy? Even at the slightest sign of danger—a snake in the house, say, or a stranger's unseemly gaze from the across the street—Arthur felt an overpowering need to take command of the situation, despite how shallowly primitive that sometimes made him feel.

You're the gruff macho leader.

"Let me see what I can find," Arthur said, pushing past Linda. *I'm doing it again,* he thought, but he couldn't help himself. He confronted a battalion of ointments and balm brands on the endless rows of shelves and realized he didn't have a clue which one to choose. He could feel Linda watching him expectantly, perhaps still assuming he knew what he was doing.

He wasn't aware of anyone else standing behind him until he heard a man's voice speak his name.

"Art? Is that you?"

He turned to his left and saw David, Jim's partner, standing just behind his shoulder. The young man looked thin. David wore his blondish hair cropped short, and his eyes always appeared to be calmly fixed on something off in the distance. He carried a grocery basket that held a sparse assortment of pharmaceutical items. Arthur noticed two large bottles of Ibuprofen in the mix.

"Hey," said Arthur woodenly, acutely aware of David's general gauntness and drained complexion. "How are you?"

"I'm okay. Just coming back from campus. Picking up some things along the way."

David moved to shake Arthur's hand, but Arthur deftly evaded the gesture by patting his shoulder. An awkward pause hung between them. *Can't take that back.* Arthur smiled foolishly. His face tingled; he could sense it reddening.

David's gaze drifted down to his basket.

Belatedly Arthur remembered Linda, who was standing beside him in a blend of confusion and pain. "Sorry. This is Linda. Linda, um, David."

"I've heard Arthur talk about you," David said, offering Linda a polite smile. "I'm glad to finally meet you. I think that—holy crap, what happened to your hand?"

Linda lifted her hand and exposed the red blistering that had risen between her thumb and forefinger.

"Did I mention that David's Pre-Med?" Arthur said.

Linda ignored him. "A spider bit me," she told David. "We're not sure what kind."

David bent closer and examined the wound. "Try an oral antihistamine—here, this one's a generic brand." He plucked a blue and yellow box from the center shelf. "Works just as well, but at half the price of the name brand. As soon as you get home, wash the area thoroughly with hot water and then apply ice. Keep your arm raised for an hour or so. If you're not feeling better in thirty minutes, a trip to urgent care might be in order. I'm sure Mr. Moore will take good care of you."

David glanced at Arthur as if seeking his agreement. Despite his best intentions Arthur looked away once more, this time making a pretense of checking his watch.

"Well, hey, I gotta run," David said. "Nice seeing you again, Art. A pleasure meeting you, Linda."

"You too, David. Thanks a bunch."

Arthur watched him walk away in a muddled silence.

Back in the car, holding her hand up high as David had instructed, Linda asked, "So David and Jim are room-mates?"

Arthur hesitated. "They are, yes."

"Or do they live together?"

"What do you mean?"

"You know…do they live together?"

"Sounds the same to me."

He could feel Linda studying him, sensed the tickling weight of her gaze.

Don't look. Don't look and she'll drop it.

Linda shrugged and turned her gaze to the passenger window. Relieved, Arthur turned left on Sutter Street.

"Well good for them," he thought he heard her mutter.

Steaming coffee mug in hand, Arthur slid open the door to the back porch and stepped outside. No golfers visible. The pond looked calm, its surface undisturbed. Soft winds carried a pine scent and distant clouds frosted the wooded horizon. The sun glared from what felt like only a few hundred yards above.

As he was about to shut the sliding door behind him, the phone rang. Arthur winced. He turned, headed back inside and picked up on the fifth ring.

"Teeeh-eh-eh-dy, my man," said Jeff. "It's me. Got a pen? I'm about to rattle off an important date or two."

"Oh?"

"Indeed. *Mann's Watch* in Los Angeles. They'd like you for the August 30th panel."

"Really?" Arthur's gut twittered. At some level he still hadn't gotten used to the prospect of public exposure.

Whether an interview, lecture, debate, even a goddamn reading, any new engagement temporarily reunited him with his wary novice self.

"No, April Fool's," said Jeff. He paused. "Of *course* really. You'll be joining a CNN Washington correspondent, a *New York Times* journalist and actress Mandy Johnson. It's a roundtable discussion on a variety of topics. The Harvard guy is a bit of a rightwing stick-in-the-mud, but he's not done a lot of TV. If he gives you shit, remind him of that affair he had a few years back with the grad student."

"Uh, okay."

"*Mann's Watch* has a 57 percent left-leaning demographic. You're sitting pretty."

Over the phone, Arthur could hear Jeff's exhalation of smoke. *Cigar or cigarette?* he wondered. They served as Jeff's appetizers and desserts.

"So," Jeff said, "Dare I email a first-class plane ticket your way?"

"I'll drive, Jeff."

"All the way to Los Angeles? Crazy, man. Planes are still the safest way to go, Teddy."

"Yeah, yeah."

"Hey, I'll see you at the book fair next weekend, right? I'd say we ought to have lunch there, but I'll be in and out. Should be a time."

"I'll be there."

"Fantastic. Hey, how's the new book coming? Or the revision, I should say. The clock's ticking. You know *Unholy Ghost* just dropped off the *Journal's* best-seller list."

"Thanks for the motivation. I—uh," Arthur paused, unsure.

"I, what? I know trouble when I don't hear it."

"Listen, Jeff—I want to run something new by you. An idea I've been kicking around."

"Just as long as it doesn't keep you from writing."

Arthur cleared his throat. "I've been following the Benjamin Holden case. The sniper who just got caught. One of those who've been terrorizing the Boston-Philly stretch."

"The cult wacko?"

"Well, yeah, that's the guy," Arthur hesitated, forced himself into the next sentence. He felt unplugged, watching himself talk. *Going and going—what for?* "I was thinking about doing a book on...evil."

A long pause rose from the other end.

"Jeff?"

"How well is *that* gonna sell?" said Jeff. In a more subdued tone, he said, "Well, maybe a lot, I suppose. Watcha got?"

"I could profile a number of cases, including Holden's," said Arthur. "What makes him tick. What makes him do the things he does. I want to arrange an interview with Holden. Dissect and illuminate people like him, maybe discuss the inner workings of terrorism. I could juxtapose sociological and psychological perspectives with the more religious views. I already have a working title: 'Sin: How Evil Proves God Wrong'."

Jeff exhaled. Arthur could imagine, amid the cigarette smoke, a cloud of unspoken opinions swirling around his manager's brain.

"Proves God wrong," Jeffrey repeated.

"Maybe I've exhumed some of my youthful arrogance lately," Arthur said. "But I like it. What do you think?"

"I think you'll need a baptismal before visiting Holden," Jeff said. "Just to be on the safe side."

AFTER A PITTANCE of hot and restless sleep, Arthur awoke to a radiant morning. The summer storm had passed; the windows at the front of the house flooded his world with eager gold sunshine. Arthur shuffled to the refrigerator and opened a can of espresso.

He wandered upstairs. Jim's canvas of a surreal desert greeted Arthur at the top of the steps, as it had for the last three years. He liked the canvas and considered it one of his son's best efforts, although he couldn't help feeling overwhelming sadness in seeing that barren yellow and gold-tinted landscape, sparsely populated with semi-anthropomorphized cacti drooped over in bristly brooding. Jim had named the painting *Cogitating Cacti*. Arthur had often wondered if the name was an attempt at whimsy, or something more Freudian.

He scrolled through email after email, his eyes flooded by the textual waterfall. Newsletters from online groups. Advertisements. Letters from readers that, judging by the few coherent subject lines he registered, were extreme in either their praise or contempt. Notices from Amazon. 9/11 conspiracy emails that he nowadays relegated to the trash, although he couldn't bring himself to unsubscribe from those news services. Low-rung authors and e-zine editors taking an astronomical shot at an exclusive interview. One message from Jeff.

He scanned a few of the personal messages and trashed those with misspellings and capital letters—ASINININE CUNTRY??!! one exclaimed.

Not enough minutes to spare, he thought. Not enough brain cells, either. He clicked on a news site, his gaze snagged instantly by a bold headline.

New Sniper Victim Discovered

Another body, crumpled at a gas station just outside Boston. Single bullet wound through her skull. A student at Tufts University, she'd been traveling home to Chambersburg, Pennsylvania, for the summer.

Something surged deep in Arthur's viscera, partly from

basic oh-isn't-that-terrible? headline empathy, partly from a mounting anxiety that this human disease was spreading, and partly from a vague sense of responsibility, as though his morbid fascination with this whole case had helped push this murder along.

"'Bigger than anyone can imagine," claimed the convicted Benjamin Holden, in a message released to the press. "You can't stop the ritual cleansing 'cause we do God's work and God's work ain't never gonna be stopped."

Amid images of the victim's high school yearbook photo and several tastefully angled snapshots of the crime scene, Arthur studied the newest mug shot of Benjamin Holden. Holden's skin appeared dark, not from genes or tanning but from sheer weathering, ingrained dirtiness. Curly ashen hair spiraled down around his ears and past his eyes. The hair looked absurdly out of place on Holden's face, and Arthur wondered if it might have been a wig. A bushy crater of a goatee ringed his mouth.

Arthur locked his gaze on Holden's eyes. The man stared through the screen, as if by intent alone he could circumvent space and time. The eyes radiated crazy. To Arthur, the ease with which any normal person could identify an insane person's gaze was probably one of the few decent arguments in favor of the metaphysical. Because empirically there was never anything actually, physically wrong with a madman's eyes. The pupil was there, the iris, the sclera. Yet the ineffable wrongness—the *off*ness—was unmistakable, like thick smog that smothered their humanity.

Likely Holden exaggerated the size and power of his group. Authorities had determined that only two other snipers remained at large. Regardless of numbers, their maniacal devotion held strong. Should Arthur feel tempted to doubt it, the copious images of the murdered Tufts student—some sad and others smiling—that splashed themselves across his computer screen served as stark reminders.

Arthur called up a variety of articles about the Judges. He did not know the exact source or nature of whatever deep-seated itch he aimed to scratch. But after almost an hour of sitting before the screen, he paused to dig through his top drawer of business card contacts to locate a specific card bearing the information of William Dyer, or "Bill," a district attorney friend of Jeff's he'd met at a party a year or two ago. Arthur wasn't certain how to proceed, but he felt confident that Bill Dyer might be able to clarify a couple of things for him.

He dialed Bill's business number. As the phone rang he studied the computer screen, across which an AP article about Holden's military background continued to scroll.

The shootings had been occurring further north. Arthur remembered the Baltimore Orioles game on the thirtieth, the one he was supposed to attend with Jim and David. He felt a sudden surge of anxiety.

No. Shut up. Shut up.

He couldn't cancel that. Jim would never let him hear the end of it.

The ringing stopped, broken by a crisp female voice. *Secretary, probably.*

The thought of canceling the Orioles game rose again in his mind, unbidden. Arthur had already seen enough evil for one man's lifetime, and he felt no desire to place himself—or Jim—in its direct path.

After a day of work and utter solitude, Arthur took an evening shower, donned his bathrobe and ate dinner in front of the TV. As he placed the dishes in the sink he noticed the silhouette of the gray-clad Recurring Fisherman standing at the edge of the pond. Arthur considered the sighting odd. Usually the man came around dawn.

Light-headed after two and a half glasses of wine, Arthur felt little compunction about stepping out his back door and hollering, "Hey!"

The fisherman didn't move.

"Hey!" Arthur cried. "Excuse me!"

The man finally turned and acknowledged him with a smile—*a goddamn and contemptuous smile,* Arthur thought—then returned his attention to the pond.

Arthur felt slighted, ignored, insignificant. An urge exploded through him to show this cocky jackass just how significant he was, and could be. He charged down the back steps, the bottom half of his bathrobe bouncing and flapping about his legs.

As he closed in, the fisherman started cranking up the line.

Hurry, hurry asshole...I'm coming you know....

"What're you doing out here?" Arthur yelled. "This is illegal. And you're trespassing on my yard!"

The man gathered his line and pole. He shrugged off Arthur's verbal attack, muttering something inaudible.

"Excuse me?" Arthur called.

"I said don't worry about it," the guy repeated, sauntering away.

That's not what he said, Arthur thought.

Arthur lunged at the man from behind and shoved him forward. The fisherman cried out as he stumbled and dropped his pole. He flailed and struggled to right himself, but his footing gave way and he splashed into the pond. For a moment he appeared more confused than angry. Arthur stepped back, both thrilled and stunned by what he had just done. The commotion had awakened the rest of the pond's inhabitants. The surface rippled with activity, creases of moonlight winking through the dusk. The fisherman's feet eventually found the bottom. His flailing stilled.

I could kill him, Arthur thought, then immediately felt an onslaught of queasiness. What was wrong with him? *So goddamn violent.* So driven by instincts that existed below the surface of his own consciousness. Too much solitude and wine, maybe. Or perhaps too many hours alone spent gathering information on the Judges of God.

Maybe.

"Asshole!" the fisherman hollered, still sputtering as he waded back to the shore.

Arthur turned. Without a word he strode back into the house.

Arthur had nurtured this idea, brewing it up almost as one does a secret fantasy, yet still he had no idea how the thing would turn out. Despite his extensive studies in developmental psychology, and regardless of the countless souls he'd met and mastered during his career as a public commentator, he realized this particular meeting would be…what, fateful? *No.* He had to not put so much weight behind it. Yet it *would* be different. It would assert itself and become branded in his memory forever. Did he wish to grant Holden that privilege? *Best not to overthink it,* he decided.

He sat alone in the visitor's room at Brookhaven Correctional Institute, resting his elbows on a cheap wooden table while he waited for the guards to reappear. Chills flittered through him. The room smelled of mildew and sweat, underneath which he caught the faint, dull barb of old piss. Waiting. Arthur's left leg grew restless.

Just leave and drive home now. Fuck this project.

His being here felt unreal. It seemed like a dream projection, like he was a character in a film. Doing this. He tried to moderate his breathing. He doodled absently on a notepad—what were originally coherent pictures like eyeballs and stickmen had devolved into squiggles and spirals and random lines as time had passed.

How deep are you willing to go?

The fascination he felt bordered grotesquely on satisfaction. Maybe people like Holden validated something in him, embodied and affirmed a strain of nihilism which, deep down, had long been a begrudged principle of Arthur's worldview. Academically, perhaps, he espoused chaos. Holden lived it. That he, Arthur Moore, longed to sit before Ben Holden and expose himself to someone so far gone... it almost felt like he would be validating Holden, maybe even worshiping him in some fashion. Worshiping the God of Random Chance—or rather, quite simply, Randomness itself, which, after eons of aimless whirling and wandering, had taken on human shape.

The metal door squealed open. Arthur flinched at the noise, but immediately collected himself. It wouldn't do for him to reveal his anxiety. He glanced toward the door as a pair of buff guards escorted Benjamin Holden into the room.

He's here. Fuck...he's here.

Holden wore an orange short-sleeved prison outfit. His hands were cuffed at the front and his ankles were shackled, forcing him to shuffle toward the table. His expression was one of detached, depraved whimsy, yet he also seemed fully cognizant of his present situation. Something about his face seemed painted on, frozen; like a mask placed over his true identity.

Arthur rose automatically to greet the man and shake his hand, but he caught himself halfway up. He resumed his seat, feeling foolish, as Holden approached. To Arthur's relief, the guards stationed themselves inside the room on either side of the door, assuming stoic watch.

"Mr. Holden," Arthur said. "Thank you for seeing me."

Holden's grin widened. "What a privilege," he said.

Arthur smiled thinly. "You feel privileged?"

"No, privilege for you," said Holden. "You've come to hear the Word. I'm your priest. Ready to receive confessions." His hot, delirious stare enveloped Arthur: "I know you, man."

"I've nothing to confess," Arthur said. "But I want to understand your cause."

Why?

"You can't understand nothing. And you don't want to. You're gonna use me as your next little sound bite in your next interview or something, when you talk about why we should abandon God. I'm a crazy man, right?"

To Arthur, Holden seemed like an energetic tidal wave, temporarily fixed at the crest of an imminent cataclysm. Pure randomness, simply biding its time until the wave broke and crashed upon its next unwitting victim. At that moment Arthur felt oddly like a domesticated house cat attempting to bat down a lion, or to lecture it on how it ought to behave. When in truth the lion could only obey the primeval impulses that fueled its savage existence.

"You're not a crazy man," Arthur said, trying desperately to steady his shallow breathing, "based on the reality in which you live."

"And what reality is that?"

"One where God, who created the entire universe, is actually a temperamental and violent tyrant. Apparently your God, despite having the ability to throw an asteroid at the Earth or explode the sun, quietly commissioned a tiny bipedal organism with a rifle to kill a few other tiny bipedal organisms. For what, may I ask? That's the part of your reality I don't quite understand."

"God doesn't shout. He whispers. He speaks to those He knows can hear, in order that those who hear Him and obey Him might help turn around man's sinking ship. Ultimate purity requires cleansing and gutting, requires bloodshed."

"Do you remember sending me a letter?"

Holden smirked. His eyes remained dead cold. "I've sent out lotsa letters. I musta sent one to you too. Only right to give people a fair warning."

"Warning of what?"

"Of what awaits them. Not only here," Holden tapped the table, "but in God's kingdom."

"Would we even go to God's kingdom? I thought he'd have nothing to do with us."

"Everyone gets to go to God's kingdom," Holden said. "But not everyone stays."

"Why is that?"

"What good is Hell," Holden said, "without having tasted Heaven?"

"So all those people you killed—God rerouted them to hell?"

"That's for God to decide. I'm just his intermediary. Messenger type."

"What did those people do, those you killed?" Arthur asked. "Why did you choose them? It seemed so random."

"Random," Holden repeated. He laughed, a sound more like gas escaping. Arthur imagined it was how a corpse might laugh. "That's the reality *you* live in. To you it's all random, right? Well, what if one of us finds you and puts a bullet between your eyes? Would that be a random act?"

"Is that what God wishes?"

"You don't deserve to hear God," Holden said. "You stopped listening long ago. But He hears everything you're saying about Him."

III

SPRING AND AUTUMN IN VIRGINIA WERE THE
hushed seasons, easy on the eyes and skin, but the winters
and summers bore headstrong personalities, enshrouding
the land and its life with their presence. And summer had
recently entered through the earth's every pore.

Arthur made his way through the sweltering fairgrounds, wiping the perspiration from his forehead. Thankfully, he'd been promised that the booth for the Virginia
Atheists Society (VAS) stood in the shade this year. Typi-
cally they held the Colonial Williamsburg Book Fair on the
hottest weekend of the year—a conspiracy for sure. It didn't
affect turnout, although the fair hosts made a bundle selling
bottled water to overheated browsers.

Thousands thronged the maze of pointed white tents
beneath the overconfident sun. Brief, merciful breezes
carried the odors of unique foods, a variety of discussions
and the gripes of hot cranky children, all backdropped by
microphone-buzzed voices from the Author's Stage, where
writers offered their wares to a sparse audience normally
seated just to rest.

Knowing his own tendency for being perpetually tardy
over the years, Arthur had managed to arrive at the fairgrounds a few minutes before his shift, the sweat already
pooling under his arms. A group of his fans had amassed
in front of the booth, but had yet to form the necessary line
to receive a signed copy of one of his books. As he entered
the booth he nodded and smiled, touched by their cheerful
validation of his presence. No paint or pie throwers or vandals here today. Twin energies of approval and admiration
pervaded the group, lowering the pulse of his paranoia.

Though not terribly keen on social events, Arthur did

enjoy the personal nature of these kinds of fairs and festivals. He found that physical contact with a few fans provided him with gratification unmatched by the millions of abstract, faceless people who watched him on television or heard him on the radio. He'd often thought that people underrated the significance of a single man or woman. Trillions of intelligent cells comprised a human being, and they all worked together to perform innumerable functions. Someone once estimated that the number of possible synaptic and neurological connections in the human brain surpassed the number of all the atoms in the universe. And in every one of his readers stirred all that celestial genius, all that conjunction and coordination, all that chance and possibility and experience woven between mind and matter—absorbing his words and adjusting an entire system of thought and lifestyle according to his influence, however large or small it might prove to be.

Human bodies, Arthur often thought, were wasted on human beings.

Among the sea of vaguely familiar faces, Arthur quickly noticed his manager milling amid the crowd. Jeff greeted him half attentively, as if stretched thin with imminent obligations.

Arthur remembered last year's fair, and his group's decidedly unattractive booth. Aesthetically that physical booth had differed little from its neighbors, but the people manning it—his colleagues and friends—had appeared so old and so grim. They sat with crossed arms and legs, their frown-tilted lips adding gratuitous creases to already well-worn faces. Toward the end of the fair, the word "dispirited" had been bandied about, irony intended. Arthur heard similar comments from the passing crowd and began using them himself in the later critiques he put forth to the group. The off-putting facade, after all, only reinforced the stereotype of the atheist as an untrustworthy grouch. One hardly needed Holmesian skills to understand why the nearby Christian and New Age booths frothed with patronage— they simply had better "vibes."

On that day a year ago, Arthur had approached his colleagues.

"Guys," he'd said. "Lighten the hell up."

As the celebrity of the group, his word was gospel. "Good call, Art," Steve Wallace, the Vice President of VAS, had said, "good to give ourselves a colorful kick in the pants."

The presentation had been revamped. This year, however, Arthur thought perhaps they had chosen a booth display too garishly (and almost comically) antithetical to the grim crypt he had criticized a year ago: two vertical hanging banners flanked the outreach desk, both featuring a wide-smiling group of twenty-somethings thrusting thumbs-up at the camera. Above them read the words *My Choices, My Life,* the VAS logo punctuating the space below their sneakered feet.

Arthur absorbed the poster and turned to Wallace, who was once again manning the booth. "I don't remember seeing this one at any of the meetings."

Wallace looked at him curiously. His large straw hat cast a rhombus of shadow over his face, which held vague resentment. "Well, Art," he said, "you missed the last two meetings."

"I know. I apologize. I've been out of the loop."

"Glad you made it today."

"So am I."

Feeling a mix of eagerness and reluctance, Arthur turned to the gathered customers. He signed copies of *Unholy Ghost* for a gaunt-faced college student and a middle-aged brunette. The third in line, a younger man maybe in his late twenties (Arthur had lately noticed an increasing number of young adults in his demographic) smiled at him and, as he scribbled his signature on a second edition of *Faith & the Future,* asked him, "So, what's the next book?"

A book on demons, Arthur nearly replied in dark jest. Except he'd scrapped that project. Had, in fact, not even touched his notepad or computer since returning a month ago from the visit with Holden. Something about Holden had cast a rotten stench, one that had clouded and filled and clung to Arthur's psyche. During his drive home from the prison—and for a while thereafter—it seemed to Arthur as if he'd sleepwalked through some terrible dream rather than had an actual visit with Holden. But the tremor in his core, which had since thankfully stilled, had been real, along with the occasional nightmare. Especially that one where he'd met Jim somewhere and had pointed out the gaping hole in his son's head. Jim touched the wound delicately and said, "Oh," before collapsing like a heap of laundry at Arthur's feet.

The new book's twist, Arthur would have added, *is that there are demons. But they've no horns or claws, just ordinary ears and nails.*

Just human.

"I'm exploring," Arthur told the young man, offering his longstanding, canned response to any such inquiry.

More readers approached Arthur quietly with their crooked, awestruck smiles. The folks whom Jeffrey, with a lilt in his voice, dubbed Arthur's "Pavlovian public." Or, worse yet, his "flock." Sure, it was all jokes and jabs, even if a small part of Arthur resented the insinuation that people had come to hang on his every word, and were as conditioned as those who might flock to the clerics and gurus and ministers. He once imagined that his voice liberated people, opened them up. But he'd recently come to suspect that this notion might be false, as deluded as any espoused from the Sunday pulpit.

TOWARD THE LATTER HOUR of his shift, Jeff reappeared at the booth. Shaking hands with other VAS members proved a challenge for him, as he carried in one hand a melting ice-cream cone and in the other a half-smoked cigar. In Arthur's opinion, these items revealed the narrow spectrum of Jeff's life choices. His rotund body reflected a legacy of countless personal indulgences that spanned from childhood well into his adulthood. If a thing (or person or place) provided pleasure, Jeff wanted it.

"Art, my man," Jeffrey said. "How's the morning?"

"Sweltering," Arthur admitted. "But looks like we're winding down. Sold a good chunk of our lot." He looked at the contents of Jeff's hands. "I hope you don't mix those up."

"I wouldn't worry about it. Black cherry and nicotine go pretty well together."

"Didn't you say you were meeting someone here?" Arthur asked.

"Right. She's at a reading at the moment. We're meeting for lunch."

"I see," Arthur said. He knew next to nothing about Jeff's entanglements. From what he'd surmised, Jeff remained a player in the ever-expanding field of sexual conquest. "If I settle," Jeff had once confided in him, "I'm afraid I'll get fat. Or fatter."

Yet for some reason unfathomable to Arthur, Jeff attracted numerous women, and often surprisingly beautiful ones at that. Was it his wealth that drew them, his power, or his playful zest for life? It certainly wasn't his looks or, frankly, his intelligence. To Arthur, who merely tolerated Jeff, it made no sense at all.

"She's a lovely gal," Jeff added. "I think this one's different. May even be a keeper. Is Jim coming today?"

"Maybe tomorrow. We're catching an Orioles game

later tonight."

"Sounds like a time."

A knot of people had gathered in front of the booth, waiting to purchase, peruse or praise, and Jeff—ever the good manager—quietly moved aside so that Arthur could return to his work.

Arthur continued signing and smiling and chatting with his fans until the end of the morning shift, all the while sucking down copious amounts of store-brand water from the cooler under the outreach desk. When the last autographic seeker had finally departed, he checked his phone. Linda had left him a message saying she planned to arrive in the next hour and would meet him at the VAS booth. With time left to kill, Arthur donned his sunglasses and flapped his arms in an attempt to erase the sweat stains that circled his underarms. Acknowledging the futility of the gesture, he shrugged and wandered off to explore the fair.

ARTHUR NOTICED THAT MANY familiar names had returned to this year's fair. He paid silent homage in passing to Vino Press, a publisher of wine and gourmet cookbooks, whose booth attendants were setting up for a two-hour wine-tasting session. Two years ago their chardonnay had granted Arthur salvation after a particularly vocal confrontation with a Richmond preacher.

New booths dotted the fairgrounds, too. He noted a Mormon booth called Golden Tablet Publishing situated near a booth displaying Hindu and Buddhist texts. In close proximity stood an Islamic booth, helmed primarily by hijab-wrapped women. The fair, approaching its tenth anniversary, had become undeniably more diverse. A good thing? Arthur wasn't sure. It was what it was. America the beautiful. America the hodgepodge.

America the pious.

He stopped by a New Age publisher called Lunar Press, prominently showcasing a book called *The Gospel of Universal Self*, by Natalie Farrow. He stood for a moment, studying the cover: a silhouetted human figure floating in space, with a picture of the deep cosmos filling out the contours of the figure's torso and limbs.

He opened the book and thumbed through the pages with interest. An elaborate scratchboard illustration headed each chapter, providing an earthy, pagan motif. He found the chapter titles to be typical Westernized, New Age-y versions of Eastern mysticism: Inner Sanctuary, Quantum Distillation for the Mind, New Thoughts about Enlightenment, The Supernova God, and so on.

As he scanned the pages he became aware of voices echoing within the booth. He was struck by the tenor of enthusiasm. The friendliness seemed forced to him, even off-putting.

The booth's attendants, exclusively female, dressed on the verge of hippiedom—privileged hippies, as Arthur opted to dub them. To his growing annoyance, they engaged passersby with radiant shouts of "Namaste! How are you today?" or "Come join us as one!"

Arthur closed *The Gospel of the Universal Self* with a thump and tossed it back onto the table. Turning to leave, he nearly collided with a woman who'd been standing behind him.

"You like?" she asked, nodding toward the book now lying askew on top of the stack.

"The usual woo-woo," he said, with a tired smile.

"I was going for just one woo, actually."

Too late, he recognized her face from the cover photo.

Natalie Farrow smiled at him. She was, he estimated, at least a decade his junior. She wore a long pale-yellow sundress, which glowed in contrast to her rich, inky Celtic hair pulled tight in a ponytail. Her eyes shone a crystalline blue. In her full, expressive lips, Arthur imagined there dwelt an innumerable host of sensual smirks, tantalizing pouts, flirty frowns and come-hither smiles. Her present grin teased.

Arthur paused, caught in that fearful delight of sudden attraction.

"Tell you what," she said—by the gleam in her eye it was clear to Arthur that she recognized him—"You can have it. Gratis."

Arthur glanced down at the book, as if contemplating her request.

"Please, take it," she told him.

"That's okay," Arthur said. His skin tingled under the spotlight of her gaze. "Thank you though. Good luck with it."

He nodded, a tip of the hat without a hat, then brushed past her and left the booth. Arthur could feel Natalie watching him as he once more enmeshed himself in the milling crowds of the festival.

WHEN ARTHUR RETURNED to the VAS booth he spied Jeff reclining happily on a lawn chair outside the tent, surrounded by a small crowd. The ice-cream cone gone, only his cigar stub remained, clenched in the corner of his mouth. He made wild gestures toward his audience, a ballet of hands and fingers, as he imparted some story that enraptured the smiling crowd. "That was all the goddamn guy *wanted*," Arthur overheard, followed by a burst of laughter from Jeff's audience. Arthur hoped the anecdote wasn't about him.

Arthur long ago surmised there were two types of managers: sharks and seals. One ate its way to the top, while the other performed tricks for its supper. Thankfully, Arthur knew Jeff to be a seal. Perplexing sometimes, but effective in the long run. People feared sharks and often fled from them. They stayed, and paid, for the company of seals.

Jeff spotted Arthur and waved him over. "Hey! Making the rounds?"

"Yeah, scoping it out."

"Where'd you go?"

"Just around. Have you seen some of the booths here?" Arthur said, partially directing the question to novelist Gary Thomas, who'd usurped Arthur's chair and pen from the morning and seemed to welcome any distraction from the crowd's apparent indifference to his book.

Gary nodded. "Is the Mormon booth back this year?"

"Why, were they here last year?" Arthur didn't recall having seen them.

"Mormons don't pass up anything these days." Jeff's focus drifted to a spot somewhere behind Arthur. He rose. "Pardon me, Teddy. Be right back."

As Jeff buzzed past him, Arthur turned to Gary and asked, "You ever hear of a Lunar Press? Puts out some woo-woo yoga-spirit stuff."

"That shit's blowing up."

"I know, don't remind me. It's starting to fill religion's cracks."

"Well, baby steps, Art. Baby steps."

"Right. Takes a long time to calm a species's nerves."

"Teddy, hey, wancha to meet someone," Jeff called out from behind him.

Arthur turned and once again found himself face-to-face with Natalie Farrow. Jeff had one arm tucked around her waist. Arthur wondered if his cheeks looked as crimson as they felt.

"Meet my new partner in crime," Jeff said.

Natalie's mildly amused smile lingered. "We meet again, Dr. Moore."

"Good to, uh, see you again," Arthur stammered. "No need to call me doctor."

"But you've already diagnosed me with woo-woo syndrome," Natalie tilted her head. "Or was it cancer of the intellect?"

She gazed at him with the playful mischief of a child proclaiming, "You're it."

"Oh Teddy…" Jeffrey said, shaking his head with a humorous grin. "Nat told me you slipped her a visit."

Arthur suddenly recalled a concept he'd formulated long ago, that of the cosmic comic—a celestial miscreant who played with people's lives. Of course he did not subscribe to the idea of intelligent design, which implied a designer. But doubtless there was a pattern at work in the cosmos. In a chaotic world, the existence of so many synchronicities and too-orderly coincidences was almost enough to demand he concede that *something unseen*, somewhere out there, possessed a conscious and intervening personality.

"I'm sorry you heard the woo-woo comment," Arthur said. He searched in vain for something else to say, anything—a clever quip or a cool-guy remark. Nothing came.

"You're not sorry," Natalie teased. "You're walking and talking like Arthur Moore. That's what the world expects of you."

"Is it now?"

"Sure." Natalie gestured to Jeff. "This lug here is never sorry. He's always Jeffrey Howes, from bone to soul."

"That's a long journey down," Jeff said, planting a kiss atop her head.

Arthur smiled, noting his friend's obvious infatuation. "You're a traitor, Jeff," he said. "You're *cheating* on me with her."

"Oh, you know it," Jeff agreed. "I've already snagged her a few gigs. The TV show *Hot Talk*, for one."

"You're still his one and only," Natalie said to Arthur, her expression both inviting and accepting. He had a sudden, fly-by fantasy of leaning in to kiss her.

Just then a female voice called his name. All three of them turned to see Linda trotting over, wearing an oversized visor, large-framed sunglasses and a pink-and-blue-checkered blouse.

"Arthur," she squeaked. "I'm sorry I'm late."

Was her arrival good timing or a terrible case of bad luck? Probably, Arthur admitted to himself, some combination of both. He leaned over and offered Linda a dry, perfunctory kiss, still conscious of his urge to linger while exploring Natalie's mouth. Gruffly he cleared his throat and made the proper introductions. After all, he was walking, talking Arthur Moore. And the world expected that.

"What are you two doing later?" Jeffrey asked. "Would you like to join us for dinner tonight? My place? I've been trying out some new 'pees."

"Peas?" Linda asked.

"Recipes."

Arthur snorted. "Are we really making everything short and hip now?"

"Nah, just Jeff," said Natalie. "I can vouch for his chef's hands, though. My stomach's still intact."

Jeffrey chuckled. "You liked the curry chicken I made the other night."

"Loved it," Natalie said. "That's what I said. I can vouch." She planted a kiss on Jeff's cheek.

Arthur watched their interplay, smiling humorlessly.

The cosmic comic strikes again.

"I can't tonight, remember?" Arthur said. "I'm going up to Baltimore with Jim."

"Oh, right!" Jeffrey said. "The Orioles game."

"That'll be fun," Natalie said. "They're playing the...

Angels, right?"

"I believe so, yes."

"Linda, you're not going with?" Jeffrey asked.

"No, it's a father and son thing," she said. "But I'd love to get together for dinner sometime." She put her arm around Arthur and he reciprocated. Sudden self-consciousness pricked him.

"As his manager, Jeff," Linda continued, "you can let me in on some of this guy's secrets."

"I don't know," said Jeff. "I'm still trying to hammer a lot out of him myself. He's like a ketchup bottle."

"Isn't *that* an image," Natalie said. "I thought *I* was your ketchup bottle."

"No, you're the hot mustard," Jeff said, hugging her tighter. "In a squeeze bottle."

Linda shifted. Arthur could feel her discomfort. He found himself resenting her for it. *Lighten up*, he wanted to say, even though he likely felt just as tense.

He asked Linda, "Want to check out the fair? They have a wine-tasting booth you'll enjoy."

"Sure," she replied. "But first things first. I want to buy your book. And have you sign it, of course."

"We gotta run, Teddy," Jeff said. "I'll give you a call a bit later."

"Teddy?" Linda asked.

Arthur rolled his eyes. "My middle name. He knows I don't particularly like it. He's funny like that, or thinks he is. No big deal."

As soon as they were out of earshot Linda said, "I noticed Natalie was wearing one of my necklaces. One I made."

"What?"

"The turquoise one. It's an irregular, eighteen-karat, beaded stone necklace. It's one of my favorites."

"Oh wow, that's amazing." Arthur threw a furtive glance

back through the crowds, but Natalie and Jeff had gone. He was taken by the sudden urge to see Natalie once more. "Why didn't you say something?"

Linda shrugged, looking distracted. Whenever she tried to conceal an inner conflict her face usually betrayed it— Arthur could easily spot the taut lips, her hardened eyes.

"No big deal," she said, dismissing his question.

A tropical beach lay before him, deftly kissed onto the canvas in that airy, controlled-chaos impressionistic style Jim had mastered. Beyond the palm-dotted shoreline, the sea crested into a geometric abstraction, fractals of cosmic majesty flowing into unfinished white space.

"Not done yet, but what do you think?" Jim asked Arthur. Paint-streaked clothes that looked older than he was covered Jim's frame. He'd centered the canvas on an easel by his dining room window to capture the light. Together the two men stepped back and assessed the work.

"The idea being that we're the incongruity in the universe. Out of the random, building-block patterns is seeded this fluid—this organic ball of life. A little oasis."

Arthur leaned against the kitchen counter, contemplating the painting. *How did this come out of my son? How did something this wonderful come from something that came out of me?*

He wasn't sure what to say. To varying degrees, all of Jim's stuff was good. Even so, the artistic process, from seed to fruit, bewildered Arthur. He saw it not as a process of building but as one of elimination, whittling the outlandish number of possibilities down to one that ultimately satisfied.

"I don't normally show off my works in progress," Jim

said, "but I've been going back and forth on this one. Kind of a love-hate relationship."

"It looks great," said Arthur. "I like that you included the Horsehead Nebula up there."

Jim laughed. "That's actually a donkey."

"Really? Why?"

"Prince Myshkin. When he saw an ass, all things made sense."

"Ah, going for the Dostoyevsky reference. I thought maybe it was a sign that God was a Democrat."

Jim laughed again.

"But I like the blending of styles there," Arthur said. "You did a good job with that."

"Thanks. I'll power through the end of it sometime. I definitely want to get this digitized and in my online portfolio."

"Fantastic." Arthur looked at his watch. "Are we ready to go? We should probably leave in the next ten minutes."

"Sure thing," Jim turned away from the canvas. "Let me go wake up David."

"He feeling better?"

Jim made a wishy-washy gesture. "So-so. I think he's getting there, but he's still not fully recovered."

Jim slipped into their bedroom. Arthur could hear their subdued talking, a rustling of Jim's weight on the bed, then the sound of a quick kiss. Arthur took the opportunity to turn off the kitchen light. The sun was still shining; lamps and fixtures had no place being on.

Arthur was always impressed by the clean and tidy nature of their apartment, its right-angled sparseness, the symmetry of the furniture that hinted at an affinity for feng shui. By contrast, Jim's room in Arthur's house had exhibited varying levels of disarray that Arthur used to refer to as unkempt, cluttered, chaotic or Kosovo. Mostly it had oscillated between cluttered and chaotic.

Arthur wandered over to the large bookshelf in their living room. He noted drawing and art books, medical books, Ayn Rand novels and a smattering of other philosophy and history books. Arthur had gifted Jim quite a few of them over the years. Tomes, Jim called them. "*Another* tome, Dad?" he'd say, whenever Arthur held out yet another soon-to-be-neglected recommendation.

Relegated to half the bottom shelf was a meek cluster of novels—a few by Steinbeck, also gifts from Arthur—with bookmarks jutting above their crusty loaves of pages. Except for a recently completed copy of Dostoyevsky's *The Idiot*, which for three years Jim had struggled to finish, the other novels were more commercial.

Where are my books? Arthur wondered. It was the writer's code and expectation that all affiliates should own and display their books.

Maybe they're in the bedroom.

He was about to turn away from the bookshelf when one spine in particular caught his eye.

The Gospel of Universal Self. Natalie Farrow.

Arthur plucked it from the shelf and gazed once more at her author photo. Seeing her face again, his chest gripped.

Who'd it belong to? *David?* Had to be. Jim couldn't imagine his son would fall for such mumbo jumbo. But, a medical student? Had pseudoscience become that convincing?

Many of Arthur's opponents came from organized faith movements. Recently, however, the New Age liberal spiritualists had joined his enemies in the trenches. While not as ingrained or reactionary as Christian or Islamic fundamentalists, these wind-chiming enlightenment types posed a more subtle, yet no less sinister, threat to the minds (and mind) of the culture. They slapped jargony labels on bogus ideas and in turn lured away those wedged between faith and reason; people who might have disavowed their formal house of worship but who remained unwilling to abandon all notion of God or spirit, and who now sought to explore the woods beyond the primordial forests of organized religion. There they often fell prey to the New Agers, so would never make it to the clearing—to the light—of scientific rationalism.

And if the book were David's, that brought up another disturbing question: was Jim buying into it? Could he buy into it?

You're overreacting.

Arthur saw no other books by Farrow on the shelf, nor any of similar content. Perhaps the book had been a gift?

Jim emerged from the bedroom, David following close behind, still looking pale and weak. Arthur thought his smile appeared forced.

"Ready for some ball?" David asked, his voice sounding frail.

"Of course," Arthur replied. "But we can't go if you're going to wear that ridiculous hat."

David scowled playfully, though he did seem to suspect Arthur might be serious. "Hey, I grew up in New York. Love me or leave me."

"I prefer the former," said Jim, putting his arm around Jim's shoulders.

"The baseball fan in me almost prefers you wear a cap that says 'God is great'," Arthur said. "How many World Series have the Yankees bought so far?"

"Dad…" Jim chastised, shrugging into an oversized blue windbreaker.

David laughed, which turned into a cough.

"How are you feeling, Dave?" Arthur asked.

"Hah, that's funny. I think that's the first time you called me Dave."

"Is it?"

"Yeah," said David, patting his chest. "I'm okay, still feeling a little lethargic. But I think getting some fresh air might help rejuvenate me."

Arthur noticed Jim glancing at David with a somewhat skeptical expression that appeared from Arthur's perspective to be tinged with fear.

"Everything okay?" Arthur asked.

"I hope so," Jim said. "Let's go."

IV

THE RAIN STARTED IN THE FOURTH INNING, dampening every person in Oriole Park. But the precipitation never graduated past a drizzle, so the game charged on without delay. Arthur, Jim and David sat on the first deck not far from the box-seating area, dining on hot dogs and peanuts and wildly overpriced beer. Arthur granted himself the privilege, rarer these days since he'd entered middle age, of indulging in shoddy ballpark food.

He enjoyed losing himself in the energy of the game, anticipating every pitch, feeling each powerful crack of the bat on the ball, and reveling in the attendant cheers or boos for each new play. Occasionally however, he roused himself out of the reverie long enough to glance around and make certain that he hadn't been recognized. Three years ago, a drunken Braves' fan had called out his name and then dumped half of a warm Pabst Blue Ribbon down his back, soaking him all the way through to his undershorts. The horror of that unexpected assault still caused him some consternation when out in public.

The crush and weight of crowds often bothered Arthur, to the point that he routinely looked for the quickest routes of escape. It didn't help that Benjamin Holden and his faceless acolytes lurked in the back of his mind.

Cosmic randomness.

But he felt a little better with Jim by his side.

Thinking of Natalie Farrow also helped. Something about her lovely face and her enigmatic smile now acted as a sort of emotional balm, though he didn't know exactly why.

David, a rank novice when it came to understanding baseball, interrupted Arthur's internal musings about Natalie Farrow to ask basic questions concerning the players and rules. Jim happily fielded them, and Arthur felt thankful he didn't have to explain the game himself. Although he knew David had spent the first five years of his childhood in Eastern Europe, he still found it strange that in his subsequent twenty-three years as an American he hadn't osmotically sopped up more about baseball. But David's intensive pursuits left little attention for anything else.

As the night wore on, David grew increasingly pale. Arthur refrained from saying anything, although he could feel his own anxiety level mounting.

By the bottom of the eighth, the Angels were up by seven over the Orioles. Sensing that David's stamina was lagging, Arthur suggested they leave early to avoid the inevitable parking lot traffic.

"Dad," said Jim, "you know we're just going to turn on the radio and hear that they came back and beat the Angels by two in the ninth."

"I sincerely doubt it."

"We came all this way," David agreed with Jim through his chattering teeth. "Might as well stay."

"Do you want my jacket, Dave?" Arthur asked. "You look like you're freezing."

"S-sure, thank you."

"You feeling okay?" Jim asked, for the first time appearing aware of David's discomfort.

"Yeah, I'll be fine."

The Orioles scored a final run, not nearly enough for the win. The game ended with a disillusioned groan from the crowd, which then began filing dejectedly out through the aisles and into the parking lot.

"God sure wasn't with us tonight, eh?" one man said to Arthur as he passed.

Maybe He had a collapsing galaxy to deal with, Arthur mused silently.

In the parking lot Arthur hurried ahead of Jim and David, eager to reach the privacy and safety of their car.

"Dad!" Jim cried suddenly. People nearby gasped.

Arthur turned back to see Jim bending over David, who had collapsed in a heap to the ground. Cradling David's head against the pavement, Jim awkwardly tried to gather up his unresponsive limbs.

An electric tremor shuddered through Arthur.

Shot...David's been shot—

No. No blood.

David hadn't been shot, thank Christ for that. But his face held a grayish pallor and he wasn't moving.

"David!" Jim cried out. "Jesus, David...come on, baby—can you hear me? Can you move? Look at me."

Several people in the crowd dialed 911. Arthur checked David's pulse and felt a faint flutter. The young man seemed to be drifting in and out. Not unconscious exactly, yet not entirely there.

After what seemed an interminable period, Arthur heard the distant wail of an ambulance. He met Jim's gaze, reached over and squeezed his son's forearm reassuringly. Jim's eyes glistened with unshed tears.

"He's going to be alright," Arthur said. The words sounded paltry and useless, even to him.

The ambulance drivers quickly placed David on a stretcher and hustled him off. Jim rode with David to the hospital, while Arthur followed behind them in his own car, trying to ward off hazy ashen images of funerals and of tombstones and of future possibilities now so surreally imminent.

❧

"It looks like Thursday may be our best bet this week," Jeff's voice sounded high and cheerful over the phone, "for you and Linda to join us for dinner."

Arthur paced back and forth across his living room. "Linda can't make it Thursday, unfortunately," he said. "But I'm free."

"That's great," Jeff said. "I plan on whipping up some spaghetti. But no ordinary spaghetti. This stuff will blow your socks off. The recipe for the sauce is a family secret."

"My mouth's watering already."

"I'm sorry Linda can't make it. I'd like to get to know her better."

"We can do the four of us some other time."

"How is David doing, by the way?" Jeff asked.

"He's okay. Hanging on. The hospital in Baltimore discharged him two days ago. He's resting now, as far as I know. They still aren't sure what's wrong with him."

A lengthy pause stretched between them. Arthur knew Jeff was waiting for him to say more.

"Well," Jeff finally said, breaking the silence first, "Nat is certainly looking forward to having you over. She says she's dying to pick your brain."

"I'm a little afraid to ask…" Arthur said.

"It's going to be a time."

"Yeah, right. So how's seven?"

"Seven's good."

LINDA ANSWERED HIS CALL on the first ring.

"Hello, you," she said warmly.

"Hey," Arthur said. "I know we were talking about going to dinner on Thursday—but Jeff and I need to meet about some things, and Thursday night was the only time he could make it."

"Oh…okay. You guys can't meet before dinnertime?"

"No, he's booked up solid. He's all over the place this week."

Arthur recognized the moment as a milestone in his relationship with Linda—his first lie. An inevitability really, once people stayed together long enough. Though this one was only a white lie (or so he comforted himself), one that generated little more than a fleeting sense of self-consciousness when he spoke it. Even so he felt a brief stab of pity for Linda, then realized how condescending he was being. Linda was a grown woman. And should she ever find out, she'd recover. And learn to adapt.

"Listen, I'll set something up for us as soon as I'm able," Arthur told her, convincing himself that the noble gesture absolved him of his inconsequential sin.

"That would be wonderful, Art."

Natalie answered the door, wearing a long, white dress draped around her statuesque figure. Her silky black hair tumbled loosely around her shoulders, backlit by a halo from the chandelier aglow in the hallway. A wild, yet strangely elegant, fragrance wafted around her, something

Arthur found deeply intoxicating. What if he took her right then and there, pressing her up against the entryway, eagerly capturing her mouth with his own? He could. It didn't matter, the prospect of Jeff bearing witness to his indiscretion, the prospect of horrifying her. But would she be horrified? No...he didn't think so.

The urge, the desire, whatever it was, peaked when she smiled. The razor mischief glint in her eyes just enhanced her natural beauty. He could barely contain the impulse to grab her by the arms and pull her close against his chest.

"Here he is...our special guest tonight," said Natalie. For a moment Arthur wondered if she planned to allow him in. He glanced over his shoulder at the darkened street, fighting a mild sense of paranoia that Linda might somehow be watching them.

"Everything okay?" Natalie asked, finally stepping aside.

"Sure, fine." Arthur entered the high-ceiling foyer. As always, the spaciousness of Jeff's house had the power to inspire mild agoraphobia in him until he became acclimated to its vastness.

Natalie took his coat. He could hear Jeff rattling about way back in the kitchen. The entire house smelled of garlic and spices, and his mouth began to water in anticipation of the coming meal.

"C'mere," said Natalie. She leaned close to hug Arthur and, for the briefest of seconds, he imagined his fantasy made quick and weirdly manifest. He returned the gesture.

"That Teddy?" Jeffrey called from the kitchen.

"It's Teddy," Natalie confirmed.

Arthur stepped toward the kitchen but she rerouted him to the living room, a slender hand on his forearm. "The 'master' doesn't want anyone in his workshop," she explained. "Would you like a glass of wine?"

"Sure."

"Jeff has a Cab he's been wanting to try out on you."

"That would be great," Arthur said. "He wants privacy, hmm? I've never known Jeff to be so secretive about his cooking."

Natalie shrugged as she walked to the bar and poured the glass. "I was wondering myself, if he's always been so culinary. He's the first man I've met who's cooked. It's a real treat for me."

"To be honest. I can't really say. I've known Jeff several years but it's always been business. I don't know much about his private life."

"He's unpredictable. That's one of the things I like about him." Natalie smiled, handing him the glass. "Though maybe that's very smart, having a manager who's also a boyfriend."

"Could work," Arthur said. "Thanks for the wine."

Natalie poured herself a glass. "Please," she said, motioning for Arthur to accompany her to the suede couch. Natalie followed him, sitting close, and for several seconds Arthur sat in awkward silence, his nomadic gaze wandering the room and pausing occasionally on the flat-screen television, the last resort for a dead conversation.

"How's Linda?" said Natalie. "I'm sorry she couldn't make it,"

"I'm sorry, too," Arthur said. "She's meeting her daughter for dinner tonight."

"That's nice..."

More silence. Arthur's mind raced for something to say. He thought of the turquoise bead necklace, which Natalie again wore, and the curious coincidence that Linda, a freelance jeweler, had made it. But he refrained. Best not to connect Linda at all to tonight, lest it spawn some unfortunate future moment revealing his fib.

Between them, he knew, existed a beast of a conversation, yet both—certainly Arthur—chose for now to tread lightly on small talk.

"So how'd the fair treat you?" Arthur asked, after a sip of his wine. "Sell some books?"

"A fair hunk," said Natalie. "Hopefully to the right people."

"Oh? What do you mean?"

"Okay, I know this'll sound a little crazy, but I secretly wish I had a way of screening my appropriate audience. You just wonder with some people why they're getting your book, and if it will just sit collecting dust on a shelf from now until they or you die. It might." Natalie made a dismissive, waving gesture. "Sorry, I know that's silly and superficial."

"Not superficial at all," Arthur said.

Natalie shrugged.

"I understand what you mean," Arthur said. "I'd rather have one solid reader I can inspire than hundreds who dip in and out, or shrug it off and forget about it."

"Like you did with mine," Natalie said, her gaze twinkling. "Dip in and out, I mean."

Arthur felt himself growing red. He took another sip.

Natalie grinned. "I'm teasing you, doctor."

Jeffrey stepped into the room then, wearing a white apron, and gleefully announced dinner.

BEAMING, JEFF BROUGHT OUT plates stacked with undulating meadows of spaghetti and set them on the table before Arthur and Natalie. Glimpsing the portion, Arthur's eyes widened.

"Don't worry," Natalie said to him. "By the time you're done with the first helping you'll be asking for seconds. This is Jeff's magnum opus."

"The sauce came from my Italian stepmother's recipe,"

Jeff said. "It's all terribly top secret."

"Call me up if you ever need a guinea pig," Arthur said.

"Nah-uh," Natalie said with a smile. "That's my job. Would you like more wine?"

"Sure."

Natalie refilled his glass. Jeff declined more wine, and she poured some for herself.

"I'm probably reading way too much into this," said Arthur after his second bite. "But by any chance is serving spaghetti an inside joke?"

"How so?"

"You know, the Flying Spaghetti Monster?"

Natalie took a long sip of her wine. "I didn't know you were a closet Pastafarian."

"I'm not. If I were I'd be in a pirate costume."

"What is this?" Jeff said, eyebrow arched.

"Pastafarianism," Arthur said. "A satirical church. Pokes fun at religion."

"Pokes fun?" Natalie said. "More like skewers."

"Or boils," Arthur said. "Skewering is my job."

Natalie drove a fork-spun whirl of spaghetti into her mouth. "Touché, Mr. Moore."

"So what is this pasta church?" Jeff said.

"They worship the Flying Spaghetti Monster," Arthur said. "You know, you certainly can't prove it exists, but you can't prove it doesn't exist. That type of thing."

"I see," Jeff said. "That where string theory comes from? And the DNA double helix?"

Arthur shook his head.

"Hah, yeah I can see it now," Natalie said. "Each noodle represents a different path through space-time, a parallel universe. And it's all happening on the same plate."

"How do you explain the meat sauce?"

Natalie shrugged. "Dark matter?"

AFTER DINNER THEY ADJOURNED to the back terrace, Jeff grabbing another bottle of wine on the way out the door. Before them, distant window lights burned like a constant vigil in the dark hills of the neighborhood, somberly overseen by the shimmering full moon above. A summery freshness perfumed the air that reached Arthur in a nostalgic place, recalling childhood eves of sprawling free days.

Jeff lit a cigarette and sat in such a way that the soft summer breeze strayed the smoke from Natalie and Arthur.

"Sorry folks," he said, "just one of my assorted vices."

"Want to help me to get him to quit?" Natalie said to Arthur.

"He's smoked for all the years I've known him. I almost wonder if it gives him his secret managerial power."

Jeff laughed. "You better believe it."

"As long as he keeps it away from me, I'm okay," Arthur said.

"Yeah, well I have to smell it on him," said Natalie. "It's like going to bed with an ashtray."

"You used to like it."

"When I smoked, yes."

"Which was—what? As little as three weeks ago."

"More than that, jackass."

"I don't mind the smell so much," Arthur said. He patted his chest. "I have weak lungs."

"That's too bad," Natalie said with genuine concern, so much so that Arthur felt a little taken aback.

"Speaking of frailty," Jeff said, "how's David doing?"

Natalie straightened. "That's right, I was sorry to hear about his little incident."

"He seems to be okay, for now," Arthur said. "Stable. He's resting. We're still not sure what exactly is wrong with him."

Natalie cleared her throat. "David is your son's partner,

right?"

"Yes."

Natalie leaned forward. "Have they been tested for HIV?"

That she so brazenly asked this question startled Arthur. He admired her forthrightness.

"Jim's assured me that they've been tested," Arthur stared into his wine glass, momentarily silent, "well, several times already."

"I'm sorry if I've made you uncomfortable," Natalie said.

"No, not a problem. I guess I'm just overly paranoid. And it doesn't help that I took a while to totally accept the relationship." That last bit had just slipped out, much to Arthur's surprise. Normally he didn't admit to his original feelings of discomfort with Jim and David, even to himself. "I'm still worried, though. They're not sure what David has."

"Hey," Jeff said, "the reason I brought you two out here?" He pointed toward a tent of black tarp standing near the far edge of the patio. "My new telescope. Actually, my old telescope—built it myself, twenty years ago. Dragged it out of the garage the other day."

"You know Jeff once majored in astronomy?" Natalie asked Arthur. "Before he sold out to fleece writers."

Jeff smirked. "Until the math sent me a bit too far down the rabbit hole, yes."

"I think Saturn's visible now, isn't it?" Arthur said.

Jeff gazed into the glittered night. "Think so."

"We just look for the unblinking star, right?" Natalie said, joining Arthur who stood hunched over the eyepiece.

Jeff pointed upward. "Follow the elliptic, a path that runs generally east to west, always a straight shot across the sky. The brighter the dots, chances are that's a planet."

With Jeff's finger pointing they eventually found Saturn

through the eyepiece. They took turns gazing at the distant yellow ball and the perceptible rings encircling it. Arthur suddenly wished Linda were present to add her unique bubbliness.

Jeff peered last through the telescope as Arthur and Natalie sat back down. "You know, it's interesting," he said, "I think I remember reading that Saturn's rings are actually a rare and temporary phenomenon. Supposed to last only a few million years."

"You mean it didn't always have them?" Natalie said.

"I don't think so. We're lucky enough to witness it."

"Must be divine coincidence," Arthur said, toasting his glass skyward.

Natalie laughed. "Just like you sitting here across from me, doctor. I'm sure Jeff mentioned I wanted to chat with you about some things."

"Absolutely."

"And please, no more 'doctor'."

Natalie poured another glass of wine for herself and continued. "Sure thing, doctor."

Arthur offered her a grimace.

"So," Natalie said, eyes rolling thoughtfully up at the sky, as if expecting her next words to float down from the dark. She lowered her gaze to Arthur. "Just to sort of put this out there—I'm tired of seeing pastors and preachers duking it out with hardcore secularists. The media leaves little room for nuance. It's obvious why, of course, as having the two extremes bouncing off one another is best for ratings. Someone projects from the seat of religion, another from the seat of atheism, and nothing is gained except more spit particles in the heated air between. Am I right?"

"The coliseum," said Arthur.

"Beg pardon?"

"That's what I call it. Cerebral sparring. The Christians

and the Romans."

"Hah. Right. Well, frankly, I'm not sure what will be achieved by pitting the two extremes against one another. Throwing scripture at science and vice versa will not sway anyone to seriously consider the other side."

"There are exceptions. Dr. Francis Collins decoded the human genome and he's a devout Christian."

"Yes. But his arguments, at least the passion for his arguments, generally stem from his faith. I'm talking not about using in an argument what is known to either side, but more...hmm, I suppose instead bonding over what is unknown. Though I know with the 'God of the Gaps' argument that hasn't been going too smoothly either."

Arthur nodded, his world floating light in a pool of Cabernet. Jeff watched them from the shadows, eyes asquint, dragging his cigarette, unleashing smoke to the night.

"Are you familiar with neuroplasticity?" she asked him. Arthur nodded cautiously. "How we can rewire the biochemical and synaptic structure of our brains?"

"Yes, exactly. I find inescapable metaphysical beauty in that. I'm hesitant to use the word 'soul,' but I think you know what I mean. By what process do we affect the material in our heads, and thus the rest of our bodies? I realize there are 'monists' and 'dualists,' the former of the opinion that our mind and body are one matter, the latter allowing for a more mystical separation of the two. I'm more of the dualist view, as I can't really understand how thoughts happen. They have to come from somewhere, right? Sure, you think a thought, and a measurable electrical impulse goes off in your brain. But what drives that impulse in the first place? By what process does the brain, thinking on itself, change its own architecture? What's the energetic prime mover at work there?"

"Quite a jungle of inquiry," he posed.

"Sorry."

"No, it's okay. Though I can't know what no one else knows—"

"I realize that. I'm only asking your opinion."

"Also known as upward versus downward causation."

"Elaborate, please."

Arthur spent a moment gazing into the sky. "Well, downward causation is the more metaphysical aspect that you were referring to, where the thoughts come into our head from the ether. Upward causation, on the other hand, posits that all thinking is empirical, that it arises from within the neural network of the brain and that it is instigated in varying chemical reactions, usually by external environmental factors. If you're hit on the arm and your arm hurts, it doesn't mean the pain receptors suddenly dropped in from the sky. They were there all along, until something environmental made them come alive."

"Okay," Natalie said. She took a long sip of wine. Briefly Arthur wondered if the alcohol might loosen her inhibitions. He felt aroused, but tried to ignore it. A thought occurred to him that his libido was the only voice of truth in the room, that all this conversation was mere decoration.

"But you're right," he said. "When you say that, in consciousness studies, reconciliation between the material and the immaterial is a very, very murky subject into which science has only begun to dip its toes."

"You're certain that, when the murk clears, it will show nothing but material."

Arthur shrugged. "If it ever clears. I can't be certain. But I'd say the scorecard for material versus immaterial has become a tad one-sided as science has progressed, wouldn't you say? Less and less room for the God of the gaps to hide."

"There's still the problem of what got the cosmic ball rolling in the first place."

"Ah!" Jeff said, as if to assert his presence.

"Well sure, but that's a cop-out."

Natalie regarded him uncertainly.

When are you going to catch up to me? He imagined her to be thinking. *When are you going to see the light?*

"Have I lost you," he asked, "or have you lost me?"

"I have another question," she replied, ignoring his attempt at levity.

"Shoot."

"Interdependence."

"Interdependence of what?"

"Of everything," Natalie said. "Everything on Earth depends on something else to survive. A man needs to sit down, needs to make a chair, and the chair needs wood from a tree, needs a floor to stand on, and both the floor and the tree need soil to stand on, and the soil needs the planet and the elements to make it so … you can go back as far as you'd like."

"Nothing inherently exists, is what you're saying."

"Right. It's a staple of some Eastern traditions. Namely Buddhism. Buddhist monks talk of emptiness, which is a huge part of balancing yourself as an enlightened being. The Dalai Lama once noted that physicists continually uncover finer and finer components of matter, from atoms to quarks, but can't pinpoint where it ends."

Arthur's head bobbed thoughtfully. "I don't doubt that some ancient traditions stumbled on some very poignant truths, or revelations, long before we actually observed them in the lab. But I'm not clear as to your question…"

"Perhaps it's not so much a question as it is my own… belief, I guess. If everything can be traced back to emptiness, if nothing exists the way we perceive, then what is existence if not ethereal? How do you take a reductionist, materialist perspective when all this around us, even our bodies, might be illusory? When the subatomic particles that compose us have a very irrational and tenuous basis in what we perceive to be reality?"

"There's the Zero Point Field," Arthur said.

Natalie nodded, approving his point.

"You know the theory?"

"I know of it. The universal tissue, as I see it."

"Sort of."

"I'm a little shaky, though."

Arthur chuckled. "So am I. We can't not be. The principle involves the notion that space is filled with particles of negative energy. These particles manifest in our realm very ephemerally as tiny electromagnetic fluctuations, popping up all over the universe. They never completely lose momentum but are the lowest amount of 'force' possible in an energy state. So this field of queasy uneasy particles may be the very ground of existence, governed by uncertainty and complete unpredictability."

"There's a book on the Zero Point principle I remember called *The Field*," Natalie said. "Have you read it? By a Lynne McTaggart, I believe."

Arthur paused, if trying to place the name. "No, I haven't." But he had. At a conference years before someone had handed him a copy—for all he remembered, it could've been McTaggart herself—and over that subsequent week he had digested it in total, had reread key sections, had in late-hour wakefulness turned over its ideas. Then, VAS member Gary Thomas, novelist and engineer, had seen him with the copy and, stern-faced, said, "Art, you can't be serious. *This* tripe? This is more pseudoscience." Pinched in sudden embarrassment, he'd stared at Thomas, who finished with, "Don't let them get you *that* easy. Wouldn't be good for us."

"According to McTaggart," Natalie said, "her theory shows we are swimming in a sea of quantum light."

"Okay," Arthur said reluctantly.

"Aren't the metaphysical, or even spiritual connotations, pretty self-evident?"

"Why? Because of the light factor?"

"Well sure. Light itself has been a staple of the religious experience since the very beginning of thought. As you said, some ancient traditions may well have stumbled upon an intrinsic field of knowledge long before Western science confirmed it. It's all how we describe it. Whether it's God's light or quantum light, it doesn't matter. The titles are merely compressed air or black symbols on a page. What's real—or unreal, I suppose—has no label."

"Sure. All the same stuff. Defining itself through us."

"You sound like a pantheist more than an atheist," said Natalie.

Arthur remained silent, unsure himself.

"Which means you'd be in my boat," Natalie finished.

"Coleridge said there's no difference between pantheism and atheism."

"Do you believe that?"

Arthur shrugged. "To a degree, yes. Though I think pantheism allows for greater leeway in the celestial watchmaker idea than does atheism, which tacks a little more 'happy accident'."

"Celestial watchmaker," Jeff interjected, glancing over from his prior contemplation of space. His tone was not that of a question, yet still inquiring.

"Basically," Natalie said, "a nickname for a God that tweaked the universe just so, tinkered with it and wound it up so that it might run by certain mechanisms, and then sat back to wait for it to run itself down."

"I see."

"I take issue with the 'accident' notion, though," Natalie said. "The happy accident. Saying that life came about

through a series of unintentional catastrophes and muta-
tions implies the existence of a prior intention gone awry. If
you believe in 'accidents,' you're allowing for a God, just an
incompetent one."

"Not really. It just refers to a deviation from the norm.
But sure, it's not the best choice of words," Arthur said.
"Though we'll take any divine demotion we can get. If we
can go from perfection to incompetent, then going from
incompetent to absent isn't much of a stretch."

Nodding, Jeff said, "Well, I've got that meeting tomorrow, so I should probably hit the sack."

"Thanks for tonight, Jeff," Arthur said, shaking his hand.

Natalie rose alongside Jeff and kissed him. "Thanks,
hon," she said, before sitting back down.

"Please don't throttle each other out here without me to
referee," Jeff said, winking. "I don't want to come out here
tomorrow morning and find you both lying in a pool of
physics and philosophy."

Both laughed. Arthur tried to envision Jeff's scenario as
his manager slunk through the sliding glass door and disappeared from the porch.

"Alright," Natalie said. "So just to touch a bit more on
the pantheism topic. Many such as yourself demand that
our worldview be seen through the prism of reason and
rationality, that we use only what is visibly or experientially
true as tools for dealing with our individual and collective
affairs."

Arthur tipped his glass toward her. "Good way of saying
it."

"Okay, well, pantheism agrees with that pretense.
However, from what I know of your ideas, pantheism also
allows for more of what is experientially true to be taken
into account than does atheism. I suspect atheism likes to
restrict its beliefs to things objectively documented between

the covers of textbooks."

"Not necessarily. But go on. What do you mean that it 'allows for more'?"

"Allows for more of what is experientially true about the human condition to be taken into consideration, rather than simply viewing things as collections of atoms and molecules."

"Okay…"

"I mean, it is experientially true that life is both objective and subjective, and in fact may be only subjective, as far as we know. It's observably true, also, that we are the universe, right? You're an Arthur-shaped chunk of the universe listening to a Natalie-shaped chunk of the universe talk about…well, the universe."

"Sounds so masturbatory."

Natalie chuckled. "In a way, sure. But when, as the whole cosmic body, you're the only game in town, what else is there to do?"

Arthur blinked a few times and shook his head, amusedly.

"So pantheism," Natalie continued, "is the idea that no separate God exists, that God is the universe, and vice versa. Now, I personally further the concept and subscribe to panentheism, where God transcends the material universe into realms beyond our understanding, where the cosmos may be little more than a blood cell in God's veins. We and everything else are just small, infinite pieces of God bent on experiencing and evolving itself back to knowing itself as God. The 'infinite' part is Einsteinian. Energy just is, and is indestructible. The universe is one giant ball of constantly recycling energy, and we are no more separate from this energy than are waves from the ocean. Our yearning to experience life is evident in just that: clearly, we all—or most of us—desire to live, and to experience life in whatever way most pleases us. And that experience is only possible through separation from the whole, even if it's an illusion."

"An illusion?"

"Sure. A moment ago I mentioned interdependence, and the ground of all existence, within which all things are connected and, dare I say, 'one.' This idea, I believe, is also supported by the phenomenon of nonlocality, in which two separated particles will mirror one another's effects instantaneously, faster than the speed of light."

"Right."

"If the universe originated from a single, all-entangled, white-hot seed, one can assume that all of existence originated from that one single seed. How can such a thing experience its own wonder without interacting with something else? So paradoxically, separation was needed to ultimately experience the truth of oneness, which, I believe, we are honing in on in the scientific field. But I also believe this knowledge was with us for eons, going back to when we started walking erect and looking skyward. Knowledge buried so deeply in our DNA that its call was scarcely audible to our primitive minds. The idea that there's a God, or a life force, in all of creation birthed some of our older religions, like shamanism and paganism. We heard increments of it as evolution proceeded, through texts like the Bible and the Bhagavad Gita. But our minds could only translate our deep cosmic knowledge through the use of symbols and stories. That was the extent of our primitive capability for millennia. Of course, I also believe Eastern practices such as Hinduism and Buddhism operated on a clearer frequency to access this knowledge than did those who produced Western theology."

"That's all conjecture, though," Arthur said. "I think you have a point in saying the universe wants to understand itself. But the idea that there was a discerning intention behind the big bang because the universe wanted to understand itself still occupies the realm of faith. If the universe existed as a singularity before separating into a trillion pieces, how could it have been aware of its own lack of experience? How could the universe have rationally thought, 'I want to experience myself?'"

Arthur paused, allowing her time to digest his words. "Also, a desire to live, or a zest to live, if that's what you're referring to, will clearly be naturally selected for and proliferate versus no desire to live, because it's a better survival trait. And several theories of the cosmos don't involve any sort of mystical explosion. M theory, for instance, has lines of undulating membranes separated by a thin dimensional veil. On the off chance these membranes cross and collide, the explosive impact generates a universe. And there could be many such collisions and many explosions and hence many universes, some of them floating dead through the void, totally unsuited for life. No accident, no intention."

"And these membranes came from…?"

"Theorists looking for answers. Theorists uncomfortable with the notion of God." Arthur smiled and shrugged. "Or else they're simply the noodles of the Flying Spaghetti Monster. Who knows?"

⚹

"I just got a gig at Earth Works," Jim said breathlessly over the phone.

A bewildered smile crept across Arthur's face. He stared at his computer monitor. Behind the digital document of his manuscript sat multiple windows: a fresh game of solitaire, the new post at Hyperthought—the blog of scientist and inventor William Turgess—and, toward the bottom, a tasteful showcase of skin, ready when the mood struck him.

"You work there already," Arthur said. "Did you get promoted?"

"No, no!" Jim said. "An art gig. I've been commissioned for a mural on their east wall—that's the street side."

"Jim that's great," Arthur said. "Congratulations."

"Yeah, David wants me to show you a few of the designs I've drawn up. Our friend Camille is a wonderful illustrator, and she'll be helping me put it up. She's done murals before."

"I don't think I've met Camille," Arthur said.

"She's pretty cool. I can certainly use her help. Mr. Hathaway's promised a dedication ceremony when it's complete."

"Good for you, Jim."

"Thanks."

"How is David, anyway?"

Jim sighed. "He's hanging in there. They think it might be Lyme disease. We're hikers, you know. Every other test under the sun has come back negative, which is good on one hand. But it's starting to wear me down."

Silently, Arthur let out a long exhale, one that had been building for quite some time.

"I'm glad it's not HIV," Arthur said. That thought, mercifully, could now retract its stinger from his brain and fly away.

"No," Jim said. "No need to worry about that, Dad."

"It'll be okay, Jim," Arthur said.

"Right, Dad."

He couldn't tell if his son was being facetious or empathetic. For a moment, silence hung between them.

"When are you leaving for the *Mann's Watch* panel?" Jim asked in a careful voice.

"About a week and a half."

"And you're driving, I take it?"

"That's the plan, yes."

"Going alone?"

Arthur considered the question. "We'll see."

"Oh?"

"Let's leave it at that," he said, with a rueful laugh.

THE SAME MOTIONS—back and forth, up, down—the same moans, mostly from her, and the same impersonal feel, as though he were working a machine. Seldom during sex did Linda actively touch him, preferring instead to lie on her back and allow him to initiate whatever gesture or motion pleased him. Arthur begrudged this, begrudged it more and more with each new mechanical bout of lovemaking.

Linda was actually well aware of her tendency to be "vanilla in bed," as she put it, though to Arthur's slight annoyance she stopped short of apologizing for it and took no initiative to change the immobile missionary position she preferred. "I like to stay with what works for me," she said. To maximize his stimulation, Arthur imagined Natalie beneath him, recalled also specific moments from his marriage to Wendy, especially from the earlier years and especially from the honeymoon at the ski lodge in the Rockies, where no space capable of accommodating two bodies had been off-limits to their more libidinous explorations. Though he'd certainly not been a virgin before settling down with Wendy, for Arthur she'd validated all the coital hype.

He and Linda lay still in his bedroom, sex evaporating from their skin, while the darkness outside threw a windy midnight shadow party in preparation for a storm. For a few moments their wordless breathing filled the room, until at last Arthur spoke. Even though it was his own voice breaking the silence, the sound still startled him.

"Linda."

"Yeah?" Her voice passed through a satisfied smile.

"Do you remember me mentioning the *Mann's Watch* panel on August thirtieth?"

"Sure."

"Would you like to drive with me to LA? We'd need to leave about a week before the panel. And it'll take us another week to drive back home. It won't be a short trip."

A few seconds passed. Linda snuggled closer and placed a hand on his arm. "I would absolutely love to go with you," she said. "That would be a lot of fun. I haven't driven across the country since I was a teenager."

"Hmm," Arthur responded, already doubting the wisdom of his decision to invite her along.

"Anyone going to watch the house?" Linda said. "Jim?"

"Actually Jeff's offered to do it. He'll stop by once in a while."

More silence.

"I think," Linda said, in a sudden shift of topics, "I might go to church tomorrow."

Arthur furrowed his brow. He knew she hadn't been in a while. "Oh?"

"It's my daughter," she said. "You know she's been studying abroad."

"In Spain, yes."

"Yeah. Sonia's been attending services there with her new boyfriend. And she's been pressuring me as to why I haven't been going."

"Okay."

"I don't really have a good answer for her. And there are things I miss about the church I used to attend before I met you."

In a low voice Arthur offered, "I can go with you, if you'd like."

Linda's head whipped toward him. "Really?"

And now I'm locked in, he thought. Dead bolted. He already felt the weight of the commitment pressing heavily upon his chest. In truth, Arthur despised all religious forms of social obligation, steeped as they were in soul-poisoning ritual. He'd not allowed himself to be put through such torment since he was a child, when his mother would every Sunday drag him and Johnny off to services.

Perhaps sensing her own overanxiousness, Linda's demeanor swiftly lightened. "That would be nice, Arthur. It's Grace Presbyterian in Williamsburg."

He hesitated, then offered her a grudging, "Alright."

"I can assure you you'll be welcome," Linda said. "Probably more than by most ordinary Christians. It's a mellow atmosphere."

He stroked Linda's hair. "Sounds good."

"Where you going, Johnny?"

Arthur runs after his brother, through woods that have ceased to be familiar. They're too deep now, the cloistered trees imposing, bending, leaning like eavesdroppers into some private dialogue. He and Johnny have strayed too far from the comfortable proximity of home. Mom would be angry. She would probably spank them both if she found out.

Johnny wears camouflage, carries a gun. A real gun, Arthur realizes. A gun like soldiers carry.

Johnny's eyes widen. "Someone is after us, Arthur."

Chills race down his spine. Arthur peers around but sees no one.

"Who?" Arthur asks.

"The man."

"Johnny," Arthur says, "we better go back."

"Don't be stupid. We can't go back," Johnny says, stop-

ping at the base of a large oak tree. Johnny stares upward. "We have to climb. We have to see. We have to catch him first."

This kid isn't my brother.

A gunshot reverberates through the forest. A bullet slashes through the foliage very close to his brother's head.

Arthur freezes and stares at Johnny, whose mouth hangs dumbly open.

"That man's coming," says Johnny.

"What man, Johnny?" Arthur scans the brooding forest but doesn't see anyone there.

"Help me, Art," Johnny pleads with him, "Help me get up to the top."

But Arthur only stands there watching helplessly as his brother shimmies up the tree.

A FULL BLADDER rousted Arthur from the dream. Bleary-eyed he rose to his feet, his body breaking out in shivers from the chilly caress of the early morning air. The darkness outside had begun to retreat from the minty glow of dawn. He stumbled into the bathroom and had already begun to relieve himself when a distant splash of water caught his attention. Still standing over the toilet, Arthur turned his head and peered out the bathroom window.

The gray fisherman hovered near the edge of the pond, his rod trembling as he pulled on it, little more than a bobbing shadow against the water. He'd caught something, though it didn't seem nearly feisty enough to be Moby. Arthur watched for a moment, growing more awake as his irritation set in. He was about to open the window to call out when the splashing died down and the fisherman grew still.

The fish wriggled off the hook and swam away, leaving surface ripples that slowly smoothed out behind him.

Arthur sensed the fisherman staring back at him, and had the queer notion that the man had known all along that he'd been watching. Even so, Arthur kept vigil until the fisherman finally reeled in his line and moved away into the crimson dawn shadows.

GRACE PRESBYTERIAN—or, as it was apparently known to its congregation, "Grace Prez"— stood as an unremarkable, steepled brick building, its most delightful feature the well-manicured courtyard sporting benches and shading umbrellas that Arthur assumed served as a popular post-pew congregation spot. Out front by the sidewalk, the marquee offered the cute, questionably uplifting phrase, "Soular Powered by the Son."

Arthur and Linda walked in through the arched doorway, Arthur lowering his head to mimic the general reverence of the crowd. An elderly couple greeted them, the husband thin and gaunt in contrast to his jolly, well-rounded wife.

"Hi Linda, how are you?" the woman said as they embraced. "I haven't seen you in quite a while."

"I know—I'm sorry, I've just been…bleh." Linda waved away the rest of her sentence.

"Well, we're glad to have you back. How's your daughter?"

"Sonia's fine. She's studying abroad in Spain right now."

"Oh really?" said the woman. "Does she speak the language?"

"Yes she does. She's met a Spanish beau and everything. It was funny—a few days ago she asked me how to say something specific in English."

"How funny." The woman turned to Arthur. "I'm Marilyn. This is Victor."

Linda flushed momentarily, clearly embarrassed by not having initiated the introduction. Arthur didn't mind. In fact, until she addressed him he'd not even truly felt present. More like he'd wafted in on the breeze like a curious specter.

"Nice to meet you, I'm Arthur," he said. They shook hands.

"You look very familiar," Victor said, scratching his chin. "Have you joined us before?"

"No, I haven't. But you may have seen me on TV. I'm an author and columnist."

It occurred to him how well those words encapsulated the modern-day absurdity of the social entertainment coliseum.

"Oh wow, a celebrity among us," said Victor.

"I'm not very big," said Arthur. "It's mostly just been local radio and cable shows."

"Still impressive." They drifted toward a seat among the gathering congregation. Marilyn brushed her hand across Linda's arm. "What a find. I'm certainly glad you two could be with us today."

"I am too," Linda said.

The reverend, a man named Matthews, stood at the pulpit, dressed in a shiny rill of robe. He looked quite young to Arthur, an amicable face tucked beneath a well-trimmed beard and a neatly combed shock of blond hair.

Arthur's gaze crawled across the crowd, and then came to rest again on the reverend. *This man speaks for everyone here*, Arthur thought. *Indeed, yes, he speaks also for mitochondria, for protozoa, for june bugs, for mosquitoes, for deep-sea anglerfish, for the prehistoric giant sloth, for the warthogs and the hyenas devouring them. He speaks for dead lifeless planets, for asteroid belts, for every imploded galaxy and every star that went bust two billion years ago.*

Fitting.

In a soothing cadence, Matthews began the service with opening prayers before eventually launching into his weekly

Sunday sermon.

"Salvation," said Matthews, his voice echoing ominously in Arthur's ears. "Some may describe salvation as the work of the individual, when in fact it is not up to us. It is a gift from God, granted us by His divine will. It is grace. It is strength and goodwill. It is His light. Just as we had nothing to do with our physical birth on this Earth, so too do we have nothing to do with our spiritual birth. In his life story Billy Graham notes that in order to be born again we must take four basic steps: recognize, repent, receive, and confess..."

Arthur glanced furtively at Linda. He studied the rest of the congregation, looked at Victor and Marilyn, and he smelled the wooden air. He knew the angular, archaic dusty ambiance of this place. As Matthews spoke, Arthur recalled his childhood in Pennsylvania when he and John would sit squirming beside Mom, the precious weekend draining away minute by minute, his young veins thickening with urges to run and scream and disrupt everything, his young brain parting the sea of rhetoric and focusing ahead on when he would be leaving here, leaving this place that told him unnaturally about nature while the real nature, the raw fluid thing, God's true grounds, called him away from this desperate artifice of man.

And, just as he had then, Arthur found himself gulping down dry pungent air. He needed some kind of release—a laugh, a cry, a scream. Something.

Leaning over to Linda, he whispered, "I'll be right back."

Marilyn threw him a concerned glance, but said nothing.

"...Spirit is endless," Mathews continued from the pulpit. "There can be no restrictions on spirit, for it moves through us all as swiftly and as universally as the wind. And when we are baptized we may be more in tune with this

Spirit, to experience through our senses some manifestation of God's kingdom..."

Quietly, Arthur moved down the aisle and slipped out into the morning. Gray summer thunderheads now blotted the sky, enveloping the blue. He breathed in deeply, felt the waning sun on his face and the strengthening, rain-scented breezes washing over him.

The words John had spoken on that day floated suddenly back to him: *Someone likes me up there.*

Behind John's disembodied phone voice Arthur could hear all the commotion, the choppy gargle mass of voices and the constant cry of sirens. And he could feel, even through the impersonal phone receiver, the swirling energy of terror, which that day, unbeknownst to all, had only just begun.

"It's very eerie," John continued. "I'm looking right now at the wreckage. It's like the North Tower is hemorrhaging smoke."

John did not actually see the first plane make impact. Like many all around, below and above him, he was jolted out of his desk by that tremendous and alien thunder, felt a trembling underfoot that brought to mind some angry subterranean deity awakening beneath the plaza. Natural curiosity carried him, along with thousands of others, to the north-facing windows that framed the other tower, which stood there, ruptured and smoldering. Natural caution then sent John filing out from the South Tower. Once outside, his neck craned up so he could study the disaster while the crowds roiled and moved all around him, he phoned Arthur.

"I have it on," Arthur said, the phone to his ear and his gaze on the TV, where anchorpersons and reporters speculated about what might have sent an airplane so catastrophically astray. "Looks like you dodged a bullet, thank God."

Though the phrase popped out automatically, John quickly capitalized on it. "Yeah, seriously," he said. "Fifty-fifty odds. Someone likes me up there, I guess. Or maybe God just likes South Tower people better."

At the time Arthur felt a weird sense of privilege, having a personal connection to the televised tragedy. It provided him with sudden and awkward confirmation that all the things he saw on the news actually did happen, that they didn't occur in some other dimension of reality.

"Okay," John had said. "Looks like they're telling us to head back in."

"Head back in?" Arthur's gut tensed. "As in, go back to work?"

"Yeah, they're trying to trim down the chaos out here on the streets."

How stupid is that? Arthur thought. Yet he kept quiet. The incident did seem like a freak accident—as John suggested, a fifty-fifty dice roll in which he and his thousands of fellow South Tower denizens emerged with favor. Besides, ever since childhood Arthur found it difficult to express his opinions about what John, ever the elder, wiser brother, the one with the firmer and more authoritative grip on the world, ought to do.

"Be careful," was all Arthur said.

As children they'd often petitioned the universe for signs, setting up "If X happens, then Y" kind of situations between two random, unconnected events. "If we hear a cop siren tonight," ten-year-old John uttered once in the darkness of their shared room, "it'll be a snow day tomorrow." This recreational groping for celestial validation suggested a subconscious reliance on the loyalty of the cosmos, on the fact that God—in Santa Claus fashion—owed them for being good. It was a habit that persisted into Arthur's adult life, though he would never have admitted it. Whatever faith he'd had as a youth had contracted over his maturing years to this oasis of the irrational, this place to which he might psychologically retreat when the world became too chaotic or indifferent, where he would try to pick out some coherent story from the mess.

After hanging up the phone Arthur continued to watch the TV coverage of the plane crash. As he stared at that monolithic image of the smoke-blackened tower, Arthur thought, *If John gets through today, it means there is a God.*

That moment had not brought an end to his faith, because he never considered himself a true believer. Some spiritual mechanism inside him had long since gone defunct. Why try to touch the untouchable, when there was so much immediately surrounding one to touch? Never made much sense. Yet Arthur had needed some grand, absolute confirmation to shut down whatever spiritual aspect might still persist within him, even though he knew it was simply he who was making the rules and always had been.

Returning to the present, he looked back at Grace Church, standing stark and white against a backdrop of pine trees.

What am I doing here?

He remained outside until his breathing slowed to a normal pace.

Can't be afraid of this.

He turned and went back inside. He smiled at Linda.

V

ARTHUR STOOD ACROSS FROM JIM AT THE kitchen table, gripping the backrest of the chair for additional support. "I'll only be gone two weeks," he said. "At the most."

"Why can't you just dope up on a plane and go to sleep, like everyone else?" Jim asked, his fingers drumming fast and rapid on the table's wooden surface.

"You mean, why don't I just stay here?"

Jim shrugged affirmatively.

"It's difficult for me," he said. "I realize it's stupid. But you know it's difficult for me."

Arthur's fear of flying had been with him his whole life. Even as a child, during the two episodes that his family had traveled by air, Arthur could not escape that terrible sense of vulnerability. If someone flipped the wrong switch in a car or a train, the resulting accident did not involve a thirty thousand-foot plummet. Baseless as he knew the fear was, it kept expanding with time, finally reaching an irreversible crescendo on September 11th, 2001.

Jim's eyes revealed his unspoken incredulity. How many important words, he wondered, lay dormant inside of his son? Jim always held back a reserve of unspoken thought, preferring to speak his feelings in codes of color, in the swirling dabs of his paintbrush. Right now his son had no canvas before him upon which to unleash his thoughts and emotions, but Arthur felt he could tell what was going on, and why Jim, normally so independent, was pleading in such a roundabout manner for him to stay home. It was David. David, stretched out in bed, sleeping so much of every day, like an enervated old man stuffed inside young skin. The exact nature of his illness remained unknown. *Unexpected.* Jim always reacted badly to the unexpected. That was his father in him, Arthur mused. Overreactive resentment of the world not obeying the plans he'd laid out for it. *Stop fucking with me,* he imagined Jim might be thinking. *Just leave me alone.*

Arthur studied his son, brought his finger to the scar on

his own chin. He'd come to the school on that day years back but arrived late, in time only to see the ghastly toll the other boys' fists had taken on his son's delicate face and body. He knew it was his fault because he was late picking up Jim from school. And all the while he drove his bleeding son home he thought, *I did this, I did this.* Not just arriving late but everything, every disjointed moment he'd shared in the life of his son.

"Dad," Jim said that night, his tender thirteen-year-old face bruised and cut. He sat on the edge of the armchair cushion, staring at the floor. "I think I'm gay."

Arthur, bringing him water, stopped in his tracks.

"I don't know what to do with that, Jim," he'd said.

Arthur knew that ideas of religious origin polluted even the modern secular mind, became so established that most people lost track of the roots of their own conditioning. God didn't like homosexuality, of course—that was where social rejection of gay people got started. God didn't like it, and even when people forgot God they didn't—couldn't—relinquish God's equally imaginary and twisted set of beliefs. Arthur's body and Arthur's brain had themselves bought into such nonsense, overruling his conscious rationality. The conditioned limbic, reptilian brain reacted faster than the human intellect.

You did this, he'd thought. *And you're already too late to fix it.*

"I'll be back in just a couple weeks," Arthur said. "You and David will be fine."

"You know," said Jim, "David and I were talking about moving to Los Angeles."

Arthur blinked. "What?"

"Who knows if it'll ever happen. But once he finishes med school we were thinking of going to LA. It's a better climate, socially and weather-wise. And it's got a huge arts community. And ...”

"And—you'd be closer to your mom," Arthur finished for him.

"We would, yes. You'd be fine out here by yourself, would you not?"

"Jim—"

"Dad, it's alright. We'll talk about it when you get back."

Arthur took particular notice of his son's penetrative green eyes, which seemed to admonish him.

Just don't be late, they said.

ONCE INTERSTATE 81 HIT KNOXVILLE, Arthur and Linda merged onto Interstate 40, passing the Great Smoky Mountains, the cities of Nashville and Little Rock. They continued on across the southern United States, where Pilot truck stops and garish billboards proved the most plentiful sights beyond rolling green pastures and isolated forests. Most advertisements bellowed about some restaurant or buffet. One in particular, for a "Steakosaurus Café," challenged drivers with its monstrous meaty mascot to *"Eat a Dino's Fill!"*

Occasional Confederate flags hung from numerous fences and building facades. Biblical signs also began to materialize—some to Arthur's amusement, others to his chagrin. *Being Born Again Don't Take 9 Months,* said one. And, not two miles later: *By the way, the Bible is on the Non-Fiction Shelf.* Others seemed more hostile: *Repent or Perish in the Lake of Fire.*

Images from Arthur's childhood wafted out of the tiny hamlets of sagging homes and trailers, surrounded by wind-tussled weeds. Clean and quaint they were, somewhat decrepit yet somehow still charming. He'd been here before, had lived and played in a town much like these, had been considered one of the "folks." Now it seemed impossible that those years had ever existed. While often glorified by country stars and politicians as comprising the heart of America, in his experience countless people who lived in rural regions were actually bored, frustrated, willfully ignorant and horny, relieving themselves through crutches that too often became fixations or addictions: drugs, booze, sex, food, religion—or any dangerous combination thereof. They were all drugs anyway, the "opiate of the masses," as Marx had famously observed. Whether people self-medicated through pills or in pews, in some sense they were all escaping their too-tiny lives of quiet desperation.

"Do you believe in hell?" Arthur suddenly asked Linda.

Linda shifted in her seat. "I don't know. I believe in love more than evil, if that makes any sense. I mean, I think there's a malevolent presence in the world. Whether it's something like Satan, who knows?"

They passed a homemade banner hanging from the side of a barn: *Nuke The Sand Niggers.* Linda gazed at it reflectively.

"Though sometimes I don't think we need his help," she added.

BY OKLAHOMA they felt the first true wave of Southern humidity. They had also nearly exhausted all the tapes and CDs both he and Linda had brought along for the trip— including two runs of ABBA's *Gold* album—and, as Arthur said, they were almost back at the top of the order.

Somewhere out in a rolling green nowhere, the car slanted suspiciously and began to tug left. Arthur heard the *flub-flub-blub* of soft rubber and pulled over to confirm one of his biggest automotive fears.

A flat.

"I don't know anything about cars, sorry to say," Linda said, her head out the window. "To me it's always been men's work."

"Well, not this man." He checked his AAA card, which had long ago expired.

"Did you know how to change a tire?" Linda asked.

Yes, goddammit. Yes, because I'm a man and a grown one and it should be innate.

Goddammit.

"John taught me when I was a teenager," he said.

"Who?"

"My brother."

"Oh," Linda said, with a sullen nod.

And if you could somehow take over for the next few minutes, Johnny, that'd be most appreciated.

The tire had been punctured by what appeared to be a rusted nail. Arthur popped open the trunk, unloaded the luggage and unearthed the spare tire and jack. Having reached the end of his knowledge base, he confronted the flat with hopeless confusion.

Son of a bitch.

"Do you need help with anything?" Linda offered.

"No, no, I'm okay." He walked once around the car, as if searching for answers in the dirt. Arthur stared again at the deflated tire.

"Look!" Linda exclaimed, pointing now. "I think somebody's stopping."

Arthur glanced up. About a quarter-mile away, the rusty pickup had already flashed its emergency blinkers. Arthur watched the vehicle swerve to the side of the road in a cascade of dirt.

"Oh, Christ," he muttered.

"What's wrong, Art?"

As the truck drew closer, Arthur noticed the encrusted paint job, the fishing nets and paint cans in the back and the wide metal baleen of its grill. The driver was likely some redneck returning from a bout of hunting and fishing and drinking. Who knew what could be in store for a stranded, middle-aged couple on the highway, if some rambunctious simian wanted to have a little fun? What if the driver stalked them after they repaired the flat? Blew out the other three tires? What if—?

Arthur hadn't moved, but the truck was slowing down, gravel crunching under its wide wheels. One of the headlights was broken.

The driver stepped out, a thin man in denim overalls with a wiry beard, wearing a ball cap. Red Sox. Like Jim's. Arthur raised an eyebrow.

"Hey there," the man said. "Got some trouble?"

"Yeah. Flat tire."

"Not a gearhead?"

"Not exactly." Arthur gestured to the man's ball cap. "Sox fan?"

"Not originally," the man said. "My son lives in Boston. I've learned to like 'em." He knelt down beside Arthur in front of the tire. "Well you found the spare, that there's a start. Want me to show you the ropes?"

"Sure. It's been a while."

Mr. Red Sox walked around to the front passenger's seat, where Linda sat flipping through a brochure. "Ma'am?" he said.

"Oh, yes?"

"Would you mind getting out? Less weight. Makes it easier to jack up."

"Sure." Hastily Linda climbed from the car and scurried closer to Arthur.

Mr. Red Sox knelt down, went to work. He slid the carjack in place, turned and twisted it to the appropriate height, then unscrewed the nuts and removed the flat before returning it to the trunk where the spare had once been. He then lifted the spare into place and retightened the nuts.

Arthur watched the process intently, too afraid to look over at Linda for fear of her expression confirming his already deep feelings of inadequacy.

Mr. Red Sox stood and offered a satisfied wave to the newly installed tire. As Arthur began returning their luggage to the trunk, the man asked, "Where you goin'?"

"Los Angeles," Linda answered, as she settled back into the passenger's seat.

"Oh man. Yeah, well, you'll definitely want to stop at the next tire place and get a new one, 'cause spares are only meant to be temporary—get you the rest of the way to point B. There's one in Oklahoma City I can point you to, ain't much further. Here, let me give you directions…"

Linda leaned out her open window and called back, "That'd be great. Thank you so much."

"Yes, thank you," Arthur said, unearthing his wallet. "How much do I owe you?"

The man waved him away. "Oh, don't worry about it, man."

"Are you sure?"

"I'm sure."

Arthur hung there in a limbo of guilt, incredulity and gratitude for a long moment, then finally extended his hand. "Thank you so much, Mister…?"

"Just call me John," the man responded, as he took Arthur's hand with a firm, dry grip.

The bodies thrashed, melded, little more than indistinct shadows as they unleashed themselves upon the person sprawled on the ground between them, the person cowering and screaming, the person Arthur could see only through

fleeting openings between flailing limbs and cloth. They were a block away as he ran to them, but it felt like he was running on sand. With every step the altercation receded, eluding his touch or involvement, as though it existed in its own closed world being projected here from elsewhere, unalterable though maddeningly visible. He could see the kicking legs, the arms thrust up in vain defense. And he saw the eyes and that they were the eyes he had known these last thirteen years, the eyes of his own son and they were horrified beyond measure, reflecting evils that should never, ever touch a child's soul. He ran and ran. Arthur had never before felt such a symbiotic connection with another human being as he did in that endless moment. He could feel each blow as if it was being delivered to his own body, and he could hear every thought in his son's frightened mind being vaporized in the wordless breath pulsing from his lungs. A feeling of helpless rage overtook him and it drove him relentlessly forward.

Suddenly he was upon them. They were touchable. Arthur ripped the attackers away from his son, whose pulpy face glistened a ghastly red from the blood. A violent backlash, then one of the young fuckers struck Arthur's chin and opened a wound that would scar him the rest of his life. He hungered to spill their blood, make them feel what his son was feeling.

Jim lay twisted, injured and groaning on the sidewalk. He loved his son, Arthur realized. He did. He loved him no matter what. He was Jim's father, and Jim was his son...and it was really as simple as that. As devastatingly complex as that.

ARTHUR AWOKE SHAKING, and looked at the clock.

2:34 a.m.

From a distance issued the melancholy cry of a cargo train rumbling across the Texan landscape. Arthur had been driving for three days now. He paused, befuddled in the darkness, until he remembered they were spending the night in an Amarillo motel.

He listened to Linda's soft breathing as she quietly slept. *You shouldn't have left Jim.*

Arthur rose and padded to the window, pulled the curtain aside and peeked out at the barren black streets. *What if the world ended?* Was this where he wanted to be? Who he wanted to be with? Had he become the person he hoped to be? Arthur gazed at the empty streets before him, thoughts flurrying through his brain. Could overthinking drive one crazy? A professor had once said of Nietzsche with dark humor: "Philosophy sent him to the nuthouse." Probably not the full story. Certainly not the full story: syphilis was the more likely culprit. But the notion had planted a seedling of paranoia in Arthur.

He retrieved his cell phone from the bedside stand and gingerly texted Jim, one of the few text messages he'd ever sent.

How r u? Hope im not wking u.

A few minutes later:

Ok. Just woke up. What're you doin up?

He replied: *Too tired 2 sleep, I guess.*

THE FOLLOWING MORNING as they packed to leave, Linda pointed to the droning television.

"Hey! Isn't that what's-her-name?" she said. "Your manager's girlfriend who we met at the book fair? Natasha?"

"Natalie," Arthur said, poking his head out through the bathroom doorway. Indeed there she was, poised cross-legged in an armchair, smiling an overeager smile. In the bottom right corner of the screen was a logo that read *Hot Talk*, the show Jeff had mentioned at the book festival in Williamsburg.

Linda said, "She's very pretty, isn't she?"

"Sure." Though truthfully she didn't look nearly as lovely on television as she did in person. All the gloss and makeup undercut her alluring earthiness, made her appear more conventionally model-esque. She didn't look bad, of course. Arthur remembered feeling similarly about himself, watching his own interviews on TV and thinking, *I'm much better looking than that, aren't I? I'm much more...real looking.*

"Too pretty to be a writer," Linda said playfully.

Arthur wondered if she saw him as homely enough to justify hiding behind a book.

He studied Natalie. She projected a formidable intellect, and a fiery confidence that seemed palpable through the screen.

"Some seventy percent of Americans believe in Satan," Natalie told the reporter, leaning forward in her armchair. "Seventy percent. That's rather remarkable to me, to be honest. Almost three-quarters of this country believe the source of the world's pain is created by some monstrous, traitorous angel. Pain and suffering exist on earth because we live in a physical world. And physicality demands dichotomy, duality. The yin and the yang. It's what defines relativity, what inspires life to flourish. So if he is down there, big ol' Lucifer deserves a thank-you. Because without the hot, you can't know the cold."

The interviewer, a young gel-haired man in tight-fitting attire, his eyebrow raised with what seemed like perpetual skepticism, said, "I suppose that's true."

"I have to tell myself to embrace that paradigm of opposites myself," Natalie said. "I'm just as guilty as the next person of wanting to shout down the opposition, instead of seeing them as mere instruments for clarifying and reaffirming my own position."

"Who do you consider the opposition? People of faith?"

"People of faith, sure, and atheists, frankly. Or hard-nosed secularists."

"There's definitely an atheistic movement that's grown in America," said the host. "You have the Four Horseman, they call themselves, right? Richard Dawkins, Sam Harris…"

"Arthur Moore," Natalie ventured.

"Hey," Linda said, beaming. "That's you."

Natalie glanced at the camera, as if sharing an unspoken secret with the audience. "Though he's not one of the self-proclaimed Horsemen."

"Sure." The interviewer shifted in his seat. "So how do you address those voices in the atheist community?"

"It's hard to say," Natalie said. "These guys bug me. Because they say they're free thinkers, but are they truly willing to think freely? Maybe more than the average worshipper, but dogma is not restricted to religion. These theophobes seem almost happy to celebrate meaninglessness. I have a suspicion that, if science were to prove empirically the existence of the spiritual, they would feel disappointed. And I'd ask, why? I mean, it's a hard mental exercise, but for a moment try to strip away all religious baggage and just ask yourself: given all we know of the wildness and the weirdness of existence, which is only getting wilder and weirder, why does the existence of an ethereal aspect to life seem so utterly impossible? As a crude analogy, why can't what we call 'spirit' merely be the melted form, or evaporated version, of the 'ice' that we call physical reality?

"Actually, regarding Dr. Moore," she continued, "We've spoken on occasion. I think, to his credit, he believes, or suspects, more exists in this world than he's willing to let on. But I also suspect he might succumb to peer pressure from others in the science or secular communities."

"Bit of an indictment there."

"Not really. It's human nature to join groups, or tribes, and to plant your flag accordingly. If you then deviate from your club's agenda, you run the risk of exclusion. I'm sure guys like Arthur Moore know there are other, more sophisticated or creative ways to look at the questions of spirituality, but they keep to what's expected of them. They hold tight to the atom. They can't waver. Not now, after they've invested so much in staking out their position."

Arthur felt a tingling flush spread across his body. He fought a sudden urge to heave the television set against the wall. Who the hell was she to fucking *insult* him publicly like this? To assume, after one brief discussion, that she knew everything about him and others like him? She was trying to show she had the emotional jump on people, and that she understood them better than they could ever understand themselves. Ironic that she'd spoken of his arrogance—or "chutzpah," as Wendy would say—yet now displayed the same in spades by analyzing someone she barely knew.

Arthur had ceased listening. He strode across the room and switched off the television.

"Are you okay?" Linda said. "She kind of dug into you there. That was unexpected."

Arthur didn't respond. Instead he asked, "Would you like some breakfast?"

Though he'd grown up a few thousand miles from the nearest desert, the dynamic Western topography reminded Arthur of his boyhood love for the Wild West—John Wayne tales in particular—while also summoning to life his favorite Martian landscapes from stories penned by Bradbury or Heinlein. He gazed in near continuous wonder at the mountains, so sculpted yet so chaotic, broken occasionally by twisting spires of red rock that looked like earthen flames extending toward the stars. A short detour brought them a few hundred miles south of Arches National Park, along twisting roads neither had ever driven before. The sun had already set behind the jagged slopes to the west, rouging the sky in front of them a lovely pink. Minimal daylight remained.

"It's such beautiful country," Linda remarked, "and we almost passed it by. Thank God for detours."

Arthur had a sudden idea and pulled into the next rest stop.

"Let's explore a bit," he told her, "before it gets too dark."

Linda grinned. Although thoughts of Natalie still circled around in the back of Arthur's mind, he hoped he could dissolve them with a brief excursion, and a few lungfuls of the crisp, raw air.

He pulled a blanket out of the trunk and pointed to a trail snaking through a small meadow, into foothills already steeped in evening shadow. He felt a bit nervous leaving behind the security of the rest area on a whim, but the orange overhead glow from the sodium lights reassured him the car would be safe, and Arthur made sure that he locked the doors behind them.

They wandered a short way up the trail until he spotted a flat, smooth clearing between two gigantic saguaro cacti. There they spread out the blanket, sat down and stared skyward. The prodigious stars winked down at them, teasing of distant knowledge. Saturn, identifiable as the single, bright unblinking bead of light, trailed along behind the narrow crescent moon. A meteor scraped the upper atmosphere. Linda gasped and pointed at its fading wake in the sky. A soft, warm breeze whispered across the desert, in concert with the hum and buzz and far cries of insects and animals. The vastness of the surrounding vista reminded Arthur of the tenuousness of his brief, insignificant life.

Finally Linda spoke.

"So what do you think?" she said. "Do you think we'll be cruising around in William Shatner spandex in the next few hundred years?"

Arthur chuckled. "Who knows? All depends if we survive the transition from level zero to level one."

Linda twirled a finger through one of her curls. "Is Earth like a Mario Brothers game?"

He chuckled again. "I don't think so. I'm talking about the different levels of cosmic civilizations. In a level one society, the people harness the power of their home planet and figure out how to control its climate, earthquakes and so on. Level two means they harness the power of their home star and colonize their own solar system, while at level three they become multi-solar and begin to spread throughout their entire galaxy. Level threes are able to harvest resources from multiple suns and their worlds."

"Do you think our species will ever get beyond level zero?" Linda asked. "I mean, without blowing ourselves up?"

"Some think we're in the transitional phase."

"Good for us."

"Well, in all honesty, that's considered the most dangerous time for a species. There's an assumption that most civilizations don't survive it."

Linda shifted in her seat. "That's a happy thought."

Arthur gently squeezed her hand. "I like to think I'm doing what little I can to help human beings survive."

"By beating down God?" Linda asked him with atypical forthrightness.

Yeah, you're helping to save the world. Sure thing. You're Superman. And Linda...what are you? A blind sheep—the kind that will doom us all?

"I'm trying to beat back superstition," Arthur said. "We can't allow our technology to bypass our logical thinking. Otherwise we're bound to wind up a once-promising iron husk of a civilization." He craned his head farther back, drinking in more stars. "We'll be nothing but a big archeology project for alien life forms to explore once they finally come."

"So, do you believe—" Linda started, "In other civilizations? Beyond our own?"

"Sure, why not? Seems unfathomable they wouldn't be out there somewhere."

"And the prospect of people living on other planets doesn't strengthen your belief in, well…God? Or the divine?"

"Well, I don't know for sure if there is life out there, so I can't really say one way or the other." He began to feel increasingly like he was addressing yet another interviewer. He wasn't, of course. He was here with Linda. Linda, with whom he discussed things like wine, movies, sports, kids and current events—discussion fodder he only now realized had taken him far from the subjects he found most personal and significant. Had long hours of trivial small talk built up into something that only felt big, but wasn't? Was this entire relationship a jumble of hot-air desires and imaginings, puffing themselves up into a seemingly solid connection, yet with nothing real or tangible between them?

No.

Arthur firmly rejected that idea. There had been a solid connection; of that he was certain. That it seemed to be vanishing now was the issue, not that it never existed.

As though privy to his thoughts, Linda asked, "Sorry. Is this too much like work for you?"

He offered a silent smile to let her know he didn't mind.

"Because I'm curious," Linda said. "Because, well…

why is our existence proof enough that there may be other civilizations out in space, but not enough to indicate that a higher intelligence created us? And maybe created all other species too?"

For a long moment Arthur stared silently into the heavens. "Because extraterrestrial life is based in physical probability. God, on the other hand, is a supposedly supernatural entity, one for whose existence no one has been able to—or could, in my opinion—provide tangible proof, even if they scoured every nook and cranny and black hole in the universe."

Linda picked up a clump of dirt and pressed it into his hand. "This is tangible, isn't it?"

"It is, yes," Arthur said. "But I know of no traditions that worship dirt."

Linda frowned. "You know what I mean." Behind her eyes Arthur could almost see the mental mechanisms cranking and grinding to life, revving up for subjects she'd perhaps not discussed in a long time, if ever. "Existence... well, exists."

"That's a Zen statement," Arthur said. "I like it."

Linda's smile was genuine, yet strangely melancholic.

"Truth be told, I'm impressed you're not challenging me every minute you can," Arthur said. "Sounds silly, maybe, but I think that's admirable."

"I've told you a couple times before that it's not very important to me, Art," Linda said. "You have your beliefs, and I have mine. That's all. We're all here together. Why not let everyone believe what they want and bless them for it?"

"You're certainly not like most Christians."

Linda shrugged.

"A pleasant change, as I see it," he continued. "Gandhi once said he would be a Christian if it weren't for all the Christians."

"Well," she said, "who am I to disagree?"

THEY ARRIVED IN CALIFORNIA the following afternoon. After passing through the desert communities of Baker and San Bernardino, they finally spotted the Los Angeles skyline towering up ahead, its buildings aligned like worn gray teeth near the continent's edge. Signs became more frequent, as did civilization, and within the hour all was concrete and glass and billboard.

The *Mann's Watch* producers had arranged a two-night stay at the Bel Air Hotel, several miles from Hollywood and tucked into a wooded canyon on a hillside just above Sunset Boulevard. While checking in at the front desk Arthur sensed a flicker of recognition in the female concierge's gaze. A humorless stare followed.

"You're that atheist, right?" she asked.

"Well...that, or author...or fellow human being," Arthur said. He recalled Richard Dawkins's interview with the pundit Bill O'Reilly, how the graphic at the bottom of the screen had identified the Oxford professor as merely "atheist," as if the label summed up his entire existence.

"My cousin read your book," said the concierge. She offered Arthur a grudging smile. "He liked it."

"Thank you."

"You'll be staying two nights?"

He and Linda shared a knowing glance. "Definitely the two nights. But we may stay longer."

"Let us know when you decide, so we can make sure you'll have a room," she said, smiling wider.

They met a bellhop named Boyd who assisted in transporting their luggage. Along the way they passed a large window overlooking the pool area, where Arthur noticed two men hosing off and scrubbing down the pavement inside a temporarily roped-off section. It seemed innocuous enough, yet Arthur felt compelled to ask about it.

"What happened out there by the pool?"

Boyd smiled conspiratorially. "Happened before the sun came up. A doe was mutilated and devoured, right down there by the Jacuzzi."

"Oh my God," said Linda, clutching a hand to her chest.

"Wow," said Arthur. "Did anyone see it?"

Shaking his head, Boyd said, "No. But we found paw prints. Bloody and big. The police suspect a mountain lion."

"You have mountain lions here?" Linda asked.

"Sure. Few and far between, but they occasionally come around. I once spotted one while rock climbing in Malibu."

They entered the elevator and the doors slid closed behind them.

Maybe we haven't left real nature that far behind, after all, Arthur thought.

Either that, or nature was simply catching up.

Per the show's request, Arthur arrived at the studio a couple of hours before taping was set to begin. The show itself was slated to air much later that same evening. Linda kept him company in the dressing room, sipping coffee and picking at some of the finger foods the producers had made available.

"Do you still get nervous?" she asked, meeting his gaze in the reflection of the mirror he was using to knot his tie.

Arthur hesitated. "I get nervous every time before I actually walk on the set. Once the questions start, I'm okay."

"Amazing."

Linda leaned forward and cupped a handful of mixed nuts. Quickly Arthur dropped a pill on his tongue and rinsed it down with a swig of bottled water.

"Patrick Mann is a pretty good host," Arthur said. "Quite fair. Though his audience has been known to get a bit rowdy."

"Hmm," Linda said, as if quietly disapproving.

"It'll be fine."

"You said this is a panel discussion, right?"

"That's the format, yes."

A knock rapped against the door.

"Yeah?"

A sallow-faced assistant, wearing headphones and holding a clipboard, poked his head in. "Dr. Moore? When you're ready they need you in makeup."

"Got it."

The young man left. Arthur turned back to Linda, who rose and slid her arms around his waist.

"Kill 'em dead," she said.

"You mean knock 'em dead?" he corrected with a grin. "Otherwise it's redundant."

Linda rolled her eyes. "You know what I mean."

TAPING ROOMS AND STUDIOS always proved so much smaller in reality than they appeared on television, where it usually seemed like the host was addressing a stadium filled with listeners. Within these cramped quarters, flooded by the heat from countless klieg lights, Arthur felt his interviews seemed more like intimate, high-tech campfire yarns. He became a storyteller in these moments, sharing a tale and inviting the rest of the world to eavesdrop on it.

During the show he sat next to a Mandy Johnson, a much younger singer/actress whose panel presence indicated a naked grab for ratings. To his left sat conservative Harvard scholar Robert Karlson, who, in his bow-tie and plaid smoking jacket, looked like a fashion relic from the seventies. Arthur sensed his only connection with Karlson might be the older man's subtle, but evident, disapproval of the fact that Mandy Johnson had been positioned as his peer.

Patrick Mann reclined across from them in his swivel chair, looking as casual and comfortable as an after-dinner smoker resting off his meal. Even so, he was sharp and on task and quick to engage all three panelists. They covered a wide variety of topics—from education to the Middle East turmoil to climate change. Respectively, Arthur considered the religious taint at work in each situation: the tension of competing ideologies when designing curricula, the hopeless quagmire of hatred between Islamic factions in the ancient sands, the arrogant notion of human environmental and species dominion, as well as how the apocalypse was truly supposed to unfold. He spoke none of it aloud of course, instead flinging off what he perceived as little more than wood shavings of his actual opinions.

Arthur noticed a familiar splintering within himself: the ability to exist in one state as Arthur who was detached and unengaged, as well as Arthur who was engaged and obliged the external world with ready-made words, offering himself to this ongoing intercourse of ideas.

"Okay," Mann said, shuffling papers. "We're running out of time, so let's go now to the audience for some final Q and A."

The three of them sat poised and ready while the audience sat attentive, a festering reservoir of human judgment. Arthur wondered about the people behind those hundreds of watchful eyes. They'd thought about him. Opined on him. Whispered back and forth about him among themselves.

A thin woman with short, frayed hair stood and approached the microphone that the sound crew set up in the aisle. She said, "Yeah, my name's Brenda, from Agoura Hills. I have a question for Dr. Moore."

"Brenda from Agoura Hills," Mann echoed, "go ahead please."

Arthur straightened in his seat and lifted his eyebrows slightly in expectation.

"On the radio program *Eggert Hour* not long ago, you referred to this country as asinine. How sir, can you possibly refer to this country as asinine, when it's been so very good to you?"

Arthur sat back, exhaled slowly. "Anyone who cannot see the asinine strains in their own country is either willfully blind, an idiot or a liar. I was just pointing out what I felt, or feel, is an asinine strain of humanity in this country: the proud scientific and sociopolitical ignorance that gets reflected by so much of our population, even in some of our so-called leaders. The rules have been tweaked, the game rigged. Yes, this country has been good to me, but it hasn't been good to most people and it's only getting worse..."

"How can you say that?" chimed in Professor Karlson. "Hasn't been good to most people. There are plenty..."

"Wait, professor, let him finish the thought," Mann interjected.

Karlson threw up his hands and sat back.

"The wealth is being drained from the community swimming pool," Arthur said. "It's going somewhere, and where it's going is into the hands of a privileged few, those who participate in this ongoing institutional affair between our entities private and public. And these few relentlessly use their resources to make sure that those they've bilked think that all this hoarding of theirs, and in some cases outright theft, is their social Darwinian birthright, and that to decry it is unpatriotic; that to be against the rules they've written in support of themselves is to heap contempt upon the country itself. But I think we've sadly sailed far from the original principles of the founders. Imagine...George Washington said to beware of those who use patriotism to suit their own agenda. James Madison said that our government should work to prevent an 'immodest accumulation of wealth.' Think on those two admonitions. Think on what's happened in the last twenty or so years, and try to imagine our founding fathers approving of some billionaire being able to write legislation with his checkbook, then using the pages of the newspapers he controls, or the voices of the TV channels he owns, to deflect from himself the suspicion of the very citizens he's undermining.

"We have in this nation what I call the distracters and the distracted. Both groups, in a way, have blinders on. The distracters are all about making more money; the distracted are concerned with trying to scrape up adequate money to get by. And as someone with humanistic values I believe in the worth of the individual, but neither group sees the other in individualistic terms. The distracters see a mass of trained animals with pockets they can pick. The distracted see massive institutional or corporate bodies with whom they can't relate in a meaningful way."

Mandy Johnson piped up. "But I think in this age now, in the Internet age I mean, there is so much more awareness and communication going on between people across classes, nations, whatever, and I think this has helped spur a lot of, y'know, discourse on these kinds of issues that weren't ever brought to the forefront before."

"But the distracters," Arthur argued, "have grown so large and so untouchable that even the butt that sits in the Oval Office can't effect real change, much less regular people who have grown cynical and apathetic. Kurt Vonnegut, also a humanist, said there's only one party in Washington: the Winners. Meanwhile the Losers, being the other ninety-

eight percent of the people, have no representation. Our
cultural soul is gangrenous with money—in politics, sports,
business, the arts, even in science. Is this what we want? To
hold such plastic and hollow positions in life? It's just..."
Arthur made a helpless gesture and decided he was finished.

Some scattered applause sounded. The woman who'd
asked the question had long since resumed her seat. She
stared at him, straight and quiet.

Patrick Mann turned to the audience, where a younger
man with thick glasses, a massive shrub of a beard and a
tight Che Guevara shirt had already approached the microphone.

"Evening," the young man said. A college student
maybe, perhaps even a graduate student. "My name's Ken,
from where doesn't matter. Earth, I guess you could say."

Nervous chuckling rippled through the audience.

"This question is also for Dr. Moore. It's documented
that your brother died in the World Trade Center on September 11th. I'm sorry for your loss, man."

The sympathy was nonexistent. With equally nonexistent gratitude, Arthur said, "Thank you."

"I'm wondering how a man like yourself, a free thinker
with such a personal connection to the tragedy, can look at
the official narrative of that day and not constantly speak
out against what are obvious holes, holes that imply a foreknowledge, even active meddling, by our own officials in
this greatest of terrorists acts on our soil—"

Almost in reflex, Arthur lifted his hand. "Please stop.
Please...shut up."

"Shut up? This is the greatest cover-up in our history
and you just want to tie the blindfold tighter? What kind
of person are you? How insulting to the memory of your
brother!"

Arthur rose from his seat. Patrick Mann sent hand signals to the security officers, who poured forth from the shadows and down the aisles to accost the questioner. The rest of the audience murmured, some clapping and others booing.

One of the officers seized the man, who flinched. "Don't touch me, dammit! This is cowardice, fascism. You're all tools of Big Brother. 'The distracters,' you called them. You're nothing but sheep. They won't stop. Look at the snipers now, the Judges of God. They're soldiers, experiments, mind-controlled agents!"

The ranting dimmed as the officers led the man from the studio, to raucous applause.

"Take your meds next time, moron," Patrick Mann called after him, to the delight of the studio audience.

Arthur remained standing, staring at the exit through which they'd taken the man. His thoughts simmered near to the boiling point. Slowly he resumed his seat, where he stared unseeingly into his water mug until someone spoke his name.

VI

OCCASIONALLY THE UNIVERSE WAS CONSID-erate enough to bypass situations that might create awkward or unfavorable exchanges. Certainly this seemed the case when, as they sat in rented beach chairs on the Santa Monica sand, waves curling inches from their toes, Linda left for the bathroom seconds before Arthur's cell phone started vibrating. The name on the screen said Wendy.

Let it go to voicemail.

He picked it up. "Hello?"

"Art, hi!"

Arthur smiled, though not, he imagined, without a little wistfulness. Even when they were undergoing separation and then the divorce, Wendy's phone greetings always seemed excited, as if each call were a first contact between them, their relationship begun afresh. Regardless of his mood her joy always seemed contagious—hell, it still was. He was glad for that, if regretful that she could still have such an immediate effect on him.

"I was expecting to leave a message, truthfully," Wendy said.

"No," he said. "Every once in a while I pay attention to the outside world."

"How're you doing, Art? Did I catch you at a bad time?"

Arthur looked up and down the golden coastline where he could see only smatterings of people. It was a weekday, uncrowded. A seagull flew overhead, momentarily the only thing between him and the sun blazing in the cloudless sky.

"I'm... busy as ever," he said. "But you're certainly not bothering me. I'm actually on your side of the continent."

"I know. Jim told me you were coming. I also happened to catch *Mann's Watch* last night. You really went off there at the end. And you looked positively disgusted at having to tolerate Mandy Johnson."

"I did?"

"I can still read you pretty well, Art."

"I didn't want to give Linda any reason to be jealous."

Wendy laughed. "I see. Linda. She's the new girlfriend?"

"Indeed, she is. Drove out with me. We've been together for only about a month and a half."

"That's good to hear. How did you two meet?"

The neutrality of her tone bothered Arthur in some indefinable way. No faint echoes of regret or jealousy, of curiosity or intrigue. In this moment she sounded bureaucratic, rather unlike herself.

"Online," Arthur said sheepishly.

"Ah," Wendy said. "That's right, that silly website called Millionaire-Matches, wasn't it?"

His gut twinged. "How'd you know?"

"Jim told me. Like I said, we talked a couple of days ago. I'm… I'm concerned about him," she continued. "Thrilled that he's painting, but David's sickness is taking a toll on him. Have you seen them much lately?"

"We got together the day before I left for California. He didn't particularly want me to leave, but I think his art will be a healthy distraction for now. And David's a strong guy. I'm sure he'll get through whatever this might be. The doctors still don't know what's wrong."

Wendy sighed. "I feel terrible about that, but I'm so grateful it wasn't HIV."

"Why feel terrible? I'm grateful too."

"You know, that was the first big thing on my mind when Jim came out to us. I never said anything about it, but…"

"You weren't alone in worrying," Art said. "Of course you weren't alone."

"Thank you," Wendy said. "By the way, I'm thinking of flying out there to visit him for Thanksgiving."

"That would be nice."

"Mm-hmm. Well anyway, I wanted to ask if you'd like to have dinner with Dan and me tonight. Linda is welcome too, of course."

Scarcely giving it much thought, Arthur said, "Sure." He picked at a fingernail. "How is Dan anyway?"

"He's run ragged from work. His firm laid off some people recently so he's had to compensate. But he's tame." He could sense Wendy smiling as she spoke. "I've got him on his best behavior."

Arthur chuckled reluctantly. "That's good."

"So I'll make reservations at Pasta Palace tonight. Seven p.m. You sure it's okay?"

"Of course." He hoped she couldn't hear too much hesitation in his tone.

"Great. Here, let me give you directions to the house…"

He scribbled her instructions on a notepad. A passing voluptuous young blonde in a red bikini caught his attention, but he still got it all down and said goodbye before Linda returned from the restroom.

"Wendy just called me," he told her.

"Your ex? Really?"

"Yeah. She invited us to dinner with her and her husband."

Linda frowned. "That's a little strange, don't you think?"

"It is. Yes." He hesitated. *You can stay in the hotel.* "So I take it you'd rather not go?"

"It's not a big deal to me, one way or the other."

"We're on good terms, you know." *Stop justifying it.* "Three thousand miles of country between us has helped that, I'm sure."

Linda nodded.

"If you're not okay with it, I understand."

"No, I'm fine. She was part of your life, and she's your son's mother. It's nice to keep in touch with those you were close to. I've always thought it sad that most people don't."

"We didn't for a while," Arthur admitted. "We needed breathing room."

Linda frowned. "It wasn't acrimonious or anything, right? I didn't get that impression from what you told me."

"No," said Arthur. "Maybe breathing room wasn't the best choice of words. What we really needed was enough time to learn how to live apart from one another and be okay."

"You said she converted to Judaism shortly before the

divorce, right?"

"It's more complicated than that," Arthur said. "I mean, she *is* Jewish, by blood. She grew up Jewish but never really practiced. But while we were married, practically out of the blue her brother converted to Catholicism. Wendy tried to hide it, but the whole thing ate at her. And I didn't particularly know why and neither did she, really. She just felt her brother had abandoned the whole family, even though none of them had ever been very spiritual. I think she said they went to temple maybe twice in her whole childhood.

"But anyway," Arthur continued, "as a way of countering her brother she began exploring Judaism. She started practicing. Became involved in the local Jewish community. And I became a casualty of her spiritual transformation. Hate to say it like that, but it's sort of true. She married Dan, who's Jewish."

"Did all that have any effect on Jim?"

"No. The last thing she wanted was to push her faith on Jim." He paused, gazed out toward the ocean that went on forever. "Since her brother tried so hard to persuade her to become Catholic, she felt strongly that people ought to be free to make up their own minds about their beliefs."

"Do they still talk? She and her brother, I mean?"

"Here and there, I think. I'm not entirely sure. He didn't go to her wedding. She didn't go to his."

"That's a shame. If anything, faith is supposed to bring people together."

Arthur threw up his hands. "I'd say that plan backfired." After several seconds, he said, "So you'll be okay meeting them?"

"Of course."

Arthur presumed Linda felt obliged to agree. He regretted that, but he also had no interest in offering her too much of a way out—at least a way out that involved him missing the dinner. As much as he hated to admit it, he wanted very much to see Wendy again.

"I think it'll be nice," Linda said. "To be honest I thought I'd meet your son before your ex-wife, but that's the way things sometimes go."

A group of gulls soared by, squawking their coastal symphony. One of them landed and was chased by a young boy until his sunbathing mother called out for him to stop. Arthur turned his attention to a point just beyond all the commotion on the shore, where the chilly blue waves of the Pacific slid across the sand in a foamy celebration of their inevitable return to the ocean. All of this living exuberance, he suddenly realized—all the joys and pains, the fears and hopes and anxieties being experienced—including his own confusing emotions and inner thoughts, were taking place in a precious, flickering moment of shared space and time, impelling all of them into the unknown future beneath the glaring sun's indifferent stare.

LUSH LANDSCAPING ADORNED the front yard of Wendy and Dan's new home—a sweet and cozy one-story abode with a rippling roof covered by a scarlet cascade of Spanish tiles. Its tinted windows faced the street as if in curiosity. For Arthur, Wendy's house summoned in him an inexplicable sense of déjà vu. In his youth he'd frequented many areas of Los Angeles, although he'd never been in this particular Santa Monica neighborhood. Yet perhaps by virtue of having known Wendy and her tastes, he felt a mysterious, slippery familiarity with the house she'd chosen.

"All set?" Linda asked. She spoke to him as though he were a child about to step onstage for his first musical recital.

"Sure."

When they were halfway up the walk, Wendy opened

the door and greeted them, smiling widely. *Not unhappy*, he registered, with regret. He'd prefer even reticence or residual discomfort to her seeming indifference to their shared history, even the bad times. Wendy had cut her hair, and her once straight dirty-blonde hair now played about her face in an artfully unkempt mop. *Enticing.* Her clothes, summery and rather bohemian, seemed to Arthur to reflect yet another chapter of her new life. She was no longer the woman with whom he'd once shared a ring, because she hadn't wanted to be that woman anymore. He saw before him a refreshed soul, a cleansed countenance that carried no trace of him.

"Art, so good to see you."

They embraced and he felt his entire body conform once again to her shape, that warm and familiar form still unaltered by the countless hours and miles they'd spent apart.

She finally pulled away from him. "You must be Linda," she said, extending her hand. "I'm Wendy."

"Very nice to meet you."

Caught in that awkward moment of deciding whether to hug or merely shake hands, in a burst of goodwill the two women chose to hug. Wendy broke it off first and ushered them through the front door. Dan emerged from a room down the hallway, handsomely clad in a silky blue dress shirt and brown slacks. He'd grown a patchy spread of facial hair since their last holiday card photo. Maybe to make himself look more distinguished, Arthur mused, or maybe in anticipation of Arthur's visit, to try and inject a bit more testosterone into the mix, to subtly project himself as the alpha male...

Arthur opted to snip that line of thought.

"Hey Dan," Arthur greeted him. They shook hands.

"How are you, Art?" Dan said, his eyes revealing a hint of reservation. "We caught the show last night. That was quite an impassioned speech you gave."

"Thank you."

"I enjoyed it." Dan paused, puckering his lips and fixing his gaze on a point above Arthur's head. "You made some valid points. Although I'm not sure if—"

"We'd better get going if we're going to be on time," Wendy quickly interjected. "I was hoping you might've come earlier so we could show you around the house."

"It looks very nice," Linda offered. "I like the front land-scaping."

"I know the yard's not up to Art's high standards," Dan said, patting Arthur's shoulder. "But we like it. Cost us a good thirty grand."

Arthur's weak laugh was involuntary. He noticed Linda blinking back surprise.

"I didn't know I had exotic lawn standards," Arthur mused.

Dan released his shoulder, mouth tightening. "I thought you hated cacti." He turned to Wendy. "Isn't that what you said? 'Arthur's gonna hate the cactus?'"

"Who hates cacti?" Arthur wondered aloud, bewildered and amused at the same time. "They're plants."

He glanced at Wendy, who shrugged and raised her hands in a helpless gesture. "We should get going."

Wendy turned on the living room lamp. She glanced automatically at Arthur and noted his classic wince.

"Still can't stand having lights on when the sun's still out?" she teased.

"I'm afraid not."

She closed the living room blinds. "It'll be dark by the time we get back. I actually think you instilled some of that artificial-light weirdness in me too. I'm always finding ways of reading by sunlight or else going outside."

"I can vouch for that," Dan said.

Arthur nodded, feeling secretly gladdened to learn he'd had some impact, however infinitesimal, on the woman that Wendy had ultimately become.

"We ready to go?" she said.

"Actually, would you mind if I washed my hands really quick?" Arthur asked.

Wendy's smiled warmly as she put on her suede jacket. "Sure, the powder room's right down the hallway, second door on the left."

He followed her directions, lowering his gaze so he didn't have to look at the many smiling photographs of her and Dan that lined the hallway walls.

When he'd finished washing his hands, he found Wendy waiting for him in the hallway.

"I know the date's getting close," she said. "How are you?"

"Gets easier with every passing year. Doesn't mean it'll ever stop hurting."

"I'm sorry I haven't called you over the years around this time. I always feel guilty about that. I loved John too."

Again, Arthur simply nodded.

"Come here," Wendy said softly.

They embraced.

THE SMALL ITALIAN RESTAURANT stood near the Washington Circle in Venice, aglow in the citrus light of sunset. Bicyclists rode up and down along the boardwalk, beneath long rows of stoic palm trees stretching out along the coast. Salt-tinged breezes, smelling vaguely of kelp, triggered something primal and wondrous in Arthur.

Wendy still likes Italian, he thought. He wondered if Linda liked Italian food. The fact that he didn't know the answer intrigued him.

"By the way, how was Greece?" he asked Wendy, as they

traversed the parking lot toward the front door. "It was Greece, right?"

"Greece was incredible. Three entire weeks of cruising the Mediterranean. We took a Literary Cruise to various sites from the *Odyssey*. We stayed in Athens for five days and saw all the usual amazing stuff —"

Arthur chuckled, holding the door for both women. "The usual amazing stuff? Have you two become immune to the world's wonders?"

Wendy laughed. "Yeah, well, I'm sure it is usual for tourists. But it's no less amazing for us."

"Where'd you go?"

"The temple of Poseidon, the Acropolis—exquisite in the moonlight—and oh! the National Archeological Museum, which Jim would have adored. The museum houses over twenty thousand pieces of Greek art—"

"From ancient to late antiquity," Dan chimed, as if remembering from a brochure.

"Yeah. We then spent the rest of our time in Crete. Went scuba diving, saw the Venetian walls, Dan played golf, and I got a gorgeous bronze tan. Just amazing."

"Certainly sounds like fun," said Linda.

The hostess, smiling perfunctorily, led them to their table. Black-and-white photos of unknown people in unknown places lined the walls. A smattering of customers sat at the surrounding dark-wood tables. Arthur noticed an older couple dining nearby, sullen and silent, their attention fixed on their respective dishes as if seeking some refuge from intimacy in the pasta. He wondered if they reflected the destination of all couples: mutual disinterest and eventual stony silence.

"Returning to reality was pretty difficult," Wendy said. "But I like to think I sopped up some ancient Greek wisdom. As kind of an intellectual souvenir."

"Have you been to Greece, Art?" Dan asked.

"I haven't," Arthur said. "It's definitely on my list, though."

Wendy glanced sideways at him, smiling.

Shut up, Wendy.

AN ATTRACTIVE BLONDE WAITRESS came over and addressed them, her demeanor pleasant and bubbly. Dan ordered a bottle of Chianti for the table—a little presumptuous, Arthur felt—and all the while Dan flirted rather shamelessly with the waitress. Arthur glanced at Wendy with concern, but either she didn't notice or was pretending not to.

The waitress hurried away, ponytail whipping. Dan's gaze followed her all the way back to the kitchen.

"So I guess we're all having Chianti?" Wendy asked.

"Is that not okay?" Dan raised his hand, ready to snap his fingers and alert the waitress to a possible change in their order, but Wendy grabbed his arm.

"No, don't worry about it."

"It's fine," Linda chimed, a bit too quickly.

Arthur said nothing, figuring silence indicated his approval.

A busboy delivered a warm, steamy basket of fresh garlic bread. The waitress appeared shortly afterward with their Chianti. She uncorked the bottle and poured a taste for Dan. Arthur watched him make a production out of judging the wine's fragrance and flavor, swirling it around in the glass and burying his nose deep inside the crystal before taking a sip and swishing it around in his mouth.

"Good stuff," Dan raised his glass in approval. "I think you'll like it, Art."

"As long as it doesn't taste like cactus," Arthur quipped.

Dan chuckled humorlessly, his eyes fixed on Arthur with silent, prodding analysis. Arthur raised his own glass and offered a silent toast in what—he hoped—would appear to Dan as a mutually agreed-upon truce.

The conversation returned to Wendy's account of their trip to Greece. Always the great mediator, Arthur thought, watching her deftly control the conversation's flow. Wendy had always been able to smooth out any awkward exchange into something more agreeable, or at least tolerable. Maybe it was she, once upon a time, who had kept their marriage tolerable long past its actual expiration date.

Arthur half listened as his ex-wife unpacked yet more anecdotes from their travels. Thankfully, nobody mentioned his *Mann's Watch* appearance again.

Their meals came, enormous plates of pastas and sauces and enough garlic to make his eyes water. They ate in relative silence, though at one point Arthur heard Dan whisper, "Watch the carbs, hon." Wendy, holding a second piece of garlic bread poised at her lips, shot him a piercing glance, and Arthur felt an instant of fierce vindication.

Dan poured himself a second glass of wine, and seemed surprised to note it was the last of the bottle. "Anyone want another?"

"I think you've had enough," Wendy said.

A stretch of prickly silence followed. Growing uncomfortable, Arthur excused himself for the bathroom, glancing back to be sure he wasn't abandoning Linda. She smiled at him serenely, and Arthur felt a sudden renewed gratitude for the kindness and gentleness of her company.

He found a door marked *Maschi* and crossed to the sink, where he splashed water on his hands and then his face. In the bathroom's dim light he appeared sallow, half dead. He contemplated the prospect that he now existed more as information, as a cloudlike representation of the various forms of media that bore the likeness of Arthur Moore, and that he himself, this physical body and whatever it represented, was in truth no more substantive than was that other Arthur, a cyber Arthur who floated out there forever opining in black vastness. The bathroom suddenly felt to him like a refuge from a world too exhausting and oppressive to reenter.

The door opened. Arthur reached for a towel and was startled to see Dan entering.

"Hey," Arthur greeted him.

Dan did not respond. For a long moment he glowered at Arthur, then said, "Listen up."

Arthur stiffened, "Yeah?"

"Look, this isn't easy for me to say." Dan's face muscles tensed. "But I don't want you having any more contact with Wendy."

"Excuse me?"

"You heard me. I realize she called you, and I can't blame you for answering. But you're divorced now. You live on opposite sides of the country, and Jim is an adult. I would prefer it if this would be the last conversation we ever have. Capiche?"

Arthur laughed despite his growing anger. "Capiche? Who are you, Don Corleone?"

Dan glared at him.

"Are you serious?" Arthur said. "I email her maybe once a month. And it's usually about Jim or David."

Dan's eyes calcified. "I am serious. I know you two correspond, sending emails and holiday cards to each other—"

"Yes, and?"

"—which in and of itself seems to me pretty disingenuous, actually, given what you...do."

The moment suddenly took on a dreamy, unreal quality. Arthur wondered if, given one snap, one shake or one splash of water, he might awaken, his surroundings instantly changed.

"You're kidding, right?" he said, still struggling to wrap his mind around Dan's demand.

"I'm not kidding, and I'd appreciate it if you'd take me seriously here."

Arthur's forearm twitched. Another customer entered the bathroom, glanced curiously at the two men and disappeared into a stall.

"That's all I have to say, Art. I appreciate your understanding." Dan turned and left the restroom.

Arthur stood there a moment longer, feeling queasy. His skin felt clammy and his chest felt tight from his barely contained inner tension. He rinsed his face in the sink once more to try to calm himself, then returned to the table. He found Dan already back in the rhythm of the conversation, laughing at something Linda had apparently said. Arthur stood for a moment behind his chair until Linda and Wendy noticed him. Slowly he sat, expressionless.

"Everything okay?" Linda asked.

"Oh yeah," Arthur said, with what felt and probably looked like a hollow smile.

Linda patted his leg and squeezed his thigh.

"I just discovered that Linda makes and sells jewelry. How wonderful," Wendy said. "She was telling us about selling her wares at science fiction conventions."

"And the…'otherworldly entities' she would encounter there," Dan said.

"It's good business."

"Probably good clientele for you, too, Arthur," Dan said.

Arthur crossed his arms and furrowed his brow, feeling his face twist with a mix of scorn and utter bewilderment. He noticed Wendy rolling her eyes at Dan.

"Art's not that kind of psychologist," Wendy corrected Dan. "You know that."

"Ah, right," said Dan. "Not the nut-on-a-couch kind."

Before Arthur could reply, Dan slapped a palm on the table. "Well, this was fun. We should do this again sometime."

Arthur couldn't contain the laughter that rushed out of him.

"What was that for?" Linda asked him.

Dan's face stiffened as he studied Arthur. His dark pupils narrowed into pinpoints, and within them Arthur could read a single, silent word: *No.*

"I'm not sure," Arthur said. "What *was* that, Dan?"

"How should I know?" Dan said. "What's so funny?"

"What's funny..." *Stop*, said an inner voice, but Arthur ignored it. Again he was being transported into that dreamy, unreal place. "What's funny is that this will be the last time I see you, Wendy."

Dan's plastic smile vanished.

"What does that mean?" Wendy asked, looking back and forth in confusion between her husband and Arthur. The sudden violence in their exchange visibly frightened her.

"Right, Dan?" Arthur said. "I mean, am I wrong?"

Linda recoiled from the abrupt and fiery dialogue, focusing instead on draining the last drops of her wine.

Dan glared at Arthur with a look Arthur might have described as sorrowful betrayal if they'd been better friends. "Why, Art?" Dan said. "Why ruin the evening like this?"

"Oh it's me now. I'm the instigator who's ruined the evening."

"Please tell me what's going on," Wendy begged them.

"We'll talk about it later," Dan said.

"Why not now?" Arthur pressed. "It's pretty simple. While we were in the bathroom together, Dan asked me not to have any more contact with you, ever."

Wendy turned to Dan, whose expression had turned to

stone.

"For heaven's sake, why would you even suggest a thing like that?"

Looking exasperated, Dan said, "It's healthier if you two don't have any contact. Healthier all the way around."

"Healthier for your ego, you mean," snapped Arthur.

"Shut up, Art," Dan replied.

Linda remained silent, gazing anxiously out the window as if she wished she were anyplace else but at that table.

"Dan, where is this coming from?" Wendy asked him. "Arthur and I hardly see each other as it is, and we speak maybe two or three times a year. There's nothing for you to worry about."

"No you don't," Dan said flatly.

"Excuse me?"

"I've seen your emails."

For a long moment Wendy remained silent. Arthur knew well that look from their years together, and for an instant he felt a flash of pity for Dan. Wendy turned to Linda and said, "I'm so sorry about this, Linda. Really, it's not at all what I intended to happen."

"Please, it's not your fault." Linda waved her off, and Arthur felt a stinging sense of embarrassment that Wendy had rushed to apologize to Linda before he had.

"Okay, end of discussion," said Wendy, swiping a straightened hand across the air. She caught the waitress's eye, and in a flat, caustic tone said, "Check?"

ON THE WAY OUT Dan walked several brisk steps ahead of the rest of them, his hands jammed in his pockets and his head cast down toward the sidewalk. A human train, Arthur thought, barreling heedlessly on, well oiled by his own ego certainties and energized by competition and conflict. When they reached the parking lot Arthur tugged on

Wendy's sleeve.

"I think Linda and I will hang back and get a cab," he suggested gently.

She glared at Dan's stiff back: "That might be best."

"Wendy, it's okay," Arthur reassured her. "I'm fine."

"I'm so sorry," Wendy said, hugging them one after the other with surprising ferocity. "We're definitely going to talk."

Me or Dan?

"He's pretty paranoid," Arthur said.

"He can be that way sometimes."

"It'll only get worse, I'm sure. What you ought to do is turn it around on him. Often when someone is that, well, crazy, it means they're the ones who are hiding something. They accuse their partners first to shift the blame away from themselves."

Wendy's eyes narrowed. Arthur's conscience had long warned him against offering two-bit psychoanalysis to people with whom he felt close, but in this instance he found it impossible to restrain himself.

Wendy said, "It was good to see you, Art. And it was great to meet you, Linda."

"Lovely to meet you too, Wendy."

"Sorry again."

"Don't worry about it. Honestly."

"It was great to see you too, Wendy," Arthur said.

"Have a safe trip home," Wendy said as she headed to the car where Dan stood waiting.

For a brief second Arthur watched her leave, then he reentered the restaurant, requested the number for a cab company and called. Within ten minutes of rejoining Linda at the curb, a yellow Prius taxi arrived. Probably fresh off the bar-studded beach circuit.

"These Priuses are cute," Linda said. "I feel like I want to pop them in my mouth like candy."

The silly comment, which Arthur realized was her way of trying to distract him, only annoyed him further. The cab slid out into the stream of other headlights. Arthur could feel his linguini churning inside of his stomach. His clammy hands trembled. It felt as if a large icy tumor was expanding in his solar plexus, displacing all his other vital organs. He glanced at Linda, who stared sightlessly out the side window.

"Hippy-Drippy Coffee," she muttered, nodding toward a glowing sign, "that's clever."

Arthur indulged himself in a moment-by-moment recall of what had happened in the restaurant. While definitely unpleasant, the whole incident also made him feel strangely alive. Such a flare-up of personal drama felt in an odd way rejuvenating. There was strange honor in realizing that when it came to him and Wendy there remained an instant's drama to be had, if only in Dan's warped mind. Ironically, the incident had only reinforced for Arthur what now felt like an unbreakable connection with his ex-wife.

He suddenly wondered how Natalie Farrow might have reacted to the situation. Arthur could picture her dumping her bowl of pasta on Dan's head, a fitting treatment for the whiny baby in a high chair he'd truly shown himself to be. He could see her drawing a verbal or semantic rapier, poised ready at his side. He imagined Natalie revealing more of herself, not less, and certainly not shrinking away from the conflict out of some embarrassed sense of courtesy.

"I apologize for that," Arthur said. "Really. I'm terribly sorry."

Linda snapped out of her self-imposed trance. "It's okay, Art," she said with a sigh. "That screwball kind of stuff happens with families."

"That's for sure."

Silence reigned for two stoplights, until Linda said, "Are we heading back soon, I guess?"

As if he hadn't heard her, Arthur said, "Have you ever been to Steinbeck Country?"

"No. Can't say I have."

"You know who I mean, right? John Steinbeck?"

"I know who John Steinbeck is, Art."

"I was thinking about us taking a little detour. I could use a bit of an escape before going home."

Linda's chuckle carried a hint of condescension, as if she were a mother granting special leeway to a misbehaving child.

"That sounds lovely, Art."

They drove the coastal route up into Northern California. It had been a little more than twenty years—*twenty years?*—since Arthur had traveled this rugged length of highway. To his pleased surprise they encountered little fog. The sun stretched carelessly across the sky, daring any cloud to encroach, and the ocean surface glittered with shifting amoebas of reflected light. Leaping pods of dolphins occasionally broke the water's calm.

Just north of San Simeon they pulled into Elephant Seal beach. Many of those large namesake denizens lay basking on the sand, while others undulated in the frothy surf. Two massive bull males fought briefly, nipping at each other's throats with gigantic tusks while emitting a sequence of watery, belching clicks.

"I wonder why they have those big trunks," Linda pondered, another in a long line of her verbal musings of the day. "They seem more a nuisance, hanging down in front of their mouths like that."

"I never thought about it," Arthur said. Her comments, innocuous as they were, had begun to annoy him. He wasn't sure why, exactly. Maybe it was the way she spoke: her tone sounded spiritually parched to him, that of someone who seemed disinterested in the words that came out of her mouth, as if she was speaking simply to combat the silence.

He had hoped to clear his mind by driving north, perhaps to rejuvenate the passion he'd once felt for Linda and thereby to give the relationship one final chance, but sitting with her in the car for all those hours, just being alone with her, he'd finally realized that he simply did not care for her the way he was supposed to. He felt no new spark of interest, and no perspective she'd offered had managed to alter his standing perception that she was...shallow .

Though he no longer entertained romantic feelings for Wendy, he was beginning to realize that seeing her may have helped to highlight his lack of interest in Linda. Arthur couldn't tell if it owed to their long history together or to a genuine persistent connection—or maybe both—but even just talking with Wendy made him realize he felt more couple-like with her than he did when doing anything remotely romantic or intimate with Linda. Far brighter flames—intellectual, sexual and (odd as it seemed in his own mind) even spiritual—burned inside Wendy. Linda paled like a candle near the heat and warmth of her sunshine.

Arthur also had to acknowledge his increasing thoughts about Natalie. Natalie, who—like Wendy—seemed more fluid and restless, shifting and challenging. Unlike Linda, Natalie had not packed the entire world into neat little social or philosophic boxes.

Arthur remained outwardly content, if noticeably quiet, as they continued their journey through Big Sur to the city of Monterey, where they stopped to walk the streets and sight-see. They visited the aquarium and several locations that had, as Arthur explained to Linda, inspired the Steinbeck novels *Cannery Row* and *Tortilla Flat*. At the waterfront they came across an array of fisherman whose lines were cast into the rippling murk below, many of whom looked as though they made a tired life of it, as though they'd forsaken all things behind them on the land in favor of an unsteady communion with the sea, its mysteries and its fickle offerings.

They checked into a hotel and spent two additional nights in Monterey, using the days to explore the surrounding countryside. In Salinas they picnicked on a hill beneath the shade of a large, twisting oak tree, the leaves of which swayed in the gentle breeze.

"This is lovely," Linda said, placing a hunk of cheese on a cracker.

Lovely, he thought. No, this was *extraordinary*. Lovely could not do justice to the four billion years of awesome craftsmanship that had gone into creating even a single blade of grass. Thirteen billion years actually, if one went back to the universal beginning.

Arthur mused often about Steinbeck, the literary face of this country. He particularly enjoyed the mystical flair in some of Steinbeck's earlier works, especially *To a God Unknown*, his second novel. To read the rich passages that described the country was to read of a place that, the way Steinbeck described it, could have easily passed for something fantastical. And yet they were merely naturalistic depictions, poetic passages describing the earth, the sun, the trees and the rivers, as well as the exchanges between these things and the planet's people. Simply describing their existence through man's eyes was enough to infuse them with fantastical beauty. To celebrate them as they were was to acknowledge the astonishing wonder of the world without any need for separate, refutable beliefs about how it all came to be.

Heading back south they took the G-16 highway just south of Monterey, through the dramatic golden-green valley between the Pacific Coast Highway and the 101. The beauty of this particular rural interstice was wholly unexpected and seemed likely to become one of the more memorable experiences of their trip. It hosted an incredible view of coastal mountains standing like noble guardians against the brewing thunderclouds that had reclaimed much of the formerly unblemished California sky.

At a pullout stop, Arthur watched the gray storms roll in. Linda fidgeted by his side, seemingly hesitant about linking arms with him. In the distance the thunder bellowed across the hills. The air assumed a static charge they could taste.

By the next day they were well out of California, and by week's end they entered western Virginia. Already the entire trip felt to Arthur like a dream, perhaps even more surreal because in a dream much of whatever happens remains logical in the mind of the dreamer. Somehow though, much of this journey—the flat tire, Los Angeles, *Mann's Watch*, Wendy, the coast—felt patently unreal, like a collection of disjointed scenes from somebody else's life story.

Before long they were winding through the green Kingsmill estate. Arthur spotted a number of golfers who were visible through the pines as he turned onto West Landing Road. There the land opened wide, revealing Arthur's stately house rising up near the end of the fairway.

He'd awakened and was home again, as if he'd never left.

VII

"I SHOULD PROBABLY DROP YOU OFF FIRST,

right?" Arthur asked, keeping his eyes on the road. He stopped for a threesome of golfers to cross.

Linda sat forward. "Oh." Arthur could feel her looking at him but didn't want to return her gaze. "Okay."

Somewhere in the universe, he thought arbitrarily, *ten thousands worlds died in the space of that pause.*

"I just figure it'd be easier," he said. "Since you have to unpack and everything."

"Sure."

Where they would've turned left toward his house, they turned right, rolling meditatively through corridors of pine and the noble solemn homes of their neighbors. The detour was only twenty minutes. Arthur kept his speed steady and on the slow side, fearing that any further acceleration would make Linda think he was rushing to get rid of her.

Her house was one of the more classically colonial-looking: red-bricked, two stories and shaded by a thick cluster of trees. Arthur went to pull up by the front door when Linda stopped him.

"I can just go in the side," she said, with a hint of what sounded like defeat in her voice.

"Alright. Do you need help?"

"I think I got it. Thank you, though."

He climbed from the car anyway, unloading her suitcase and backpack and walking with her to the side door, where they hugged and shared a perfunctory kiss. It was difficult for Arthur to parse out the emotions lingering in her expression; what he construed as disappointment may well have just been exhaustion or a combination of both or, knowing certain women as he did, insulated rumination on some offensive remark or look or gesture he might have unthinkingly made during the trip.

"Thank you, Art," Linda said. "For the journey."

"Sure," he said, smiling. "Thank you for being my copilot."

Linda nodded and hauled her luggage up the small porch to the side door. He waited until she was inside before leaving.

ARTHUR NOTICED JEFF'S LONELY SEDAN parked in the circular driveway. He felt a stab of regret at having asked his manager to "check in" every once in a while, which to overeager Jeff likely came across as "house-sit." Presently wanting solitude, Arthur found any company a bit of a nuisance, particularly one as energetic as Jeff's.

The front door opened and Jeff stepped out, waving. Arthur rolled down his window.

"Hey ho!" Jeff called.

"Hey ho?" Arthur said out the window. "What are you, the eighth dwarf?"

"Not anymore. They kicked me out for being too big."

With bellhop alacrity, Jeff pulled open the car doors and began unloading Arthur's luggage. Arthur emerged from the driver's seat and together they carried or rolled everything toward the house.

"Thanks, Jeff," said Arthur.

"You got it." He glanced up. "Oh, by the way, I don't think I ever asked you about this, but I notice you have two chimneys."

Arthur climbed the porch steps, head lowered, every step firm and definitive. "Right."

"So is one in the twilight zone somewhere?" Jeff said. "There's only one fireplace as far as I can tell."

Arthur chuckled. "There is no second fireplace. I put in another chimney for aesthetic balance."

"Aesthetic balance?"

"Yeah, well actually it was Jim's idea. He's the artistic one. Has a good eye for that stuff, and when he suggested it

I figured hey, he's got a point. Why not?"

"Okay."

Inside, they amassed the luggage by the bottom of the staircase.

"How's the fort?" Arthur asked

"Still standin', as you can see." Jeff offered an airy wave toward the ceiling. "Natalie and I came by every couple of days just to keep the place company. Stayed here a few nights too. But don't worry—we kept the lights off during the day and we brought our own wine."

A sudden image of Natalie unclad and sleeping under his roof, beneath his covers, excited Arthur, made him feel an untoward intimacy because it was his bed, his domain, and Jeff was a simple variable who could easily be changed—maybe.

A smile tugged at the corners of Arthur's lips.

You're a jackass.

"I'm glad you guys had a good time," Arthur said.

"Sure did. How was the trip?"

Arthur didn't quite know how to answer that. He shrugged noncommittally. "Fine. Spent some time with Wendy."

"Oh really?" Jeff crossed his arms, his eyes narrowing a little. Arthur recalled one of Jeff's scotch-scented lectures on socializing with exes, how "one shouldn't go there," especially, he'd said, with ex-wives.

"Charlotte and I just know too much about each other," Jeff had remarked, referring to his own failed marriage from a decade ago. "We're stained with each other." Yet when it came to Wendy, Arthur resented Jeff's brittleness. He remembered how flirtatious Jeff himself had been with her, though such interaction was always mutually understood as safe and snug in the "friendly" zone. Even so, their divorce had delivered one of its stronger glancing blows to Jeff.

Afterward Wendy had begun to feel like a chronic health condition to Arthur, one he avoided mentioning to Jeff for fear of having to endure yet another lecture.

"It was pretty brief," Arthur said. "She called me because she saw me on the show."

Jeff eyed him dubiously. "Whatever."

"We all went out to dinner." Arthur laughed, but even he could hear the humorlessness in his tone. "Unfortunately, it turned into dinner and a show."

Jeff frowned. "What happened?"

"Wendy's new husband—"

"Dan, right?"

"Yeah, Dan."

"He still the same pretentious twat?"

Arthur released a long, exasperated sigh. "More or less," he acknowledged. "He got all bent out of shape about Wendy and me still speaking. Just paranoid and insecure."

"Well sure," Jeff slapped Arthur's bicep in a friendly way, "look at the act he's following."

"Thanks, I guess. Though it should be pretty obvious to Dan by now that the curtain closed long ago on my opening act."

"How about a glass of wine to rinse off the traveling dust? Syrah, perhaps? Or maybe a nice zinfandel?"

"Syrah," Arthur replied.

"You just missed Nat," Jeff said. "She left to do a signing not twenty minutes ago." He poured Arthur a glass of ruby-red Syrah: "And there you are."

Arthur sipped it gingerly, enjoying the instantaneous feeling of relaxation that flowed through him. His thoughts turned once again to Natalie. For whatever reason, the teen-ager inside him—the one he'd thought long dead since his divorce—was apparently still alive and feeling aroused, fix-ated on a crush with that same lusty, animal intensity he used to feel back in high school. Unnerving, to say the least.

"What was Nat's deal on that *Hot Talk* show, by the way?" Arthur asked.

"You noticed that too, did you?"

"I did. I watch all my superstars when they're doing PR," Arthur sipped more of his wine. "I have to say, I don't particularly appreciate public psychoanalysis by someone I barely know."

Jeff nodded agreeably. "She did make some mention of worrying that she'd gone too far. She gets on these rolls, and she sometimes forgets to pull back. She's got a lot of fire in her, you know," Jeff grinned. "It comes out in both good and bad ways. And I could say the same thing about you, Teddy."

"When in my life have I ever attacked a specific person in public?"

Jeff's snort was immediate and harsh. "Are you kidding, man? I could compile a book covering the number of potshots you've taken at the Pope. Or at any one of those presidential spiritual advisors or bright-toothed televangelists—"

"Yeah, but—"

"But this time it's *you* in the sights, so it's crossing the line." An amicable smile, that of a friend lovingly jabbing another friend, tempered Jeff's accusatory tone.

"I'd appreciate it if she'd not flirt with those sorts of ad hominem assaults," Arthur persisted, in a quieter voice.

"Tell her yourself."

Arthur waved it away. "Forget it."

"Anyhow, there may be more immediate concerns," Jeff said. He leaned in closer to Arthur and whispered, "She thinks your house is haunted, y'know."

"What?"

"Nat. She thinks this place is haunted."

"Why would she think that?"

"She said she just felt strange vibes."

Arthur raised his eyebrows in disbelief. "Oh boy, here we go. Vibes?"

"The funny thing is that I woke up once in the middle of the night and could swear I heard her talking out in the hallway. Couldn't hear what she was saying though. I asked her about it in the morning and she said she had taken a call."

"So?"

"Well, I happened to notice that her cell phone was still on the nightstand."

"Weird."

"Yeah, she doesn't seem to want to engage the topic much, at least not with me. So I've just sort of dropped it. Doesn't matter if she's schizo," Jeff grinned, "everything else about her balances out."

Arthur sat down and began sorting through three weeks of newspapers and letters that Jeff had piled high on the kitchen table. Jeff leaned into him, and in a softer tone offered, "Nat's unbelievable in bed, you know. That alone makes up for a lot of crazy."

"Thanks for that image," Arthur replied, all the while thinking, *the classic predator male.* Another one of their differences. How thoughtlessly Jeff could buy into that primal impulse to brag of his sexual conquests. Such tendencies went back to Adam, of course. Polite society had mostly managed to whittle it down from raping and pillaging to sharing a knowing grin and a few crudely explicit words with one's friends about the willing "hotness" of one's mate.

"That fire of hers," Jeff continued, seemingly oblivious to Arthur's rising discomfort, "it comes in good and bad ways, as I said. She's actually writing a book about sex now. I read the first few chapters last night. The publisher's going to put an in-house illustrator on it for the pictures, too."

"No photographs?"

"Not sure. I think there may be some. But she's got a whole repertoire of her own, things probably no one else has done."

"I'm sure, Jeff, out of all the seven billion people in the world, that when it comes to sex she's not the first one to try anything."

"She's not alone, that much is for sure, "Jeff leered. "I'm right there with her."

Arthur suddenly felt as though he'd lost some competition, a game that might have been unfairly rigged. In that moment he resented Jeff—a mere variable in the equation of Natalie's life—far more than he cared to admit. Seeking a distraction, he set down his wine and reached for the most recent newspaper.

"Hear about the shootings?" Jeff asked.

"No."

"Those jackoff God's Judge snipers shot someone in Alexandria on Monday. Yesterday a father out shopping with his daughter was shot here in Yorktown. The daughter was only injured, but her father was killed."

A flame of anger ignited in Arthur's chest. "Jesus."

"I know."

Coverage of the killings had made the front page. Arthur skimmed the article. He felt relief noting that, since Benjamin Holden's arrest, the papers had stopped seeking him out for quotes. Best to seal that asshole away for good, slap duct tape over his mouth and prevent him from ever again addressing the gullible public. Even better, allow the people to forget all about his existence.

Arthur was also pleased to realize that his trip out west had helped loosen Holden's grip on his own psyche. It wasn't entirely gone, however, a truth revealed by the reaction he felt the instant Holden's name had come to mind.

Arthur often imagined an inverse world where emotions could be observed and quantified as easily as physical phenomena. In such a world, would madness have space to congeal like a malignant social tumor? Would fear be able to grow like black mold, festering and multiplying in unlit places? Or might these negative aspects of human character begin to spoil as visibly and swiftly as any other neglected fruit?

"I'll be right back," he said suddenly. Abandoning the paper, he headed into his study and dialed the phone.

Jim answered on the fourth ring.

"Jim? Hey, I just got in."

"Hey, Dad," Jim said. "How was the trip?"

"Everything went okay. How have you been?"

"I've been a little distracted with the mural. And now that David's back in the hospital—"

Arthur stiffened. "What? What's wrong?"

"Yeah, a few days now. I told Mom. She didn't tell you?"

"No." Arthur wondered briefly if Wendy had embraced Dan's new commandment about their relationship. "Maybe she just didn't want me worrying on the trip home."

"Hmm."

"What happened?" Arthur pressed. "Do they know what's wrong?"

"Pneumonia. He can barely breathe."

"Oh, my God. I'm so sorry to hear that."

"They think maybe it was an infection all along. Something hiding in his lungs. They don't know shit," Jim sighed. "It's morbidly comforting to know there are so many gaps David can fill in the medical field, if he ever becomes a doctor."

"*When* he becomes a doctor."

"Right."

"I'm home now, if you need anything."

"Thanks, Dad. I'll let you know."

Arthur recalled Jim's earlier talk of moving to Los Angeles, but decided not to raise it. It hadn't been the first time
it'd come up—during moments of vulnerability and resentment, when Arthur became the target of his ire (whether
justifiably or not), Jim sometimes slipped in the possibility
of moving across the country to be closer to his mom. The
threat would slide out quietly, the conversational equiva-
lent of inserting a teardrop's worth of poison into someone's drink. Jim knew the idea would shut down some part
of Arthur, as if to imply, "Mom's better than you, right?"

"Listen, I just heard," Arthur said, "that these snipers are
apparently roving south, getting active closer to your neck
of the woods. So keep a vigilant eye out, okay? Watch yourself."

"I will, Dad."

"Seriously. I mean it."

"Okay, Dad. Don't worry."

"Okay."

They said goodbye and hung up. Arthur stood silently
for a moment, then
returned to the kitchen, where Jeff sat reading the newspaper. He retrieved his glass of wine and took a long swig.

"Thanks again for watching the house," he told Jeff.

"Sure thing, man," Jeff said. "How's Jim?"

"David's sick again."

"What else is new?"

Arthur sniffed the air. "Do I detect a hint of...cigar
smoke?"

"Yeah, I was hoping you wouldn't mind."

"You couldn't have smoked outside?"

Jeff looked wounded. "I don't smell anything. Besides,
it's been chilly lately." He waved toward the ceiling. "I do
think your smoke detector's broken, though. Mine usually

screams like a banshee whenever I light up. I have to say, I
found the silence comforting."

"I guess I need to replace the batteries." Arthur walked
to the window and watched a couple of golfers trudge their
way past the pond. In it, the reflections of a series of high
cumulus clouds moved like tectonic phantoms across the
sky. "Did you happen to see a guy fishing out there, by the
way? Down by the pond?"

"Fishing? No," Jeff snorted. "I can't imagine anyone
wanting to fish in there."

"There's been a guy in a gray windbreaker who hangs
out down there occasionally, early in the morning."

"Well no wonder I didn't see him," Jeffrey said. "I'm not
a morning guy. You know that."

"Right."

"Does it concern you?"

"Well for one thing, it's illegal." Arthur rubbed the back
of his neck. "And second, I don't want him catching anything. There's a fish in there, it's got to be at least this big,"
Arthur measured a space of about four feet with his hands.
"I call it—"

"Moby, right?"

"Yeah. I told you?"

"Sure," said Jeff. "And that's cute. Arthur Moore, ich…
itchio…" he paused, struggling to find the right word, "fish
activist," he finally finished.

"Were you going for 'ichthyological' activist?"

Jeff shot him a finger gun.

Arthur chuckled, sipped his wine and continued gazing
at the pond, where the wind was softly brushing the surface
clean and smooth and black.

ARTHUR WAVERED on whether or not to spend September 11th alone. That morning he turned on Miles Davis

instead of the television, deliberately avoiding the news. He made himself breakfast, finally finishing off the home-made blueberry jam David had given him for Christmas the year prior. He ignored his lengthy list of emails and instead wrote for an hour before the words dried up. He plucked *Of Mice and Men* from the bookshelf wall and read for several hours. Shortly before noon he finally snatched a few golf clubs from his storage closet and, noticing few golfers on the Kingsmill course, decided to play a few holes.

When evening loomed and the sun began to wane, Arthur donned a jacket and strolled through the woods down to the shores of the James River, noticing along the way the early signs of autumn tinting the trees. He sat atop a cement wall jutting out toward the water and watched the river roll end-lessly on, lapping gently against the roots of nearby silhou-etted cypress trees, which rose from the shallow waters like gnarled calligraphy strokes against the backlit sky.

The evening's cool warmth supplemented perfectly the meditative sounds of the water. He closed his eyes and listened to the buzzing and chirping in the foliage behind him, an arrhythmic music that predated humankind and, he presumed, would continue unabated long after his tribe of tall, squabbling apes had acted out their final sin. Arthur appreciated that sense of permanence, even drew comfort from it (though not on a personal level) when he realized his own presence or extinction would in no way really affect anything. His absence would not be a wound to be sutured or a permanent scar on the universe. He would flake cleanly off the world's face.

Who knows I'm out here, right now? Realizing he was the only one in the world who knew created a sudden leaden feeling in his stomach.

As the twilight deepened he rose and made his way slowly back to the house. By the time he arrived night had fully fallen. Checking his phone Arthur saw several missed calls, several voice mails. Two were from Linda, but he didn't feel like calling her back. Dropping his cellphone in his desk drawer, he shuffled into the kitchen to pour a glass of wine.

◦≬◦

In his office the next morning, Arthur hesitated over his phone's dial pad. Finally he called Jeff.

"Hey Teddy," Jeff said. "What's going on?"

"I was wondering if you could you give me Natalie's phone number." Arthur added, "David has a copy of her book and wants to get it signed."

"Oh." Jeff sounded surprised. "Hey, I can get him a brand new signed copy, if you'd like."

He's wise.

Arthur's mind raced to seek another excuse for needing Natalie's number. "I also wanted to speak with her about what she said about me, like you suggested. And I do have a few more questions I'd like to ask her."

"Topping off the brainiac ping-pong match you had the other week?"

"I suppose."

They chatted a few more moments before Jeff coughed up the number and they hung up. Arthur hoped he hadn't sounded too desperate.

He knows.

Arthur didn't feel he was actually making a conscious decision to be alone with Natalie. Rather, something deep in his chemistry seemed to be pulling and tugging him unavoidably into the scheme.

The phone rang twice before she picked up.

"Hello?"

"Hey, Nat. It's Arthur. Art Moore."

Half a second ticked by. "Art? What a pleasant surprise."

He tried to gauge her reaction. A little slow on the uptake, but she sounded happy to hear his voice. Had she forgotten about him already? Or was she genuinely surprised to hear from him?

"What's up?" she asked.

"A couple of things, actually," he said. Two reasons for reaching out felt far more legitimate than one. He steadied his breathing, wanting to sound casual. "I'm finally reading Gospel of Universal Self. Thought I'd run a few questions by you, if you don't mind."

"Of course not."

"It's my son's partner's copy, actually. Would you mind autographing the book for him?"

"Of course."

"I was also wondering...well, this may sound strange. But..."

"Yes?"

Arthur chuckled nervously. "By any chance did you tell Jeff my house was haunted?"

She hesitated. "Not haunted, really. I just...felt a presence there."

"I'm intrigued," Arthur said. "I didn't know you were into the paranormal."

"Not in a ghost-hunter way," Natalie said, a slightly offended edge to her tone. "But in the big picture I think everything is paranormal."

"Would you mind? ... This may sound strange, but I'm curious as to what you think might be going on here. Or at least what you thought was occurring."

"You won't see anything more than you already have," she said.

"Still, I'm interested. And, of course, I'd like to discuss your book. How about Thursday?" He would have ample time to snag the copy from Jim and read enough to bone up on the book. "In the evening? Around seven, perhaps?"

"I can do that," Natalie said. "See you then, doctor."

"See you."

JIM LED ARTHUR to the bookshelf, where he stood scanning the toothy array of spines. "Which book did you want, again?"

Arthur gestured to the third shelf. "*The Gospel of Universal Self,* down there." The title still felt strange to say. Its mixture of words seemed alien on his tongue, yet were strangely validated by the mere act of his speaking them aloud.

Jim cocked a quizzical eyebrow, but plucked the book from its place and handed it to his father. "Honestly, I didn't even realize we had this. And it doesn't seem up your alley, Dad."

"I met the author," Arthur said, perusing the cover as he had that day at the book festival. "She's Jeff's girlfriend. I thought I could get it signed for you guys."

Jim settled onto the couch amid a disheveled pile of crinkled, incomplete pages of graphite sketches. "I don't mind one way or the other. I'm not even sure if that copy is mine or David's. I seem to recall that we picked it up in a bulk purchase at some yard sale. I doubt either of us have read it."

"Just like *Unholy Ghost?*" Arthur asked with a rueful smile.

"Sort of," Jim grinned apologetically. "I got derailed by Dan Brown, I'm sorry to say. But hey, at least I'm reading, right?"

"So if your diet was nothing but candy and chips, your excuse would be, 'Hey, at least I'm eating?'"

"Sucks your name wasn't Bob," Jim said. "Bob the Snob.

Nice rhyme there."

"Hah, sure." Arthur flipped through the book. "Thanks again, Jim. I'll bring it back with a signature."

Jim shrugged.

"You working on mural sketches?" Arthur asked.

"Yeah, so far I have a few favorites. I showed one to Ethan, the owner. He thought it was a bit dark, though."

"That one, I presume?" Arthur pointed to a richly penned rendering of a bald, eyeless man holding a knife and fork while sitting alone at a dinner table against a celestial background. On the table sat baskets and dishes filled with a wide variety of living plants and animals. Resting on the man's dinner plate was planet Earth, looking like a steak about to be carved up and blissfully devoured by the unaware blind man.

"That's the one," Jim said. "I call it *Mankind's Last Supper*."

"Well done. But, yeah, I suppose it's a little dark for a health store mural."

"I'm trying for a more upbeat approach. I'm thinking of going with this one..." Jim leaned forward and shuffled through the pages. He pulled out a charcoal sketch of two cupped hands about to catch a massive falling water droplet. Reflected in the drop was a forested, mountainous landscape topped by a crescent moon.

"Very nice," Arthur said. "Did you finish that other piece you showed me? The tropical beach and donkey and all that?"

"No. Once again I got derailed by other projects. Mainly this mural."

"Understandably. Well...I'll get out of your hair." Arthur made his way to the door with Natalie's book tucked under one arm.

"Okay, Dad. Thanks for coming."

"Sure. How's David doing, by the way? You visiting him again soon?"

"Tomorrow night. They say he's on the mend. He just needs gobs of antibiotics. I miss him. It's weird, because it's hard for me to be creative when he's not around. Even when he's in the other room studying, I feed off his vibe."

Arthur nodded. "I'm sure he'll be fine."

"He will be." Jim's voice wavered, "would you like to go with me tomorrow? I know hospitals aren't your cup of tea exactly…"

"Are they anyone's cup of tea?"

"Well, David's I suppose, being the budding doctor and all." Jim sighed. "I worry sometimes he's gonna burn himself out and get sick again by just trying too hard to get himself back on track."

"He's tough. And smart. He'll make it."

"Yeah."

"Anyway…"

"By the way," Jim said. "I saw your *Mann's Watch* appearance."

"Uh oh."

"Tell me: which one are you? Distracter or distracted?"

Arthur deliberated for a second: "Depends on the day, I think."

BY THURSDAY NIGHT Arthur had hastily read a little more than half of *The Gospel of Universal Self*, scouting its pages for the broader recurring concepts. He felt like he was both studying for a test and prepping for a first date, two anxieties he never thought would meet. The mixture proved unwelcome but not unexpected.

He dog-eared one page featuring a passage of particular interest: "I believe one of the most crucial notions we as a species have to understand is that our so-called 'animal instincts'— our predisposition to greed, lust, violence, etcetera—are to be treated as tools to measure our spiritual evolution. So to people like Bernard Shaw who couldn't, or can't, fathom why a Creator would engineer imperfect creations, I ask this simple question: how would you know or experience perfection without first being imperfect? It is a beautiful system when you think about it. After all, you can't get to high school without starting in first grade and taking the necessarily awkward growth steps. As Christ says in *The Course in Miracles*, 'Free will does not mean you get to determine the curriculum; only that the amount of time you invest in exploring it is entirely up to you. We must never again use phrases like, 'Oh well, it's just human nature' as an excuse for aberrant behavior. Otherwise, like any poor student, we're likely to have to repeat the same grade over and over."

To her credit, Arthur found many statements compatible with secularist tradition; they expressed basic truths about humanity's past and future that would behoove any human being to heed regardless of class, race or belief system. Yet her casual mentions of God and Jesus, ostensibly as real to her as a door and its doorknob, irritated him, which kept him from feeling full appreciation for her work.

Thursday night proved cloudy, hinting of the first autumnal storm. Despite the chill in the air, Natalie arrived wearing a tank top beneath a sheer long-sleeved blouse over a long skirt, and sandals with raised heels. He noticed she was again wearing Linda's handcrafted turquoise necklace.

"Hey Nat," he said. "Thanks for coming."

They shared a self-conscious hug.

"Sure thing," Natalie said. "Thank you for inviting me."

How odd, he realized, though strangely pleasurable, to imagine Natalie having been here before with Jeff. She seemed relaxed, even at home, as she settled comfortably into the living room sofa. *Fluid*, he thought. *Loose. Cool.*

"Would you like anything to drink?" Arthur asked. "I have a nice merlot decanted."

"Just water for now."

He poured her some water and felt obliged to grab a Coke from the fridge for himself. When he returned to the living room with their drinks, a heavy, awkward silence lengthened between them. *Think of something to talk about.* Two options he ruled out: the weather and 'How was your day?'—topics too strained to even contemplate.

"How was your day?" Natalie asked, politely sipping her water.

"Oh, it was alright. Business stuff, mostly."

"And what does business stuff entail?"

"Writing, I suppose. Or trying to write."

"I'd have expected more than that," Natalie said. "You're becoming an industry unto yourself."

Arthur chuckled. "Hardly. Ask Jeff."

"Why go through Jeff when you're right here?"

"Maybe he's too busy making an industry out of you."

"Oh dear. That'd be much harder."

"Harder? In this country? You give an intelligent voice to faith and spirituality. People crave that here."

"They crave drama. From Angels versus Demons to Yankees versus Dodgers to Democrats versus Republicans to Atheists versus Pastors. The Coliseum, as you called it. Aptly too. Sword clashes sparking passions."

"We do like our extremes."

"Sure. They enclose us. Without these twin polarities we'd only feel comfy boring openness and loneliness. But that's why I can see President Moore long before President Farrow."

Arthur nearly choked on a mouthful of Coke. "How's that figure?"

"You're an atheist. That's a hard line: a well-defined corner. Many may not agree with you, but they know your position and can sum it up in a sound bite. Or they think they can. You have a following. You're the Yankees against the Dodgers."

"Please, I'd rather be the Dodgers," Arthur said, grinning slightly. "I can't stand the Yankees."

"Okay, sure. But my point is that in political elections that one definable word is key. You say it, snap! The people fall in line appropriately. But who am I to Joe Electorate? I'm neither traditionally religious nor atheist. I'm a New Age nutjob. Too nuanced, frankly. Too ambiguous."

"I see what you mean."

"I'm totally not insinuating that somehow I'm more complex," Natalie said.

"I get that." Arthur rubbed his chin. "In any case I'll have to ring up Jeff in the morning and let him know my plans to make a run for the White House."

Natalie laughed. "Do you foresee Linda as your first lady?"

While obviously playful, the question startled him. "I'm not sure she'd be equipped for that lifestyle. Not that I'd be, either. But Jeff could do it."

"Probably so," Natalie agreed.

"Would you be his first lady?"

Natalie tossed her head back and laughed. "Hah! You know I don't do well with labels." She moseyed over to the living room coffee table, where he'd prominently placed *The Gospel of Universal Self.* "Is this David's copy?"

"It is indeed," Arthur said.

She picked up the pen he'd left beside the book. "Anything in particular I should say?"

"You can make it out to both David and Jim if you'd like."

"How lovely." She scribbled out a note and her signature, then handed the book to Arthur for his approval.

To David / Jim,

To many happy years as One. Thank you!

Natalie Farrow

"Your signature is actually legible," Arthur said. "In my experience, the two kinds of people who have the worst chicken-scratch handwriting are doctors and writers."

"And you're both," Natalie said with a chuckle. "I'd like to see your signature."

"Hah, right." He rubbed the back of his neck, trying to ignore his petty desire that she might reciprocate and ask for an autographed copy of one of his books. "So I read *Gospel*. I found it fascinating, I have to say."

"Thank you. Any particular thoughts?"

"I dog-eared a few pages." He picked up the book, opened it to a random page. "Oh, and one quick question I wanted to ask you—you refer to Jesus and this *Course in Miracles* book a couple of times throughout. I don't think I'm familiar with that book. I mean, it does sound familiar. But you toss it around like it's as commonly recognized as the Bible."

"I think it's a shame the book isn't as commonly known, but I guess that's to be expected. After all, the Bible does have a religious monopoly here, doesn't it?"

Arthur offered a 'what're you gonna do?' kind of shrug.

"The Course can be very dense and very academic," Natalie continued. "But then again the book was written with academics—with teachers and instructors who would impart the material accessibly to students—in mind."

"What's the connection to Jesus?"

Getting less awkward, he thought, trying not to reveal his excitement. *Over the hurdle.*

"A psychotherapist named Helen Schucman channeled

the course over a seven-year period in the 1970s," Natalie explained. "Keep in mind that, beforehand, Schucman was an atheist, and she'd been raised Jewish. But there was a period in which she was having a very tense relationship with some of her colleagues, and one in particular named William Thetford. The way I heard the story, one day, exasperated, she said to Thetford, 'There's got to be a better way.' Soon after she started 'hearing' what she described as a voice that wasn't literally a voice but more an urge, an inspired compulsion to write down things of which she wasn't aware until they were out and on paper. This voice spoke personally of Christ, of the nature of God, our purpose, which is to discover our true identity and to discover love in our relationship to all things and to all people."

"Okay…"

"She channeled the Voice for a while and kept it hidden, because she was embarrassed to show the writings to any of her colleagues. Finally she ended up confiding in Thetford, and both of them went to work collaborating on its editing, organization and publication."

"That's interesting."

"It's a remarkable book. And it's Jesus' correction of modern Christianity. He says the lesson is not in the crucifixion, but in the resurrection. The book uses Christian terminology but is far more Eastern in philosophy than the Bible. It informs people that there's no Satan, for instance. And it further says that in ultimate reality, there is no evil."

Like a turbulent slide show, images of John and of Benjamin Holden and of Jim's bloody and pulpy young face flashed through Arthur's mind.

"Believing in evil doesn't mean you have to believe in God," said Arthur. "I certainly believe in evil."

"Sure. Evil exists. But it only exists as an illusion so that you may know love. You can't have creation without contrast."

"Hmm."

"Think on it. Dichotomous truths exist side by side. Good and evil exist in our physical world of relativity, but behind this world there is only good, an all-encompassing neutrality and acceptance." Natalie shifted in her seat. "The course claims its overall, take-away message is: 'Nothing that is real can be threatened. Nothing unreal exists. Herein lies the peace of God.'"

"I see."

"Since its publication many other books have been written that have distilled its concepts into more commercialized forms. That's what I tried to do with *Gospel*."

"I think you put together a fine book," said Arthur, racking his brain for something useful to say.

"Thank you, Art. I appreciate that."

Silence for a few seconds, then Natalie tilted her head. "I might take a stab at that wine now."

"I'd say it seems a good time." Arthur headed to the wet bar and lifted the decanter of merlot. "You were saying?"

"Oh, I wasn't saying anything."

He poured them each a glass. "Thought I saw some comment lurking in the back of your eyes."

"Impressive, Dr. Moore." Natalie accepted the glass he proffered. "Thanks. I was just going to say that it helps to have a spiritual foundation like *A Course in Miracles*. That way I see myself more as a messenger and not some original prophet, if you will."

"I think I get what you're saying," Arthur said. "To be honest it's always made me laugh a bit when I see people writing and speaking and touring to promote some form of self-realization or enlightenment. It seems that all such efforts indicate they're not 'enlightened' themselves, because they're seeking money and validation for their efforts."

He worried he'd gone a bit overboard so he paused to gauge Natalie's response, but her expression still appeared agreeable.

"I mean," Arthur continued, "if the way they were inside was the way they preach to others how they should be, they'd be fine sitting at home, being fulfilled in themselves and not caring about the goings-on in the world. Right?"

"Well, you're speaking pretty generally. I don't know anyone, including myself, who claims to be 'enlightened.' I get what you're saying, but I do think we all have a duty to help repair the world and our individual conditions with the tools we feel are most appropriate to us. We do the same thing, you and me. We're both writers. And sometimes, when the world demands it, speakers."

"Sure," Arthur said. He sipped his wine. "Sorry, I hope I didn't step on any toes."

"No toes to be stepped on," Natalie said with a laugh. "I'm enlightened."

Arthur chuckled.

Natalie leaned forward, playful mischief lighting her eyes. "So!"

"Yes?" Arthur raised an eyebrow.

"What would you like to know about the ghosts running rampant in your house?"

"Ah, right. The ghost."

"I'm a little annoyed that Jeff told you, by the way," she said. "I spoke in confidence. Or at least I thought I did."

"He's my manager. He hides nothing from me."

"He's my manager too."

Arthur raised his glass in a mock toast. "Touché."

Natalie sipped pensively at her wine. "Frankly, I now feel a little embarrassed discussing this with you. I'm aware that you think me trite or superstitious or perhaps a valid candidate for Bellevue."

"Like I said, I'm curious myself about the afterlife. Besides, I'm a psychologist, not a psychiatrist." Arthur smiled, encouraging her on.

"Just so you know, I'm not feeling any presence right now. I only felt a presence a couple of times while you were away."

"A presence? As in…a spirit?"

"As I said before, a presence. Not hostile, just … there, like an impression hanging on the air, a shadow. It talks to you, but you're so closed off that it's like it's speaking into a phone where the other party has already hung up."

"Does this presence have a name? What does it say?"

"Have you lost a loved one?"

Arthur tensed. "At my age most everyone has lost a loved one, no?"

Natalie cocked her head at him, saying nothing, but he could feel her gaze boring into him.

He rose stiffly, turned away from her and watched sightlessly out the front window. "Yes, I've lost my mother and my brother. I don't know what happened to my father. Was this presence you perceived male or female?"

"Gender labels don't exist with souls. That's like asking whether gravity is male or female. But I sensed it felt no great urge to communicate with you. It's more just watching out for you. It knows things will be okay for you."

"Things are okay for me."

"Are they?"

"Sure."

"Alright." Natalie set down her wine on the coffee table, stood and began pacing the living room, arms crossed. "Did you enjoy the shade of the oak tree?"

"What?"

"The shade of the oak tree. In Salinas Valley, when you were picnicking with Linda."

There was a brief period, seconds at most, where Arthur didn't quite comprehend the enormity of what Natalie just said. Her words had to first filter through an intellectual membrane, a defensive net in his psyche that routinely caught and deflected statements absurd or unreasonable. But there was nothing untrue about what she'd said. Slowly he was filled with the realization—a sense beyond the mere possibility—that she'd truly displayed some form of clairvoyance.

He could feel Natalie staring at him. He avoided making eye contact, worried it might reveal his incredulity. Eventually though, he felt compelled to meet her gaze.

"Did I just spook you?" she asked.

"Well, it's certainly odd that you would know about our picnic. Did you talk to Linda?"

"No, I've not spoken to Linda." She remained focused on him, as if daring him to refute her. Though her tone sounded coldly certain, her level gaze felt soft and empathetic. She eased closer to him and placed a hand on his shoulder, which for a moment he resented as patronizingly maternal, until she slid her hand across his bicep and began tenderly stroking his arm.

She said, "You're familiar with Steinbeck's work, *To a God Unknown*?"

Arthur cleared his throat. "It's one of my favorites of his, yes."

She could've spied it on my shelf, or maybe asked Jeff.

"So you remember the oak tree," she continued. If she sensed the mental battle that raged inside him, she paid it no heed. "How the main character believes the spirit of his father lives in the oak tree to help him watch over the land?"

"Right."

"That's all. This presence is just your oak tree."

Arthur smiled, if only to release some of his discomfort.

His skin felt hot and tingly, very present and very alive, but not in a positive way. More like he'd stuck his finger in an electric socket and received an unpleasant jolt.

"It's okay Art, I understand," she said. She retrieved her near-empty wine glass and finished its contents.

Arthur pointed to her glass. "Refill?"

"Sure, thanks."

He poured them both refills, then said, "So tell me…how did you become interested in all this?"

Natalie raised her eyebrows. "All this…?"

"All this spiritual stuff, I mean."

"I know what you mean, doctor. For starters, I was brought up Catholic. I was pretty devout for the first sixteen or so years of my life. Then I began to ask questions. My mind didn't do ceilings. It just kept bumping up against them and then breaking through them. That was difficult at first, because I couldn't find a philosophical shelter big enough to contain the way I was thinking." Natalie paused, reflecting. He wondered if she was editing her story to make it sound more palatable to him.

"But I read a lot," she continued "A whole lot. Soon I found myself at the Mountain Wellness Center in Arizona, run by Neil Valentine: he was one of the authors I'd come to read, well…a lot. We saw each other. Intimately, I mean. He really helped me—physically, emotionally, spiritually. It was a wonderful experience."

"I'm glad you found it so," Arthur said.

"I'm a believer in the 'whatever works' theory," she said. "Within reason, of course."

"I am, too."

She shot him a look of wry amusement. "I'm not as sure as you are about that."

Again he felt himself tense, as if he was somehow failing to live up to her high standards.

"Why not?"

"If I told you, right now, that I'd gotten all my wisdom and knowledge from a tiny troll who lives inside my closet, and that he's always been my protector and supporter, you wouldn't have anything to say to try and change my mind?" Natalie ran a quick hand through her hair. "I'm just saying, you're attached to your own prescription for what works."

"I'm not that kind of doctor."

"I'm talking about the things you say and do between the covers."

Arthur couldn't help but smile. "Please tell me you're referring to my book covers."

It was Natalie's turn to make her way to the large window that faced the patio, the darkening golf course and the even darker, mysterious woods beyond.

"Oh, Arthur," she said. Her tone lightly chastised him, though her gaze remained locked on the heavily shrouded forest. "Everything about you is so much more honest and telling than you actually are."

WHEN IT HAPPENED Arthur wasn't exactly sure—later there would be hazy rifts in his memory, mere patches of awareness. He did recall placing his hands upon Natalie's shoulders, and that she didn't seem to react. He squeezed a bit tighter and then lowered his hands to her waist. Breaths became more frequent than words. Their touch felt like an electrical contact, binding them. Then Natalie moved. And in the next patch of awareness, when at last Arthur had relocated himself in the ordinary world, he found himself holding Natalie, now half undressed and eager, against his bare chest.

For several long moments they shifted with the capricious winds of their impulses. Natalie's skin felt soft and smooth, the lines and curves of her body the fruit of some master sculptor. Unexpected tattoos dotted her flesh, the most enticing of which was a serpentine dragon coiled at the small of her back. Her hair shone like a moonlit water-fall.

They'd started in the living room, but continued up the stairs into Arthur's bedroom. Arthur shut the door, still feeling the sensual brushstrokes of Natalie's tongue in his mouth. In her carnal prowess they segued to a graceful, almost artistic synthesis.

When at last they finished making love neither one spoke, as though the release had washed away all words.

Lying beside him, Natalie's soft breath pulsed against his shoulder, the tickle of it slightly annoying him. Outside, an imminent storm rumbled. Lightning flashed, illuming the room for the briefest of seconds and producing on the far wall an optical illusion that reminded Arthur of his brother John climbing a tree. He watched the shadows play for a while, then gradually fell asleep.

"Arthur?"

No response.

"Arthur, wake up. I think something's wrong."

He opened his eyes and registered that Natalie was shaking him awake. Loud rain clattered against the window. In the distance more thunder rolled.

He looked at the clock: 3:11 a.m.

"What is it?" he asked.

"I smell smoke," she said.

He sat up and noticed it instantly: an odor, hot and pungent, like an active barbecue, but mixed with other, stronger chemical smells.

"I smell it," he said, now fully alert.

"Did you feel the house shake earlier?" she asked.

"Thunder?"

"I think so."

He shook his head. "No, I was asleep. Do you think lightning hit the house?" He threw back the covers. A thin wisp of smoke was already curling beneath the bedroom door and across the carpeted floor. He knelt down, held his breath and peered beneath the door jamb, where he noticed a ghoulish, pulsing light dancing all along the hallway. His body went numb. "Jesus Christ."

He backed away from the door, the smoke-heavy air already stinging his lungs. Natalie reached for her purse on the nightstand and dug out her cell phone.

"I'm calling 911."

Arthur, unsure of what to do next, moved back toward the door. Behind him Natalie said, "Yes, something's happening. A fire's broken out..."

He could hear flames crackling just beyond the door, then he heard the splintering crash of something nearby. A sudden vision of his entire house, dropping and crumbling into a heap of black debris, flashed through his mind.

He reached tentatively for the doorknob and withdrew, finding it warm to the touch. Smoke continued to seep into the bedroom, heavier and blacker than before. Dizziness increased. He could feel his chest growing tighter with every breath.

Now or nothing.

Grimacing, he seized the doorknob and opened the door just a crack.

Fire lashed the far end of the upstairs hallway. A wall of flames licked the ceiling, having already swallowed up the hallway rug. Smoke billowed, sweeping whirls of drywall ash along with it. Arthur stood frozen in disbelief and willed himself not to panic. Something childlike in his brain insisted there was a way he might simply switch off the flames.

"Arthur—!" He heard Natalie's plaintive voice somewhere behind him. At the moment, she didn't seem real. Maybe, he thought shakily, she was calling out to him from that same timeless, far-off dimension they'd earlier visited. With any luck she would stay there, safe and sealed off from this inferno.

The encroaching heat began to overwhelm him, the flames lunging, taunting, licking clean his home, his livelihood, his life. For a wild instant he thought, So this is hell.

Defeated, he closed the door. Even so, the air in the bedroom thickened, growing oppressive from the voluminous clouds of ash. His lungs felt like heated stones in his chest, yet his head was as light as a feather.

He turned and spotted Natalie huddled beneath the window in the darkness of the bedroom, her cell phone still clutched tight against her ear. Everything seemed to be happening in slow motion, all the world's gears cranking down, down. Relinquishing. Giving up.

"Fire department's on their way," Natalie shouted. "Can we climb out the window from here?"

He moved toward her, opening his mouth to answer her, when the sudden crack of timber sounded overhead. There was a crash and Natalie screamed. At once the heat and the hell flames engulfed him. Agony rippled through Arthur, and he sensed the shock of his organs as they sought desperately to keep him functioning, to keep him here.

Soon, the pain began to fall away, the world receding to splinters and whispers and then, at last, to nothing.

QUESTIONS

I

SEATED AT THE EDGE OF HER COUCH CUSH-
ion, television flashing some banal and outdated game
show, Natalie Farrow felt stoned, even though she wasn't
and hadn't been for years. The sensation triggered some of
the less-pleasurable aspects of her prior experiences: feelings of prickliness, of being enclosed in too-tight spaces.
Slight—or perhaps even not so slight—paranoia.

Her cell phone rang. Natalie muted the television and
answered.

"Hello?"

"Hey, Nat," said a familiar, sullen voice. "It's Jeff."

"Hey there." She leaned forward and tugged a cigarette
from the pack on the coffee table.

Why can't you end it? she thought, unsure if the thought
was referring to him or herself. *Why can't you just end this?*

"Arthur was released from the hospital today," Jeff said.

She closed her eyes and let out a silent sigh of relief.
"Good," she said, keeping a neutral tone. "That's wonderful
news."

"He'll be staying at his son Jim's, at least for a while."

"I see."

Jeff sighed. In a lighter tone, he finally said, "Would you
like to see him?"

She lit the cigarette with shaking hands and inhaled deep, long.

See him.

"You told me he didn't want to see me, Jeff."

Jeff hesitated. "Yeah, but that was before."

"Before what?"

"Before he thought he'd live to see another day."

"Did he ask for me?"

"Um—well, not exactly."

"Look, I told you I need some time to myself." She took another drag. "I told you I didn't want to talk about Arthur with you."

"Yeah, but that was weeks ago. I'm just telling you he was released, and they think he's going to be okay. That's all."

"I'm glad," she said. "Thank you."

"Look," Jeff said. "Maybe it's time you and I talked about...well, about what happened that night."

"I'll talk to you soon, Jeff."

Natalie hung up, then took one last drag and smashed out her cigarette. She felt she understood Arthur's request for distance, even if it was hurtful. She'd needed time—still needed it, really—to process what was going on inside her. To some degree she felt rushed, confused, angry. Ignored, also, in her own repeated requests for solitude these last few weeks.

"I get it, Natalie," Jeff had said of her "hookup" (his word) with Arthur. "I get it. I get it, and we can work past it."

Jeff probably saw her night with Arthur as a singular inevitability that, once fulfilled, would never reoccur. Arthur, he might be telling himself, was out of her system now. A speed bump. She and Jeff could keep going. The word "please" became the pushy sentiment haunting his every word when the topic of their relationship had arisen. Yet Natalie was unsure how long they could continue. Every intimate moment with Jeff now seemed like a silent argument, another truth tucked away beneath surface physical distraction.

She sat staring for a moment while the jubilant game show host unveiled the prize to the victorious contestant. All muted—she didn't give a damn about game shows—it looked to her like an elaborate mime routine.

Her phone rang again. Jeff, calling back.

"It's not your fault," he said. For once he sounded sincere. "It's not as if you set the fire yourself. You went one way and Arthur went another. You saved yourself."

"Well thanks for that," she drawled.

"No, I didn't mean that in an accusing way. I understand. Anyone would. Who knows what might have happened to you if you'd been standing right there beside him."

They're on their way. She could still hear those comforting words from the 911 dispatcher, ringing in her ear in the split second before she watched the burning house collapse itself all around Arthur. *He's gone, she'd thought. Gone, gone, he's fucking gone...*

She'd turned her face back to the window, where the golf fairway sat in moonlit calm. Her eyes stung and her face moistened with tears and her nose ran as she shouted and pounded at the stuck window—*pull up dammit, pull the fuck up*—while the heat swirled all about her. At last the window popped loose and slid open on the cool evening breeze. Carefully she centered her weight on a nearby drainage pipe, which bent and squeaked and dipped beneath the pressure. Breathing hard, she slid down the pipe and dropped to the angled tile rooftop a few feet below. She was already scaling her way across it when she heard the forlorn whine of the sirens closing in, howling through the dark woods toward this house, this house…yet sirens were always for someone else, weren't they? Unfathomable. Impossible. Adrenaline diluted all into dream texture and then a tile broke and, with one loud, crisp *snap* she fell. The ground rushed up to meet her and then a searing pain shot all the way up her right leg and into her pelvis.

I'm done for. Arthur's going to die, and I'm going to die. Arthur. Oh God, Arthur. Her mind pulsed in and out of consciousness. At times she became aware of the stars above her being slowly consumed by smoke. Which stars were they? What was happening on the planets around them? They were dead probably, those stars up there, snuffed out long ago.

Long ago.

She then saw faces floating above her within the ashen clouds, stern and stubbled and shadowed by helmets of fire. The pain in her leg had become a neon throb. Consciousness slipped away again, but she came to once more to find herself being placed on a portable stretcher. Gravel crunched beneath its wheels and it made a squealing noise like a small animal in agony, going, going, *going.* They loaded her into the ambulance and the siren blared while the two paramedics began to work on her leg. One, a young African-American man, spoke to her sharply and shone a light in her eye. "Your pupils aren't dilated," he said. "That's a good thing."

Natalie stayed in the hospital for three days with a severely sprained ankle and a concussion. She spent most of that time watching TV, and even declined Jeff's offer to bring her some books. The second afternoon she spent doodling aimlessly for hours on the back of an envelope.

"What," Jeff had asked her that morning, from the foot of her bed with his fingers nervously tapping against the railing, "were you doing at Art's that night?"

She'd seen that same question haunting his eyes for

hours, days really, before he finally spoke it.

She hadn't answered.

Miraculously, Arthur had sustained only first-degree burns on his arms and face. His more significant injuries were internal, mainly to his brain. He'd flatlined, Natalie had heard, when they drained the excess fluid from his cranium due to a subdural hematoma that caused bleeding inside his brain. Yet he came back. His doctors had succeeded in stabilizing him in a coma, from which he'd blearily awakened after several days.

You saw it happen, in your dreams. You saw that it was going to happen and yet you did nothing...

"I guess I'm just not in a very good place with myself, Jeff."

"Because you saved yourself? Because you thought fast? Nat —"

"I'll talk to you soon, Jeff," she said curtly, and hung up.

Jim drove on in pensive quiet, well accustomed to his father's silence. They veered off the highway, heading to Kingsmill. The season was turning faster than expected. An autumnal chill stung the air, the clouds stacked thick and gray against the pale-blue sky. Late afternoon sunlight dribbled through the clouds.

Although Jim usually felt comfortable when his father remained silent, this time he could feel a distinct heaviness in the air. He wondered if it warranted mention.

Leave him be, Jim thought. It seemed like the best idea, at least for the moment.

Arthur stirred. "You're sure you don't mind stopping by the house?" he asked, at last breaking the silence.

"There's not much there to see just yet," Jim cautioned

him, "but sure."

Jim had often mused in the past that their relationship bore hidden fractures from the weight of so many mutually concealed thoughts. "Dark matter psychology," he'd once called it. Yet since the fire he'd been uncertain whether those ancient fissures still remained between them. Something had softened in Arthur's eyes, his spirit noticeably more pliable.

He glanced over at his father and noticed Arthur watching him.

"What?"

"Nothing," Arthur said. "Just...thank you. Very much. For taking me in. I know it's going to be an inconvenience for you both these next few weeks."

"No inconvenience at all, Dad."

"You sure David's okay with it?"

"He's fine." Jim smiled. "He's looking forward to doting on you."

"I do rather feel like a child," Arthur admitted.

"David and I have talked about becoming parents some day." Jim's smile widened. "Maybe this will be good practice for us."

Arthur let out a soft chuckle, and then turned back to the shifting gallery of scenery.

"The workers out at the house have been at it practically round the clock," Jim said. "Right after the fire all that remained was a twisted little chunk of apocalypse."

Arthur laughed.

Jim glanced at him with open curiosity. Strange, he thought, that his father should seem so unperturbed by the loss of every life artifact that he'd ever accumulated.

"It was really kind of David to visit me," Arthur said.

"He's been feeling better these days. The moment he heard about what happened, there was no way he wasn't coming."

"I never once visited him."

Jim sensed a rueful undertone in the comment. "You're a busy guy. He understands that."

"So is he."

Jim felt it prudent to drop the subject. Silence returned as they wound along the asphalt veins that ran parallel to the golf course. Between the fairway and the house the pond sat still and silent, its surface undisturbed by life.

Arthur laughed out loud when they reached the house and Jim pulled into the driveway.

"I'm glad you find it funny," Jim said.

"What else can I do?"

They parked behind two large dump trucks full of scrap wood and other miscellaneous debris. Arthur seemed utterly absorbed in gauging the immensity and totality of the damage. Belatedly, Jim realized the photographs of the scene he'd shared with Arthur during his convalescence hadn't adequately prepared him for this up-close experience of the destruction.

He studied Arthur's face and noticed emotions there that were usually foreign to him.

"My God," Arthur muttered, shaking his head with disbelief.

"Workers'll be back first thing tomorrow," Jim offered, hoping the information would cheer him up.

They picked their way through the ruins with a mix of caution and curiosity. The foundation remained solid, thank heaven. Arthur seemed relieved to note that the west wing, which contained the den and the library, had only been grazed compared to the rest of the house, despite water damage and a layer of ash that now covered the shelves and books in a thick gray paste. The rest of the house, however, had been charred beyond recognition. Like ancient ruins, a few blackened, broken pillars of framing jutted starkly against the darkening fall sky.

"I wouldn't go too much farther," Jim said.

Arthur stopped obediently just outside what used to be his den. He peered through the charred, mangled spires at the second hole of the golf course just beyond. He seemed entranced by the wide-open view, though still somewhat pensive.

"What a weird feeling," he told Jim. "I've never before been able to see the pond from the den." He jammed his hands into his pockets and edged a bit closer, taking care not to slip on the charred wood and bits of debris that crunched beneath his soles with every step. "It's rather sur-real, actually. I like it. Makes me wonder if I should keep that view when we rebuild."

BACK ON THE HIGHWAY, Jim switched on the radio but kept the volume low as he flipped through various streams of babble, song and static. A creeping sense of responsibility had begun to weigh on his heart. He realized that the quality of his care over the next few weeks, coupled with David's emotional support, would serve as Arthur's first tentative foothold on what promised to be a long, return climb back to the outside world.

"By the way, Jeff's called me about a dozen times these last few days," he told Arthur, "telling me he needs to talk to you."

"I turned my phone off," Arthur said. "I left him a mes-sage a couple of weeks ago. Told him I'd get in touch when I was ready."

"He's concerned about you. But knowing an opportu-nity."

"Opportunity?"

Jim gestured toward the radio, where NPR now droned.

"I'm guessing he meant some media opportunity."

"Oh."

At Jim's apartment building they piled out. Jim offered to carry the brunt of Arthur's luggage, which wasn't much. David emerged from the smaller back bedroom as soon as they opened the door. Although that room had long functioned as Jim's informal art studio, he and David had earlier blown up the queen-sized air mattress they'd purchased the day before. They'd also added a night-light to a small bureau that stood in the corner, and David had thoughtfully topped the mattress off with fresh sheets and warm blankets with pillows. He'd even laid out a clean stack of towels for Arthur to use. *Not exactly the Taj Mahal,* Jim thought. But for the near future it would serve as his father's temporary quarters.

"Hey," David greeted them both.

"Hi David," Arthur returned.

"So good to see you up and about, Arthur." David gestured toward the back bedroom. "You're all set up in here."

Arthur entered the room and set his bags on floor beside the bed. "Looks fine to me. Though isn't this…?"

"Dad, seriously," Jim cut him off. "Don't worry about it. Artistry is highly portable."

"Thank you both for putting me up," Arthur said. "And also for putting up with me."

"You kidding?" David smiled. "We're happy to do it."

"Don't think I'm not aware of my good luck," Arthur said. "And to think I even have a doctor in the very next room, in case something happens."

Grinning, David asked, "How're you feeling?"

"Better than a few weeks ago." The answer came out clipped, almost dismissive. Arthur added, "There's not much to complain about beyond some persisting headaches."

"Just take it easy," David said. "Honestly let me know if you need anything."

"Thanks, David."

Jim said, "David and I thought we'd make dinner at home tonight. Just to kick off our little arrangement here."

Arthur gaped at Jim: "You're cooking now?"

"We are tonight," Jim answered, swinging his car keys around on his finger.

Jeff's signature knock disturbed Arthur's afternoon nap—loud, rapid and unapologetic. Arthur, who'd been stretched out on the couch, sat up suddenly and glanced around, feeling mildly confused as to his surroundings.

"Jim?"

Another knock. *Most definitely Jeff.*

"One minute," Arthur called as he acclimated to waking up in a living room that didn't resemble his own. His right shin had sustained a painful bruise that ached whenever he tried to stand. It throbbed now, and he grimaced. A moment later David sailed past him to answer the door.

"Don't get up, Art. Relax. I got it."

"Thanks." Arthur settled back into the sofa. "Is Jim around?"

"No. He's at a meeting about the mural."

Jeff stood in the apartment doorway, his pale face silhouetted by the afternoon sunlight. Arthur could see he looked drained, his normal humor conspicuous in its absence. He entered the apartment and shook David's hand. "Good to see you, man." He offered Arthur a forced smile. "And who do we have here...the lord and master, resurrected at last."

Arthur sank still lower in the sofa as his sense of discomfort expanded. "Hey there."

David must have sensed the tension between them. "I'll be studying in my room, if you guys need me." He headed down the hall and vanished inside the master bedroom.

Jeff perched awkwardly on the edge of an armchair next to the couch, fingers entwined and his lips making a soft, idle popping sound. He seemed not to know where to rest his gaze, and it darted around the room like an anxious bird.

Arthur felt a sudden rush of pity for his friend, so strong he'd have sworn that if he could touch it he'd feel something warm and smooth, like a satin curtain. Jeff just sat there, looking small and momentarily lost for words, so different from the Jeff he'd come to know. It shocked him to realize in that moment how entwined their worlds had been for such a long time. Obviously no man was an island, but for the first time Arthur could see visible traces of his own influence on Jeff, in the way he combed his hair and his crooked grin. It suddenly occurred to him that people were not the hard objects they often imagined themselves to be, running around bumping and tumbling into one another like rocks on a slope. *We are,* he realized, *more viscous than that. More like fluids, constantly mixing.*

Several more long seconds of silence passed.

Is he waiting for me to start? Arthur wondered. Does he want me to explain, confess…to tell him? Tell him…what?

Finally, Jeff spoke.

"Sorry for barging in like this," he said. "I wanted to see you for myself. I feel like we haven't gotten to talk mano-a-mano since you got out. And, you know, I wanted to hash over some things."

Arthur nodded. Though he didn't feel ready to have this chat, he knew he couldn't avoid it any longer. "Hash away."

"I drove by the house the other day," Jeff shook his head. "Still can't believe that's where it used to be. I feel like it's still intact somewhere out there, and that it'll come back someday. Like it's only gone out for a cleaning, or to the shop."

Arthur gave a tepid chuckle. "It's a new opportunity for me," he said. "I finally have an excuse to iron out some kinks in the original design."

Jeff furrowed his brow, stood up and pointed to the kitchen.

"Any beer in there?"

"Yeah, I think so."

"Think they'd mind?"

"Help yourself."

Jeff opened a bottle of Heineken and returned to his perch on the chair. More awkward seconds sidled by while he sipped it.

"You been following the chatter out there?" Jeff asked him. "I sort of hope not. But I do think you should be prepared for it."

"I've heard rumors," Arthur said. "Cable news discussions with pastors about my soul's destination, and some other stuff about the nature of karma. Oh, and that one radio preacher in South Carolina apparently said the 'Devil hisself' came out to snatch me for every bad word I've ever said against Jesus." He shook his head. "Frankly, I don't think I've ever badmouthed Jesus 'hisself.'"

"Maybe not, but your book sales are up by sixty percent," Jeff informed him with a laugh. "Maybe you should die and come back more often."

"Oh, man," Arthur shook his head, darkly amused. "Society, eh?"

"I guess just about everyone is eager to hear from you, to finally get your version of the story."

Eager to hear from me, Arthur's brain parroted. "Everyone, huh?"

Jeff rested his beer on the coffee table. "Have you considered doing a quick appearance, or making a public statement?"

"No, and I won't. Not now."

"It wouldn't be a big deal," Jeff urged. "I'm not talking some big hoopla, or even an interview. Just talking to one or two people."

"Isn't that an interview?"

Jeff sighed. "A simple sound bite is all we need. To get to the truth and end all the speculation."

"And just what would that accomplish?" he asked.

"Teddy, please." An instant of irritation crossed Jeff's face. "The reason I'm here with you, or that we even know each other, the reason you're at all a household name—it's all been grand speculation, right? Until now, I mean. I don't wanna trivialize everything that's happened. I don't. I want to help you stop *them* from trivializing it. From bastardizing it. Because you've experienced something most people haven't. For once you weren't just talking about what happens when we die. You were actually, clinically dead. So I'm thinking that whatever you say from this moment on, it won't be just speculation. Am I right?"

Arthur looked away. "I don't know, Jeff."

"Your religious friends in the media have jumped all over this," Jeff pressed. "Christ, man, you're an outspoken atheist and your home was struck down by lightning. Even I have trouble believing that it was just a stroke of bad luck."

"You think God thunder bolted my house?"

"Not really, but the accusation begs an answer, doesn't it? And of course you have tons of defenders, and well-wishers too. I got the mail stack if you're interested. I actually thought about bringing some of it along, but I decided against it. Anyway, here you have a chance to tell the world what you went through, that you had a literal trial by fire and came through it stronger than ever. You didn't get chummy with Jesus and you didn't share toasts with Buddha...am I right?"

"Actually, I went to purgatory," Arthur said, with enough gravity in his tone that Jeff, by his startled expression, appeared to take him seriously. Arthur grinned. "You know, I went through a fire purge to purify my wicked soul...along those lines. Or at least that's what many people would like to believe."

Jeff shrugged. "Who knows. And really, who cares what they say?"

"Exactly. People will believe what they want to believe, no matter what I say. It doesn't matter."

"No, I mean..." Jeff looked to Arthur like an agitated teacher attempting to reason with a stubborn student. "Who cares what other people say once you—the only person whose say matters—finally say something."

"The fog will clear at some point."

"Let's hope so." Jeff finally lowered himself into the chair and changed the subject. "Have you heard from Linda at all?"

Arthur's stomach clenched. "She sent me flowers the week after I woke up," he replied. "Nothing further, though. So, no. Not really."

"Got it." Jeff scrutinized the beer bottle and began peeling off fuzzy fragments of the label.

"Look... Jeff," Arthur began. "About Natalie."

Jeff took a long swig of his beer. With a solemn nod, but without meeting Arthur's gaze, he said, "Yeah...about Natalie."

"I'm sorry."

Jeff said nothing.

Arthur rubbed the back of his shaved scalp, his fingers running tenderly over the sutures. "I didn't mean for this to—"

"Forget it," Jeff said. "Natalie's a grown woman. She makes up her own mind. A guy like me…" He stared down into the bottle like a fortuneteller trying to read the tea leaves. Although it could've been his imagination, Arthur thought he noticed moisture build in Jeff's eyes. He glanced away to give him a little privacy.

"I always assumed she might stray," Jeff continued. "Hey, I'm just glad it was you, right? Someone worthy of her affections."

"Again, I'm sorry."

"Please don't embarrass me anymore about this." Jeff looked up then and smiled, but his eyes still seemed cold, unforgiving. "I forgive you. I'm just glad you're okay. And she's Natalie. You don't think I know that?"

Arthur frowned. "What do you mean, 'she's Natalie?'"

"Well, I mean, I sort of knew going in that she was a free spirit."

"That she is."

"The world can be kind of a playground for a pretty, intelligent woman. Sorry, but that's how it is."

Arthur wasn't exactly sure to whom Jeff was apologizing, or even what for. "Are you still managing her?"

"I'm still managing you, right?" Jeff smirked. "I'd be insane to drop up either of you hot taters. And anyway…" he trailed off.

"What?" Arthur pressed.

"We're kind of still seeing each other. Sort of."

Arthur blinked. "You are?"

"Yeah," Jeff said. "Who knows what's going on? I think we're pulling off the Band-Aid to see if the cut still bleeds."

"You need to just talk."

Jeff shrugged. "I know." He paused a moment. "She told me you were very stimulating. To be honest, I'm surprised she impressed you all that much. I mean, she knows her stuff, but I've also known you to dismiss people outright for saying or writing the kinds of things she does."

Arthur felt an urge to counter the statement, but the bigger, better part of him recognized its truth. "People are individuals," he said. "What I might have said or done to someone similar to Natalie doesn't mean she'll get the same treatment."

"Right." Jeff drained the rest of his beer. "Right." He rose and tossed his bottle in the yellow recycle bin near the kitchen entry. "I should let you be, Teddy," he said. "Thanks for indulging me in my random check-in."

"Sure." Arthur pushed himself unsteadily to his feet. Jeff proffered his hand but Arthur, half on instinct and half against even his own will, opened his arms: "Thanks, Jeff."

Jeff raised his eyebrows, clearly taken aback, but he leaned in and the two men briefly embraced.

"Rest up, okay man?" Jeff said on the way out the door. "Rest up for when you come roaring back. Should be a time."

A thin smile plied Arthur's lips: "Quite a time, indeed."

Jim recalled how, many years ago now, he'd once watched in fascination as Mr. Jackson, his eighth-grade science teacher, had stretched black cloth over four small posts and then placed a billiard ball in the center, creating a low-hanging depression.

"The fabric is like space-time, as Einstein saw it," Mr. Jackson explained. "The ball is like a planet, depressing and distorting the space around it and funneling all the smaller, nearby bodies into the fabric's warp. And there you have it, class...the theory of gravity." He concluded by firing a marble moon around the rim of the indentation. Jim had stared, enraptured, as the marble moved into a steady orbit around the denser, larger billiard ball.

Jim often perceived his father in much the same way. Arthur's presence commanded all space around it, drawing in all the nearby energy and attention. Little mystery then, why his career in media had grown beyond the written word. Arthur's charismatic presence also explained for Jim why his father seemed to have taken over his and David's entire apartment, diluting the limited independence Jim had scraped up in his shaky, young adult years. Jim accepted the possibility—one that David tended to favor—that because he was Arthur's son he'd inflated his father into something far grander in size and scope than he genuinely was. But that didn't explain why so many others tended to spiral around him.

He returned his attention to the sketch he was working on while his father drifted about the kitchen, setting up the afternoon tea kettle.

"I'm making some tea," Arthur said. "Would you like any?"

"I'm okay, Dad. Thanks."

"Are you sure? It's no trouble."

"I'm sure."

The doorbell rang, a raspy buzzing sound that David had once described as "a giant bug fart." Grateful for the interruption, Jim hurried to the door and opened it.

Camille Rhodes, his partner on the mural, stood there bearing a large sheet of paper that he could see contained a detailed sketch. Her wide, crooked smile beamed infectiously at him from above the paper's soft curl. He adored her smile's crookedness, and the fact that one of her upper teeth was smaller than all the rest.

Smiling, Jim said, "Uh oh. What have we here?"

"Sorry," she said, "I just had to show you." Spying Arthur in the kitchen, Camille stopped and lowered her sketch so quickly she crinkled it against her thigh. "Oh crap, I forgot. I'm so sorry. I didn't mean to intrude…"

"No worries," Jim said, closing the door.

Arthur fired off a quick wave. "Please," he said. "Don't mind me."

Camille wore her usual combination: a baggy gray sweater and ragged bell-bottoms that pooled over her sandaled feet. A rubber band secured her short ponytail. She carried herself, as usual, with an air of dreamy indifference. It startled Jim to notice how quickly his father's presence had affected her demeanor, and not in a positive way. Camille's uncaring enthusiasm had instantly shifted to one of guarded self-consciousness. Without even trying, Jim thought ruefully, his father had lassoed her into his powerful orbit.

"Camille, this is Arthur, my dad. Dad, this is Camille, my partner. She's working on the mural with me."

Introductions completed, they met in the divide between the kitchen and living room, hands extended. Camille approached Arthur with the expression of a star-struck tourist on Hollywood Boulevard.

"So nice to meet you," she said. "Again, I'm sorry if I've interrupted anything."

"Please," Arthur said. The kettle was starting to whistle so he removed it from the stove top. "Would you like some tea?"

"Um, sure."

Arthur fixed them each a cup of Earl Grey. He sipped his tea, his free hand tucked in the pocket of his corduroy pants. "Did I hear that you two met through David?"

"That's right," Jim said, smiling. "And Camille is the nicest present he ever gave me."

Camille laughed. "Where is Davy Crockett, anyway?" she asked, blowing on her tea to cool it down.

"He's at school," said Jim. To Arthur, he said, "Camille and David go back a long way."

"We met in high school," she said. "But we diverged, obviously, in our respective fields."

"You're a doctor of a different kind," Arthur told her. He smiled at Jim warmly. "You both are."

Jim felt briefly taken aback by the uncharacteristic remark, but said nothing.

"So where'd you go to college?" Arthur probed.

"Royce-Regents, in New York City. I graduated a year ago. I'd love to go to grad school for fine arts, though. Kinda why I'm doing this mural. To build my portfolio. And, you know," Camille glanced over at Jim, "to leave a signature on the local landscape."

"Or on a store wall," Jim said. "Whichever works."

"Do you live nearby?" Arthur asked.

Something about the politeness of his father's inquiries irritated Jim. They seemed like a soft interrogation, a sizing-up of her.

"I'm staying in Williamsburg with my aunt," Camille told Arthur. "I'm originally from North Carolina, though."

Arthur gestured to the paper in her hand. "Show us what you brought."

She hesitated. "I wanted to show Jim an idea I had for a section of the mural."

Jim instantly regretted not pulling her into a more private meeting, where she'd likely be far more comfortable showing off whatever she'd drawn. The irony was not lost on him that while Camille's work would soon be publicly displayed on the exterior of a building, she still felt deep reservations about presenting it to new people.

Arthur and Jim both eased in for a closer look as she

unrolled the newly creased drawing. It represented the water-drop part of the mural that reflected an earthly landscape. Jim noted that Camille's revision had taken a more macro approach than his own, by widening the panorama of the country and filling it with more creatures, some surreal hills and then configuring the entire landscape into a vaguely humanoid form: a sort of pantheistic maternal figure whose silvery hair streamed off into a blaze of thunderclouds. The change was not small, nor was it entirely big. Jim liked it immediately.

"I thought we could tweak the landscape section a bit," she suggested to Jim. "Make it less generic. Not that it was generic or boring before," she hastened to add.

"Camille, seriously," Jim said, "this project is as much yours as it is mine."

Her grin widened. "Aw, you're sweet, Jimbo."

"It's true." For several weeks now Camille had been Jim's partner in dreamland, his companion in creation. She'd provided for him a laughing, merry, occasionally stone-faced escape from the reality of his father's tragedy and hospitalization, as well as from David's ongoing health malaise. The two of them had created a little bubble away from it all. Now, Jim suddenly realized, that bubble had burst. Camille and Arthur now occupied the same world.

"I really like this female figure shape," Arthur traced the subtle feminine form with his finger. "Mother Nature, I presume?"

"Kind of," Camille agreed. "You could call her that."

"I wonder if you might make those mountain peaks into her breasts," Arthur said, his tone revealing a hint of humor. Camille laughed, but Jim felt himself stiffen. Odd that his father would be so suggestive with someone he'd just met.

"That's not a bad idea," Camille replied. "Maybe I can

have them spewing a milklike magma fluid."

"I'd hate to think what might come out of that crack in the lower earth."

"Well that's easy," Camille said. "If she's Mother Nature, then we did!"

"I didn't mean *that* crack."

Jim continued to smile, even though he felt baffled. For years after he'd come out he'd resented Arthur's stubborn unwillingness to discuss anything remotely sexual. Arthur always kept those cards close to his chest, and Jim had eventually trained himself to accept it.

"I really like this rendition," Jim told Camille. "Let's do it."

"No changes?" she asked. Her expression pleaded with him, as if she wanted some bit of criticism to verify that his overall approval was genuine.

"Not from where I stand," he said. "Once we get it up there we'll see where it takes us."

"Okay then." Camille's gaze met his and held there for several moments. "We're buckled into this ride together, my friend."

JIM ROSE EARLY THE NEXT MORNING and quietly entered the kitchen, where he fixed a thermos of vanilla tea and snagged a nutrient bar for a hasty breakfast. Occasionally his gaze drifted to the closed door of Arthur's room.

He felt an aching pity for his father, as if the man were a vulnerable and defenseless child. Arthur Moore had ignited many fires in many minds, sometimes willingly, sometimes unwittingly, and amid these fires he must have stood as he had in the flames that had nearly claimed his life: confused, feigning strength, burdened terribly with the inexplicable as reasonless heat engulfed him.

Dawn had already begun to fold back the night into shadows and corners when Jim left the apartment. He arrived at Earth Works just as the sun crossed over the horizon. Camille was already there, dressed in clothes that had come out of what she called her "art closet." Her shirt and pants were both streaked with meteor showers of paint. Behind her stretched the partially finished mural.

Camille had begun unloading their paints and brushes from the small storage shed. "Morning Jimbo," she said as he approached her, "notice I left the 'good' out."

"Still too early to be good?" he said.

"Well, let's see how it goes from here."

Jim downed the last of his tea and proceeded to help unload the rest of the supplies, including an industrial-grade twelve-foot ladder. They then began painting in companionable silence until Camille, dipping a roller in the black canister and adding a black background coat to the cosmos, finally spoke.

"It was cool meeting your dad yesterday," she said. "And I like that he's staying with you. Little surreal too, since I know him from all his YouTube videos and news clips."

"Yeah," Jim said, a little distracted, "I get that."

"I haven't read any of his books, though."

"They're pretty good," he said, in instinctive reaction. In truth, he'd never read a single one of his father's books from cover to cover. At best he'd skimmed enough pages from each that it might amount to a book's worth if one was being generous.

"Between you two there's enough genius to conquer the world," Camille said. "He's got academic smarts, and you've got artistic genius."

Jim stopped painting for a moment and faced her. In a playful tone he drawled, "Hey, who says I don't got academic smarts?"

Camille giggled. "You just did, with that fake Southern

accent and grammar."

"Like any good artist, most of my IQ is in my gut."

"I only wish more of mine was in my boobs."

Jim froze, his newly dipped paintbrush dripping into the can. "You didn't just say that, did you?"

"Hey, I'm allowed to be a girl sometimes."

"You're gorgeous, Cam," he said. "Don't be redonk."

"Please tell me you didn't just say 'redonk'."

"I'm allowed. I don't got the smarts, remember?"

Camille laughed again and rolled more black paint onto her mural section. "By the way, when did your dad get home? From the hospital, I mean."

"A couple of days ago. Why?"

"Honestly, given everything that's happened he seems to be doing phenomenally well."

"Yeah, he seems almost rejuvenated," Jim said. "The doctors were flabbergasted by how well he recovered. And how quickly."

"I imagine that would be true for anyone who almost died. Feeling rejuvenated, I mean. Grateful."

"Maybe," Jim said, sounding doubtful. To him it seemed like the changes in his father's attitude involved something far more than mere gratefulness, but he had no idea what the difference was so decided not to mention it to Camille. "I haven't met any other people who've almost died, though," he added.

Camille said, "I haven't either. I'm just glad he's doing okay."

"Me too."

"He was with someone else that night, wasn't he?" Camille asked. "A woman, I seem to recall. Sorry if I'm being too nosey…"

"No, it's fine," Jim assured her. "He was indeed with someone else that night. She escaped in better condition than he did, that's for sure. She managed to climb out the bedroom window."

"He didn't follow her?"

"I don't believe he ever got the chance. Things started collapsing around him before he even knew what happened. It's a miracle he wasn't more seriously hurt than he was."

"He was sleeping with her, I presume?"

Jim hesitated. "I think so, yes. Though I've never met her, and he's never said a word about her."

"So they fucked," she said, "then they scattered to save themselves."

"Maybe. I guess only they know how it really went down," he replied.

"Sounds so...primal." She picked up a brush and applied gold speckles to one of the spiral galaxies. "Although I don't mean to trivialize what your dad went through."

"No, it shocked the world into him," said Jim. In a quieter voice he added, "And I think he'd agree with you."

II

LINDA RENWORTH TENDED VIGOROUSLY TO her small greenhouse garden, pruning the roses and azaleas and planting baby tomatoes and green onion seeds that she'd bought from the Earth Works market over in Yorktown. Though the Williamsburg market was closer, she knew Arthur's son Jim was working on a mural at that store. And while she'd never even met Jim, no doubt her curiosity would have driven her to seek him out and sneak a peek at him had she gone to that location to do her shopping. She hadn't wanted to tempt herself like that.

At some level, Linda had always felt like an incomplete

person, not quite up to the standards of the other people in her life—not even her own daughter. It was possible, she conceded, that much of her insecurity was based on her own assumptions and perhaps projected. Even so, hers was not the sort of life pattern that was easily broken. For years now she'd been in the grip of a nagging sense of worthlessness that dictated much of her internal life. *Why didn't Arthur introduce me to Jim?* she wondered. Had he been too embarrassed? Or had he simply wanted to keep his life compartmentalized? It pained her to realize that she might never know.

Linda realized that her residual hurt and anger seemed way out of proportion to Art's original act of betrayal, especially given the paltry two months she'd spent as Arthur's girlfriend. Although they'd been, at least for her, an intense two months. Once she'd learned he'd been alone in the house with Natalie Farrow that night, she'd chosen not to visit him in the hospital, though her conscience eventually pressed her into a compromise that involved the sending of flowers.

Strangely enough, Linda felt right at home in this kind of hurt. It seemed suffering had found her again after making a brief detour, and had continued right where it began on the night her ex-husband Stephen had left her for Angela Touley. Only the faces and names had changed. The pain felt exactly the same.

She'd always known she was more neurotic—more complicated—than the simple, polite persona she presented to the public. She'd made strenuous efforts to conceal what she considered this less-predictable side of herself, trying to hide her volatility even from Stephen well into their marriage. In retrospect, she realized that compulsion signaled a red flag about her level of trust and comfort in the relationship. She'd always felt the need to be courteous, to "roll with the punches," as her mother used to say, whenever they had to move yet again because her father's naval job commanded a change. Ironic then, that her apparent complacency had been among the things Stephen had cited as being responsible for the diminished passion between them. "The world seems to go in one ear and out the other with you," he told her, one night when too much gin had loosened his tongue. "And it's like you don't want to capture, or even to hear, it. Or," he held up his hand, his fingers bent as if grasping an apple, "don't care to taste it."

Had Arthur felt the same way?

Fighting back sudden tears, Linda set down her watering can. She deposited her spade and trimmers in the side yard storage shed, then sat in the gazebo swing for a while, absorbing the autumn sun. She closed her eyes and listened only to the wordless sounds of the wind. When the phone rang inside the house a few minutes later, Linda dutifully hurried to answer it.

"Hello, Mom," Sonia said.

Linda felt a weird blend of anxiety and enthusiasm. "Hi, sweetheart. How funny. I was actually thinking of calling you earlier this morning. It's rather late there now, isn't it?"

"Not really. It's only ten-thirty. Ferdinand and I were just about to go to dinner."

"How are you?"

"I'm doing great. We were checking our calendar this morning, and I called to let you know that we'll be flying home for Thanksgiving. I managed to reschedule a few things."

Linda hesitated. "Oh, that's...wonderful."

"You don't sound very excited."

"I'm fine, darling. Really, I'm mentally planning the dinner already." Not long ago she'd imagined them spending Thanksgiving at Arthur's place. That memory seemed so unreal to her now, like a fragile dream that her mind tried to seize in the instant before she awakened, but that always dissolved a bit faster than she could collect it.

"Have you been going to church?" Sonia asked her, sounding stern. "Ferdinand has this wonderful church in his village. It's so quaint, an adorable little Spanish chapel."

"That's great sweetheart," she said. "Yes I have been going lately. And I'm certainly looking forward to seeing you. And meeting Ferdinand."

"You'll love him." Sonia chuckled, "I've been teaching him some English. It's fun. He wants to learn."

"That's kind of you," Linda said. "I don't want you to have to play translator, though."

Sonia fell silent.

I'm being too bossy, Linda realized. She tried to ignore how much Sonia's romantic, early relationship enthusiasm echoed her own behavior, like an intoxication that drove her to do almost anything for the man that she adored.

"I don't mind, mother," Sonia said. "I have to go now, though. We have reservations. Just wanted to let you know about Thanksgiving."

"Okay. I love you. Talk to you soon."

"Bye, Mom." Linda heard a man speaking rapid Spanish in the background. Sonia laughed, then the line went suddenly quiet. With her daughter's energetic voice still resonating in her head, Linda made herself a cup of coffee and ambled over to her computer to see if she'd received any new responses to her profile on Millionaire-Matches.com.

Jim arrived home that evening to what he initially thought an empty apartment, until David emerged from the bedroom wearing a collared red shirt tucked into sleek-fitting tan denim jeans. They greeted one another with a kiss.

"Looking spiffy," said Jim. "Camille said you two were going out to dinner. I thought maybe you'd already left. Where are you going?"

"Whaler Inn. She's craving seafood. Aren't you coming with us?"

"She extended the invitation, but I'm exhausted. I just want to chill. I'm always in awe of her energy."

"She's a firecracker, for sure," David said with a laugh. "Truthfully, I don't feel much like going out myself. I think school's backed me into a rut I don't know how to get out of. Camille tells me I need to be more social though, and I feel bad I've only seen her a couple of times since she's been here."

"Don't worry," Jim said. "She gets plenty of updates from me. How're the stomach cramps?"

"Still off and on. Ibuprofen seems to help."

"Hope so." Jim glanced around. "Where'd Dad go, by the way?"

"I think he's out taking a walk," David said.

"His car's gone."

"Then maybe he went for a drive." David leaned forward and added, "Hey, I have to tell you something. Today Art and I had the most personal conversation we've had since we've known one another."

"Really?"

"Mm-hmm. It was strange. Earlier today I heard what sounded like crying. When I peeked into the living room, I saw your dad sitting there on the couch just …well, crying."

"Was he watching a movie or something?"

"He had your laptop open."

Jim frowned. "Really? That's weird."

"It was very weird."

"And?"

"I asked him what was wrong. He said 'nothing.' Then he asked me about how I finally came out. As gay."

"And what did you tell him?"

"I felt a bit awkward, but I told him the truth. I told him my mom had more of a problem with it than my dad, all of that. For a moment there it almost felt like I was describing someone else's life, or maybe like I was sharing a past life experience. I really think he was curious. But I do think it's sweet that he's trying to get to know me a little bit better."

"That's good," Jim said, wondering, only half jokingly, who this strange new father person was.

"I got the impression," David continued, "that he wasn't asking for my sake. It was more for himself."

"What do you mean?"

"Well, he's not gay, obviously. But he didn't ask anything about my lifestyle, or any details about how I started dating men, or what it was like for me to realize that I was attracted to men. He seemed much more interested in the process of someone revealing their true colors. Anyway," David said, heading for the front door, "I wanted to tell you. Give you something to knock around in your head while you're all alone tonight." He buttoned his jacket. "I have to go."

"Okay. Have a good night. Tell Cam I'll see her bright and early tomorrow."

They kissed again and David left. Jim stood for a long moment staring at the closed door, trying his best to process the conversation. From the living room window he watched David descend the stairs. He could hear the soft reverberation of every step, and suddenly he had an ominous feeling that David, and the prior perfect episode that had been their life together before his partner's sudden, mysterious illness, was a beautiful dream from which he was soon to be plucked.

He poured himself a short scotch with trembling hands. It had, he realized, been more than fifteen years since his own coming out, since he'd exposed his own true colors. He could see the moment as plain as ever, could still see Scott Gregory, a shaggy-haired eighth grader, standing by the staircase on the second floor of Jefferson Middle School, chuckling and whispering with two friends.

"Let me copy off you," Scott had begged him that morning, during Mrs. Janus's math test. Jim ignored him, cupping his palm over the answers to shield them from Scott's view. For the rest of the exam he could feel Scott's angry glare. When the bell rang Jim scurried out and headed for the stairs. He wanted to get to history class before Scott caught up with him.

It wasn't to be. He switched books at his locker and spotted Scott strolling by just before he closed the door. Head down, Jim walked toward Scott and his friends. They quieted as he approached. Scott murmured something, but Jim had already scooted past him and started down the steps when he heard his name ring out like a shot behind him. "Jimmy! Hey Jimmy!"

Can't avoid it. He turned, peering up at Scott's fine-cut face, smiling between the twin satellite smiles of his friends. Scott cupped his own genitalia. "Suck it, Jimmy. Go on. Suck these balls and I won't wail on you for fucking me over in math."

Jim froze. The tardy bell would ring at any moment. Almost nobody else was around. Of course Scott meant it as an insult, but Jim thought he detected something genuinely longing beneath Scott's mocking tone. It frightened him as well as excited him. The friction generated by these two conflicting feelings rubbing up against one another sparked Jim's own arousal. He wasn't sure how to react. Was he smiling? He'd no inkling what expression might have come over him during those past few seconds. Whatever it was Scott reacted by smirking, then gesturing toward the bathroom.

"Let's do it," Scott said.

Jim noticed the other guys narrowing their eyes in bewilderment. Meanwhile, his heart was doing a tap dance against his gut. *It's going to happen.* He tried his best to conceal his excitement. He needed to make it seem like the insult it was intended to be.

The tardy bell rang as they entered the bathroom. The foursome bustled toward the farthest stall. Jim noticed that on one of the walls someone had etched a crude depiction of female breasts. Scott ordered him down on his knees and Jim obeyed. Scott then unzipped his pants and his penis emerged, eye-level with Jim, who had never seen another kid's cock in real life. Strangely enough, it did not feel strange or wrong. Quite the opposite. Scott's member was pinker, much smoother than his own. Almost delicate. Nested in coils of sparse blond hair.

Jim closed his eyes, leaned forward. A sudden blow to his temple sent him crashing to the floor. He thought maybe a bird had flown in through the window and smashed into his head. But he looked up and noticed Scott's right hand, still raised in the air. Scott's left hand had hastened to cover his groin. Jim lay quietly on the moist, cracked and fucking disgusting middle school bathroom floor. A sonorous voice, Scott's disbelieving voice, now filled with a mix of incredulous humor and something resembling terror, rained down on him: "You're fucking *serious*, Jimmy?"

Knobby-boned fists began pelting his tender flesh. Everything turned black then, broken only by occasional flickers of sunlight that penetrated his swollen eyelids as it flooded in through the single restroom window. Jim imagined his entire body filling with blood, every organ ruptured and relinquishing its duties, giving up.

They left him lying there on the floor, motionless and barely conscious. After a while he shivered, sniffed through a clotted noseful of blood. Everything throbbed. He didn't want to move, thought he might just eventually die lying there and that that would be alright, because anything on the other side of this life must be better than this. What if he just didn't move? Or if he waited until nightfall to crawl away?

Finally, though, he struggled to his feet and approached the mirror. He stared at a green loogie sliding snaillike down one cheek. He didn't looked too bad, he decided. Puffy eyelids, messed up hair, one nostril bleeding, a faint blue bruise on his cheek that would surely be black by tomorrow morning. But his ribs had hurt to the touch, Jim recalled as he thought back now on the episode, and his crotch had burned like fire where one of the boys had brutally kicked him.

That memory still held the power to wound him. Jim rifled through the kitchen freezer, pulled out a Stouffer's frozen lasagna and popped it in the microwave for his dinner. He opened a soda and, standing by the counter, stared across the apartment and into nothingness.

Scott and his friends had found him again later that afternoon, behind the school after classes, where his father would always come to pick him up. They'd set upon him once more, their sporadic chants of "shit-pusher!" and "faggot!" echoing in Jim's ears with every blow. Then from nearby he heard a man call "Hey!" and the attack on him eased, though it did not abate.

Between splashes of movement, within the frenetic shutter snaps of light and dark, Jim noticed his father arrive and then enter the fray. Arthur lunged for the boys and, one at a time, wrenched Scott and the others off of Jim with a ferocity that Jim never knew he possessed. Although Scott angrily flailed back at Arthur and struck Arthur's chin with his fist, Arthur had pushed him aside without hesitation and gathered Jim up to his chest.

Jim's thoughts leaped forward once more, leaving the beating far behind as they traversed the subsequent moments, hours, days and weeks that followed. In truth, he remembered those intervening moments far less than the second seminal incident that had crystallized as a memory: the moment he'd succumbed to the impulse to tell his father the truth.

Actually saying the words *I am gay*—the long withheld follow-up to his original, *Scott thinks I'm gay*—had left Jim empty, though not in a bad way. Speaking them aloud, the words finally rinsed away the false, unnatural toxin that was the lie, the way a cleansing rain might wash one's windows clean.

The morning that he had confessed the truth to his father Arthur had approached him in the living room, carrying a glass of water. Jim sat in an armchair, half-perched on the cushion's edge. He kept his gaze focused on his shoes the entire time he spoke. Strange to remember now that he had noticed how one was untied. Jim had felt, rather than seen, his admission sinking into Arthur, curdling inside his father like a spreading flow of spoiled milk.

He would not lose his father's love, he'd realized. Deep down, that was never a worry. But he knew Arthur disliked surprises, detested change. Jim suddenly felt that, until that very moment, he'd been living his life as the fraudulent son, the shell of whom had now cracked wide open to reveal the true son inside. And to some degree that meant their entire relationship, which had been based on the unspoken lie, would need to begin anew.

When he'd finally looked at Arthur, Jim saw his father

rubbing his teary eyes. A slow exhale, filled perhaps with newly confirmed suspicions and an awareness of future burdens, escaped Arthur's lips. "I don't know what to do with that, Jim," Arthur said.

The microwave beeped just then and pulled Jim back to the present. He carefully retrieved his steaming dish and adjourned to the couch where his laptop rested, apparently having been last used by his father. He stared at it, remembering David's remarks. He tried to imagine the impossible—his father sitting right there, looking at something on the computer screen while sobbing gently and quietly. It felt as though he were trying to conjure an alien parallel universe.

I don't know what to do with that, he marveled. In that moment he genuinely appreciated, perhaps truly for the first time, the enormity of how it felt to be at a loss for what to think, or how to respond to someone, when something had happened that the mind couldn't quite comprehend.

Jim opened the laptop and stared at the screen's wallpaper, a minimalist painting by Rabo Karabekian. He clicked on the Internet browser and checked the day's history cache, where he noticed a listing for a website called NDERC.org.

He opened the link and, to his surprise, found himself looking at a website for the Near Death Experience Research Center.

Sunset cooled into dusk, and windows and porch lights winked confidently from the houses all across the neighborhood. All except a single porous abode on West Landing Road, now sitting in a silent, oppressive gloom. Arthur had hoped he might catch a lingering crewman or two still at the house, but the moment he arrived he could tell that nobody moved within the charred and stunted remnants of his home.

He parked on the far side of the street, away from the overflowing dumpsters and piles of rubble. He ventured up the driveway past two work trucks the owners had left parked in the front, and continued across the grassy lawn toward the shadow-dappled golf course. He wandered along the second hole to the place where it doglegged into the darkness and met the pond.

There was movement in the fairway—two, no, three, four grazing deer, alerted with pricked ears to Arthur's presence, distinct light reflected in dull amber eyes. He stopped and looked at them with a smile they would never comprehend, and he wondered what about them he might not comprehend, or would never be able to know. It was, he realized, a meeting of two highly disparate views and experiences of the universe. But, as Natalie might say, fundamentally all such wildly varying forms came from the same seed and were molded from a singular energy that now peered simultaneously through his eyes and those of the deer.

He strode closer to the pond, where it seemed he had not stood for eons. Weeds whispered nearby—probably a turtle keeping its cautious distance. He paused at the edge of the grassy drop-off by the water with his hands in his pockets, fighting a fleeting impulse to teeter forward, closer and closer, until he fell face-first into the pond. The idea, ludicrous enough to bring a chuckle to his lips, seemed oddly enticing.

He'd once read a literary essay about alcoholic authors' thematic fascination with water. No one could really pinpoint the reason for it, but right now it appeared to make sense. Like all addicts, alcoholics—particularly writers, Arthur imagined—sought to lose themselves, to melt away into that maternal element.

He removed his shoes and socks and sank his toes deep into the marshy wetness of the grass. For the first time in his life he felt like a fixture of Earth, treelike and tangibly connected to the greater reality, no longer a loose particle bouncing around in a striving, desperate and uncomprehending way.

The moon rose through the trees and cast a glowing sheen on the surface of the pond. Arthur watched the water, noticing every flit of movement, every inky ripple, as if some large unseen quill were periodically dipped into it. Each tremor triggered within him a sense of anticipation that Moby might suddenly appear, but the disturbance was never big enough nor did anything break the surface of the watery, hidden cosmos by his feet.

They lay in bed, Natalie beneath Jeff. He slowed the cranking gear of his flesh against hers, winding down with great, gratified heaves as he rolled away from her and kissed her shoulder. The sheets became a drying bog of sex. A full moon shone through the bedroom window, like the unblinking eye of some giant voyeur.

Natalie had heard it said that people with higher IQs had a more difficult time reaching climax. Though humbly resistant to the implication that she possessed a superior intelligence, she understood well the distraction of too much thinking. At its peak sex was half physical, half mental. The former fell swiftly in line. The latter demanded focus; sometimes an intense, wrangling focus.

Since the night of the fire at Arthur's house she'd not truly had sex with Jeff. He'd had sex on her when she'd made herself available to him, all the while emitting the necessary noises and going through the expected motions. Yet she felt strange during these experiences, as if she were watching a friend or a sibling have sex. Oddly enough, however, the sex still sated her, because some essential part of her needed touch, craved it actually, no matter the context. Yet that biological part of her now had a strained relationship with what she liked to think of as "higher" Natalie, the one that required intellectual and spiritual closeness for maximal intimacy, and to round out the best that the bodily pleasures could offer. "How was that for you?" Jeff whispered into her ear. The inquiry had become more frequent in the last few weeks.

"It was good, Jeff," she reassured him.

"You sure?"

Natalie shifted beneath the sheets.

Why are you scared? a voice prodded her. *Just end it.*

"Can I ask you something?" Jeff said.

"Sure. What?"

"Did you really feel a presence there, in Arthur's house? Like a ghostly presence?"

"Yes, I did," she said.

"What did you feel?" Jeff pressed. "Specifically."

Specifically. A prod and twist into deeper tissue.

"Not specifically. I'm not that attuned. I just got snatches of energy and whispers of, well, personality I guess. Intention."

"And you think whatever it was, was benign? I mean, not malicious or anything?"

Natalie felt detached from the present, from where she was, who she was with. *I don't care anymore.* About what, exactly, she wasn't sure.

"It was 'good,' yes," Natalie said. "At least I got a good feel from it, whatever it was. But..."

"But?"

"I'm still not really sure if this is related, but I had a

dream while you and I were there, at Arthur's house, when he was on his trip. A pretty lucid dream."

"Alright."

"I'd call it a vision although I'm...I don't know...maybe I'm just embarrassed to use that word aloud. And I don't know if it was a vision—"

"Babe," said Jeff. "What was it?"

Natalie stared at him. Babe. He wanted to press on with her, she did not. But any word, any action that might release her from him stalled within her. She felt guilty, confused.

"Quite frankly," she said. "I dreamt that the house was on fire."

"No shit."

"I just saw flames everywhere, eating everything. I wasn't very afraid at first and I didn't feel the heat because, well, I was the dreamer, the spectator. I saw Arthur there too and he was burning. I mean, burning. I don't know why I was being kept safe. I didn't feel the heat. I didn't feel the flames. I think it was the presence I felt, communicating with me. Showing me. It was like it wanted me to let Arthur burn. 'Leave it be,' it seemed to say, and I felt as if it was holding me back from going to him. Arthur was on fire, but he wasn't thrashing or screaming and he didn't seem to be in pain, even though he was being swallowed up into...well, I guess into practically nothingness."

Jeff appeared confused.

"I don't understand it any better than you do," said Natalie. "I really don't. I just got a sense that, throughout whatever it was, it was telling me Arthur would be okay. But I've never had such a literal dream before. I figured it was something symbolic. I don't know..."

"So you think Arthur was meant to...burn?"

"I don't know," Natalie said.

"Well, what's done is done," Jeff said. "Arthur's okay

now."

"Yeah."

They'd touched on her indiscretion with Arthur only briefly, Jeff treating it, or trying to treat it, like she'd accidentally spilled something on his shirt. *Oh, that'll come right out.* His reaction, clearly based in insecurity, irritated her. Yet beneath the weight of her inward confusion, and despite drifting through a fog of ambiguous, unsettled feelings, Natalie had resumed her part in this relationship, if there actually was one and not some tattered remnant pretending to be whole.

"I'm going to make you some midnight pancakes," Jeff said, climbing out of bed. "That'll set your mind at ease. Blueberries, right?"

"You don't have to do that. I'm not hungry."

"I am. I'll eat whatever you don't." Jeff pulled on his pants and shirt over his husky frame. "Think of it as an early breakfast."

Natalie appreciated the gesture, even though the pancakes were surely an on-the-fly distraction.

"Where do you have the butter?" Jeff called as he rummaged in the kitchen. "I don't see it anywhere."

She got up and wrapped a bathrobe around herself. "Should be a new one in the bottom fridge drawer there."

"Ah, got it."

She went out to her porch and drew a cigarette and smoked, strengthening the crisp, smoky-orange smell of the autumn night. In the kitchen, Jeff clanged through dishes and cupboards.

Idly Natalie brought out her phone. A birthday alert sounded—*Neil Valentine.* Her throat closed. Neil's birthday tomorrow. Though it'd been years since she'd last seen him, it disturbed her to think she would've otherwise forgotten.

Neil, she thought. *You made me me.*

She'd first seen him at one of his seminars at the Mountain Wellness Center, a spiritual retreat in Arizona he'd founded after the unexpected popularity of his book, *The Divine Dialogues*. Natalie was just one of hundreds of eyes in the audience, though there were moments when they met gazes, when, as Natalie journaled later, their spirits shook hands before they'd even shared a word.

Somehow, Natalie knew she'd be received more substantially, more thoughtfully, than the rest of the crowd that had gathered post-lecture around Neil Valentine's signing table. She maintained no illusions that her fortunate good looks had not played a factor, but there was an ease with Neil, a deeper symmetry that fit and that she recognized instantly. Beyond mutual attraction, she sensed he was what she, a restless twenty-three-year-old journalism major, needed.

There was something a tad awe-inspiring about looking back on the first brush with a significant ex, recalling a time just before an entirely new person and new dimension and, in many cases, a new you would be added to your life, when you had no idea about the avalanche of impassioned memories—good and bad, sweet and sour—inexorably coming your way.

"It sounds like you're following my path," Neil said later, when they'd met for coffee. Neil, ex-consumer of liquor and caffeine, had stuck to decaf tea. "But following it the clean-cut, institutionalized way."

She wanted to be a writer, and had in fact attended the seminar not only for personal edification but to cover it for the small-circulation magazine *Ego*, where she'd been working. Neil Valentine's book had begun to circulate into greater and greater cultural spheres, first within the New Age community (though privately Neil despised that term, claiming, "It's all one age, the Human Age, the time in which we either find ourselves, or don't") then into the broader public, spending four consecutive weeks on the *New York Times Best Sellers* list. One time, if she remembered correctly, *Dialogues* had even sat one slot atop *Faith & Reason*, Arthur Moore's flagship work.

That Neil's book had come from such a dark place—for nearly a decade he'd lived on the streets, doing, as he said, "anything to scrape by"—most assuredly galvanized sales. Natalie had read and reviewed it for Ego, but, having only skimmed it the first time, any revelation was superficial. It had intrigued her, though; Neil was five years her senior but still young, and was even younger when "the Force" spoke to him (his euphemism for whatever divinity he palpably channeled into its pages), helping reconcile his inner and outer lives, to answer the deepest questions percolating within. After purchasing a copy of Dialogues from him directly, after truly sinking herself into its depth, Natalie knew this was what she had been seeking. The curtains had been parted wider, allowing in greater light.

While Natalie often cited *A Course in Miracles* as major inspiration for *The Gospel of Universal Self*, it was The Divine Dialogues that had proven a far more poignant catalyst, if only because of how personal it'd become when studying at Neil's side. While Neil never specified the identity of whatever "Force" had spoken through his pen—whether God, Ra, Zeus, or Cthulu—the wisdom of the passages, as peaceful as they were forceful and certainly unique for a man in his late twenties, had led many like herself to believe something *other* had dictated much of the book's content.

"Think of all the stages of your life," Neil lectured once, "as representing three phases: death, tomb and resurrection. In death, we part ways with the past, step out of old modes, shed previous skin. This begins our tomb stage, which can last a long time and feel like purgatory, a neutral, indecisive, often melancholic stretch of time when you're trying to find your path. But in persisting, you ultimately come to resurrection—a snug new shell, a new self. We all go through these stages, in waves big and small, long and short."

Much applause had followed, raucous to an almost pandering degree. Many hands were raised.

"These lectures are necessary," Neil remarked later at dinner, "but I don't like to give them."

"Why?" Natalie asked.

"Did you see how many hands went up with questions about how to live their lives? Or what course of action should be taken about problem X, issue Y, conflict Z?"

Natalie nodded, remembering the suffocating desperation surrounding her in that audience.

"This despite how often I say that my word is *not* gospel," Neil said, "because everyone needs to follow their own truth, and realize that I'm here solely as a guide to self-realization."

"You're the man with the microphone, though."

Neil nodded resignedly. "I am, yes. And with every talk I get an up-close, real-world illustration of how cults are born. How religions are born."

They had traveled together, sometimes on group excursions with wealthier patrons of the Center, other times by themselves. Most of the journeys were an extension of their spiritual seeking, their life's work: rugged jaunts through the wilder areas of India and Cambodia and Southeast Asia, visiting vine-wrapped Buddhist temples and holy shrines, sometimes on the swaying backs of elephants.

"Do you ever take a *vacation* vacation?" Natalie asked once with minor spite, wondering if they might not just go to Tahiti or somewhere and simply relax, toast drinks on the beach, maybe snorkel.

Neil smiled with so much assurance—which usually proved calming but was maddening to Natalie when she was feeling irritable. He kissed her and replied, "It's always a vacation, all the time, everywhere. We just have to make it so."

Of course, that was the whole idea of the Wellness Center, to render the "vacation" within oneself, to carry inside you an unspoiled pocket of paradise. "We see the world through our biases; we bend the world accordingly with inward tools," Neil said. "The only reality we know or that exists is that of the internal. You are responsible for giving the universe its experience of being human, just as a dung beetle has the honor of giving that same universe the experience of," here he smiled, "beetling dung."

For a while Natalie struggled with the idea of contentment or "inner peace," that goal of every serious student of meditation. *Why would I necessarily want this?* she thought. While she would happily see the world's problems disappear, they also sparked in her many passions that fueled her writing, and she loved to write, to lose herself in the intellectual sandbox of words and ideas. That she would actively try to drain herself of those passions seemed a disconcerting thought.

"Writing is your meditation, then," Neil said. "Writing is your path."

Meditation, she learned, was not so much about abolishing passions but focusing them, using them to facilitate a wider, greater consciousness.

Sitting on the porch, the acrid scent of her cigarette hanging on the air, Natalie crossed her legs, acutely aware of a desire unfulfilled now commanding attention. The tickling echo of Jeff inside her, his drying moisture staining the innermost areas of her thighs.

Throwing a quick glance at the window looking in, she

lowered herself in her chair and began to finger her tender labia, circling about, drawing into her pelvis increasing swells of energy between each measured breath. *Orgasmic meditation* was the term. Better with two people, of course. Neil had introduced it to her, though, since the first few times had been spent intentionally not climaxing, the *orgasmic* part was a bit of a misnomer...until the time she finally *had* climaxed, unleashing total gratification: the height of emotion and sensation, the very reason the physical universe had been made, had been patient enough to wait billions of years to grow nerve endings.

Halfway to climax, she stopped, suspending her every molecule in electric anticipation. She breathed, steady, imagining with each inhale the sexual energy being dispersed throughout the rest of her system. It was the life essence, usually wasted. For all anyone knew the big bang had been a giant orgasm, with humans being the natural inheritors of that first energy.

The desire began to simmer. She fished out and finished another cigarette, then went back inside. While Jeff continued about in the kitchen (Natalie had long suspected cooking was a form of meditation for him, the way writing was for her), she retrieved her laptop.

She Googled The Mountain Wellness Center but could find no evidence of it. The website was down, and there was little news she could find of what may have happened. Disappointed, she sent an email to the address she remembered from long ago.

Neil,

Thinking about you. Happy birthday. Would like to hear from you if you're out there.

Nat

She listed her current address and phone number, then sent it.

Realizing that the Center may have closed brought a sudden profound sadness. Part of her felt orphaned.

Natalie stared at the desktop image on her laptop: *The Gospel of Universal Self*'s front cover image, the humanoid shape stippled with distant celestial bodies. She remembered Neil's semi-joke of himself as the reverse Buddha, how he'd found God on the streets and become wealthy thereafter. Sometimes he'd mentioned running away, skirting his celebrity image, but never had she thought such idle musings valid. "People need help," he'd said. "People need my help."

What happened?

Time distorted. The next thing Natalie knew, Jeff was holding a plate of blueberry pancakes before her.

"Would you like these here?" he asked, "or in bed?"

Natalie stared at the short stack. "Jeff," she said, tingling as if she were doing something wrong. "We should probably talk."

Sitting at her computer, Linda opened her Millionaire-Matches inbox. Beyond his passable handsomeness, she wasn't sure why this Mark Gavin intrigued her. By his pleasant but succinct messages, he seemed the more aloof type—similar, actually, to how Arthur had been during the first stretch of contact.

For about two weeks now she and Mark had kept in casual regular contact. Slowly, Linda was acclimating herself to the idea of going out again, of doing the dating thing, interviewing, analyzing every little statement, every brush of physical contact. She felt like the whole exhausting process, game, really, required a welling-up of Herculean energy. But she knew her heart would not let her alone, as it seldom did with anyone. The urge for intimacy burned through all bitterness and exhaustion.

Mark's religious profile specified "spiritual." She couldn't recall Arthur's response in that category, although she assumed he must have been N/A. Linda felt relieved that Mark was different.

With some hesitation, she searched for "Arthur Moore." His profile came up and showed no activity for the past several months, which both relieved and saddened her. *Why are you thinking of Arthur?* She wasn't sure, other than that whenever she started to look around again she tended to dwell on her most recent relationship as a point of immediate reference.

But there was something different about Arthur, wasn't there? Something that burrowed deeper. That cut deeper. Certainly she'd responded to his stature as an author and commentator, a person with "important" opinions, regardless of their content. That a veteran public figure had chosen her had excited and validated her. Unabashedly superficial, but true.

But that wasn't all that'd been different about Arthur. As opposed to so many men she'd encountered, he made no secret of his intellect and more cultured passions. Arthur was a thinker. He actually *thought*: all masculinity in his mind. He was middle-aged and still seeking new discoveries and challenges, never shrinking back into sports and poker and beer and mumbling simian harrumphs at the dinner table. Sure, he could brood, become withdrawn and occasionally forlorn, but to Linda those things revealed an attractive depth.

All that he had buoyed in her, though, had fallen. All validation invalidated. The Linda that had grown out of their relationship had been pruned.

Linda responded to an email from Mark. She then moved reluctantly to a multi-forwarded message from her daughter, which contained a sugary story—complete with pictures—about a Christian soldier returning home from Iraq.

Sonia had been relaying many chain emails to her, most of which added a religious message to the usual request or demand for further distribution. Linda realized that such letters had come to form the bulk of correspondence with her daughter. Twice Linda had tried to send Sonia a chatty personal email, but had received no reply. She was contemplating sending Sonia another message when the doorbell rang.

She opened the door and gasped.

Arthur Moore stood distant-eyed on her porch, one hand in his pocket. Burn marks lined one side of his neck. An island of scarred flesh accented his stubbled jawline.

"Hi Linda," he said quietly.

She knew two sudden urges, one of adoration, one of anger. She wanted to shut the door in Arthur's face, but knew she never could. Maybe it was simply the Christian in her, the "Christ hand," as Reverend Matthews called it, "that which our fear keeps balled up in a fist, but which we need only to unclench, and extend."

Arthur had wronged her, yes, and in the month since the night with Natalie, since the fire, his violent brush with death, much had accumulated in Linda, not the least of which were brainstormings—some less-savory fantasies—of what she might say in this very circumstance.

But now....*now*, staring at him, all commentary and emotion, contemptuous or noble, retreated from her like cockroaches running from the light. Past all the transparent conceits now stood the touchable soul she had once held, and who had once held her.

Arthur smiled. He had lost weight but he had been

relieved of more than pounds. Linda could tell some new quality animated him. It was invisible yet undeniable, as were many indefinable things.

"Come in," Linda said. *He's only been inside my home twice before,* she thought, surprised by the tiny odd revelation. Once to pick her up for the trip out west, once to have dinner. Most of their nights had been spent at Arthur's, a routine that had gone unquestioned.

"Like anything to drink?" she asked.

"I'll have some water, thanks."

She retrieved a glass of water from the kitchen, cursing herself for not acting more...how to act? Reserved? Angry?

Linda returned and handed him a glass of ice water.

"Thank you."

"How are you doing?" she asked tentatively. "How are you feeling? Please, sit down."

Arthur took a sip of water and sat on the couch. "Glad to be able to feel the sting of ice again, that's for sure."

Linda wasn't sure how to respond.

"I've been doing well. A little tired."

"That's excellent."

"I didn't come just to say hello," said Arthur. "I wanted to apologize to you, in person."

"Art—"

"I know I hurt you. After what you said—your husband, or ex-husband, had an affair and everything—I think it was particularly shitty what I did. I figured that's why I didn't see you the weeks I was in the hospital."

Linda shrugged, nodded. Her eyes tickled hot with impending tears.

"You sent me flowers," Arthur said. "I appreciated the gesture."

"Of course," Linda said, "of course."

"Linda," Arthur said. "I'm sorry."

She lowered her head. "You liked Natalie."

"I liked you too." Her glance was fast upon him. With a mild stutter, he added, "I don't know what I want, or what I was doing."

"You know what, and maybe this is kind of sad, but I'm a little used to it. Maybe I even expected it."

Arthur's eyes softened with gentle concern. Linda had a sudden urge to melt before him, to cry and to love him as though he were her own child.

"Expected that I would fall for Natalie?" Arthur said. "I'm not seeing her, by the way."

"Expected that you would eventually move on," Linda said. She was fully aware she was sliding into full "self-pity" mode, disparaging herself to elicit compliments, hugs, friendly pats. "I'm a stopover, not a destination."

"That's absurd," Arthur said. "I've been in flux for a while. It's been festering. Natalie was...an experiment, I guess. Again, I'm not sure what I want. I haven't been sure for a while. And," Arthur leaned forward on the couch cushion, "I do want to keep you in my life."

Tears bubbled hot and stinging in Linda's eyes. A laugh squirted from her throat, almost involuntarily.

"I understand, Art, I do," she said. "It doesn't mean I'm fully okay with it. I want to have you in my life too." She exhaled. "But that might take time. I've begun dating again. Or at least I'm trying to. My profile's back up on Million-aire-Matches, by the way."

"That's great. I hope you find somebody...more worth-while."

"I met a man named Mark Gavin," she said.

"I hope you've seen him first."

She smiled. "You know how I am. I like surprises. I didn't even really know you'd been on TV before our first date."

"Hah, right," Arthur said. "The good with the bad, huh?"

"The way I roll, Art."

"Hey, Jeff's hosting a gathering before Thanksgiving," said Arthur. "Would you like to come? You can of course bring your new guy, if things work out. If you'd like."

"You're inviting people to Jeff's party?"

"Just the intellectuals."

Linda smiled, faintly. "My daughter and her boyfriend are coming from Spain for Thanksgiving," Linda said. She looked at the coffee table as she spoke, unable to look too long into the softness of Arthur's eyes. "We'll be doing our own thing. But thank you."

"Of course."

As Arthur sipped from his glass his eyes closed meditatively. "I won't take up any more of your time. Thanks again for letting me pop in on you like this."

After some hesitation, Linda reached forward, took Arthur's hand lightly in hers and gave it a firm squeeze. "Can you tell me one thing? What was it like, Arthur?"

"Sorry?" he asked, then read the question in her eyes and knew what she was asking. "The fire?"

"Yes. And…everything else. That happened. What was it like? To die?"

"What was it like," Arthur repeated. A rickety smile broke on his lips. "I don't know, Linda. I've thankfully been spared that knowledge, for now."

Then he left.

Jim emerged from the bedroom at dawn and saw Arthur up and already dressed, munching on a bowl of cereal at the kitchen table and reading a water-damaged copy of John Steinbeck's *To a God Unknown*. Jim hadn't mentioned discovering the Near Death Research site in his computer's history cache, but hoped his father would bring up the topic when the spirit moved him. He worried Arthur might consider his snooping an invasion of privacy.

The questions, however, wouldn't keep forever.

"Hey there," said Arthur. "Good morning. Looks like you're getting pretty good at this."

"What? Getting up?"

"Yep. I remember the effort it took to haul you out of bed when you were in school."

"I think I've matured a little since then, Dad."

Silence settled in as Jim fixed his usual thermos of vanilla tea.

"You going to the house today?" Jim asked.

"Yeah. I told the crew I'd be there by eight. I just wanted to enjoy the morning."

"You want me to make coffee?"

"No, none for me this morning. I should probably get going." Arthur tossed a smile at Jim. "How's the mural coming, by the way? I'm tempted every day to drive by and check it out. But I'm respecting your wishes not to look till it's finished."

"Thanks, Dad. Yeah, it's goin' pretty well. A little over halfway done. Camille's great, she's been working harder than I have."

"I can't wait to see it."

"Thanks. Well, I'll see you later."

Arthur closed the book and put his cereal bowl in the sink. *The dishwasher, Dad! In the dishwasher!* Jim thought, but said nothing. He waved to Arthur as his father disappeared behind the closing door and the apartment once more buzzed in silence. Then he headed back to the bedroom to kiss David goodbye.

To his surprise he found David sitting on his side of the

bed, hunched over and very pale, right hand caressing his abdomen.

Needles pricked Jim's chest. "What's wrong?"

David looked up at him, eyes wide with a kind of helpless pain that froze Jim's veins.

"I think maybe," David said, "you should take me to the hospital."

JIM COLLECTED THE NECESSARY FORMS and drifted into the emergency waiting room and sank into one of the chairs. He sighed, feeling like a cyclone winding down. The thumps and pounds of his body diminished. David had been taken in for surgery; the doctor—as David himself had sullenly mused on the drive over—had said it was appendicitis.

Jim remembered Camille. *Shit.* He hadn't called her about not showing up this morning. He checked his phone, expecting a series of missed calls and voicemails but finding only a single lonely text message from her, time stamped at 7:32 a.m.: *Where are you?*

He called her phone but got voice mail. "I'm so sorry, Cam, but David's sick. I'm here at the hospital, waiting for a doctor to tell me something. Look, I'll be there as soon as I can, alright? Cover for me, okay? I'll buy you a rum punch at dinner tonight."

He hung up and glanced furtively at the other faces. Some were middle-aged, some older. One guy, about his age, sat slouched and staring at the ceiling. All was so still in the room save for the quivering fingers, the heads rolling back, the eyelids closing and opening with hesitant slowness as if the people wished to fall asleep and forget for a while. Often Jim felt closer to strangers than he did to casual acquaintances. Weird notion, sure. But with strangers the relationship was always understood, existing at the broadest level, in the silent acknowledgment of two members of the same species sharing a harsh world.

JIM ENTERED THE HOSPITAL ROOM, his partner's eyes fastened expectantly on the doorway. Color had yet to fully return to his skin but David's relief was instantly clear. He held out his hand toward Jim.

"I knew I shouldn't have had the shellfish the other night," David quipped, as Jim took his hand.

At the foot of the cot stood the doctor, a short Indian man with bold glasses and a sparse goatee unconnected at the sides of his mouth. He did not look terribly older than Jim or David.

"It's a good thing you brought him in when you did," said the doctor, whose name, Jim learned after a quick firm handshake, was Dr. Bera. Addressing David, Bera said, "Do you want to fill him in, or should I?"

"Do we have to?" David said with small smirk.

"Tell me what?" Jim said.

"The appendicitis was caused by a condition called fecaloma," said Dr. Bera.

The term alerted Jim. *Sounds like melanoma.* From his bed, David held up a hand. His lips formed a playful frown, an expression Jim knew as unspoken, slightly amused self-deprecation.

"Basically ... I had petrified balls of shit stuck in there," David said. "Blocking up the appendix."

Jim winced. "Oh man. How'd that happen?"

"Usually occurs because of damage to the intestinal lining," said Dr. Bera. "He mentioned to us that he'd been ill recently. That could well have done it. It's a bit of a freak thing."

"I don't doubt." Jim leaned over and kissed David's forehead. "Damn."

Jim's cell phone rang. He brought it out. The screen said Mr. Hathaway, accompanied by a picture of Earth Works' facade. A small lump formed in his throat.

"One sec," he said, and stepped out into the hall. "I should get this real quick."

Maybe Camille had asked Hathaway to call, or maybe the man had been annoyed enough by Jim's absence that he'd taken it upon himself to call and lecture him, per Hathaway's style when something didn't go right.

Jim picked it up. "Hello?"

"Jim."

Hathaway's voice sounded deeply shaken, not at all condemning.

"Yes, Mr. Hathaway? I'm sorry I didn't show up this morning. I had to rush David to the hospital."

"Oh," he said. "Is everything okay?"

"Now it is. He had appendicitis. But he was in surgery and he's fine now. So, I'm sorry, it was just a crazy morning and I didn't have the presence of mind to call you or Camille."

"Jim," Hathaway sighed. "Something happened this morning."

"What?" He thought maybe some vandals had taken to the mural overnight, one of his biggest worries. "What's wrong?"

"The police are here," Hathaway said. "Camille was... shot here in the parking lot. By the mural. She's...well, she's dead, Jim. Gone."

Ozone coursed through him. His mind whitewashed. "What?"

"The police are pretty sure it was one of those goddamn snipers still running around. The God's Judges assholes."

"Christ...oh God..."

"It was pretty early so not many people saw anything.

But they figure it was from a long distance. It was the same caliber bullet, no gunpowder residue around, and she was… she was just lying there sprawled out, face down like she wasn't expecting anything like that. Had a paintbrush in her hand for God's sake."

Jim remembered Camille's text message: *Where are you?* With this news it had garnered a horrible sense of desperation, as if she'd been asking why he wasn't there to help her.

To save her.

"What time was she…?"

"They placed the time of death around eight this morning," Hathaway said. "I suppose we were lucky that I'd closed the shop today, though that's why no one noticed for so long. I found her when I came by to check on a shipment."

Jim recalled the text-message time stamp – 7:32.

Half hour later and…

Was I the last person she talked to??

Camille. Camille oh Christ I'm so sorry. Jim thought about her aunt here and her family down south and he thought about David, *oh God David,* who'd known her for so much longer in New York, and he thought about her future dreams for graduate school and the rest of it all that would now join the past as seamlessly and unceremoniously as a breath in the wind.

When Jim was younger, his Uncle John's death had frightened and confused him. Having not seen John in a few years, however, there'd been a merciful buffer between Jim and the sting of the news, for which he had steeled himself after watching the Twin Towers crumble and plume. John had joined thousands of others in a wide-brushed stroke of fate, a collective tragedy, and, as surreal as the whole period had been, Jim had also taken strange comfort in his uncle's death being one of many. In a way, the whole country had mourned John. Though he was loath to admit it, there was some nobility in that: the nation felt as an extended family, sharing in his grief.

With Camille, he felt the tremors. Knew the hot invasive stink of death. Its skeletal fingers had flipped a coin and Camille had lost. With all that had happened recently, Jim felt achingly vulnerable, as if the Fates encircled his flesh, teasing him, savoring him.

Reluctantly, he agreed to come by Earth Works. He had no idea what to tell David, what to tell his father, his mother, anyone. None of that mattered in these hazy, smoldering moments, during which his mind could do nothing but meditate on the freak absurdity of it all—how he owed his life to hard balls of shit.

III

LINDA PARKED, TOOK A BREATH. THEN SHE climbed from the car and hurried toward the crowd bustling into Grace Presbyterian, joining its current of murmurs.

It was indisputable, she mused, that something beyond DNA or genetics or biology connected people. All human minds, all souls, were but knots on one twine, one big, complex cat's cradle. Constantly, humanity was in dialogue with itself—it just didn't hear most of it.

Today, though, it spoke one thing: fear. The air itself had a scaly, unsettled quality.

It happened at Earth Works, she thought, her mind unable to stray far from that reality. Arthur's son's friend. She remembered Arthur telling her about Jim getting the mural job, the cute bubbly pride he'd tried to suppress but which had been clearly evident.

Outside, she felt exposed. Yet the sanctuary of Grace, its communal atmosphere, proved a mental balm. Within its walls, among the familiar faces, all these eyes and minds attuned to the same wisdom, she was no longer a single vulnerable body but a cell fortified in some greater whole.

After the Sunday service, during which Reverend Matthews's sermon had addressed Christ's ominous statement, "I bring not peace, but a sword," Marilyn and Victor approached her in the courtyard.

"Linda, I hope I'm not intruding too much by asking," Marilyn said. "But are you and Arthur still together? How's he doing? I know you told me all that happened. But what happened with you two? If you don't mind my asking…"

"No, Mary, I don't mind," Linda said. "We're not together anymore."

"I'm sorry to hear that."

Marilyn scrutinized her like a concerned teacher.

"Would you like to have Thanksgiving dinner with us?" Marilyn asked. "Victor's cousin and his wife ended up not being able to make it this year so I think we can squeeze you in."

"Thank you," Linda said, genuinely flattered by the invite, even though it felt like blatant charity. "My daughter Sonia and her boyfriend are coming into town, though. We're just going to have a private dinner."

Marilyn's eyes cooled. *What obligation do I have to you?* Linda thought.

"I'm happy to hear that," Marilyn said. "What's her boyfriend's name?"

"Ferdinand." *Let's go,* she thought. *Let's get out of here.* "Thank you again for the invitation."

"Of course. You're very welcome."

Clouds masked the sun. Linda shivered. She said her goodbyes to Marilyn and Victor and walked hurriedly to her car and got in. Sighing, she started the ignition. The return drive took her through wooded streets and avenues where, she imagined, the flanking trees might contract into a tightening tunnel, into some dark dead-end in which she might be lost.

⌘

"Are you ready to go?" Arthur said, standing in the doorway to Jim and David's bedroom.

Jim scavenged quickly for something to do with his hands. He closed another button on his dark suit. "Yeah, think so," he said. "Soon as David comes out, we're off."

"What do you think…" Arthur hesitated. "What do you think you're going to do with the mural?"

"I'm gonna finish it, soon as I can," Jim said.

"Well that's good. That's good." The latter part sounded forced. "I wouldn't tell Mom though."

"Too late. She's requesting David and I go out there a little early for Thanksgiving. She's a little nutso at the moment."

"I don't doubt it," Arthur said. "So you'd be gone… what?"

"From the Tuesday to the Sunday, it looks like."

"And David can afford it? Time-wise?"

"He's making himself afford it."

Jim hung by the door, ready to go. Arthur turned momentarily back to the book in his hands, a beginner's life-drawing guide he'd scrounged from Jim's collection. David was still in the bathroom.

"So how's the *Geraths Guide* reading?" Jim asked.

"The what?" Arthur said.

"That's what you're reading. It's part of a series of drawing books called the *Geraths Guide*. What are you doing reading a drawing book anyway?"

"I thought it looked interesting," Arthur said. "I'm always amazed by what you guys do. I may even give it a shot. I've been tinkering with drawing a bit for the rebuilding of the house, to show what I want done."

"I could've helped with that."

"I don't want to bother you, Jim."

"Well, if you want any pointers I'd be happy to throw them your way. You know that."

"Just pointers?"

"In my experience a serious artist can't help the casual artist all that much. Both eventually become frustrated by the differing levels of dedication."

"I see."

"No offense."

Arthur waved off his words.

David emerged from the bathroom, dressed in a black suit and tie and wearing glasses in lieu of his contacts. He moved with reluctance toward the door, head lowered. He looked desperate to cajole himself out of a dream.

Jim put an arm around him and kissed him and the two went to the door.

Arthur stood up. "So you guys will be back later tonight?"

"Yeah. Sometime. Probably late."

"Drive safe," he said. He met both Jim and David's eyes, then said, "I'm so sorry, again."

David nodded. "Thanks, Art."

Then his father said something that startled Jim.

"But don't worry. Okay?"

He sat back down.

Jim blinked. If not for having to leave, and if not for the self-consciousness that would inevitably stay his tongue, he might well have turned and said; "*What the hell do you wanna tell me, Dad?*"

ON THE WAY TO CAMILLE'S HOMETOWN of Tolesko, North Carolina, they passed often through miles of fields and woods, occasional stretches of forest so overgrown, so authentic and primal, that Jim experienced momentary bursts of merciful forgetfulness, where he felt not himself but some formless sightseer. The highway didn't exist, nor did the car, nor David, nor he—not as a person, anyway. Rather he was like a sentient wind, touring the majesty of pristine lands.

Then, he would come back to the present, see David, understood they had not spoken for what seemed like a long time. Resentment brewed in Jim, though he wasn't exactly sure why and he felt bad about it.

"I'm here still," Jim said, reaching over and taking David's hand.

"I know," David replied. Jim noticed that David did not squeeze his hand in return. "I'm thankful."

Jim pulled his hand away. "I'm glad you are."

David's expression curdled. "Why wouldn't I be?"

"Never mind."

Jim tried to wave away petty thoughts. Here Camille been murdered in cold blood and he, James Moore, wondered why he wasn't the one being coddled? David had hugged him, sure, as they cried, and said in a tone as close to humorous as the days would allow, "Thank God for my appendix, huh?" Still, for whatever reason, Jim had expected more.

The funeral service was held at the family Lutheran chapel, an old church in a yard of robust maple and oak trees. Neither Jim nor David were well-acquainted with any of Camille's family members, though more of them knew David. The attendance impressed Jim, though.

Would this many people have come to my funeral? he wondered.

A young boy stood at the entrance passing out a booklet containing photos and notes about Camille's life with a hymn printed on the back. By the church podium stood two blown-up, flower-laced pictures of Camille Rhodes's paintings, one from her childhood, giddy and color streaked, another from sometime recent. Seeing them, Jim's stomach turned.

The pastor, a tall man with thinning hair and a small mustache, approached the podium. Jim rested his hand on David's, gave it a plump squeeze then quickly moved it off.

"We might ask ourselves," the pastor said, "how such atrocities could possibly happen so close to us, to those we love? We see strikes of lightning on the evening news, not in our backyard. But we cannot succumb to the same descent as those that took Camille. We cannot allow such people to weaken the strength of our communion with God…"

Over the altar hung a cross, bathed in ethereal light-shadow.

"The Rhodes family has requested we join them in a hymn," said the pastor. "If all of you will kindly turn to the back of your pamphlets…"

A collective rustle stirred through the crowd. The singing began, and Jim joined in with a soft voice. With a furtive eye he watched other people around him and thought perhaps he could tell who was going through the motions and who might be feeling genuine comfort from the hymn. He thought about his father, of all people, and wondered how he might react to this.

You know exactly how he'd be.

He then thought about Uncle John's memorial, held a few weeks after his death. A good many strangers had attended. Dad had been furious at his mother, or Gran-Gran, for insisting on a Catholic ceremony for John. Jim himself was no closer today to accepting any of this formal ritualistic hoo-ha than he'd been years ago.

He'd never really understood the commotion between his dad and Gran-Gran, as nothing about their argument broke through their surface masks for the occasion. More surprisingly, no one had really asked what John would have wanted. Then again, given John's minor aloofness in the years leading up to his death, maybe everyone was afraid to acknowledge that they honestly didn't know.

While Jim never considered himself close to his uncle, he imagined that, as he'd grown, he'd come more and more to fill his uncle's ideological shoes, though he hesitated in calling agnosticism "ideological." Why not pluck yourself from the rink? Jim always thought. Why not enjoy life as much as possible without planting flags and making teams? Of course, the rink had no exit and every person had a flag and a team, whether acknowledged or not.

Such thoughts prompted another memory—Jim as a kid of maybe ten or eleven, having just stayed a week with Uncle John in New York and returning with him to Virginia, complicit in John's loving little scheme to surprise Arthur and Wendy with a short visit of his own. Jim had been sitting next to his uncle on the flight to Richmond, where John ordered two cocktails. By the time he'd drained the second, most of his attention had rolled over to the window, where the daylight bled down into the horizon and the stars shone and the Richmond lights winked back dark countryside.

"It's funny," John said to him, a feathery smile on his face. "Look at the city there, Jimmy." He pointed, his thick finger on the glass larger than two city blocks. "Somewhere in all those beads of light is a church or two. Or synagogue. Or mosque. Whatever. Could be that one, that one, or that one. And these beads of light down there are claiming to speak for all that up there," he gestured toward the stars. "When you see it from up here like this, that kind of seems pathetic, right? I mean, what difference does Jesus make to those stars? Or to some silicon-based creature that lived ten million years ago on some planet in the Andromeda Galaxy? Like your dad says, we think we make this shit big, even though we shrink it into something staggeringly small."

He and David now sat in what would be one of those little beads of light glimpsed from the sky. Jim thought about Camille way up "there," higher than any airplane or breathable air or any space and gazing down at all of everything but somehow also watching them specifically, in this pew.

Hope you're up there, Camille, Jim thought, *with your brush to the mural of creation.* That image first struck him as corny. The more he dwelt on it, though, the more poetic and apropos it seemed, and he blinked at the tears welling in his eyes.

About forty minutes into the service, David took the stage.

"Camille," he said, a crack in his voice, "'we were ice and fire,' she once said. Always she swore she'd come up with a better comparison since I repeatedly told her I didn't like being the ice. She sat on the art end of things, and I sat on the science end of things and when we first met in New York we were both so into our own things that it's amazing we kept in touch as we did. That's because we felt a shared connection that neither her creativity nor my microscope could pinpoint..."

Jim's mind wandered. David's voice became a distant echo. Jim closed his eyes and thought of the Judges of God and of terrorism and of child rapists and serial murderers and he entertained an invisible field of random antagonism across the universe, musing that humanity's unique blessing was its protected conscience—walled off, mostly, from these corrosive forces. Yet people like the Judges of God had surrendered to this indifferent chaos; in the tradition of many a violent and sociopathic person, they had *become* it, had dissolved into these currents that rendered little distinction between their bullet and the fatal heart attack.

"What I found remarkable about Camille," David said, sniffs and sobs rising in the audience, "was her passion. Her passion about art, about life. Camille wanted nothing less than to change the world. To change the world through art."

The people around Jim became one homogenized flat thing, like a canvas upon which his mind could splash gruesomely titillating fantasies. Jim saw Benjamin Holden and the two other faceless shadows still at large, and on that interior canvas he bludgeoned them and cut them while relishing the thundercrack of bone and the rivulets of blood tracing the contours of their skin. With a blade Jim opened their throats and their bowels and he reached in and shredded each tendon and severed non-vital parts so as to keep within their tortured persons the anchor of life and all the pain it had to offer. They would scream out their indifference until they could do so no more. They would be pushed to a place in full view of the peace experienced by their victims, while they themselves would forever be denied entrance.

Arthur pulled into the parking lot of the Sportsman's Grill, ten minutes late for his meeting. He paused in the car, gathering thought and breath. Since the hospital he'd not felt the need to take an anxiety pill but wondered if it was only a matter of time. All that moved in the world seemed only to be moving in him. Everything else appeared frozen beneath the milky-frost clouds, a stillness defied only by the humble, twirling descent of autumn leaves.

The glow, he thought, remembering. *The light...had a*

sense of humor.

He climbed out of the car and made his way into the restaurant, exchanged smiles with the hostess. That otherworldly bond, that electric whip of connection he'd felt with many others, flared only for seconds. It had been strongest when awakening in the hospital. Over the ensuing weeks it had waned steadily.

He surveyed the restaurant. Arthur felt a sense of relief realizing that Jeff was late, too. He followed the hostess to a booth by the window and ordered a cup of decaf. His gaze wandered toward the center of the restaurant. He had first met Linda here, at her recommendation. He'd been late then, too, had walked in and found her nursing a cup of coffee at a table in the center of the dining room. He'd approached her, hand extended, and she had risen and hugged him after which *(picky paranoid jackass I can be)* he'd requested they move to a corner table or booth because "this one" seemed "too open."

He'd noted a visible loneliness in Linda back then, and Arthur knew now that his actions may well have deepened it, maybe even made it a chronic thing. That was largely why he'd asked that Natalie not visit him in the hospital. Childish? Maybe. To him, though, Natalie Farrow represented a symbolic container for some other, departed Arthur. Absurd, of course. And insulting to Natalie. But the feeling was real. And despite its absurdity it had proved to be therapeutic. Small delusions seemed necessary on the path to reconstructing any new reality.

Jeff arrived moments later, flustered and out of breath. He approached Arthur.

"I find myself ducking and running back and forth to my car now," Jeff said. "Fucking sniper lunatics." They shook hands. "How's it going, Art?" The waitress arrived to pour Art's coffee and Jeff ordered a Diet Coke. "Sorry I'm late.

Had a meeting with one of my other clients that went a little overtime."

"No problem," Arthur said.

"How was the memorial service for Camille?" Jeff asked. "I still can't get over that. How's Jim doing? How's David?"

"They're doing as well as they can," Arthur said. "They're going out west soon, to see Wendy. She'll mother them both for awhile."

"Well that's good." Jeff received his soda, thanked the waitress. "They're going for Thanksgiving, I presume?"

Arthur nodded.

"What about you? You coming over?"

Arthur said, "Yeah, I am. Can I ask you something?"

"Sure. Anything."

"Will Natalie be there?"

Jeff hesitated. "Yeah, she will be. I think. Will that be okay? I know you said you didn't want to see her."

"No, um…" Arthur gave a wan smile. "It should be okay."

Jeff sat back and exhaled, his gaze fluttering, finding no place safe to land. "We're done, by the way. Officially."

"I'm sorry to hear that."

Jeff waved him off. "It had to happen. And while it was more her, it's also mutual. We're on okay terms, though. We're different people. We were bound to dissolve. She's a little too intense for me. I never actually thought I'd say that. But it's true."

Arthur absorbed the implications of that in silence.

"But I'm glad you called, Art," Jeff said. "I know you said you wanted your time or your space or whatever, but I tell you, you've got your pick of the litter: interviews, lectures, new books…"

Time or your space or whatever. *Callous dismissal.* None of those things, none of those people—writers, interviewers, schools, professors, those apparently waiting in the wings for his public emergence—none truly cared about what he had to say. Only its impact. This goddamn exploitative machine clanking about him, so fascinated with the shell and not the meat, and which in too many cases dismissed the meat by hollowing out all the complexity for easy delivery and digestibility.

For the year or so preceding Christopher Hitchens's expected passing, many had speculated whether or not the thorn-tongued pundit might slacken his anti-theism as the end approached. Yet Hitchens never wavered. And once he was gone there was no way to confirm what he might have seen, or come to know—if anything.

Arthur Moore, however, was different. His detractors anticipated that he might come forth to acknowledge God's hand in saving him, might humbly admit he'd been wrong. His fans and colleagues anticipated a brass-balled show of philosophical integrity rivaling or even surpassing that of Hitchens. For he might be an *atheist*—atheist, went that serrated word, oh my!—swayed not even by a return from death and eager to proclaim that no pearly gates existed, and that no Palestinian man would be offering a welcome glass of water-turned-wine to new arrivals.

"Jeff," said Arthur. "I'd rather not."

"You want to wait another few weeks?" Jeff said. "As I said, you were dead, for Chrissakes. I'm sorry to sound crass, but…"

"I don't want to wait another few weeks," Arthur said. "I'd rather not have to wait for anything."

Jeff sat back, crossed his arms. "So you're saying, what? You want out of the game?"

Arthur said, "Out of the Coliseum, yes. Gone. I need to sort through too many things and I can't be distracted by the media circus. "I'm not ruling out more books. But I need to decide what those books might have to offer."

"Heard you withdrew your membership to VAS."

"I did. I'm cutting down my commitments."

"Did some of them come to visit you? In the hospital? I know Steve came."

"A couple times," Arthur said. "He was impressed with my recovery."

"As we all were."

Arthur sipped his coffee.

"And we're grateful," Jeff added. "So why are you cutting VAS—us—off?"

"I'm not cutting—"

"Oh, stop the shit, man. I talked to Steve the other day. He's concerned about you, but knows you have a lot on your plate. I think you owe them an explanation, considering the platform they've given you. It's professional courtesy. If not for them then for me, so I won't be bugged anymore, and so I won't have to bug you."

"Alright," said Arthur. "I'll stop by at some point." He downed the rest of his coffee, then threw a five-dollar bill on the table and rose from the booth. "I've got to go. See you, Jeff."

"Art, man," Jeff said, palms displayed, like a man in supplication. "What's going on? What happened?"

"I'll be in touch," Arthur said, as he strode away.

The bell above the door chimed his exit.

⚜

After sitting for a long while, Natalie opened her eyes. Her apartment settled back into form.

She couldn't remember the last time she'd tried the lotus position, or "mainstream meditation." Probably almost a year ago. She never thought she was meant for it, that the universe had overstuffed her mind with too many thoughts and that it had given her the writing pen as her paramount release valve.

But there was something to be said for the lotus position. Though it'd been only fifteen minutes, in opening her eyes once more she felt a small, heartening sense of returning from somewhere else, of descending calmly back to the world.

Yet she also found herself pining for the time in which she'd written *The Gospel of Universal Self*, a period she saw as one long writing meditation. It now seemed impossible that she'd ever recapture such an experience, that extraordinary peace absolved of all past and all future, a spinning center point of impassioned creation. As of late, writing had proven a sporadic, unreliable exercise—in sitting down to work, buzzing cicadas of thought would gather about her mind.

But it's all up to me and only me because it's my path and my duty, to give ear to all the inner chatter until that selfsame entity, light, soul, spark, whatever, that permanence of so many names that only listened and watched, steps clear from the noise.

This is all bullshit, she would think, in darker moments. Namby-pamby voodoo Ouija woo-woo bullshit.

Natalie rose and walked to her desk, where the printout of interview questions from the science-and-spirituality magazine *Soulful* sat waiting. She'd had them a week and had not yet put down an answer and wasn't sure when she might, or if she might.

Occasionally Jeff entered her mind. She wondered how well he had truly taken the split. Men like Jeff tended to act tough and understanding while the real feelings acidified them within.

"Have at me," Natalie had said. "Tell me I'm being a

flighty bitch—"

"You're being a flighty bitch," Jeff had said, with a grave smirk.

That was the most she'd gotten out of him. Maybe, though, she was giving him too much credit. Maybe that was all he truly needed to say.

Natalie knew it'd not been one of her wisest decisions, getting involved with her manager. The pull of his charisma had taken her by surprise; he was both playful and persistent, an attractive option for her career as well as her social life, and at the time she had been lonely in both. Her last major relationship had been Neil, and, with Jeff, it'd been nice to have a more light-hearted partner, one whose pillow talk wasn't concerned with existential questions, whose gravitas did not hold her in place or make her feel intellectually or spiritually subordinate.

Jeff was more your spiritual subordinate, wasn't he?

Much as Natalie tried to push it away, the realization kept returning: she had used Jeff. It disconcerted her, how unaware she'd been of her own motives. She'd fallen into a relationship with Jeff around the same time he signed her, granting her a kind of emotional insurance and priority. She'd wanted to experience a man unlike Neil, more a guy's guy, and Jeff had merely been the vehicle for that experience. After the fire, after having cheated on him, she'd cashed in on that "emotional insurance" for body comfort, flimsy assurance, and, frankly, sex.

Often Natalie told herself she was a "patron of humankind," a ravenous seeker of all kinds of connection. But that was only a noble-sounding cover for being fickle and selfish, taking from people what she wanted.

Then writing about what people should be doing, right?

She began disrobing.

Stop beating yourself up.

Only halfway through the shower, standing with her head lowered in the steam, Natalie realized she'd actually just taken a shower the night before.

Another hour passed before she remembered her phone was still on silent from her period of attempted meditation. She retrieved it from the kitchen table. Her heart flinched at the name and number that had, half an hour ago, left her a voice mail.

Arthur M.

Natalie stood there staring at the phone. Initially she rejected it. Either he had intended to contact someone else, it was an old message, or this was a dream.

She waited, then brought up the voice mail.

"Hi Natalie," Arthur said, with a subtle, sullen hesitance in his voice. "It's Arthur. I know a lot has happened lately. Obviously. I'd like to reconnect and clear some things up, though, if you're amenable. Would be nice to see you."

She put down her phone. In a mild daze, Natalie began preparing a blueberry smoothie. She'd respond after breakfast.

RUN, HER BRAIN ECHOED.

What're you, a child?

She sat on a bench in the courtyard of Governor's Palace, in Colonial Williamsburg. *Like I'm an agent in one of those spy movies.* Everyone around her just ornaments decorating her central drama. She wanted to smoke but refrained. Nearby, people trickled down the main street, tourists and families and actors in period costumes that made for a decent show as she sat waiting, breath steaming in the chill gray air.

For some eerie, inexplicable reason, she felt watched.

Then, Natalie turned her head and there he was, walking up from the south side, head down and hands in the pockets of a heavy hooded coat. She stood to greet him, realizing only seconds later that she was smiling. Her pulse quickened.

"Arthur," she called.

He spotted her and waved. Even from where she stood Natalie could see the burn scar scrawled across his neck and part of his face. Natalie could tell he was not entirely at ease. He smiled, but the smile seemed burdened.

"Hi Natalie," he said.

They embraced. Touching Arthur felt far more comfortable than she'd expected. For several seconds he stared at her, the hollow grin still on his lips. Empathy gleamed far back in his eyes, behind a hardening layer of what Natalie construed as frustration. This wasn't the peaceful Arthur Jeff had alluded to—rather, she saw an actor in struggling portrayal of that character.

"How are you?" she said. "How're you feeling?"

"Pretty well, actually," Arthur said. "I can't complain. I mean, I can, but I'd kick myself."

"You have every right to complain."

Arthur shrugged. He gestured down the path. "Want to walk?"

"Sure."

They began to drift away from the bench.

"Listen, Nat…" Arthur said. "I know I asked that you not visit me in the hospital."

Natalie put up her hand. "Art, I get it. I understand."

"I'm sorry about that."

They walked around the courtyard, branching off into the streets. Natalie found herself wanting to move faster. Arthur's pace was slow and measured, sometimes gratingly so.

"It's not that I didn't want to see you," Arthur said.

"I know, Art." Natalie smiled. "As I said, I get it, remember?"

Arthur turned and studied her, a distant fog shadowing his eyes.

"How are you?" Natalie said again. She meant it genuinely, but it came out clipped, forced. She breathed, tried to calm herself. "I mean, how've you been otherwise? I'm so sorry about the, well…you know, the shooting. I couldn't… it was just surreal. I couldn't believe it."

Arthur lowered his head. She felt a twinge of regret for bringing up the shooting, but it was one of the bigger thoughts she could grasp out of her windblown mind.

"I couldn't believe it, either," Arthur said. "Nobody could. Jim's still hoping to finish the mural, though. If only for Camille's sake. But I've been okay. Taking it easy. The house rebuild is coming along nicely."

"That's good."

"I'm probably going to move out into my own apartment soon, too."

"I see," Natalie said. Their gazes lingered a second. "It's good to see you." *Such a hackneyed line,* she thought. "And…I'm so glad you and Jim are okay. You have no idea."

"It's really good to see you," Arthur said.

There was something stilted about the whole exchange. Not totally unsurprising, she supposed, given the circumstances. And the presence of other people also tended to blunt more substantive interaction. *We're on display.* She thought of her relationship with Neil, which, in a humorous tone, he'd called "nocturnal": in the public light their dynamic was always heavily diluted.

"I'm a selfish hypocrite," Natalie said. "Not to mention a coward."

Arthur looked taken aback. "Excuse me?"

"I left you, Art. Then when I saw you fall through the floor…I don't know…I barely even remember the moments in between when I was on the phone with 911 and when I was out on the driveway, facing the fire engines."

"What else could you have done?"

"Arthur," she said. "I'm not going to deny that my reaction was instinctual. But—and this is something I've never experienced before—it was like my higher self, my rational mind, my belief system, conspired with my animal mind in those moments and…"

Arthur stared at her, visibly confused.

"I left you," Natalie said. "I left you there because I thought that's what was meant to happen. I thought that's what the universe intended because when I was in your house, while you were in Los Angeles, I saw that happen—in a dream. I saw you burn to nothing and I felt there was nothing I could or should do because…"

"Because you were supposed to?"

"Yes."

Natalie took out a pack of cigarettes, unsheathed one and lit it and blew the smoke skyward.

"Back on the nicotine train?" Arthur said.

"For now, yeah."

"So do you still believe that?" Arthur asked. "That you were supposed to do nothing?"

"I don't know. Only you can tell me. I know I felt awful after it happened. Not only embarrassed about cheating on Jeff, of course, but…well, feeling like a coward I guess, as I said. It's easy to believe in purpose and order when you're in control of writing about it. It's something else to take to it in the heat of utter chaos. I was just in shambles."

"Nat, stop," Arthur said. "It's alright."

For a moment they fell silent, Natalie searching for something else to say. "Jeff told me you quit your atheist society. And that you're taking time off."

"He told you correctly."

"Why?" She took a long drag.

"I want to concentrate on getting the house back in shape, among other things. Family things. I'm thankful Jim and David have taken me in. I could have gotten an apartment by now, but...I didn't want to be alone. Not yet."

Natalie nodded, understanding.

"I never stopped...I don't hold you responsible, Natalie," Arthur said. "Please understand. I just needed time to sort things out."

"Arthur," Natalie said. "In all seriousness, I didn't particularly want to see you either. I was frightened. I was embarrassed. Hell, I still am."

"Life's a scary, embarrassing affair," Arthur said, with a dry smile.

Something large, she realized, was pressing at him from within. She could sense the weight of it in his words, see it pulsing in the shadows behind his eyes.

They reached another bench and sat down awkwardly, their thighs almost, but not quite, touching. Natalie stabbed out the remains of her cigarette in the ashtray next to the bench.

"Arthur," she said, before she'd even registered a conscious urge to engage him.

He stiffened slightly. "Yes?"

"During your operation...all that happened..."

"Mm-hmm?"

"Do you...mind me asking about it?"

Arthur paused a long moment, before shaking his head. "Ask."

"What do you remember about it?"

He cleared his throat. His gaze strayed from hers. "I don't remember much. If anything. I flatlined."

"I've met people who've had near-death experiences," she said, ignoring his reply. "The first stage of their reaction is the hardest, figuring out how to tell others. Let's face it—

we don't live in a society that's very acceptant of that stuff."
A sentiment of *thanks to people like yourself* hung in the
air, but went unspoken. "Even religious people, strange as
it may seem, have trouble digesting these things. Sure, they
love talking about God. That's accepted, even encouraged.
But actually *experiencing* God is doubted, frowned upon,
and often even considered blasphemy."

"Right."

"There's a philosophy I appreciate," Natalie said, "called
death-tomb-resurrection. With every change in your life
there is a death stage, where what went before falls away. It's
followed by the tomb stage, during which you're in limbo,
often confused as to where to go next. Finally, there's resurrection, where the new period officially begins."

"Nat," said Arthur. "I'm a man of reason—"

"Stop with that," she cut in, squeezing his arm. "You're a
man of reason, yes. But the universe is anything but reason-
able."

Arthur looked at her long and hard.

"Art," she began. "I—"

"Okay," he said.

Then he told her.

DUSK HAD FALLEN by the time she pulled into her complex
and parked. Natalie craved yet another cigarette, if only
to do something with her hands. She longed to offset the
chaos of her thoughts with some automatic, repetitious
motion that might combat it. She decided instead to sit for
a moment monitoring her breath while listening to the ticking, cooling engine.

A soft grin tugged at the corners of her mouth. In some
way she felt validated, honored, hopeful in regard to her
time with Arthur, even though some residue of dubious-
ness and anxiety, the source of which she couldn't pinpoint,

still stirred within her.

He'd had an extraordinary experience. An experience he'd appeared to have both created and undergone—a bumping-up of the subjective against the objective, a melding of the spectator and the stage. Arthur made no excuses when speaking to her about his inability to fully comprehend what had befallen him. Natalie had even sensed mild resentment in his words. He seemed upset that such a burden of inquiry had been laid upon him, uninvited.

Still deep in thought, she clambered out of her car, entered her apartment building and rode the elevator up to her floor. She didn't notice the person pacing outside her apartment door until the shadow entered her field of vision and a voice said, "Hey Nat."

Immediately she recognized the man, but for a long moment didn't believe he was there, if only because she didn't want to acknowledge her intimate familiarity with the haggard face behind the beard, the green eyes that glittered like beckoning twin oases in desolate earth. A raspy smell of grunge and liquor surrounded him like a cloud.

"Neil?" she said. "Oh my God."

"Hi Natalie," he repeated. He scratched his ear and then began fingering it nervously. "Sorry. I know this might be a shock. Can I come in?"

No, wait, she thought. *A goddamn dream.* Like when Arthur had called her. The universe appeared to consolidate events.

This is real.

"Come in," she said. Natalie unlocked the door and gestured Neil inside. Only later would she realize how natural was her inclination—maybe both of theirs—to not embrace one another. Superficially, of course, he looked like a vagrant, as decrepit as he might have once been years ago while living on the streets. But Natalie felt an even deeper aversion rise within her, the kind that would prevent her from hugging a stranger.

"Neil," said Natalie. "Sorry, I'm still processing that you're here."

"And that I look the way I do, I'm sure."

"Well, I mean..." Natalie trailed off. "Can I get you anything?"

"I'll have water."

Neil settled on the edge of the couch. Natalie hastened to the cupboards, grabbed a glass and filled it with tap water.

"Thank you, Natalie," he said, as she handed him the glass. He drank half of it then set it on the coffee table. "I got your email."

In another dreamlike moment, Neil unfolded a piece of paper from his jacket pocket and presented it to her. On it she saw her own words: *Neil, Thinking about you. Happy birthday...*

"I don't even know where to begin," she said, taking a seat on an armchair.

"You shouldn't have to know," Neil said.

Natalie began to notice the slow return of other, lesser memories of her time with Neil, and of Neil himself. The moments that had fallen through time's sieve, leaving behind only the most pleasurable ones, which passing years had gilded even more richly with romance and nostalgia.

No doubt she had once loved Neil, and loved him deeply. But even then Natalie had realized that her love had not so much grown naturally as it had been instilled in her, and even been demanded of her. Even at the summit of her feelings she had felt a deep frustration, a constraining sense of self-surrendered obligation.

Time and a full beard had minimized nothing of Neil's arresting stare. He'd once expressed disdain for the religious hold he could exert on people. Natalie, though never saying it outright, had intimated, *It's your own fault.*

"This is my issue," Neil said. "My doing. Everything."

"What are you talking about?"

"I owe you an explanation, for what happened to me, to the Wellness Center," he said. "I know I shared a lot with you when we were together, but people are universes unto themselves. I didn't share everything."

Natalie's throat tightened. She had reached out to him, and here he was. Yet he addressed nothing of what she may be going through, the issues that prompted her to email in the first place. He'd come solely for himself, it seemed. To confess his sins and seek her absolution.

Look at him. He needs you now.

"What happened, Neil?" she said, aware of the thin layer of frost that glazed her tone.

He took another, longer drink of water. "When I was about nineteen," he said, "about, what, maybe ten years before the 'me' you knew, I was living in Las Vegas, homeless on the street."

"I know that," Natalie said. "Of course I knew that. That was the crisis that started your book..."

Neil gave her a mildly admonishing look, as if to say, *Wait.* "During that time I met another man, a drifter," he continued, "older. He told me he was a Gulf War vet. I took to him. Not like he was my father or anything, more like a really kind uncle. He watched out for me, Natalie. He showed me all the best spots for food, for money, for...well, for getting my rocks off. And at some point I ended up with this girl. Young girl. She was...well, she was only fourteen."

Natalie's eyes widened.

"I didn't know it at the time," Neil hastened to assure her. "She was a prostitute. I only found out afterward how old she really was. And I lost it. For whatever reason, something just erupted inside of me—it was like she was mocking me, spitting my own history back at me and reflecting my own abuse as if to say I had become a man exactly like my father and, again, I just lost it."

Natalie leaned forward. His every word pricked at her stomach. "What do you mean by 'lost it'?"

"I beat her. Hard." He sighed. "To death."

"Oh my God," she said, covering her mouth with her hand. Welling tears began to burn her eyes. "Oh my God, Neil."

"I know. Believe me, I know. That incident was the unspoken event haunting and driving so much of the despair in *The Divine Dialogues*, what I was trying to reconcile. Of course I never told you that, or anyone. I mean, I wasn't trying to beat *her*—"

"What the hell does that mean?"

"No, I mean, she was just a personification of what I was trying to beat. But anyway, that veteran guy, my 'street uncle,' he knew about what I did and he helped me, covered for me. I was terrified of everything by then. Terrified of myself and of him too, because he'd started to become someone else in the months he and I were together. He was becoming more paranoid, more religious, if you can call it that…I'm sure his time in the war accounted for a lot of it."

Natalie just watched Neil as she might an actor on television.

"Ten years later," Neil went on, "after I wrote the *Dialogues* and started the Wellness Center, who should come visit me but this old street uncle of mine. I didn't recognize him at first. He came as a patient of the center. He took classes and everything. I don't know if you ever met him. But he got me alone. I knew it was him.

"He was still crazy, but I could tell he'd learned to control the craziness," Neil went on, "which to me was even scarier. I asked him what he wanted and he said was going to start doing some spiritual work himself. Just needed some money. I was hesitant obviously, but he'd come to me for help. And he'd helped me before in Vegas. I had lived with him on the street. He knew my worst secrets, and he'd kept them to himself, as far as I knew. I also felt that, with all the stuff I'd preached and written, it'd be hypocritical of me not to help him. By then I'd made enough so that I could give him some of it. I figured he'd spend it on liquor or heroin or something, and I'd never hear from him again. He came back a couple times after that, wanting more money. The last few times he was more aggressive, talking about how he had kept evidence of what I'd done, and how we were brothers and how we needed to always help one another out. How, with one disruptive call or two, he could destroy everything I'd worked for at the center, and with the book."

Neil put his face in his hands then looked up, stretching his features against his fingers.

"There were economic reasons for me closing the center," Neil said. "Books sales had slowed, and not as many people were coming or signing up for classes. Profit margins thinned. But I was also worried about my past, about what I'd done bleeding into what I'd become. And you have to believe me that I was thinking more about the people like you who I'd helped than I was about myself. I'd given them a coherent universe. I'd helped them make sense of this insanity called life, the way I'd made sense of it for myself, with God's help. I didn't want to bring it all crashing down, to invalidate for everyone all they'd achieved in themselves, through me."

Natalie formed a slow, understanding frown. "You're in the tomb stage right now."

"I suppose so. It's lasted a while. I started to question and reevaluate everything about myself. I actually returned to being homeless, by choice. I had some money, but I chose not to settle anywhere. I began to feel that 'settling' meant a kind of congealing, a drying-up of energy and of momentum and a hardening of spirit. You know me, I've been prone to wanderlust."

"You have," she said. "That's why we decided we probably wouldn't work out. Why we thought I needed to rsurrect myself."

That's why I decided to resurrect myself, Natalie silently amended. If it'd been up to Neil she would have been at his side forever, always the magician's assistant, the smart and pretty face of his spiritual empire. *Follow your own path,* he might've said, alongside me.

Stop that.

"I drifted with money," Neil said. "But I soon realized how inauthentic that was. I was pretending. I sought reconnection with truth. And I realized that the center, as helpful as it had been for me at the time and as helpful as it may have been for some people, had been doomed from the get-go. Because wisdom *does* congeal. You can only say the same thing over and over again before it curls up and withers in your heart. Like what Nietzsche said, right? That which we can find the words for is already dead in us."

Natalie wasn't sure how to respond. She'd always despised that quote, even as she recognized its partial truth. She did not feel it a broad truth, though—just applicable in certain contexts.

"So I gave away pretty much everything I had," Neil said. "I wandered for a long time, a third of the person I used to be, a third the person I was, a third the person I was slowly becoming. And I guess I'm still becoming that person. Tomb stage, as you said."

"Neil," she said. "Why did you come to me?"

"Because of your email," he said. "And because I could. And, because…" He gestured toward the printout of her email, and she handed it back to him. Quickly he surveyed the coffee table and took a pen and flipped the paper over and began to write. "Because I want you to know where you can find me."

When he finished writing, he slid the paper back across the table. On it was scrawled a Pennsylvania address and a phone number.

"I thought you weren't settling down," Natalie said, "the nomad."

"It's nothing much," he said. "It's a trailer I rent in the woods. I go there to recoup. Kind of a home base, I suppose. A nice place to get, and be, away."

Natalie looked at the address. She rose from her seat. Even his handwriting looked different, every letter slanted and rushed, textual lemmings scrambling toward some doom. Her eyes misted over a second time.

Neil rose and approached her. She sensed a slight shift in his energy, the boring through of a newfound clarity in his eyes. He reached out and touched her arm and stroked it, comforting at first until it became sensual.

He's come to reconnect, she thought, *in more ways than one.*

"Neil..." she said.

He stared at her, a singular intent brewing in him. It was animal but also pleading, needing—a living thing craving the validation of another close body. Part of Natalie felt tempted, certainly. Another part recoiled with disgust given all he'd told her. "Reason and love keep little company," Shakespeare once said.

Neil had long been a mixture of both primal and cerebral. And although his coarsened appearance had startled her, Natalie found this sudden tip toward the primal side slightly exhilarating. It would be a cathartic fuck, she realized. An experience she still craved. And it would be with someone she knew and knew well. Yet he'd also been absent from her life for so long that he was no longer the person he once had been.

If she said yes, she'd be fucking an intimate stranger.

Tears leaked from her eyes. She backed away.

"I think," she said, sniffing, "you should probably go."

⚹

Arthur made his way down a series of hallways that smelled of bleach and ammonia, that glowed and hummed in florescent white. Artificial daylight sent a chill down his spine. Electricity had no business filling in for the sun. Hospitals were the worst offenders, too, swallowing day and night into their cold, glowing bowels.

Yet in coming here Arthur also felt a regrettable sense of returning home, of entering into a reunion with a past life.

Somewhere beyond the perimeters of this world he had come to know the inexplicable: a lightness, a timelessness. He had stumbled upon something that had opened a channel to a place of clean and pure knowing, the wellspring of intuition, resting deep in the brambles of his mind. A cerebral Shangri-la. This feeling of contentment was countered by the heaviness of Earth, of the expectations put on him to act and to speak certain ways, under certain times. Which was not necessarily bad. It felt good to be alive, to breathe the same air as Jim and Jeff and Linda and Natalie, and even the odious interviewers with whom he'd so often sat and argued. And while not burdened personally with some of the most significant aspects of what he'd encountered (if it all could truly be deemed an encounter), his burden lay in figuring how to carry what he'd experienced in relationship to others. So far, only Natalie knew the truth.

The whole world had receded, drained from me as if I

contained it. I could see it all, see that glow, not twinkling or pulsing but just there—immutable, inextinguishable...

Breathing deeply, he entered the office of Dr. Nathan Waters.

Waters rose and greeted Arthur with a muscular handshake across a polished oak desk. Tall and well built, the doctor looked more like an athlete than a surgeon. A weekend athlete, perhaps, given his profession.

"Dr. Moore," he said with a wide smile, "the walking miracle."

Arthur's grin was small and fleeting. "Thanks for seeing me, Dr. Waters."

"Are you kidding? It's a pleasure. I'm amazed I'm shaking your hand and talking to you right now."

An energetic personality, Nathan Waters did not conform to Arthur's personal stereotype of doctors—male doctors, in particular—who, at Waters's age, tended to project an exhausted air of indifference.

"All thanks to you," Arthur said, taking a seat.

Waters waved him off. "Thanks to your nuts and bolts there. They decided to kick back into gear. So what did you want to discuss?"

Arthur slouched lower in his chair, arms on the armrests, his hand splayed across the side of his face. "Something that happened during the surgery."

Waters narrowed his eyes at Arthur.

"At one point, I was clinically dead," Arthur said. "You told me as much."

"That's right."

"But ..."

The doctor leaned forward.

"I was conscious," Arthur continued. "I watched you and the nurses scramble to bring me back. I watched the nurse at my right side accidentally drop a tray of instruments. I

saw myself, pale and not breathing. I heard you keep repeating, like a mantra, 'Get him back, get him back!' I heard
other sounds in other rooms, on other floors, though they
were a little more indistinct.

"I was outside myself," Arthur continued. "I watched you
work. I moved down the hallway and saw a naked woman
walking out of another operating room. It didn't surprise
me, to be honest, even with her nudity. She seemed very
much at peace. I looked at her, and she looked at me—the
only one to acknowledge me. We passed each other, even
passed *through* each other, like...I don't know...like two
fog banks. For that second I could feel her, but not physically. It was like a sensory cloud of memory, of information.
I touched her name: Annabelle Eubanks. I could feel her
lightness, but also that it was tattered and stained with ache,
like she'd just wrenched herself from the mud and some of
it still clung. Am I dead? I thought. Somehow, it made absolute sense that I was, just as much as it made absolutely *no*
sense. I moved toward the lobby, saw my son, Jim, and my
friend Natalie and my manager all sitting there. And I even
remember seeing the roof of the hospital. There are blurry
gaps between distinct memories. Like a dream. But what's
distinct is very clear. And I can tell you right now it did
not feel like a dream or hallucination or any of that. It was
incredibly clear. And, if I didn't have doubts myself, I would
say it was unequivocally real."

It *was*. The subsequent revelation rose at the back of
his throat but Arthur swallowed it down. He couldn't just
"say" it was unequivocally real. Because what else could
be inferred by the headline he'd found—"Williamsburg
Woman in Fatal Car Wreck"—with the picture of that
bright, smiling face over the smaller caption: Annabelle
"Annie" Eubanks.

Arthur's words seemed to drip into Waters. The doctor's expression seemed cautiously understanding. "I can't deny," he said, "that you saw and felt what you say you did."

"There's also been an interesting side effect," Arthur said.

"What's that?"

"I used to take medication every once in a while," Arthur said, "for anxiety."

"Okay."

"I haven't had any urge, or need, to take anything since I woke up. It's almost like—like whatever unease I once had was just rinsed out of me."

"Hmm."

Arthur refrained from expressing concern that this new-found calm might not last. Occasionally he felt pricked by his anxiety, and mused that perhaps it had been shoved into some deep corner within him, where, over the coming days and weeks, it would test his defenses for an eventual return.

"It's probably not a surprise to you, given my career, that I've studied this near-death phenomenon," Arthur said. "I know of it. I know it well because I've fought against the conceit, the very idea, I mean, that they could offer evidence of life after death. I know they've done studies with DMT or ketamine. I believe I may have been hallucinating. Per-haps only imagining being dead. I don't know. But I can't deny the authenticity of what I felt. It was just...weighted and real. Wherever I was, if I was anywhere, had more meat than this world, yet it was so much lighter."

Waters studied him with reserved fascination.

"I know there's a spectrum for near-death experiences," said Arthur. "One to five. One being a feeling of utter peace of mind, five being, well, something beyond, an absorbing light. I don't know what I was, ultimately. Maybe a three-point-five. Maybe even a four."

"I'm aware of the spectrum," Dr. Waters said.

"And I know that such unexplained phenomenon is not uncommon," Arthur said. "Seeing a white light. Feeling the touch of 'God.' Those recorded observations."

Waters chuckled, but it felt less humored and more like an expulsion, a release of tension. "You're right, it's not. You're not the first patient of mine to acknowledge something like this. I've verified other, similar experiences: people who've registered flat EEGs but come back describing these experiences in detail, things that happened after clinical death has been established."

Waters reclined in his chair. "I've read some of your work, Dr. Moore. Like you, I'm not a religious person. I suppose you can accurately classify me as secular. Growing up, the idea of spirituality and God was simply inconsequential to my family, and it's been that way for me pretty much my entire life. But you know—and I could very well be in the minority on this, among my colleagues in medicine— the more I practice, the more extraordinary circumstances I encounter, and the more I open myself to the possibility that someone, or something, is juggling all this."

"All this?"

"Yes. All—" Waters outstretched his arms, "—this. Reality. What we perceive as reality. Whatever the hell that is. That there's some grand intelligence at work, not on a micromanaging, individual life level, maybe, but an awareness of things that surpasses that of any human."

Arthur crossed his legs, eyes narrowed.

"My growing suspicion," Waters continued, "is that consciousness may actually be like a television signal, with our bodies acting as the television. If you shut off or break the TV, you haven't stopped the signal. However, the signal's unable to penetrate the receiver. From where that signal's being broadcast, who can know? We probably will never be able to know. Is consciousness the exception or the rule of existence? Will consciousness allow itself to even know the answer to that?" Waters threw up a hand. "Who can know?"

"Before the surgery," Arthur said quietly, "before...I died, I would have had no trouble describing my presumption of a typical 'near-death experience.' Yet whatever happened to me...I can't find the words to describe the experience. I'm bastardizing the importance of what I saw." Arthur leaned back in his chair. "I almost feel...I don't know...fraudulent, I guess."

"In what way?"

Arthur shrugged. "Suddenly, now I'm trying to grasp all—" he outstretched his arms, "—this."

Waters chuckled. "Welcome to the human program, my friend."

❧

Linda loved the inimitable, house-swelling perfume of Thanksgiving. It was a yearly congregation of the best smells a kitchen could offer, deliciously entwined in the air like olfactory ornaments. It helped, too, that she had a sensitive nose. Half the delight of life, she'd always thought, were its tastes and odors. Hopefully, Heaven had a fragrant scent.

They sat at her extended dining table, Linda in the middle across from Sonia and Ferdinand, whose wood-hued face wore a wide bright smile. He appeared to hesitate with every movement, as if needing to grant himself permission to reach for his glass or a nearby dish.

"Ferdinand," Linda said, speaking with what she feared might sound like patronizing slowness, "I'm so glad you could join us, and that I could meet you."

Ferdinand listened intently to each word. Sonia sat beside him, ready to field anything lost in translation.

"Thank you," he said, nodding. "Thank you for having me."

"You have a lovely smile, too," Linda added.

The smile remained, his perpetual default reply. Mild confusion nested on Ferdinand's brow. Seeing it, Sonia murmured the compliment in Spanish.

"Thank you," he said again.

"So hon," Linda said, taking the bowl of peas from Sonia. "I take it you're enjoying things over there? In Spain?"

"Definitely," Sonia said. "I think the rhythm of life is much healthier over there. There's more of an emphasis on family and enjoying recreation time than there is here. I feel like here everyone is expected to leave home at eighteen and hit the ground running to get to the top office by twenty-five, to heck with anything or anyone that might get in the way. Women, especially."

"And how's everything in the psychology world?"

Sonia stared at her, eyebrow raised. "Mom, what do you mean? I stopped psych a long time ago, remember? I'm doing poli-sci now."

"Polly—?"

"Political science."

"Oh, that's right."

"I really like it," Sonia said. She leaned forward and scooped more mashed potatoes onto her plate. "I'm just not totally sure what I want to do with it."

Ferdinand said something and Sonia quickly answered in Spanish. Hearing her daughter speak so fluently in a foreign language conjured pride, though it was tinged with a little jealousy.

"What are you studying, Ferdinand?" Linda asked.

Sonia fielded the question for her boyfriend. "He's majoring in economics."

"I see," Linda said. "That's a brainful."

"Do you want me to tell him that?" Sonia said.

"No, don't worry about it."

Ferdinand glanced at Sonia with mild bewilderment and they shared more rapid Spanish. Linda assumed she must have translated her comment because his gaze whipped at her and he chuckled.

They dined in silence, and Linda found herself eating faster than normal. Sonia sat across from her, upright in unusually good posture, lifting her food with methodical motions.

Laugh, Sonia, laugh. How 'bout you just laugh? Linda willed from her daughter a chuckle, a chortle, a random and explosive guffaw, a baptismal of giggles. She used to laugh all the time as a girl. While making her sandwiches for elementary school, Linda would sometimes put a dollop of mayo on her own nose and then walk over to Sonia pretending to be ignorant of the white glop in the middle of her face and Sonia would tumble backward and erupt in laughter. There had once been an anything-goes lightness about her, like a chirpy and soaring little bird. Only later had that bird's wings had been clipped, and it had since been stuffed and mounted.

Though she would never say it, Linda had begun to think Sonia's young laugh reached far closer to God than anything that fell from her adult mouth.

"God realizes," Reverend Matthews had once sermonized, "that, to many of us, aspects of life and His plan seem just plain confusing, even absurd. The tool He gave us to deal with that—a tool we should always keep at the ready—is humor, none other than laughter. So before you go to bed tonight, before you offer up your prayers of gratitude to Him, seek out a joke, seek out silliness, seek out the comical absurd that will help you deal with the tragically absurd. Seek out something that will make you laugh."

"You haven't met Mark yet, right?" Sonia asked her.

They sat on Linda's couch by a flickering fireplace, mugs of steam-whispering hot chocolate in their hands. Upstairs, Ferdinand was taking a shower and getting ready for bed.

"No not yet. We've just been corresponding."

"Do you know if he's Christian?" Sonia asked.

"I know he has a spiritual side. I don't know much more than that. Usually I don't get into that sort of stuff until I meet someone in person."

Sonia snickered, but it was dry and not amused. "Usually? How many times have you done this internet dating thing?"

"Just once before, with Art."

"How is Arthur, anyway?"

"I'd rather not get into that," Linda said. "Not right now."

Linda squirmed, heated more by her daughter's admonishing gaze than the fire to which she directed her attention.

"You should try Christian-only dating websites," said Sonia. She sipped her hot chocolate. "If you're not meeting anyone at church. Truthfully I'd go with the latter, since online you don't know who you're getting."

"Right."

"Mom, I know Dad messed with you. I know he messed with your faith—"

"He didn't mess with my faith. He disrupted my going to church. There's a difference."

"You have to understand that God wants us all to be Christian," Sonia said. She set her mug on the coffee table, as if to prepare grand gestures for this point. "You can't call yourself a Christian unless you're willing to follow God's steps. That doesn't mean being with someone who's *spiritual*, whatever that means. That means being with someone who's Christian."

Lowering her head, Linda murmured, "I understand, Sonia."

"I wish you could come with Ferdinand and me to our church in his home village in Spain. It's a tiny little stone house with a thatched roof. It's wonderful. You just feel reborn every time you walk in and hear Father Ramirez speak. The man speaks with such a passion! That kind of priest is a dying breed, especially in America. I feel like we're losing God over here."

Linda kept still and quiet. *You can't get elected dog-catcher in this country without God,* she thought. *We're not losing Him.*

"I only want to see you happy, Mom," said Sonia. "And God will make you happy. You taught me, and now I'm old enough to help teach you, too. We can help each other."

"Sonia."

"Yeah?"

"Why is it you never answer any of my emails?"

Sonia sat back, inhaled long and exhaled slow. "I'm busy, Mom. I'm studying."

"I receive dozens of religious chain letters forwarded from you. You can't take several more minutes to write off a personal email?"

"I sent those letters because I thought they might help you."

"I'm fine."

Sonia rolled her eyes and looked at her fingernails, idly picking at them. "Okay."

"I just miss you, is all. I miss hearing about how you are, not about how much God loves me."

"I'm sorry Mom. I'll try more often. But I don't send a lot of personal emails."

"You texted Ferdinand not ten minutes ago," Linda said, her eyes probing, "and he's upstairs."

"So?"

Linda rose from her seat, leaned over and kissed her daughter's head. "I'll see you in the morning, honey. Good night."

❧

The phone rang three times before Arthur, seated at his office desk, picked it up. In between lifting the receiver and putting it to his ear, a brief sour wind blew through him. The voice on the other end was brittle with business.

"Dr. Moore?"

"Yes?"

Leave me alone, he thought, assuming it someone from the media, or VAS.

"This is Agent Richard Latham, with the FBI."

"Oh. Hello."

"I wonder if I might ask you a few questions."

Latham's words grabbed Arthur's attention. "Um, sure."

"As you may or may not be aware, there was a recent homicide in your area, the gunning down of a young woman—"

"I know. Of course I know."

"And, as I'm sure you also knew, your son, James Moore, was working alongside Ms. Rhodes on the mural. He happened to not be there that day."

Of course. Of fucking course. Arthur closed his eyes. *Why tell me this again?* His throat began to clog. Ominous expectation burned in his breast. "Yes."

"Okay," said Latham. Arthur thought he detected some military past in the agent's voice: a constant readiness to yell. "I know you know all this. I just like laying out things plain, to square us on the same page. Alright?"

Don't like the way you're talking to me. "Alright."

"I also have here..." Latham paused. Arthur could hear papers being shuffled and flipped. "That earlier this summer you went to visit Mr. Benjamin Holden, self-confessed leader of a small terrorist group called the Judges of God. We know the group consisted of at least three members, Holden included. We believe it was one of the two members at large who murdered Ms. Rhodes."

"I went to see Holden, yes," Arthur said, trying to restrain the defensiveness rising in his voice. "It was research for a book. I'm a psychologist."

"You're more than that, it seems. And just let me be clear: no one, not me, not anyone, is accusing you of anything. Just know that as we go forward here."

"Okay."

"I'm going to break a bit of protocol here and let you in on a little something cooking my way: we're pretty certain we have a lock on the whereabouts of the second shooter, a man by the name of Robert Gray. The problem is that we have almost no idea where the third shooter might be. We're hoping that with Gray and Holden behind bars the other domino might fall, but the picture we're getting of these guys is that they're fucking steel lipped and loyal. We suspect there may even be more people involved, not as shooters but as supporters, financial or otherwise. Right now we're unsure how these guys were able to function as they did. Or do."

Arthur stared at the wall, listening.

"We do know the name of the third guy," Latham said, "an Alexander Heyst. Now, when you were with Holden, did he happen to mention anything about Heyst that you can recall?"

Arthur genuinely tried to remember, but his brain groped spastically through a mostly gray void. His only potent memory of that day was of Benjamin Holden's cold dead eyes, aquiver with lunacy. "No, he never mentioned the other names."

"Now, for the trickier part," Latham said. "Would you think there's any reason to believe the Judges are targeting you or your loved ones specifically? Maybe as a warning?"

Chills crawled down Arthur's back. That Camille's death may have at all been related to his visit with Holden was a notion that had circulated the backwaters of his brain and that he'd desperately tried to ignore. To hear someone else suggest the same affirmed its potential truth.

"I don't know," Arthur said. I must sound weak.

"Because it's a bit coincidental, if you'll allow me to say," Latham continued, "and remember, no one is accusing you of anything...but it's a little coincidental that you go visit Holden, and then they kill one of your son's coworkers on a day your son didn't show up."

The specter of the word "conveniently" hovered in the latter part of the sentence.

"Are you saying I knew about the shooting and warned Jim?" Arthur said. "He had to take his partner to the ER. Check dates and records."

"I'm not saying that. I'm still laying it out plain, squaring us, as I said. Okay?"

Arthur sighed. "Okay."

"For the record, I don't think you had foreknowledge of the shooting. Nor do I necessarily think it was in retaliation for whatever awkward powwow you had with Holden."

"Alright."

"You went to see Holden months before Ms. Rhodes was killed, for one. If they were related, I'd expect something like this to have happened sooner."

Arthur didn't reply.

"But I'm putting my feelers out," Latham said. "If you

can remember anything, give me a call." He rattled off a phone number. "And just be vigilant. Heyst is still out there."

Jim and David sat down to dinner with his mother and Dan and an older couple they knew from temple. It was a surprisingly comfortable evening, given Dan's alcohol consumption, although Jim noticed his mother's sometimes strained efforts to make the evening work.

After the party David retired to bed, while Dan adjourned to his study. Jim and Wendy skimmed the waiting pile of dishes, Wendy washing and Jim drying.

"Dan drank a bit too much tonight," Wendy said. "I hope he didn't offend you in any way."

"Me?" Jim said. "Nah, Dan's alright. A little too…" He paused, shrugged.

"Tell me. Please."

"I think maybe he likes to compete with Dad."

Wendy sighed. "Men and their peacock feathers, I suppose."

His mother's tone was accepting as well as dismissive, so Jim chose not to pursue the topic further. He'd long observed that Dan disliked his father, which only fed Jim's aversion to his stepfather. And while he may have misinterpreted certain behaviors, Dan's overeagerness to buddy-up with him and David—especially David, as if to declare to the world *Hey! I'm cool with your kind!*—along with his obsequious tendency toward total, even self-contradictory, agreeability left an aftertaste of the amphibious in Jim's mouth. Every new interaction prompted that one dangerous question ever closer to the edge of his tongue: What's with *this tool, Mom?*

"I've been working for the past two days," said Wendy, rinsing soap from her hands. "I don't know why I'm not exhausted. Instead I almost feel wired."

"I'm not that tired either for some reason," said Jim. "Even though I'm still on Virginia time. Jet lag hits David hard. And the turkey and wine probably sent him into a coma."

"How's he been feeling?"

"Physically or mentally?"

"Both."

"He's been okay. Been quiet, doing his work. We haven't interacted much. Haven't been...well..." Jim stammered. "I sometimes feel like I'm walking on eggshells with him, y'know?"

"I do know."

A pause.

"Would you like to go somewhere Mom?" he asked.

THEY SET OUT WALKING the two quiet blocks to a small pub in Venice called The Beefeater. While crisp, the air had nothing on Virginia's icy bite, so Jim had easily foregone wearing a jacket. His mother envied this, having long ago succumbed to what she called the "So-Cal wussiness."

About a block into their walk, an odd sensation befell Jim. He slowed his pace. His mother, her arms folded and eyes down while caught up in a lopsided conversation about her worsening tennis elbow, didn't seem to notice. Prickly familiarity spread through Jim, a strong déjà vu that gave their surroundings a surreal, ominous texture.

The Beefeater was almost empty. The bald, thick-framed bartender poured his mother a white wine and Jim a beer. They chose a table with high chairs by a window nook, next to the watchful eye of a portrait of Henry VIII.

"Dan and I come here every once in a while," his mother

said. "Usually just for a nightcap." A cautious smile tugged at her lips. "And things with Dan have smoothed over. Just to answer the question I know you want to ask."

Jim blinked. "I didn't know I wanted to ask that question."

His mother shrugged and took a sip of her drink. "I think Dan and I have settled on a don't-ask-don't-tell policy with Arthur since the fire. He understood my concern, and I think he's feeling more tolerant of me keeping Arthur in my life. But Arthur told me while he was here that people who rashly accuse others of indiscretions are usually the ones actually engaged in it."

"So Dad made you paranoid?" Jim said. "I swear he spreads his paranoia like a contagion. He used to at least."

"He didn't help," his mother admitted. "But really I've noticed that Dan can be a bit of a lady's man. A bit flirtatious. Doesn't mean he's ever done anything or will ever do anything. But I don't know. It puts me on edge in a way that I just feel stuck. And I hate feeling stuck when I shouldn't even be so in the first place. It's all in my head."

"I'm sure not all of it is," said Jim. "Reality meets us halfway. At least it does the sane people."

She grinned, but her smile was thin. Seconds slid by, viscous.

"So how's your dad really doing?" she asked. "I called him a few times after he woke up at the hospital but only spoke to him once. I get the sense he's keeping his distance a bit." For a moment she appeared wistful. "How's the house coming along?"

"I haven't been over there lately, but he's over there almost every day. He's also been consumed with other things."

"What other things? Drawing? You said he was starting to draw, right?"

"Well he's taken an interest in it. He's been reading my instruction guides from the community college."

"That'd be great for you two to share," she said. "Is Art still living with you and David?"

"Yeah, he's still there." Jim ran his finger around the rim of his beer glass. His mother watched him. "He'll be getting his own apartment soon though. He's keeping busy. Had to work out his insurance crap, his bank crap, lots of little things…but…"

"What's goin' on back there?" she asked.

"Back where?"

"You know. Back behind your eyes."

"Don't you mean, what's going on 'up' there?"

"You're not *that* much taller than I am."

"Thanks, Mom."

"You were doing the finger 'round the glass thing."

Jim snickered. "It's something dad told me. I'm just wondering if he would want me to tell you."

"That's inevitable now, isn't it? Now that you've told me this much? Come on, out with it."

Leaning forward slightly, Jim said, "Okay, well, I should back up a bit. David told me he saw dad on my laptop one afternoon and that he was crying, like, actually *crying*. He didn't know that David saw him. Later, he asked David what it was like for him to come out of the closet."

His mother's face darkened at the mention of Arthur crying. "What was he looking at on your laptop?"

"I checked the browser history," Jim said, "and saw a listing for the Near Death Experience Research Center."

She recoiled slightly.

"I avoided talking with him about it for a while," Jim continued. "I mean, it's Dad. I could also tell he was hesitant, and I think seeing his reluctance only fed my excuse to not get into it myself. So we kinda beat around this thing.

Until the night I got back from North Carolina, y'know, from Camille's funeral."

His mother winced a little and rested her chin on her palm. "Right."

"David and I'd gone out when we got back. Just had a few drinks. Nothing much. But it loosened me up enough, and I was certainly distraught enough, that when I got home I..." Jim sighed, his hand up and clutched as if struggling to grasp what might've come over him. "David went straight to bed. I went straight to Dad's room and knocked on the door. He came out—"

"Sorry," she said. "I don't mean to interrupt. But I just want to say, liquored up or not, I'm proud of you."

This time Jim blinked. "Why?"

"For just going at it. That's the only way you can really get at Art. At least it was when I was with him."

"Sure. I went at it. But anyway, he came out and I said, 'What happened to you when you died?' He recoiled a bit, but didn't seem too surprised that I asked. He lowered his head and said, 'Something I can't explain'. I said, 'You're the great explainer, though.' 'No, I'm not,' he said, pretty declaratively. So then I say, 'What would your reaction be if you were me?' 'Just what yours is,' he says, 'but I'm not you.'"

As Jim spoke, his mother's jaw gradually unhinged. Her eyes were dumb with disbelief.

"Holy cow," she said. "So...what? He had some mystical encounter or something?"

"No, no, I don't know. I still don't know all the details. He didn't give them, and I didn't pump too hard, not after that first intrusive knock. Maybe I didn't want to actually hear it myself. I'm kind of like Dad in that I don't like dealing with unreasonable shit. I mean, he told me he physically went somewhere else. 'How?' I said, 'Your body was here.' I think he's still hesitant to use any word like 'soul' or 'spirit.' Dad said—and I know this is weird—but Dad said he felt 'evaporated,' like some lighter part of him lifted right off, the 'skin shed of the snake,' as he put it, 'light but inde- structible.' The part of me,'" Jim chuckled, "and I still have trouble knowing Dad said this, but he said, 'The part of me that's been around since the big bang.'"

"Wow."

"But this is what's going through his brain now, I imag- ine. How to reconcile all this. He seems pretty chilly in regard to Jeff."

"You might remember some of this," his mother said, "but in the last phase of our marriage, when I was show- ing more active interest in going to temple, your dad would occasionally say to me, 'How could you get into something so phony and man-made?' My answer was always in the vein of, 'well, God made us to get together and make Him, in whatever way we want.' He always dismissed that. Your father has a bit of a misanthropic strain in him, a distrust of institution and community, which I respect to a point. I suppose, though, that he was or is always looking for God. He just couldn't find anything of him, or her, or it, in others. He needed to head off into the jungle and look the lion in the face."

"I don't know if he met God," Jim said. "If Dad ever said something like that, I'd think I died."

His mother chuckled.

"He was very quiet while in the hospital," Jim went on. "I know he was grateful to be alive, but I think the thought of dying—of having died—bothered him. But he doesn't know how to describe what he's feeling. Toward the end of his stay in the hospital he seemed to brighten more. He was still keeping to himself the day I took him home and he was just…lighter I guess. Like a cured asthmatic taking deep breaths. I mean, he laughed when he saw the destruction of the house firsthand." Jim downed the rest of his beer in three galloping gulps that burned his throat. He coughed, then added, "in a weird way, he almost seemed glad for it."

THEY WALKED OUT into the crisp marine air and turned right down a sidewalk into the darker residential block, retracing the way they'd come.

"By the way, Mom, I meant to—"

Suddenly Jim became aware of a white car, traveling slowly behind them. He paused, alarms sounding inside his head.

"What's wrong?" she asked.

He put his arm around her. "Nothing. Just keep walking, okay?"

The car sped up ahead of them, then braked. He watched cautiously as it rolled at conspiratorial pace over the orange lamplight puddled on the road. Ignoring a stop sign at the corner fifty or so yards away, the car hung a sharp left.

They kept walking, walking, Jim feeling a measure of relief. He tried to ignore the memory of only an hour earlier, that potent sense of déjà vu, of not only déjà vu but something bordering more on ominous intuition.

Woo-woo crap.

Yet he'd had such an intuition before, on the morning of that day in seventh grade, when he'd wrenched himself from a dream he didn't remember. He recalled a faint sense of some assault, of fists on his flesh, of mortifying exposure. What it was, he didn't know. *How* it was, he didn't know. It was simply something....vicious. *Bad.*

Badness.

Then, hours later, Scott Gregory had approached him at the top of the stairs.

About thirty yards from the stop sign at the corner, Jim

halted. "Mom," he said. "Let's turn back."

His mother adjusted her purse strap. "Yeah, okay."

Nearby, he heard a car door slam. Then another. He also heard the faint rumbling of an idle engine.

Jim had his arm outstretched, ready to usher his mother in the other direction. Two figures appeared from the shadows behind them and made their way toward them.

Too late.

"Hey!" a voice called from the darkness.

The men drew closer, the light betraying a human face darkened with stubble and enshrouded in the cloth hood of a grungy jacket, one pocket bulging with the man's hand plunged deep inside it. *No mistaking this.* No mistaking what was unfolding. His mother exhaled sharply. For Jim the world tilted a bit, became unsteady and unreal.

"Give it up," said the man with his hand in his pocket.

Jim's heart rammed. *Felt this before.* More breath, pulsing. *Knew this was gonna happen. Knew.*

How?

Jim held out his wallet and the man snatched it. With awkward speed, his mother began rooting around in her purse. The man reached out and grabbed it from her. His mother gasped, began to sob.

Jim had never heard his mother cry. Rage flooded him and without thinking he wrenched the purse from the mugger's hands. Everything stalled as Jim stared deep into the man's jittery green eyes, fists clenched white. The man stepped back, waiting. Jim noticed his lip tremble. Then the accomplice cried from the shadows, "Let's fucking *go*," and the man in front of Jim whirled and scampered back into the darkness.

A moment later, the car squealed off unseen into the hush of faraway traffic.

Jim stood without a sound, shaking, not wanting to

move, afraid he might unleash on his mother his uncontrolled energy—a lifetime of build-up, suddenly with no place else to go. His mother touched his arm and he shuddered. Her eyes bore deep into his until the violent and trembling heat began to ebb.

"Jim," she said softly.

He turned and they embraced.

"I'm sorry, Mom," he said.

"My God," she said. "For what?"

IV

AS AUTUMN DISSOLVED INTO WINTER, THE bare ashen-blue trees stood naked and defiant against the cold. Blushed curled leaves amassed at their base, covering the gnarled roots in piles of red and gold. Snowflakes melted from the sky, becoming rain mere yards from earth. Everywhere the season breathed.

Natalie had become somewhat of a hermit, devoting energy to finishing her new book, *Sexpirit: Unleashing the Sensual in the Spiritual and Vice Versa.* Lunar Press wanted the full manuscript by early February and had already recruited an in-house illustrator for the visuals, whose initial samples had not impressed her. They were too stiff and self-conscious, hardly of the loose organic quality she envisioned for the book.

Seeing Arthur had proven emotionally cleansing, unclogging much of her creative self, allowing her once more to feel the cool muse-stream of words.

During a coffee break she checked her email and found a forwarded message from none other than Arthur, atop which he'd written: "Are you able to come? Last minute, I know."

"You're Invited," said the email below, "to Earth Works' New Mural Unveiling." The date listed was tomorrow. Further information featured short bios of Jim Moore and his tragically late partner, Camille Rhodes, as well as links to local press coverage of the mural's completion. "Camille's vision perseveres," said one article on which Natalie idly clicked.

She'd actually caught wind of the unveiling through the media, and wondered why she'd not heard of it first through Arthur or Jeff. Then again, this week had not found her terribly accessible.

Reading Arthur's invite summoned a crush of longing for another presence, a body and a mind there to reach out to and to touch. She could probably count on a single hand the number of words she'd spoken aloud, either to herself or someone else, during this recent stretch of writing.

She retrieved the phone and dialed Arthur. Four rings.

Then, on the other end: "Hey there."

WHEN SHE RETURNED from the kitchen with the two glasses of juice, Arthur was standing by the coffee table, a book open in his hand. Natalie saw it was *The Divine Dialogues*, which she'd brought out since Neil's visit.

She extended the juice glass. "Here you go."

Arthur started. He closed the book and took the glass. "Thank you."

"Sure." Natalie stood beside him sipping her juice, her gaze crawling across Arthur's face. With her pinky she pointed at The Divine Dialogues. "Interesting book, written by an even more interesting man."

"I know the name," Arthur said. "Hell, he may have once been on my naughty list."

"He wasn't religious," Natalie said. "Not at all. Not in the traditional sense."

"This sold pretty well, didn't it?" He glanced at the cover. "Well, yeah, *New York Times* best seller. There you go."

"Mm-hmm." Natalie felt a flicker of regret for having left the book out in plain view. She didn't relish speaking of Neil now, especially not with Arthur. Though, she mused, given his current quest it might make a good resource for him.

"Take the book," she said. And then, quoting T.S. Eliot; *"'These things have served their purpose: let them be.'"*

"Are you sure?"

Natalie nodded.

"Thank you. I'll give it a read." Arthur flipped the book over and glanced at the back cover, where a clean-trimmed Neil Valentine, the one she'd known and loved, smiled back from years past. As sad as his present circumstances were, she felt something undeniably liberating in realizing that the Neil Valentine she once knew no longer existed.

He needs your help, whispered a voice, one she tried to ignore.

"You mentioned him several times in *Gospel*," Arthur said.

Natalie studied him. A warming validation tingled inside her.

"I just read it," Arthur said, "for real this time."

She set the juice glass down, leaned in and kissed him. He reciprocated, putting down the book and his own glass. They spent several moments standing there entwined, sinking into one another. Natalie found the kiss had actually lost some of its former intimacy, but maybe that was to be expected. Arthur's lips on hers felt almost like a stage kiss— a production with little authenticity. He was not as wholly and magnanimously present as their first time.

"Everything okay?" she breathed across his neck.

His lips grazed her cheek on their way back to her mouth. "Yes."

Stop now, he's not into it. But she couldn't. Desire swelled in her, both cleansing and muddying. *Too soon, too soon,* her mind nagged her. *You're taking advantage of him.* Her urges, however, drove her to distance those notions through a total commitment to the moment, any past and any future existing nowhere outside the sensations of now, every touch and caress filling and stretching the seams of history and all existence.

They made it half-clothed to her couch, Arthur driving kisses upon her skin as if adamant to overcome his own reservations. He lay atop her and she cupped him through his trousers and felt only moderate hardness. She helped him remove the rest of his clothes and undressed herself as well. With his half-erect penis on display she could smell the apology on his breath, though it was quickly corked in kisses.

Arthur buried his face in her glistening neck and muttered, "I'm sorry."

Natalie, stroking the back of his scalp and trying to suppress her own disappointment, whispered, "Don't worry. You're not totally back in this world yet."

He's lost it. Lost the animal. Lost the drive and—

In researching *Sexpirit*, she'd read of people who'd undergone near-death experiences and come back with a diminished libido. Normally it was temporary, a symptom of having known what one woman referred to as a "spiritual orgasm." It was nothing against sex, they said, more that they had known something greater that rendered physical intercourse to them what beloved childhood toys were to adults: unnecessary.

Maybe Arthur's will never come back.

They lay there naked and breathing hard until, from the end table, her cell phone rang. She glanced over at the blue-lit screen. It was Jeff.

"Go ahead and answer it," Arthur said, sitting up. "I won't be offended."

"Sure?"

Arthur waved her on. She reached over and answered the phone. "Hey."

"Hey, Nat," Jeff said. "You're working?"

"Um, no," she said distractedly. "You're good."

"Well I'll make this short 'n' sweet. I booked you for an hour slot on February ninth with the radio show *Eggert Hour* in Pittsburgh."

"Okay—got it down."

"He said he's read your book. And you know he loves talking about spirituality and faith and all that."

Natalie looked at Arthur. "Isn't that the show Arthur was on earlier this year?"

Arthur's eyebrows lifted.

"Where he called this an asinine country?" Jeff said. "Yeah. I'd recommend not following in our buddy Teddy's footsteps."

"Thanks, Jeff."

"You going to see the mural tomorrow?" Jeff said. "Did Arthur tell you about it?"

"The big unveiling," she said. "I'll be there."

⚹

"No speech?" Arthur said from the front row.

"*This* is my speech," Jim said, and tugged on the silk cord. The massive white sheet fluttered to the ground and the mural was reborn in every eye of the audience.

Applause crackled from the spectators arrayed in plastic chairs on the parking lot. In the front row David stood and then so did Arthur, and soon the dozens of people behind them rose and washed Jim in their appreciation.

Jim looked up at the mural. Two cupped hands awaited the fall of a massive water drop reflecting an Earthscape, the celestial background clouded with stars and galaxies and nebulae. In the lower right-hand corner an unplanned feature had been added: a piece of lunar surface upon which a now-immortalized Camille Rhodes sat gazing at the wonders across the wall. In the upper right, it read: "For Camille."

Jim and his boss Ethan Hathaway offered another round of gratitude for the attendees, then the small crowd rose and broke apart, many drifting to the table stacked with crackers and a cheese plate and plastic cups next to several bottles of wine and soda. Two security guards stood watch on the grounds. A local news cameraman caught the action from the sidewalk.

The unveiling was expected to be short, and not only because of the cold; the last of the Judges of God lunatics remained at large. For several days now the media had grown leprous with pictures of a man named Alexander Heyst: burning certain eyes snuffed of reason, facial hair like ashy vandalism across his face. They'd snagged the other guy, a Gray-somebody, in a hidey-hole—actually a public storage facility, if Jim recalled correctly—in Miami. Though he was drawn to the whole case, Jim could only tolerate fragments of it; that no one knew which shooter pulled the trigger on Camille continually gnawed at him. For all intents and purposes, though, because Heyst was now allegedly the last to be caught, to Jim he was the culprit, the last to witness Camille alive and art making, the first to see her dead.

By now, though, Heyst was projected to be far from Virginia.

Ethan Hathaway approached Jim. "I'm very impressed with it, just the whole thing," he said. "Even more impressed that you found the courage to finish the work, under the circumstances."

"Thank you, Mr. Hathaway."

Also in attendance was Natalie Farrow, whose name Jim had of course heard though he had not yet met her. He was struck by the sharp prettiness of Natalie's face. All features seemed cut and angled and honed to the glimmering focal point of her beauty that needed no assistance from makeup. The contrast of her pale skin and shimmering black hair offered some profound cosmic truth, and her trim sloping figure was at once tight and loose, like a life-drawing sketch from the hand of a master craftsman. He realized that he'd love to draw her, maybe even abstract her or put her through some impressionistic filter.

Arthur noticed Jim's scrutiny and nudged him.

"She's too complicated," Arthur said, with a smile. "I wouldn't get involved if I were you."

"You're kidding, right, Dad?" Jim said. "I'm just indulging my artist's eye for aesthetics. She's all yours."

Arthur chuckled and slid an arm around Jim's shoulder. They approached Natalie as she caught their gazes and approached them.

"Jim, I presume?" Natalie said humorously, hand extended.

"The man of the hour," Arthur said, removing his arm and gesturing like a showman to his son.

"Nice to finally meet you," Jim said, shaking Natalie's said. "Thanks so much for coming."

"Are you kidding? Of course."

"Jim," Natalie said, still clutching his hand, "I just want you to know how deeply sorry I am about your friend, Camille. Your dad spoke highly of her. I wish…well, I wish I had a chance to meet her. She sounded wonderful."

"Thank you," Jim said, his eyes moistening. "She was

wonderful. I couldn't have done this without her."

Natalie smiled.

"Oh," Jim said. "Thanks for signing our copy of your book."

"You're very welcome."

"I just love this, Jim," Natalie said, indicating the mural. "You have extraordinary talent. And it's right up my alley. Thematically."

"Thank you," he said. "That means a lot."

For another second Natalie lost herself in the mural, then turned to him. "So I have a proposition for you."

"Yeah?" He smiled.

"How would you like to illustrate my new book?"

Toward the latter stages of the mural, Jim had begun to wonder frequently what project he might tackle next. This mural, after all, had become a central axis of his recent life, a nourishing distraction from David's illness and his father's hospitalization, and it had taken on transcendent purposefulness in the wake of Camille's passing. That it should ever actually be done had to some degree seemed an almost impossible prospect. But it was done now.

"Are you serious?" Jim asked her. "Really?"

"Absolutely," said Natalie. "Right now the press is using an in-house illustrator that I don't much care for. I've told them as much, too. And I'm sure I can talk to them about bringing you on board instead. We'll just have to come up with some relevant drawings and show them."

"Can I ask? What's the book about?"

Natalie said, "Spirituality and sexuality. Bringing the two together."

"Wow." A little chuckle fell from his mouth. "I'd be interested."

"Great," Natalie said. "I don't know if I'll be able to get you on the cover—they still want their own artist to do that.

But I'm certainly going to press it."

"Okay...damn, well thank you, Natalie."

"Nat."

He smiled. "Nat."

Jim noticed Arthur by the snack table lifting a drink to his lips, watching them with soft approval.

⚭

As Arthur and Jim entered the apartment, Jim said, "Hold right there," and continued on through the living room toward the bedroom. David had gone on to campus and they were alone.

"Why?" Arthur said.

"Just stay right there," Jim called. "In fact, take a seat in the living room. I'll join you in a second. I have something to show you. The mural's not the only thing I finished recently."

"Should I close my eyes?"

"If you want. Not necessary though."

There's an overflow in Jim, Arthur thought. *The cosmos pouring creation through him.*

Jim emerged from the bedroom, a canvas under his arm. He angled it toward Arthur. It was the unfinished, part-abstract, part-naturalistic piece his son had shown him that summer, the night they'd left for Oriole Park. The Horsehead Nebula hovered like a jeweled sigh above a geometric rendition that Arthur recognized as a tropical beach.

"Jim," Arthur said. "That's fantastic. The Horsehead looks more distinctive now, too."

"That's Myshkin's donkey, remember?" Jim said with a playful scowl. "I mean, he called it an ass, but I think saying 'Myshkin's ass' would sound a trifle weird."

"Hah, right. You were having trouble finishing this one,

as I recall."

"I was, yeah."

"What finally pushed you to the finish line?"

"You, Dad."

Arthur blinked. "What?"

"It was you." Jim's expression softened. He set the canvas down against the wall. "You told me you felt some kind of indestructibility. That moment you died. That you could feel some part of you that's been around since the big bang."

Arthur noted hesitation in Jim's voice.

"I don't know what went through, Jim," Arthur said. "I'm still trying to figure it out—"

"You don't have to explain," Jim said quietly, "because I want to tell you something first. Something that happened in LA."

There was an electric tickle in Arthur's stomach. "Okay."

Jim sighed. "Mom and I were robbed one night, walking back from a bar."

"Oh, my God," Arthur said. "Why didn't you tell me?"

"I'm telling you now."

"Come on, you know what I mean."

"I'm fine, Dad."

"What happened?"

"We were heading back down a dark street. A car rolled down the street, pulled up in front of us and two guys jumped out. They accosted us."

"Did you get the license plate? Go to the police?"

"Mom called the cops, yeah. Didn't see the plates, no. We told them what the guys and the car looked like, as best we could."

"Good."

"But I'm telling you this," Jim said. "Well, I wanted to tell you this...because I had something strange happen to me. I still have my credit cards, ATM card, my ID. They only got my cash. You know why? Because I took all that other stuff out of my wallet, while I was at the bar."

"Why?"

"Because," Jim said, clearing his throat, clearing away that creeping hesitation. "When Mom and I were walking, I felt a weird and uncomfortable familiarity, a sense of déjà vu. More than déjà vu. I dunno, a wave of badness. An intuition, I guess. But again, even beyond that. It was like an echo of an experience, before the experience even happened. It was as if the sensations and emotions of the mugging already hung like a bad smell in the air. I didn't know what might happen, but I knew *something* would happen. I even suggested an alternate route home, but it was a longer way back and Mom didn't want to be out too long in the cold. So I tried to convince myself that I was being ridiculous, to listen to that voice that said I was overreacting, that nothing would happen. You know whose voice I heard?"

"Mine?"

"Yeah," Jim rubbed his forehead. "The only other time I remember feeling that way was in seventh grade, on the morning I got jumped by Scott Gregory and his friends. I could feel their fists on me before it happened. I was certain of it, to some degree, but I never knew how to tell you. I didn't want you to think I was crazy."

"Was it my fault, Jim?" Arthur's face contorted with a distraught realization. "What happened that day?"

"No, no, Dad," Jim said. "Don't think that. I guess I just...I guess I just want to clear the air and admit that we don't know. We're not in control. That the world is goddamn weird, and we're not just in it, we *are* it. The world is weird and by default we're weird, too, and we can't deny that. And neither should you."

Jim exhaled. "You don't need to tell me everything if you don't want to. But where are you now? Do you think it was real, whatever happened to you? Whatever you felt? I mean, you've attacked near-death experiences before. You said in *Unholy Ghost*, I think it was, how scientists or doctors or whatever had learned how to turn them on and off in the brain, like a neural toggle switch."

"I know," Arthur said. "I know I did. But it's easy to talk. It's difficult to describe the *real*ness of it to anyone else. Somehow, I became detached from my body, from its heaviness. I passed through people. I saw you and Jeff and Natalie in the waiting room. I saw myself. All typical, I know. But it's typical for a reason." Arthur rapidly deliberated whether or not he should, or even could, extrapolate on the experience, as memory of the grander, latter portions seemed to slowly diminish with the days. "I don't totally discount that I was a victim of drugs or chemicals or subjectivity. But my EEG was flat. No brain activity for the time I was gone. And that made sense because I felt like I had no brain, or body. I felt the way water might when it becomes vapor. Lighter, like I said before, freer. Like I was of some other aspect of this reality. And I..." he paused, crossed his arms, "I passed through another woman there. She was naked. Lighter, like me. I passed through her and it was like passing through a cloud of information. I picked up her name, and I remembered it: Annabelle Eubanks. Her friends and family called her Annie. And I found out..."

"She died?"

"She was in a car wreck," Arthur said. "They tried to save her, but...yes, she died. It was *her*, the photo in the news."

Jim's eyes widened as he drank in Arthur's words. "This might sound strange, even silly," he said. "But I remember reading how nothing actually touches anything else. When we make physical contact with something, what we feel is our atoms repelling the atoms of the other person, or object. So, I mean, if the atoms didn't put up that tiny electrical force field, we'd all be passing through each other. Like vapor."

"Or ghosts."

Jim gestured at him affirmatively.

"I'm still processing it, Jim," Arthur said. "And I don't feel like I'm totally in charge of this processing. I feel like I'm just digesting something, and then, one day, I'll wake up and it'll be clear what I think about it all. But..."

Hesitantly, Jim asked, "Do you think Camille is still around? In some way?"

Arthur stiffened.

"Sorry," Jim said. "I had to ask."

"If she went through anything of what I went through," Arthur said, "I wouldn't worry about her."

Tears stung Jim's eyes. He rubbed the back of his neck.

"Jim," Arthur said. "I'm sorry you never felt you could tell me."

"About?"

"About what you felt," Arthur said. "Your intuition, whatever it was. Before the mugging. Or before that day in junior high."

"Of course not," said Jim. "I'm my father's son, in many ways. Maybe not as vehement, but I just assumed all that 'woo-woo' stuff, as you called it, all things supernatural or psychic or whatever, were just stupid and impossible."

The words pinched something in Arthur.

"But I'm an artist," Jim went on, "and I should take some blame too because I let you influence me too much, because as I see it, it's the artist's job to keep the scientist in check. Science demands ultimate knowledge and control. Art reminds you that we're all prisoners of our skulls, that ultimate control is a fool's errand, so flee the doomed Pequod and get used to it. Life is inescapably metaphysical. It's *weird*, as I said. My art is tangible and 'real' only when

I put it into sketches or into paint. But half the process is intangible. The ideas, the 'visions,' if you want to call them that. Who the hell knows *where* they come from?"

Arthur went over and sat next to Jim on the couch, where he put a hand on his son's shoulder and squeezed. Silence settled about them, until Jim pointed to the finished painting and said, "You think you know where you might put that in the new house?"

⁂

Her gaze followed idly the nautical ropes strung and knotted decoratively around the walls like Christmas lights or curtains or, in some cases, hammocks. A faux whaling vessel bow jutted above the bar. Linda regretted not ordering a drink while she waited, and with every moment Mark Gavin was late, the greater grew Linda's temptation to eschew her personal bias against drinking alone. Making fleeting eye contact with every man trickling into the Whaler Inn, she dreaded that sense of a social marquee hovering above her head, shining the words *Woman Waiting for a Date!* Or even worse: *Woman Stood Up!*

Calm down. Finally, a man with bold black-rimmed glasses and a blue blazer over denim jeans entered the restaurant. He scanned the tables. She watched him until their gazes clicked and she saw him smile. The recognition was definitive. A small knot formed in her stomach.

The man approached her and said, "Linda?"

"Indeedy," she said with a smile. "Mark?"

"Guilty as charged."

She stood and they hugged, a slight, tenuous gesture. "May I?"

She nodded and Mark quickly took the seat across from her. "You look like a Linda," he said.

"I certainly *feel* like a Linda."

The waiter came by and took their drink orders, wine for Linda and a scotch on the rocks for Mark. From emails and one phone call, she had gathered enough about Mark Gavin to know that he seemed like a decent and honorable person: two grown kids, one in college, a relatively clean divorce five (or was it ten?) years ago, and a former television producer who dabbled in the stock market.

"So you were out in Hollywood for … almost thirty years, you said?" Linda asked.

"I was, yes. I'm actually a New Yorker—so Los Angeles wasn't much different. Hotter, but just as crazy. I'm looking to settle somewhere a little more quiet. Or at least what I hoped was quiet."

"What did you produce out there? Just television?"

"Just television, yes," he said with a frown. "I produced a few cop dramas, one sitcom. I worked on the political panel talk show *Mann's Watch* for a little while too, in its first season."

"Oh, I have a friend who just went on *Mann's Watch*," said Linda. "He lives in Williamsburg."

"Who's that?"

"Arthur Moore."

Mark furrowed his brow. "I don't believe I know him. What's his gig?"

"He's an author. And commentator. Talks about religion mostly. Or calls for the destruction of it." She smirked. "I'm sort of kidding on that front. Maybe. He's one of those atheist types. He's a brilliant man, though."

Mark shrugged. Linda squirmed.

"So why did you leave Hollywood?" Linda asked.

"It just wore me down," he said. "I left when my kids were old enough. There are a lot of creative kleptomaniacs out there. I mean, I was the one who actually came up with the idea behind *Seinfeld.*"

She gazed at him with a cautious smile, unsure if he were joking with her. "Excuse me?"

"People don't believe me of course. But I met Larry David at a party in the Hollywood Hills. Larry mentioned he and Jerry were working out story ideas for a network show. I wanted to get into sitcom production too so we traded information, and I had a brainstorming session with Larry that didn't go so well. At one point I leaned back and said, 'I got nothing.' His eyes lit up, we talked a bit, and I never heard from him again."

Linda laughed, increasingly uneasy. "Um, well, so you didn't really think of the idea. Right?"

"It's okay," he said, letting out a deep hiss of breath. "The churched helped me come to terms with it. With my anger, I mean."

"Oh? What church was that?" she asked cautiously, hoping she didn't sound shrill.

"Hubbard's," he said. "Scientology."

He said he was spiritual. Linda was careful not to react one way or the other. She couldn't remember what Scientologists believed. Did it have anything to do with God, or a god?

"Are you still with them?" she asked.

"Sure am," he said with a nod. "Half a bookcase in my library is dedicated to Hubbard's work. I even have a near-mint first edition of *Battlefield Earth.* Boy what a shame the movie was though. If I ever get back into the producing game, I might just try and remake it."

They ordered two appetizers to share, the calamari platter and a shrimp cocktail. She listened politely to Mark's stories, nodding and smiling now and then. The realization of a dead-end date weighed on her. Mark Gavin began and ended at himself, an obliging self-promoter though unaware to what height his solipsism had grown. To Linda the food became more entrapment than enjoyment.

Linda's gaze drifted up and away past Mark to any other person or focal point—such as the bubbling lobster tank or aquarium—that might offer respite.

Mark wiped his mouth, then rose. "I've got to hit the head. But I'll be back." She noted the choice word 'but'—an all-too-clear indicator that he, too, understood the sad trajectory of the evening.

Linda resumed her people watching. A heftier man in a brown leather jacket entered the restaurant and strolled to the bar. She watched him call good-naturedly to the bartender, leaning on his elbows as he ordered a beer.

"Jeff?" Linda said.

He turned, a cute bit of deer-in-the-headlights look on his face as he surveyed the tables and saw her waving.

"Oh, hey!" Jeff snatched his bottle of Stella Artois from the bartender and made his way to her table. They shook hands. "How are you, Linda?"

"I'm alright, generally," Linda said. "What are you doing here?"

"Well, I'm drinking," Jeff said, grinning and holding up his bottle as one might in a commercial. "What else? Drinking while I wait for an appointment to have more drinks, with a prospective new client."

"I see. Busy, busy."

"You're telling me. He gestured to Mark's seat. "I'd sit down here, but I'm assuming it's taken."

"I'm on a date," Linda said. She made a face. "Sort of."

"Sort of?" Jeff seemed to get a kick out of that. "Does he not know it's a date?"

"No. I mean, he knows it's a date."

"Ah. I see. What started out as a date has become a trial by fire."

Linda chuckled. "Your words, not mine."

"Hmm, I'd sorry to hear that." Jeff frowned. "Hey, I have an idea. Give me your cell number."

Linda did so. Still smiling, Jeff meandered back to the bar, thumbs hopping over the screen of his phone. A moment later Mark returned, hair moistened and combed.

"Don't want that last shrimp?" Mark asked, fingers poised to pinch it from the cocktail glass.

"By all means."

Mark began talking again, sliding back into the same subjects of his life in Los Angeles, desperate to impress, so it appeared, less addressing Linda and more the rest of the establishment, any pair of open ears.

Linda's phone rang. She waited two rings before glancing at it.

"I'm so sorry, hold on," she said, "I need to get this."

Mark waved her on.

On the other end, Jeff said in a subdued voice, "Just say, 'Hi Jeff.'"

"Hi Jeff."

"Now say, 'Is everything okay? Slow down.'"

"Is everything okay? Slow down."

Both excited and on edge, Linda felt like she'd been plopped into some scene from a romantic comedy.

Mark looked at her.

"Oh my God. Where's Lance?" Linda said, still following Jeff's cue. She exhumed what she could of her high school drama class for some shocked emotion. She put a hand over her mouth. "That's so *awful*. Okay, I'll try my best. See you shortly."

She hung up.

"You've got to leave?"

"I do. I'm so sorry, Mark. It's my cousin. I'm sorry... I've got to run."

"Don't worry, Linda," Mark said. "I understand."

"Thanks." On polite reflex, she almost said, 'Let's talk soon,' but her distaste for the evening had subverted even her knack for courtesy. She fled.

"I hope he's okay," Mark called as she bustled past him.

Out the door and into the night and across the parking lot, Linda breathed and breathed, feeling high on mischief and without the least bit of guilt. When her phone rang again, she answered quickly.

"I'm in the blue BMW," Jeff said. "Lemme flicker the headlights. See me?"

"Yes," she said, laughing. She couldn't help herself. "Thanks, Jeff."

"You're welcome. Now, since I know you're free for the evening, how about dinner later?"

�;

"That's the last one, right?" Arthur said.

Jim plopped the suitcase onto the couch next to two cardboard boxes, then stood back, hands in his jacket pockets. "It is, yeah. You're all set."

Arthur lingered by the sliding glass door, which led out to the balcony of his new furnished apartment. The complex was large, sporting north and south wings each with a central swimming pool. Arthur was on the third floor, perched in nourishing view of the nearby pine woods. Thankfully, the minimal possessions he'd carried from Jim's made for a swift and sweatless move.

"Looks like a nice little place," Jim said. He drifted on a self-guided tour through the kitchen and the small hallway connecting the one bathroom and bedroom. "Would've thought you'd go for something bigger."

Arthur shrugged. "It's temporary. And I think my time

with you and David helped me be a little more economically minded."

Jim chuckled. "Maybe those hobos with the red polka-dot handkerchief hanging from a stick have a thing or two to teach us all about economy."

"Maybe."

Jim returned to his position behind the couch where he opened the flaps of one of the cardboard boxes and glanced inside, casually fingering the contents. Arthur detected melancholy in his son's demeanor.

"Got all your books here?" Jim asked.

"I believe I do," Arthur said. "Want a glass of something before you go?"

Jim patted his stomach. "I'm good, thanks."

"I guess that's it," Arthur said.

"Wait, I have something for you." He thumbed toward the door. "It's in the car. Kind of a housewarming present."

"Oh?"

"C'mon, I'll show you."

Arthur followed Jim down the stone steps to the lot. A young woman toting two armfuls of groceries passed them, and Arthur smiled at her. She reciprocated, then lowered her head. Seems shy. He paused a second, unable to remember the last time he himself had felt comfortable smiling at a stranger.

Arthur watched Jim reach into the backseat and grab a red, yarn-handled gift bag. He handed Arthur the bag, who stood for a moment, unsure of proper protocol for such a moment.

"Go on, open it," Jim told him.

Inside was a 6 x 9 shrink-wrapped sketchbook, a box of drawing pencils and another of Prismacolor pencils.

With a soft clap to his father's bicep, Jim said, "Have at it, Dad. The white sandbox, as I call it. Pure romp and play."

Arthur chuckled, leaned forward and hooked an arm around Jim's shoulder and squeezed. "This is great. Thank you so much, Jim."

"I remember as a kid looking at some of the sketches you did in college," Jim said. "Figured it'd been long enough."

"I suppose it has."

"So I'm not gonna come by in a week and find that still blank and wrapped, am I?" Jim said, indicating the sketch-book.

"Bet your life you won't," Arthur said. "Hey, I was just about to take a walk into town. Want to come with?" He held up his gift bag. "Williamsburg's just a couple of miles down the road. You can watch me draft my first sketch. Give me pointers."

"Never said I wanted to be a teacher," Jim said with a grin. "I'll have to take a rain check. I'm meeting with Natalie in a little while to go over the book plans."

"Oh, wow," Arthur said. "Okay."

Jim climbed into the driver's seat and waved over the steering wheel. Arthur waved back. Then the car pulled out and away and was gone.

THE AIR THROBBED WITH CHILL, the sky a stain of ice milk. Dressed in a turtleneck, a sweater and an overcoat, Arthur took the new sketchbook and pencils and made his way to the streets of Colonial Williamsburg. Candles lit the windows of the historic area, where wreaths and icicle lights accented doors and facades. In the Governor's Palace courtyard stood a large communally decorated Christmas tree, where Arthur stopped to attempt his first sketch.

He couldn't remember the last time he'd drawn. Probably in some remote and rare junction of energy and free time during grad school—the occasional doodle or sketch had soothed the academic wounds to his spirit. Yet it wasn't long before his anxious work ethic took ultimate hold, when Arthur felt unproductive not doing something school related, or at least as congruously challenging, something that demanded precision and technical conquest. The sense of play had been sucked out of drawing. Yet no obligations existed now, no petty loyalties loomed.

Unfettered.

He focused first on the environment, sketching the buildings and antique cannons and trees. It was still too early to try people. Especially since many of those around him were actors dressed in eighteenth-century garb. Though his initial sketches seemed stilted and flat, the more Arthur drew the more he acclimated to the feel of his hand on the page and the fluidity of his movement. He sensed that he was giving something to the world, creating something, rounding out one of its rougher edges, making right what nature had wronged…

Listen to yourself.

Dimly, Arthur knew he had felt such passion long before. The memory thundered against the horizon of his mind. The act of drawing, this cathartic exodus of pent-up imaginative energies ("God Juice," Jim had once called it) seemed to open a tiny passage to that other side and that other being he had become in the hospital.

How detached from his body he'd felt, in that eternal moment—lighter, cleaner, far more lucid in sense and memory. A place of no time, a place that felt as seamless and as motionless as submersion in a swimming pool, where the ends of one's individuality were no longer very distinct and the body blended and floated and was light. For months Arthur had carried that place, that feeling, with him but its memory was no match for the world, which was slowly filling him back up with the person he once was, a process ironically compounded by his frustrating pursuit of the answer to his experience, and his partial wish to be back there while still remaining here—as well as his fear that either an actual answer, or no answer, remained inevitable.

The anxiety, too, made a slow return. Thankfully he had yet to endure a full attack, but the more the fear and the frustration mounted, the more he could feel it coming, bladed whips at his consciousness. He didn't want to return to popping the occasional pill, but realized that if it got worse he may not have a choice.

He filled five pages. When rounding out his final sketch, one of the Governor's Palace itself, a voice behind him broke his reverie.

"That's magnificent."

Startled, he turned. An elderly woman stood over him with a pleasant expression. He blinked and looked back at the sketch. Mild tingling crept up his cheeks. "Thank you," Arthur murmured.

The woman smiled and continued along the sidewalk.

Not magnificent.

But not terrible, either.

How did I do that?

HE WALKED BACK the route to his apartment, then drove to his house in Kingsmill. Reconstruction seemed to be coming along faster than expected. Half the first floor had been finished, including the library, the bedroom and a large portion of the living room. He strolled through the progress and felt larger than himself. He spoke more with the foreman and some of the construction crew and, as he headed back to his car, on a whim Arthur reopened his sketchbook to a blank page, sat on the lawn and began sketching the incomplete home.

⁂

When Arthur entered Jim's apartment he saw David in the kitchen, arms crossed and leaning against the counter and staring off nowhere as a frozen dish spun in the microwave.

"Hey, Art," David said, scarcely moving his head. Then he did a full double take, and with a sly subtle grin said, "Forget something?"

"No." Arthur deposited his sketchbook and pencils on the kitchen table and hung his jacket on the chair.

"Jim is still with Natalie, I think," David said.

The microwave beeped and David carefully fetched his steaming tray, setting it down at the table where Arthur sat as well.

"I know Jim's gone," Arthur said. "I actually wanted to talk to you, if you have a second."

"Um, yeah, sure. What is it?" David's brow furrowed. An air of assured control and strength tempered his look of concern.

"It's something I think I should tell you," Arthur said. "I've been going back and forth on whether or not to say something, but I don't think it'd be right of me to keep it from you."

"Is this your near-death experience?"

Arthur stared at him, somehow both surprised and not. "Jim told me you—"

"Saw you, yeah, on the couch." David stabbed at his dish, a plate of what looked like tuna casserole, and blew on a forkful. That appearance of control appeared to wane in his expression, replaced by growing anxiousness. His leg shook. "Sorry, didn't mean to interrupt."

"That's alright."

"You were saying?"

What am I saying? For a brief and embarrassing moment Arthur experienced one of those blank-outs, a hyperawareness of choosing the right words that paralyzed all speech. This had happened before in interviews, but never in personal conversation, not that he could remember.

Over a few interminable seconds, he retaught himself English.

"It wasn't a typical near-death experience," Arthur said. "I mean, in some ways it was. But..."

And he explained the detachment from his body, the high and soft and unencumbered feeling and the trip—*the float?*—down the hospital corridor and seeing Jim and Natalie and David himself fidgeting, heads bowed in the depths of the waiting-room cushions. He spoke of Annabelle Eubanks and of the essence that he had felt in passing and the sense of release and then the newspaper article that he had found, complete with her smiling photo so ignorant of all that would befall her.

David sat there, fork still, eyes fastened shut. For a second Arthur wished he could suck back all he'd just said.

"So the woman you saw," David said, "did actually die."

"I don't say any of this conclusively," Arthur said. "I could have glimpsed her before somehow and incorporated her into some lucid dream I had—"

"No, stop," David said. "Don't strain to explain away or backpedal on this. You saw her, you saw her naked and you never knew this woman, who you know died the very day you almost did."

"Maybe I shouldn't have told you."

"No, sorry. I'm glad you did."

"I just figured, perhaps, with all you've been through, it might..."

"Be comforting," David said. "I get it. Thanks, Art. Really."

Arthur couldn't shake the whiff of spite, even sarcasm, in David's tone. The young man was trying to be genuine and maybe was, to some extent, but in him swords were drawn, sharpened by emotion and by profession, by even his unsteady relationship with Arthur, and all were ready to cut down the significance to which Arthur alluded.

"I'm not sure death is the end anymore," Arthur said, startling even himself by saying such a thing so succinctly.

David took a bite of his casserole, his face pensive, even darkly playful.

"I know, it's strange to hear myself say that," Arthur continued. "That was partly why I hesitated in telling you. Because, well, it's me. Let those who're supposed to say stuff like that—pastors or counselors—say it. But I realized: it's also me." Arthur started to feel awkward, his tongue groping, navigating unstable ground, talking mostly to fill silence. "If I'm saying it...you know what I mean?"

"Sure, I know," David said. "And again, I appreciate it. I do."

"You don't really believe me, do you?"

"I believe you. I've encountered patients at school who've had similar things happen. Maybe not quite to your level. But some cases I think are clearly that of a deoxygenated brain and a biased imagination. Others are harder to get a bead on. I try not to think too hard about it."

"I get that."

David shifted in his chair, threw gazes between the far wall and the ceiling. "But if dead people are still alive somehow, in some form," he said, "and I've always said this, by the way, ever since my grandfather died when I was a kid...why don't they *show* themselves? Why do they just totally remove themselves from us? If they're still around, why couldn't they, hey, swing over for a visit? Chat it up? It just seems like a game, really, putting up an iron curtain between the living and the dead." He paused. "I know it's a dumb gripe, a *really* dumb gripe."

"We want control," Arthur said. "That's what Jim says of us science types."

"*Pffft*, fuck that," David said. "He's silly like that. He wants control, too. Why else would he try and throw the world on a canvas?"

"Touché," Arthur said. They lingered in silence for a moment. "I suppose it could be that, for those deceased, speaking to the living is like us speaking to someone asleep. Some of our words might seep through, affect their dreams, but unless we give them a good shake or speak loud enough, they won't wake up."

David rested his elbow on the table, his chin on his palm. "So, death is what jolts us awake?"

"The mind can maybe only take so many absurd dreams," Arthur said, "before it's had enough."

"Sure," David said, running his fingers through his hair. Idly he stabbed more casserole. "Sure."

THE DOOR TO THE LIBRARY conference room was open. Arthur walked in, smile consciously thin, making furtive glances to the people sitting at the folded-out tables over piles of potluck delights and talking or laughing in raucous tones. On the wall hung a banner that said "Merry Christless Christmas!" the words bracketed by candy canes in the shape of infinity symbols. The Virginia Atheists Society had grown in the past year or so—inversely correlative to Arthur's own decline in attendance—and he recognized few of the younger faces.

Gary Thomas, the novelist, saw him first and approached him.

"Art, this is a surprise," said Gary. "Steve told me you'd quit your membership."

There was an oasis of grace in Gary's dry heated eyes. I'm giving you a chance to explain yourself, it said, *and if you don't dammit, I'm going to get at it myself.*

"I did," Arthur said.

"I'm so sorry about what happened," he said. "Awful tragedy. But I'm certainly glad to know you're up and moving around and doing okay. You are rebuilding your house now, I assume? Where are you staying?"

"I am, yes," said Arthur. "I'm staying in an apartment for the time being. But I'm expanding the house a bit, shaving off some things, reworking it."

"That's good you're treating it positively," Gary said. His demeanor darkened. "We were all so scared for you. Do you remember our visit when you were in the hospital? Steve and Michael and I came. I'm only asking because you seemed rather...out of it when we were there."

Part of Arthur wanted him to elaborate on the definition of "out of it," but he just nodded. "Of course I remember your visit. Very appreciative."

Gary said, "So what's the deal? If I may ask."

"What deal?"

"You know, why did you quit? And are you coming back now?"

Arthur bit his lip. "No...I don't think I am. I just thought it'd be respectful to take a more formal leave."

Gary stopped chewing and looked at him. Another person came up beside Arthur. It was Steve Wallace, the society's husky president.

"The good doctor," said Steve as they shook hands. Arthur noticed Steve blinking rather profusely. "You're a sight for sore eyes."

"Thank you." Ironic, Steve's label of "good doctor," given the man himself had been a pediatrician for thirty years. "It's good to see you too. Both of you. I've needed time to myself. To just be and to collect my thoughts."

"Certainly I understand." Steve sipped his drink. "We care about you is all."

Or care about my sound bites.

"The thing is," Arthur said. "And I appreciate your words of support, I do. But, I'm moving with another tide, and I don't think my heart is in the society anymore."

"What did we do?" Steve said. "What can we improve?"

"It's nothing like that," Arthur said. "I just don't feel it's right for me and coming here would just make me feel..." His skull was a train-wreck of thoughts and notions. "It wouldn't make me feel right."

"Why?" Gary said.

He felt more and more eyes on him. Wondering, pondering eyes. Wanting to engage him, maybe, but too timid.

Get in, get out.

"I'm just tired, is all," said Arthur. "Tired of this."

Steve's face fell. He leaned in closer to Arthur. "You said you want to be left alone, right? You know they're talking about you out there. Speculating."

"I know. I don't care. I have nothing to say to them."

"Well what happens when it's announced that you abandoned the society? What then? Rumor flames will be fanned even more so."

Abandoned. A large worm had squirmed to life inside Arthur's stomach. "So?" he said. "Why would that even be announced?"

Steve's eyes challenged. "Why wouldn't it?"

Arthur shook his head. "You know what, do what you will. I'm done. I'm sorry."

"What's the matter?"

"You guys have stopped," Arthur said. "And I realized I'm still going."

Arthur turned and started toward the exit. Steve spoke

after him.

"I don't know what to do with that, Arthur."

He stopped in the doorway and took a deep breath, those words rattling ghost chains in his mind, his memory.

I don't know what to do with that, Jim.

Then he left.

⚘

Drifting into the Newport News airport, Linda eased up on the gas. Through the sparse crowds she spotted Sonia waiting on a stone bench, looking at once vulnerable and utterly indifferent with her legs crossed and eyes focused on the tiny electric pool of her cell phone screen. Probably texting Ferdinand, who had opted to spend Christmas in Spain.

Linda pulled to the curb and waited for Sonia to glance up, observing Sonia with a playful smile as her daughter's thumbs hopped over the keys, as if getting the message off in time to beat some apocalyptic deadline. When Sonia finished, she kept the phone in her palm and peered off to her left, watching for her mother's car. It took effort on Linda's part to not stretch it out.

"Honey!" Linda called through the open passenger window. "Right here!"

Sonia snapped out of her trance, saw Linda and gathered her lone bag and piled it in the back. She climbed into the passenger's seat and they hugged.

"I'm so glad you decided to come out for Christmas, too," Linda said. "I know that's a lot of flying."

"Yeah, seriously," Sonia said. "Ferdinand's with his family and he's still scared to introduce me, apparently."

So I'm Plan B? "How was your flight?" Linda asked. "Or flights."

"Mostly spent wishing Ferdinand was next to me instead of the overgrown swine that smelled like potatoes." Sonia pulled brusquely at the knot on her scarf. "I spent eight hours next to him."

"That's too bad," Linda said with a light flourish, a sad smile.

"This is our first week apart," Sonia said. "First week and a half, technically."

Linda found herself torn between empathy—certainly she remembered that wrenching first time apart from her first real boyfriend—and a twisted little burning hope that this break might impede their relationship, or at least remind Sonia that she could still function without a man at her hip.

"To make things even worse, my seat was next to the bathroom," Sonia continued. "Thank God I couldn't smell anything, but the toilet was broken or something and it kept flushing every five minutes with this huge whoooosh sound and was seriously so annoying."

Linda didn't say anything as she merged onto the highway, her mind scrambling for a topic that would cool her daughter's fire.

"I enjoyed that letter you sent out," Linda said sweetly, "the one about Santa describing the symbols behind Christmas. How the needles of the tree point heavenward. How the red symbolizes lifeblood. How candy canes are shaped like a shepherd's cane."

"When did I send it?"

"A couple days ago."

A musical alert chimed and Sonia scrambled in her purse, bringing out her phone.

"Sorry, Ferdinand's texting me."

Linda waited while her daughter clicked back a response, then glanced out the window at the passing pines and long gray clouds. "What are we doing on Christmas?" Sonia asked. "We're going to service right?"

"My friend Arthur told me he's going to have a little get-together on Christmas Eve. So I thought we could have dinner there and then go to Grace. They're holding a communion service and a choral concert."

"Okay."

"What about—?" Sonia started before another text message chimed into her phone. "Hold on."

Linda kept driving.

Another minute and Sonia resurfaced. "What was I saying?"

"I don't know, honey," Linda said.

✂

Arthur forewent putting up a Christmas tree. He hadn't had one in many years. He did adorn the apartment with some decorations—Santa figurines, stockings and a string of icicle lights he'd purchased in Jamestown, which he hung on the mantel. For food, he set up a buffet table with items from the grocery market. Jeff had promised to bring something, too. For the final ambient accent, he set up a five-year-old boom box and CD player and put on the only Christmas disc he had found that survived the fire.

Despite many outside assumptions, Christmas had never been a point of contention. People, of course, needed ritual. Ritual was basic. And in its ideals Christmas hardly ranked among humankind's worst. Arthur had said, too, rather infamously, that after so much "overly fantastic lathering" and "competing fairy stories"—Christ's virgin birth, Santa Claus, flying reindeer, elves, the ostentatious decor, the commercialism—the holiday had, in an odd way, become de facto secular.

The doorbell rang. Arthur opened the door and Jim and David stood there. He greeted them with hugs.

"Art," David said, patting his back. "Never knew you as a hugging man."

"He's a softy around the holidays," Jim said.

"I can be," Arthur said. "Help yourself to the food." He gestured to the buffet table, behind which hung Jim's cosmic Myshkin piece. He noticed his son looking at it. "Thought that could be a good place for it," he said. "How's it look?"

Jim smiled. "Don't ask me that question. As the person responsible, I'm apt to list a million things wrong with it. But I like where you put it."

Jeff showed up and made room on the table for his culinary contributions, a berry pie and a kind of spinach casserole, in the process thundering a "Merry Christmas" in his caricatured jolly voice. Natalie arrived not ten minutes later; Arthur hugged her and they kissed one another on the cheeks. They paused, smiled. A dull, rejuvenating ecstasy filled him like a physical thing as he took in everyone's presence.

Linda and Sonia showed up last. Some introductions went around. Linda greeted Arthur with a necklace she'd made for him, putting it on like a Hawaiian lei. She gave one to Natalie and to Jim as well.

"Where's mine huh?" Jeff said.

"It's coming," Linda said, blushing a bit.

Meanwhile, Sonia walked, arms crossed, among the small crowd. Throughout the night, she kept diligent worship of her cell phone. She spoke first with Jim, probably by generational default as they were of similar age.

He saw Natalie in the kitchen, going through the cutlery drawer. He approached her.

"Where do you keep the bottle opener?" she asked.

"Here." He showed her and she thanked him.

"How are you?" he asked.

Natalie sighed, looking tired but pleased. "I'm alright. Still writing a lot. Of course the return to smoking helped with that. The nicotine sets off a lightning storm in my head when I'm at my laptop."

As if following the gesture of an invisible third party, they both turned their heads toward the living room, where Jeff and Linda stood with drinks in their hands, talking by the mantel. Linda laughed at something Jeff had whispered. Arthur cocked his head, unaware of the last time he'd heard Linda laugh.

"I've almost finished reading *Divine Dialogues*," said Arthur. "It's a very…nourishing read. Interesting. You can tell this Valentine guy just opened a vein on the page."

Natalie gave a wan smile. She chewed her thumbnail. Arthur noticed a sudden hesitance in her. "He used to say he was an archeologist of the self. Of himself, too."

"That seems an appropriate description." Arthur made a circular motion with his hand, as he tried to conjure what next to say. "Definitely feels like the guy touched some kind of higher plane."

"We share that higher plane, I think," Natalie said. "We all have the keys to it. Some of us just misplace those keys."

Arthur nodded thoughtfully.

"I'm glad you like the book," Natalie said. She leaned forward and placed her palms on his temples. Arthur thought she might lean in and kiss him. "But don't analyze too much."

"Says you."

"Right." Natalie lowered her arms. "Says me."

There was a pause, during which both glanced out toward the living room.

"By the way," Natalie said, "I sent in Jim's sample sketches to my editor. I should hear back sometime this week actually if they'll consider using his work in my book. I'm certainly fighting for it."

"Wonderful," Arthur said. "Thank you so much, Nat."

"Don't thank me," she said. She started past him, stroked his arm. "You've got a very talented son."

"I know," he said, his eyes intuitively searching out Jim, David and Sonia chatting across the room.

Arthur thought to ask Natalie what might be bothering her, but refrained.

$$\mathcal{X}$$

"Stop and think for a moment," said Reverend Matthews from the pulpit. Candles lined the altar and flanked the congregation, aglow in shadow play. "It's incredible to think God would extend such a caring hand, his Love, to a place so tiny, a tiny planet in a tiny galaxy. His love is so much greater than anyone can imagine that he gave us His Son, so that we may not live as tiny specks in darkness and sin. He wants us forever in his luminescent embrace..."

Linda listened in earnest, but she found her attention slippery. Beside her, a stiff and rigid Sonia stared straight ahead in a way that seemed unnatural. Several heads to her left she saw Marilyn, eyes closed in a meditative way as she took in Matthews' words; her husband Victor sat in grave countenance, his arms folded. To Linda, the church was filled with people who seemed so solemn, more commemorative than celebratory.

"When we share the gospels and praise God," Matthews continued, "we engage in the ecstasy of the shepherds..."

Linda found her thoughts drifting to Jeffrey Howes, to the enjoyable dinner they'd had after the Mark Gavin bombout, to their various chats thereafter, freshest of all being their time at Arthur's Christmas gathering. There seemed an easiness about Jeff's manner that Linda found refreshing, a thread of humor in everything he said that, whether thick or thin, was always there. Through Jeff, she could find consistent reassurance that things would be okay.

What, she thought suddenly, *would Jeff see in you?* He and Natalie Farrow weren't together anymore, she knew. Whether or not it had anything to do with her night with Arthur in September, she couldn't be sure, but she had sensed no real bitterness between them.

The choral concert began with "Silent Night," the congregation standing to join in song. The voices hummed and swirled together in a single harmonious lift. Linda put an arm around her daughter's shoulder and felt Sonia stiffen further, uncomfortable with her touch. Her daughter's face remained buried in her songbook—but only then did Linda notice the tiny glowing screen of her cell phone, as Sonia's ever-furious thumbs pecked out a message in Spanish.

NEARLY TWO HOURS PAST MIDNIGHT, Linda awoke with a dry throat. She put on her bathrobe and walked in a lethargic haze to the kitchen to fill a glass of water, taking great pains not to stub her toes along the darkened hallway.

Returning to her room, she noticed a swatch of light beneath Sonia's door. *It's so late,* she thought. Linda couldn't quell the instinct that had her gently tapping the door.

"Honey, are you okay? Are you still awake?" She caught a faint scent of cigarette smoke and again rapped softly. "Sonia?"

"Hey, Mom," said a reticent voice within. "What is it? What are you doing up?"

"Just got some water." She opened the door. Sonia sat at the window, where the screen was open and a cigarette smoldered in an ashtray on the windowsill. Linda pushed the door open the rest of the way and the temperature of the room—about twenty degrees cooler than the rest of the house—made her shudder. "I didn't know you smoked."

"I don't smoke—usually," Sonia said. "Only when I'm upset."

"Why are you upset?"

Sonia scowled at the cell phone in her hand. She took a quick drag and exhaled into the night.

"I've been waiting for Ferdinand to come back online," she said. On her desk, her laptop sat glowing and patient. "We were Skyping and he said he would be right back."

Linda rubbed sleep residue from her eye. "How long ago was that?"

Sonia hesitated, her gaze darkening. "Like an hour."

"Oh, honey, go to bed. You can talk to him tom—"

"No! He's coming back. He'd better come back. I don't see what he could be doing. He said he'd be back. I hate it when guys do this."

Linda brushed a strand of hair from her daughter's cheek. With a tired smile, she remarked, "Well, you'd better get to bed before Santa comes."

Sonia scrunched her face. "Mom, please stop, okay? Totally not in the mood." She began furiously tapping out another message on her cell. Linda turned to leave when Sonia said, "By the way."

"Yes?"

"Speaking of Santa—I looked up Arthur Moore."

"You did."

"Yes. I thought he looked familiar. He's got quite a story going."

"Yes," Linda explained. "He's an extraordinary person." She wanted to add *in some ways*, but refrained.

"What were you doing with him in the first place?" Sonia said.

Linda hesitated. "He's a good person, Sonia."

In some ways.

"He's an atheist, mother. I mean, not only that, he makes a living at it. He writes books and speaks about denouncing God. What were you thinking?"

"Don't we need people like him," Linda said, "to test and to affirm our faith?"

Sonia drew on the cigarette, the flame tip glowing and crackling. In a burst of smoke, she said, "Our faith is always tested and always affirmed. At least it's affirmed for those who truly believe. But there's no use, no excuse, for being intimate with someone who thinks like that. It doesn't make sense. Mom…"

"What, Sonia?"

"Okay, I know this might sound…whatever," Sonia flipped her hand in the air, "but I ask this honestly, and I mean it: if you died tonight, wouldn't you want to go to heaven?"

"Oh Sonia, for goodness' sake…"

"For *your* sake, mother. For *your* sake. And mine. I mean, why did you even stop dating him? I read about the fire. I hate to say he deserved it, but I hope he took it as the sign it probably was."

"Goodnight Sonia," Linda said, closing the door behind her.

Half-clothed, David strode from the bathroom, toothbrush jutting from his mouth. He approached Jim, who sat at the kitchen table roughing out gesture sketches of male and female bodies in dynamic, suggestive poses.

"I just got the official confirmation," Jim said. "Natalie said Lunar agreed to use my drawings."

"That's fantastic," David said, jerking the brush around

his teeth. "I'm so proud of you."

"Thanks," Jim said. "I feel like I need to bone up on my life-drawing skills. Haven't done as many things in the human form in the last year. And Natalie's book is nothing but the human form."

"The book is about sex, right?"

"Pretty much. Actually it's a little hard to do all these without getting turned on every few minutes."

"I can imagine." David walked to the kitchen sink to spit and clean his brush. He turned and watched Jim for a long moment. "And, hey, I get the hint."

"What hint?"

"I know we've had a dry spell for a while. I've just been exhausted. Between school and everything else that's happened lately I just don't have room for sex in my brain right now."

"I know," Jim said, keeping his eyes on the page. "I kinda figured."

"It's nothing to do with you, Jim. You should know that."

"I do. But I haven't been very aggressive lately because I know you've been so, well, distracted."

"Right." David smiled, walked over and kissed the top of his head. "Thanks."

"What are we doing for New Year's, by the way?"

"What would you like to do?"

"My Dad said Jeff's having a little get-together," Jim said. "But we don't have to go of course."

"I was thinking we could have a little fun here," said David, whose smile revealed more light than it had in the last month. "Just us."

"I could go for that. Sure."

"Great." David turned for the bedroom. "I'm going to crash. Night. Love you."

"Love you too. G'night."

The bedroom door closed. Jim replayed the last ten minutes in his head, his smile lingering as his aching hand brought the graphite anatomy to life on the pages before him.

The wind snapped cold and wet on the final evening of the year, the trees stiffened like the arms of old men reaching skyward in death. Though light snow had fallen in the morning, by mid-afternoon many of the clouds had moved on, granting the sun hours of warming input before it took its leave in a silent, crimson frenzy.

New Year's at Jeff's was a small affair, a smattering of choice friends and clients. Save for some glancing conversations with acquaintances about his house or appearances and books, Arthur managed to keep primarily to the circle of Jeff, Linda and Natalie, and as midnight closed in everyone watched the screen as the ball sat there high above Times Square, poised and glowing and ready while thousands of frantic hands flailed and waved like windblown leaves of grass.

As the final minute of the year ticked toward to twelve, Natalie leaned in close to Arthur.

"Do you think of that old 'calendar year allegory' every time at New Year's too?" she said.

Arthur wrinkled his brow, his eyes still on the screen. "The what?"

"That old thing where they crunch the entire history of Earth into one calendar year," Natalie said. "Where the first bacteria develops in May, and the dinosaurs roll out sometime in December."

"Ah, right. No, can't say I've thought of that."

"Because you remember where we make our entrance?"

On the TV the ball flared to life and began its descent. The entire room erupted in a shout of "Ten ...nine...!"

"We come in the last ten seconds of the year, right?" said Arthur.

"...five!..."

Natalie tipped her glass toward him. "Well, all of written history comes in the last ten seconds."

"Got it."

"...two!..."

"Here's to the next ten seconds," Natalie said.

The room shouted "Happy New Year!" in unison. The wide-smiling people began to mingle, going for their spouse or the closest person to usher in the first moment of the infant year. Natalie noticed Linda and Jeff hug and share a quick, formal kiss. Then Arthur touched champagne glasses with her, his eyes warm, like twin lit hearths. After momentary hesitation, they embraced.

V

HE TRIED TO SHUT OUT EVERYTHING ELSE around him and within him, to align his thoughts solely behind the sight in front of him: Natalie, her head on the pillow, eyes closed and so receptive and so willing (*for me?* some incredulous part of Arthur would always think, of every woman he'd been with), her splayed hair forming rays of black sunshine across the white space of the linens. The smooth candied touch of her nude skin on his.

As well as he could with a half-hard penis, Arthur maneuvered himself deeper and deeper into her. Natalie responded with tenuous pleasure and affectionate understanding. Arthur was grateful though self-conscious. *She's so patient.* He could tell his sexual energy was returning, however incrementally. To his relief, he felt more "animal" tonight. Arthur attributed his last bout of impotence with Natalie more to the suddenness of their actions, where they had just collapsed into one another like gravity-bound objects. Yet even if Natalie's words that night had been meant to assuage him, they continued now to provide a haunting background chorus.

You're not totally back in this world.

"Let's try something," she said, as they lay curled in her bed. "Lie flat on your back." Her fingers orbited a teasing path above his genitalia. "Close your eyes. Be still. Just feel it, absorb it. Don't try to build up into climax. Just take it as it comes. Narrow your thoughts on the sensation."

Finally her fingers landed on his penis. She stroked the head, then moved with silken caresses down the sides, finding and enflaming every nerve ending. In a mad riotous rush, all energy flowed to his loins and Arthur grew.

"Again, just try to focus on every bit of touch," Natalie said. "Not the endpoint."

Methodically she touched him, her tender firmness that of a sculptor plying clay. Arthur felt something of a groundswell in him. His ears filled with the excited chatter of the trillions of molecules making him. The parade of sensations was familiar, but not at this tempo: this was sex in slow motion, due glimpses of every nuance and moment normally passed in a crude grunt or thrust or streak of sweat.

"It's called orgasmic meditation," Natalie said, softly. "It's supposed to elevate your senses, disperse the sexual energy to other areas of your mind and body to increase awareness. And contentment."

Natalie quickened her pace. The fault line of his imminent orgasm rumbled, amassed in unprecedented power.

"I'm close," he exhaled.

Ever so slightly, she slowed, squeezing tighter. He came and the climax was like none he'd experienced before. Deep cleansing pulses. Invigorating. His whole interior cooling and misting like a hot surface splashed with water. Natalie withdrew and he lay there, eyes closed, mind rinsed.

"Can I do you?" Arthur asked, feeling a little like a sheepish teenager.

"You don't have to."

"I want to."

He tried to ignore her expression of amused doubt as she herself lay on her back and began issuing guidance, which mildly embarrassed Arthur.

"Slow down," she said. "Start around the area. Tease. Good."

He tickled, rubbed, began probing. The only saving grace for him now, the only thing that kept it from feeling like he was failing a medical exam he wasn't supposed to be taking, was Natalie's moans, those nourishing reminders of her pleasure. Her instructions waned and the breathing increased and Arthur kept on till her body seized and she cried out, eyes shut, the hand once caressing the back of his neck now clenching his shoulder. Arthur had never climaxed a woman with just his hand.

They lay next to one another. Minutes slid by. Gratified exhaustion eddied into Arthur. For a long moment he lingered in that twilight between consciousness and sleep, thoughts and memories flowing over his mind's eye.

"Are you okay?" she asked softly, resting her chin on his shoulder.

"Just thinking," Arthur said. "I haven't told you this, but you know the day we saw Jim's mural?"

"Yeah."

"We had a discussion afterwards, he and I. He told me

he's had strange experiences."

"Strange experiences. I'm gonna need more."

"Psychic moments."

Natalie sat up. "Oh yeah?"

"As far as I know, he's only had a couple episodes in his life, right before very, how do I say, odious circumstances. Deep gut feelings of something bad about to happen."

"And it did? Happen?"

"Apparently."

"I think everyone has intuitive capabilities," Natalie said. "We all start in psychic preschool, we all have the tools between our ears. Only a few go on to higher grades. And of course within one grade are several varying degrees of ability, just as one fourth grader might read better than another in his or her class."

"Are you still in elementary school then?"

Natalie laughed. "I don't know. I think I've lost touch with my abilities over the years since I was little, and since I was with Neil Valentine. I devoted my energy to writing. When you're writing, you're thinking, and when you're thinking, you're not doing and you're not being. I've analyzed myself out of my stronger intuitive talents, in a way. They were clearest, I think, when I was a kid."

An unspoken memory floated in Natalie's wistful eyes. Arthur asked, "What happened when you were a kid? If you don't mind me asking."

She slid down beside him again, propped on an elbow. "I've always been pretty hesitant to talk about this," she said. "It was something I was so readily acceptant of as a kid, so maybe that's partly why I think it's difficult for me to accept as an adult. But…when I was around six I started getting visits from a girl named Amanda. She just walked into my room one afternoon. I didn't question her, really. I remember feeling that it was right that she was there. I wasn't sure where she came from. Neither was she.

"So," Natalie continued. "You know both my parents were Irish Catholic, practicing and worshipping regularly. Several years before I was born, my mother got pregnant for the first time. The child was a stillborn. A baby girl. They were both devastated, of course, and that's when their marriage started fracturing. My mother tried to find solace in God while my father pulled away from the church. At least that's the story my mother told me. They tried again a few years later, though, and here I am.

"But the marriage didn't last. By the time I was seven, my parents were through with one another. I thought for a long time that they'd had me as a way of reinforcing their union, assuming that having a kid would ensure they stick together. I still sort of suspect that. My dad would leave for a while and my mom would never tell me where he went, just that he needed to be by himself and that it had nothing to do with me. They were bothered by something, and I didn't know what but my lack of knowing soon haunted me and I became a sullen kid, and way too paranoid for my age."

Natalie lay back down, gaze trained on the ceiling, then continued. "It was around Thanksgiving—I remember because I was shut up in my room and shy about seeing the guests—and this young girl named Amanda came to me. She just…appeared out of nowhere. I didn't know her. But she told me she was my big sister. She was a few years older than me. She said she was nine.

"I told my mom that Amanda was visiting me. Her face fell, like I'd punched her in the gut. 'Who?' she asked. 'Amanda, my big sister.' Really, she was dumbstruck. My parents tried to deny or hide the issue, hoping, I think, that my remark was a fluke soon forgotten, but eventually my mom finally admitted that 'Amanda' was the name they were going to give to my sister who died very, very young."

"How much did you tell them of the visits?"

"Not too much. When I saw how hurt it made them, I actually backpedaled a bit and said I'd dreamed that she visited me. But my mom became so upset, I didn't tell them anything else—that I saw Amanda after that, many times over the next few years. I don't think she ever aged during those years she visited me, and she always wore the same blue dress. Sometimes my mom would hear me talking but I always told her it was make-believe."

"Couldn't bring yourself to tell them the whole story?"

Quickly Natalie threw up her hands. "I sort of intuited then, and realize now, that I didn't want to shatter their world. I learned pretty early on that some people of faith can be terribly frightened of confronting the unknown, even if it's something potentially supportive of their faith. My dad seemed almost fascinated by what I told them, though he avoided probing the subject because it was hurtful for him as well. Just reminded him of the loss, I suppose. But a lot of believers tend to keep an emotional buffer between themselves and the supernatural. They prefer to believe things are waiting *out there* rather than knowing or experiencing them. It's too scary."

"Or they're afraid of being proved wrong, in whatever way."

"True."

"What did Amanda say of her...situation?" Arthur asked.

"I asked her where she lived," Natalie said. "If she had any friends. If there really is a God. Mostly we were just little girls in need of companionship. The times we did talk about God, she had some insight, but honestly not much more than I did. But she was still wise, much wiser than her age, because she was *comfortable* not knowing. And that's what made her wise.

"I think I asked her once if God was real. She said to me, 'Are you real?' I said yes. So she said, 'Then isn't God real?' I asked if she was real, and she answered, 'Not any more or less real than you.' I got lost after that. But I remember asking her once if God was a man. She said kind of, and told me that he was both good and evil.

"Good and evil?" Natalie went on. "I didn't get that. Not at the time. Over the next couple years, I took this to confirm what the Bible said about divine judgment and all that, and so for another ten years or so I became a pretty regular Catholic until I had a...hmm, I don't know, an enlightened moment, I guess. Sounds cheesy. Most people gradually tinker with new ideas until all aspects of the old way of thinking are discarded. I think I'd been subconsciously discarding ideas for a long time, and building up new ones to replace them. Then, one day, I found myself suddenly illuminated by all that had been brewing inside when my mind decided I was ready to handle some new ways of thinking and looking at things. And there was one silly, stupid environmental trigger for that."

"And that was...?"

Natalie hesitated. "The smell of peanut butter."

Arthur studied her, eyebrow raised.

"It's true," she said, laughing. "I'd grown up in my hometown my whole life, until my mom sent me away to boarding school. Visitors told me how my town smelled like peanut butter but I could never smell it since I'd always lived there. But whenever I came home from boarding school, I smelled it immediately."

"I see."

"The story of the peanut butter smell is how I see Eden. We didn't recognize paradise when we were there, because it was all we knew. Nothing to compare it to. But taking an earthly detour, into this world of the crying and suffering and diseased, then returning to paradise…well, we see it right away. So I began to understand what Amanda meant about God being both good and evil. You need evil to see good. More, evil is the tool that chisels good into form, makes it a thing at all. And God is everything, even the yang. Light and dark: the primal equation, the age-old contrast."

Outside, Arthur could hear the wind hastening.

"You don't have to believe all that," Natalie said. "But it's what happened."

"I believe you," Arthur told her.

Natalie's smile was light as she brushed her fingers through her hair.

"It's a little strange with me," Arthur said. "I don't think I ever really grew in my opinions."

Natalie frowned. "What do you mean?"

"I don't mean that pejoratively, that I never grew. I mean my innate setting was always doubt, but I hesitate to call it 'doubt' because that implies a reasoned pushback or picking apart of something. It was more that, from the very beginning, I just assumed the idea of God was untrue, that my church going and God worship with Mom was a phase that would eventually end. I wish I could cite some grand epic turning point where I became who I was, but I can't. People sometimes assume it was John's death that started me off on atheism and things, but it wasn't. I never turned. I just was."

"Interesting," Natalie said, "that your mom, religious as you've said she was, could never break through to you."

"Pretty much. I felt sorry for her, later. Still kind of do."

"What about your brother, John?"

"Do you mean whether or not he shared my belief system?"

She nodded.

"He was a bit like me, actually. Mom kept trying to set

our eyes forward on the pulpit, but we were too slippery and too distracted wanting to do our own things, whatever preoccupied us in the moment. We had weekly or daily gods: the fort by the stream, the dead frog in the grass, our guns we whittled from logs and sticks. Any actual or proper god was too distant and permanent. But John believed in God, I think, at first, and he believed sincerely. When I was eleven or so, he asked me if I thought if Mom thought we were going to hell. I asked why God would send us two kids to hell, before we could even prove ourselves. He said God could probably see the future and what we'd become. I said, 'Can you ask God if I'm gonna be rich?' He just lowered his head, but he was smiling."

Arthur cleared his throat. Natalie studied him.

"Whatever belief John had, it was short-lived. We didn't talk about it much. He kept up appearances for Mom's sake, longer than I did. He might've convinced himself he still actually believed. According to him, it was simply age and experience that weaned him off religion, though he was always far more sympathetic than I was to the idea of God's existence. I remember when I told him about my first book, while I was writing it. John asked me, 'Is this your public shaming of Mom?' I told him of course it wasn't. I told him the truth—the book was about the encroachment of the religiously tendentious into our public spheres. He didn't seem to buy that.

"Years later, John became quietly agnostic, of his own volition. Nothing to do with my book or my success, of course. 'It's the only rational stance in an answerless universe,' he once said. He wanted to get me to drop my designation as an 'atheist.' I said, 'Why? It just means a lack of a god.' He said, 'I know, but *you* know it means, or seems to mean, way more than that.' He was right, of course, and I knew that, as well. 'You're such a devotee of God,' John told me, 'that his Word is not enough for you.'"

"Huh," Natalie said. "I actually like that. He was joking, of course, right?"

"Yes, of course. And I saw his point then and I see it now. The two broad reasons why religion attracts people are its codes and structures for daily living, and its claim to ultimate answers. As many problems as I have with the various codes and structures, my biggest problem is with the conceit that religion explains anything about the origin and the reason of existence. No faith does. They kick off with, 'God made it all,' then roll right into the codes and structures and ethics. Well, back up, I say. *Why* did God make it all? And how?"

"Kind of ties back to what I was saying," Natalie said, "about religious people being afraid of the unknown."

"Right," Arthur said. "And I do understand that fear. I'm afraid of the unknown. It's natural. But we can either sit in bed imagining the monster, or thrust open the closet door and shine a light in there and see for ourselves that there's no monster there."

"God's a monster?" Natalie said, smile intact.

"No, I didn't mean that." Arthur sighed. "You know—"

Natalie was about to speak, but stopped. "Sorry, go ahead."

He idly caressed her bare knee. "I've read about people who wake up from near-death experiences with heightened abilities. Like psychic senses. Even seeing others who are dead, at least for the time being. As you saw Amanda."

"That didn't happen for you," Natalie said, the tone falling between a question and observation.

"No," Arthur said. "At least, I don't think so."

Natalie shifted her position. "Well, as I said before, I think everyone has the psychic muscle. They just don't exercise it, and are quick to suppress it. Mostly subconsciously. And they're also quick to deny others who haven't suppressed it. A legitimate psychic may indeed give you a telling that turns out to be wrong. It's not because they're a fraud, or even that they were wrong—it's because you took a path that didn't end up the way the psychic saw it. Usually they only see one possible branch of the future, not *the* future. Because there is no one path." Natalie moved closer to him, put her arm across his chest. "As you've always said, only you are in control."

They made their way into the airport, the crowds like colorful froth in a roiling anxious sea. *Going to fly.* Arthur tightened his grip on his suitcase, recalling when he was a child at Pennsylvania's Hershey Park, and the lumps in his stomach and throat that grew and grew the closer each step brought him to his first roller coaster.

"When's your interview with Eggert tomorrow, again?" Arthur asked.

"Eight a.m.," Natalie said.

"Wow, the first hour," he said. "I was put on near the tail end."

The words he spoke were distant echoes against the din of his whirring mind. He was flying. *Flying.* For the first time in years and years.

You're past this. You're past all this now.

You're only going to Pittsburgh.

Then, another thought, surprising for how true it rang: *You're not actually here.*

It doesn't matter.

Fragments of former Arthurs befell him. The brambles were thickening, knotting in irrevocable twine over the pathway to that peace that had so recently—and seemingly so briefly—opened within him. He longed to go back there, to reassure himself that the peace had been real, from a real source, and hadn't just been the desperate firing of dying neurons. The peace had certainly felt more real than any sensation he derived here among trees and buildings and sky.

Natalie took his hand in hers as they moved up the escalator. Her touch felt soft, warm over his nerves. They went through the security station, during which a heavy-eyed female TSA agent approached Arthur and waved him down with the wand. Watching her work, Arthur knew a sudden and mysterious surge of compassion, and he suppressed an urge to embrace her and to tell her it—whatever "it" was—would be alright.

They approached the gate and sat down. "How are you doin'?" Natalie asked him.

"I'm okay," he said. "I'm actually not as nuts as I might have expected. My brain must be getting better at overriding my gut."

"Wasn't it your brain that infected your gut with those thoughts in the first place?" said Natalie. "You're just conditioned, I'm sure."

Says the writer to the psychologist.

Natalie slid her hand through his and Arthur placed a hand atop hers. Watching the crowds streaming, trotting, bustling, every passing expression a lid over an individual human cosmos, aroused a kind of awe in him, and he imagined a grand unseen tissue connecting everyone and all things, a gargantuan organ, the very Parts of which unwittingly worshipped the Sum. Leaves in reverence of the tree.

They boarded, Arthur taking a window seat. He realized that he couldn't even remember when he'd flown last.

Doesn't matter.

He sat, eyes closing in long blinks. Breath came hard.

Natalie's hand again found his and did not stray. Stewards, stewardesses, flight attendants, uniformed crewmembers, whatever their appropriate name now, bustled up and down the aisle, snapping overhead compartments and issuing stoic requests, and beneath it all whined the revving engine.

The plane lurched and began to taxi. Arthur exhaled. The plane positioned itself for takeoff, and Arthur's head fused to the cushion behind him. Natalie squeezed his hand tighter and Arthur heard the sudden roar of engines as the plane began to gain speed down the runway.

"Almost over," Natalie whispered. Arthur nodded furiously. Outside the earth sped by, the horizon slanted and then they were in the air rising high, piercing the white veil of clouds and emerging like a breaching whale into the unblemished blue. The sun flooded the cabin, a silent yellow lullaby that, in time, sent Arthur into a fragile sleep.

"ARTHUR?"

The voice. Above.

"Arthur, up here."

Johnny is perched on the branch, attired in his camouflage and layer of leaves and toting his BB gun and smiling mischievously down at him.

"John come on down from there."

"Not yet, not yet."

This time Arthur sees the crack in the branch, sees it widen, splinter, as John sits there scared and silent. He drops his gun to the forest floor and the leaves rustle off him as he tries to slowly make his way to safety, when suddenly the branch falls and John crashes to the earth.

Arthur screams as his brother strikes the rocks at the base of the tree. The woods don't react. Slowly, with mounting nausea, he approaches John and watches in terror as the child skin begins decaying, the flesh receding, the skeletal frame and crenellated earth emerging cold and crusty. And then at the peak of this morbid show the flesh and tissue grow back and smooth into place and the blood runs heated and the eyes return with embers of life, and then John's mouth opens in a gIt's likerin and he hears these two words:

"Just kidding."

⚬

The leaden weight of February gloom permeated Pittsburgh's avenues and alleys. Steam-like city breath issued from the concrete orifices. Snow dusted roads and rooftops.

"You handled Bill Eggert pretty well," Arthur said. He and Natalie sat in rain-dirtied lawn furniture outside Joe's Sandwich Shack. Far more the Pittsburgh veteran than she was, Arthur planned to take Natalie to three of his favorite eateries, all of them serving some variation of the Philly cheesesteak. Joe's was the fanciest, relatively speaking.

"Thanks," Natalie said, smirking. "Think I chose my words more carefully than you."

Arthur grinned, but it was shallow. Every once in a while he still received letters or emails regarding that unfortunate 'asinine country' remark, which now felt like it'd happened in some distant past life. "I think he was primed to be much more patient with you."

"Why?"

"You can tell just by the way he introduced you—'our beautiful guest today.' If he'd tossed in 'brainy' as well, I might give him a pass."

"Eh." Natalie waved him off, then lifted a stringy bit of meat from her cheesesteak. Her fingertips shone with grease. "By the way, isn't it more authentic to drive a few hours and have these things in Philly? If I'm pushing my arteries to the limit, I might as well have the real thing."

"These cheesesteaks are actually better than anything you'll get in Philly," Arthur said, "and we'll burn it off. I still have to take you to the Carnegie Museum."

"I wouldn't have thought you liked little hole-in-the-wall places like these."

"Why?"

"I don't know," Natalie said. "You just strike me as someone who might look for the health inspector's grade before going into a place."

"Pittsburgh and ball games are the two places I know-ingly let myself eat junk," Arthur said with a tint of pride, "but you can be a snob in some areas and freewheel it in others."

The casualness of this response pleased Natalie.

"Just think of it as adding blubber to our bodies to ward off the cold," Arthur said.

It's like we've just met, Natalie thought. *No monster dis-cussion—no obstacles. He's still confused, but it's not me.*

They sat eating for a few seconds before Natalie broke the greasy, napkin-patting silence.

"Listen, Art, I have a bit of a favor to ask."

"Sure."

"I didn't tell you this, and I apologize for it. But, a while back, actually right after we reconnected, um…Neil came to my apartment. Neil Valentine."

Arthur seemed only mildly surprised by the news, even affected a curiosity that felt faintly voyeuristic.

"It was pretty strange," Natalie said. "He explained to me where he'd been, what happened to the Mountain Wellness Center, how someone he knew on the streets had come back and was extorting him because he knew something Neil had done that might compromise his stature and the center—"

"What did he do? Neil, I mean."

Natalie hesitated. "I don't know, exactly," she said. "But

he was in bad straits, Art. He himself wouldn't say that, I don't think. He seems to think of it as a chance to recharge his spiritual self. He's in a place out in the woods here in Pennsylvania, he told me. I checked and it's only about forty minutes outside of Pittsburgh."

Arthur studied her. "You want to visit him?"

"Would you mind terribly?"

"No," he said. "No, we can go."

"Thank you. I just want to make sure he's okay, out there on his own. When he visited me, some aspect of him reminded me of a sheep scampering from the wolf. Like he might at any moment hurtle himself blindly over a cliff's edge."

"Nat," Arthur said, placing a hand on hers. "Let's go."

Natalie smiled. "Okay, I'll give him a call, once my fingers aren't sopping."

VI

AFTER LUNCH AT THE SPORTSMAN'S GRILL, Linda and Jeff took a walk down a wooded trail not far from her house. The stripped trees stood slanted, like the characters of some incoherent language etched upon the land. Linda had never taken this trail in winter and appreciated it anew. The trees seemed merely like slumbering souls who would awaken a few months from now in a burst of green rapture.

They discussed Sonia.

"I think I'm madder at myself for not understanding my daughter better," Linda said.

"It's not your fault," Jeff soothed her.

"Thanks. I don't know. Maybe I could have been there

more for her. Her dad's affair was traumatic for her. I think..." Linda chuckled. "Sounds silly, but I think that's why she sought almost a surrogate father in God."

Jeff made an agreeable frown. "I suppose you can't aim higher. Her God sounds abusive, though." He kicked a rock in his path. "Sorry, I couldn't help it."

Linda shrugged. "I'm sorry, I know this must sound petty."

"No, it doesn't."

"And it's probably boring, since you don't have kids."

"Nah," he said, "I live vicariously through other people's kid problems."

This time Linda made the agreeable frown.

"Although," Jeff said, "I do think the role-reversal here is interesting, and kind of ironic. One of my major pet peeves are the parents who think kids are little wind-up dolls, tiny versions of themselves they can mold or use to fill a hole in themselves. But in this case, it seems as if Sonia is trying to control you."

"Sure," Linda said. "Maybe not in the way she believes she is. But she's controlling a lot of my moods and thoughts. From five thousand miles away. I'm just tired of it."

Breath steaming in the cold, Jeff said, "Maybe she's upset that you're not upset."

"Wait," Linda said. "Run that by me again. How's that work?"

"Have you told her what you've been telling me? Maybe that could be the needle that pops the balloon. Come clean. Tell her the truth. Your truth."

Linda took this in. What Jeff proposed was not unreasonable, of course, though it did scare her. Sonia was brittle. Always Linda felt she had to tread lightly, and that too heavy a step would cause an irreversible fracture.

"By the way, I hope you don't mind my saying..." Linda

said.

"Shoot."

"I was sorry to hear about you and Natalie. She seems quite—"

"Spunky?"

Linda chuckled. "I was going to say nice. 'Spunky' sounds like you're describing a teenager."

"Words sometimes pop into my head and I say them. I can have an issue with filters."

"God bless that. We need fewer filters jamming everyone up."

"Sounds like you wouldn't mind a filter or two on Sonia, though."

"No," Linda said, "in a funny way I'm actually glad she's being herself with me. I'm just hoping this is a 'self' she will shed."

"So then it sounds like maybe you might want to lose a filter or two yourself."

Linda leaned into him. "Maybe you can help me with that."

"Anything you need."

Having mentioned Natalie as a less-selfish topic, Linda felt bad they were back on Sonia, but carried on nonetheless. "The problem is that when she gets going, my head becomes so crowded with thoughts that are clear to me but that I find difficult to articulate, and articulate in a way that won't send her over the edge. She launches off on God, on life, the universe and everything, and I get stalled up."

"Nice Douglas Adams reference there."

"Sorry?"

"Douglas Adams." Jeff eyed her strangely. "You just quoted the title of the second *Hitchhiker's Guide to the Galaxy: Life, the Universe and Everything.*"

"I did?"

Jeff laughed, a barking, jovial guffaw that echoed through the naked wood. "Fantastic."

"I must have just heard the phrase before," Linda said. She felt herself blushing slightly. "I didn't know where it came from."

He slid his arm around her shoulder and offered a gentle squeeze before releasing her.

They walked a moment in silence.

"I don't mind, you know," Linda said softly.

Jeff raised an eyebrow. "Mind?"

"Your arm. Around me. It felt nice."

"Nice," Jeff echoed with a smile. He squeezed her again, and this time his arm remained in place. "Not spunky?"

Linda giggled.

"Yeah, I leave all the life and universe questions to the Natalies and Arthurs of the world," Jeff said.

"You've gotta have your own take, though," Linda said, her tone gently pressing.

"I suppose," he said. "I've always thought of life as a buffet. Why would you willfully stop at the salad and bread? And God—Sonia's God, your God, my God, even Art's God, or whoever it is out there—it's the whole bar and the whole buffet. I'm not entirely sure what that means, but I'll let you noodle with that for a while and see if you can't tell me what it might mean."

"Copout," Linda said. "But, you are making me hungry."

"We just ate."

"I know."

Again Jeff squeezed her shoulders. "My kind of gal."

Linda sat masturbating on the couch. Toward climax, the doorbell rang. She didn't let it derail her, leveling off the swell of desire that had overcome her.

The doorbell rang again.

She looked at the clock—just past nine. Not too late, but still rather curious. Hastily she pulled up her pants and rose from the couch, stars littering her vision. She walked to the door and opened it and felt the blood rush to her face at the sight of Reverend Matthews on the porch, his hands together at his front, a look of almost theatrical compassion on his face.

"Hi Linda," said Matthews. "I apologize for the late hour. But I was nearby and thought I'd stop over."

"Um, sure." Her face tingled. "Is everything okay?"

"Things are fine, thank you," he said. "May I come in?"

Linda gestured him inside. He walked in, surveyed the living room. In her field of vision the couch seemed to glow a heated red. There had to be some obvious sign somewhere of her pleasurable indulgence.

"Would you like anything to drink?" Linda asked as Matthews lowered himself into an armchair.

"No, I'm fine, thank you." He leaned forward to the edge of the cushion, hands still together. "I wanted to let you know that, when she was here over the holidays, your daughter came and spoke to me. About you."

"Sonia?" Linda said, sitting back on the couch.

"Yes. She seems to be deeply concerned about you. About the status of your faith."

Status of your faith. What is the status of my faith? she wondered. *Sixty percent? Seventy-seven-point-two percent?*

"My faith is strong, Reverend," Linda said.

Matthews' eyes narrowed. "I don't wish to pry, but you were recently close with that fellow Arthur Moore, weren't you?"

Linda's gut clenched. "We were close to some extent, yes. We dated. But we don't see either other anymore."

"I've no personal reason to question your faith, Linda. I only came here on the word of your daughter, who was worried."

"What did she think was happening to me?"

"She said you might be straying." Matthews frowned slightly. "She said you've done it before."

"I've never once stopped believing in God."

Matthews absorbed her words. "You can talk to me, Linda, you know this. Feel free to contact me anytime. I realize it's sometimes a cultural badge of honor—for women, too, these days—to just grin and bear it, but when we share with each other we share with God, and sharing is closeness and sharing is love."

Linda appreciated the sentiment. Matthews's wisdom was usually sincere and sound, even if, for her, his youth undermined his authority.

"I'm okay, Reverend," she said. She gripped the armrest of the couch, trying to quell her agitation. "I really am. I'll be there Sunday."

Matthews smiled and stood up. "That'll be wonderful, Linda."

Long brooding country flanked the Pennsylvania highway, the woods and fields like a cold whisper made solid. Sunlight shone woolly and gray through the clouds. Short ridges of snow lined both sides of the asphalt.

In a rented car traveling eastward, Arthur and Natalie sat quietly, Natalie driving and smoking, the window down. Arthur absorbed the landscape, the rustic pockmarks of civilization.

"We're not far from where I grew up," Arthur said.

"What was the name of the town again?"

"Several miles from here, not far from Fredericksburg. I'll take you there, if you'd like." They turned off and merged onto the Lincoln Highway. The craggy trees heightened, drew closer, as though impatient for the age when they may usurp the pavement. "Last time I was here was for my mother's funeral."

"Was John with you?"

"He was. This was about two years before the eleventh."

Natalie nodded, dragging on her cigarette. For a while, silence. Arthur could tell she was focused and stiff, her limbs fastened like metal clamps to the steering wheel.

"I'm a bit worried about him," she said.

"I know." The following sentence didn't feel right, though he said it anyway, "I'm sure he's okay."

"No, I mean...when I called him. He sounded very distant, almost hesitant to talk."

"You think he doesn't want visitors?"

"He said he did. I mean, that he wanted to see me. But he was really just..."

"Did you tell him you were with me?"

"Yeah."

"Could that have upset him? Maybe I—"

"No," Natalie cut in. "It wasn't that, I don't think. He just sounded terribly distracted."

"I don't know the guy, but from his book and what you told me, he sounds like a man of many burdens."

"Could say that."

Valentine's directions brought them to a small converted garage, next to a trailer home. A blue pickup truck and a two-seater car sat lonely and still next to one another. A corresponding post by the side of the road jutted from a mound of slush, proclaiming the address 10451—the number Valentine had given her.

"This it?" Arthur said.

They sat in the car, watching the area like two amateur detectives on a stakeout. The wind drew breezy ice strokes across the grass, as if trying to stir any life back to wakefulness. They waited for movement, any movement. Arthur wondered if Natalie had been entirely honest about her gut sensations.

Does she actually want to see him? Does she want to be here? "Are we going up there?" he asked.

Eyes fixed on the trailer and the garage, she said, "Yeah. Let's go."

Closing her eyes, teeth gritted, Linda dialed her daughter and lifted the phone to her ear.

The ringing began.

Sonia picked up. "Hey Mom." Between her words were loud chewing noises, what Linda guessed were gum smacks. "What's up?"

"Reverend Matthews came by," she said tersely.

The chewing ceased. "Oh?"

"He said you were concerned about me."

A beat. A deliberating pause. "I *was* concerned about you, Mom. I consulted Reverend Matthews out of love. I realized you might not listen to me, but you might very well listen to him."

Linda sensed in her daughter an odd mixture of impatience and fear. *I don't care,* she thought. *I'm tired of trying to decode her.*

"Listen," said Linda. "I want you to stop bothering me about the God you want me to have. Because frankly, we don't have the same God."

"Mother," Sonia snapped. With a breath, she calmed. "God is God. You can't change Him."

"God gave us all different eyes and different minds," Linda said. "If He wanted us to see Him and feel Him the same way He'd have made us all the same."

"Seriously, Mom? God gave us *choice*—"

"Exactly," Linda said. "And I choose not to stick by your choices. And stop sending me those damn chain letters."

"Why?"

"Because they're impersonal. I want to hear from my daughter."

"You're hearing from me *now*."

"No, Sonia, you're hearing from *me*."

A pause.

"Mom," Sonia said, in a lowered tone, "you know I'm busy. I send those emails to all my friends."

"I don't want to hear it, Sonia, okay?" Every word fanned her fire. Linda felt impassioned but also remarkably light, expunging something long coagulated in her. "It's not my fault Dad ran off. It's not my fault Ferdinand is unresponsive. It's not my fault you're not happy with whoever I choose to spend my time with. I love you and I am here for you. Always know that. But that doesn't mean I'm some kind of punching bag for you, or some sad sack case to be rescued and reformed."

"Mom, what on earth are you talking about?" Sonia said. "All I ever tried to do was *help* you."

"Well, you're not helping. In fact, you're..." Linda drew a breath, feeling light-headed, "you're becoming a pain in the ass."

"How can you *say* that, Mother! I know Dad's divorcing you broke you spiritually. But I'm here for you. Here to bring you back into God's love and—"

"Stop it, Sonia. Dad has nothing to do with this."

"Is it Arthur Moore then? Is it that atheist?"

"Sonia, no. No. It is me." Linda exhaled a long, slow

breath. Sonia quieted. "You're going to have to live with my decisions and be okay with them."

"I can't be okay with it, if I know God's not okay with it."

"You speak to God directly?"

"Every day and every night."

"He must be tired of you, darling," Linda said with a sigh, stifling a laugh. "Talk to *me* sometime then. Every once in awhile I need you as much as God does."

Linda entertained an image of her daughter right then, standing beneath the hot Spanish sun, phone to her ear and running her pink-glossed fingernails through her hair and rolling those rich brown eyes that her father Stephen, in his occasional tendency toward purple poetics, once said were like "ripe little soil plots, sprouting flowers of spirit."

"Mom," Sonia said. "I gotta go. I got class."

"Okay—"

"Bye."

"I love you, Sonia."

A moment of silence lingered before her daughter hung up.

Linda closed her eyes. For a long moment she stood quietly, aware that her body was shaking, aware of the tears pooling behind her eyes. Quickly her gratification gave way to remorse, to a nagging sense she'd burned a final bridge with her daughter. She fought a sinking feeling that Sonia would never speak to her again.

She'll get over it. She'll forget about it.

Linda hesitated, then called Jeff. He picked up on the third ring.

"Hey, Lindy," Jeff said, sounding chipper.

While honored that she'd reached a level with Jeff to warrant one of his cute (or, in Arthur's case, pesky) nicknames, she wasn't too enamored with this one.

"We should work on 'Lindy'," she said. "It just reminds

me of Charles Lindbergh."

"What's wrong with that? Man was an aviation hero."

"And a Nazi sympathizer."

"Touché. What's up?"

"Just got off the phone with Sonia," Linda said, her spinning head now slowing. "Mind if I talk at you for a while?"

Walking up to Valentine's trailer, Arthur stalled. An eerie feeling came over him. Natalie moved ahead. The place and its towering wooded backdrop appeared to Arthur suddenly painted, not really here.

Something weighty and familiar—a touchable, holdable, testable thing—filled him. It was acrid. Jim had called it déjà vu, or something like it. What was the other word he'd used? Intuition. No. More direct, more characteristic.

Badness.

"Natalie," he said.

She turned. Her brow lowered. "What is it?"

Natalie looked at the trailer, mere yards away now, then back at Arthur. She crossed her arms, seemingly fighting off both the winter chill and her own contrasting feelings. She appeared ambivalent, though frustrated.

"Never mind," Arthur said. "I don't know."

Natalie glanced down at her slush-stained boots. "I'm sorry if this is awkward for you—"

"No, that's not it."

"I promise we won't be too long," Natalie said. "Thanks again for coming with."

"Sure."

Halfway up the walk, they both stopped and stared at the figure that materialized behind the screen door. Arthur glimpsed a stoic expression, could make out almost satirical bits of the man whose picture adorned the back inside flap of *The Divine Dialogues*. Then the screen opened, cutting a harsh whine through the frosted stillness, and he was there, Neil Valentine, wild with beard, clothes rumpled, beaten against the stone face of the world.

"Natalie," Neil said. There was a yellowish pallor to his skin. His gait looked stiff. Walking toward them, he offered only a furtive glance in Arthur's direction.

"Neil," Natalie said. "Is everything—?"

She stopped at an expression he made, his lips puckered as he mouthed a silent word: Go.

"What?"

Terror welled in the man's eyes. Arthur shivered. *Something terribly wrong. Badness tainting the wind.*

Go, Neil mouthed again. He gestured at them with slight ushering motions. Arthur took a few steps back, primed to follow the cryptic instruction, but halted because Natalie remained still.

And then the *snap*, a sound like the splintering of a heavy branch. Neil cried out and fell forward as Arthur and Natalie moved to catch him. As Arthur felt the man's weight in his hands, his sinuses grazed by the stink of fear and unwashed flesh, he glanced down and saw blood sputtering from the back of Neil's leg like water from a broken sprinkler.

"Oh my God!" Natalie screamed.

All words drained from Arthur. He cast glances about the trailer and the woods and saw nothing, though the presence of another hung heavy on the cold.

"Neil? Christ, what's *happening*?" Natalie cried from a million miles away.

Breath and spittle heaved from Neil's mouth. Through gritted teeth he uttered, "Get out of here. Go. Fucking go!"

Arthur saw the man then, striding with mechanical

determination from whatever shade had concealed him. His face was both weary and neutral, somehow. A keen remorseless animal engaged in the business of survival. He wore a green camouflage jacket, the soldierlike complement to the narrow rifle clutched in both hands. *So tall.* Certainly they'd cited his height on TV though it'd been an abstract number, hardly accounted for by the photos disseminated.

Alexander Heyst.

Natalie blubbered, "Oh God…"

Heyst stopped by the side of the trailer, watching them like an amused idiot as they worked in quivering shock to try to help Neil. Arthur stripped off his jacket, thinking he might try and use it as a tourniquet. Natalie and Neil both pressed their hands on the wound, eliciting grimaces and grunts from Neil that only grew fiercer. Sweat filmed the man's forehead. For Arthur the seconds slowed; he operated as if he were in fact a tiny man shut up inside his skull, watching as this bodily vessel of his worked and stumbled.

"Get 'im inside," Heyst called out. His voice was nasal, tinny almost to a comical edge.

Though Heyst did not have the rifle trained on them, both Arthur and Natalie's every step were cautious. Born of fear, certainly, but also, at least for Arthur, an inability to even function at normal pace. Constantly some new area of him erupted in shudders, as if, one by one, his muscles relinquished the life force within them.

"There're rags and towels we can use to bandage him up," Heyst said, gesturing with his rifle to the trailer.

Arthur made only fleeting eye contact with Natalie, whose face now glistened with tears and mucus. Gingerly they lifted Neil, propped his arms around their shoulders, and escorted him in blood-dripping stutter steps toward the trailer. Heyst moved to the screen door and opened it. As they passed him and entered the disheveled living room

Arthur tried not to look at Heyst, desperately wanting to avoid those eyes so manic and adrift.

Entering the trailer, Arthur had the sense of walking into a living tomb. In a nearby corner, two heaters twanged and hummed against the chill. Piles of moldering books rose in a second corner, and clothes were strewn dramatically around the floor and all across the frayed corduroy couch, as though the people wearing them had simply evaporated.

They sat Neil down on the couch. Heyst disappeared for a moment and returned with several white cloths, scissors and a towel. He tossed them on Neil's lap, then stood watch in the center of the room, still clutching the rifle.

"Tie it tight," he said.

"He needs 911," Natalie said, though by her expression it seemed part of her couldn't believe she was actually speaking.

"He'll be alright for now," Heyst said.

Arthur used the scissors to slice Neil's pants leg up to the wound. They then applied the towel, which reddened in seconds. Neil's breathing pulsed in a constant rhythm, reassuring Arthur that at least he wasn't dying. Natalie clutched Neil's hand and spoke to him through her tears.

"Neil," she said. "Stay here with us."

Neil's head lolled toward her and their gazes met. He swallowed. "I'm here," he said. "I'm so sorry, Natalie."

Arthur wrapped two layers of cloth around the wound. His hands were sticky with blood.

"Wash off if you want," Heyst said, indicating the kitchen.

Head down, Arthur walked to the sink and rinsed off. In the dish rack he glimpsed a steak knife and considered taking it but quickly rejected the idea. In slow, measured steps, he returned to the couch and gingerly sat down beside Neil's feet. Natalie had taken a seat just above his head and was stroking Neil's hair and face in a comforting way. Arthur began to speak, the words tumbling forth as if without his consent.

"Wh-what's happening here?" he asked. His even tone surprised him, given the electrical storm that raged inside his head.

"What's happening here is that I'm cashing out my arrangement with Mr. Valentine," Heyst said.

"Arrangement?" Natalie's glance flitted between Neil and Heyst.

"Natalie," Neil said, tears dripping down his cheeks. "I'm sorry. I'm so sorry..."

"What the fuck is going *on*?" Natalie demanded. Arthur heard the hysteria creeping into her voice.

Heyst ignored her and instead told Neil, "You should probably save your strength."

"Fuck you," Neil replied.

Natalie stiffened. Arthur could see clouds of portentous thought settling in all around her. He'd never seen that kind of expression on anyone before, let alone her. She looked as if she'd passed into some terrible new reality. It made her appear utterly and achingly fragile, as if the weight of a colossal betrayal—some sudden, horrific revelation—had illuminated itself in her mind, and all she wanted to do now was send it back into the darkness from which it had come.

"You told me," she said to Neil, eyes hot and accusing, "about the man you met on the street who extorted you."

Neil stared at her, silent and still. Arthur felt queasy.

"Who was that?" Natalie said.

Swallowing, Neil hesitated. "The man...his name was Holden."

Natalie's eyelids slammed shut as if to block out the unwanted information. Arthur rubbed his forehead, prickly with disbelief.

"Jesus Christ," Arthur muttered.

"That's why you shut down the center," Natalie said. "That's why you ran away."

Arthur recalled the brisk exchange with Agent Latham. *We suspect there may be more people involved, not as shooters but as supporters, financial or otherwise, he'd said. Right now we're unsure how these guys were able to function as they did. Or do.*

"I didn't know what he was doing with the money I gave him," Neil said, his voice thinning and growing weaker. "I didn't know what I was doing. I just wanted my past out of my present. At one point I refused, refused to give him any more, but..."

"What?"

"He knew about you," Neil said. "He threatened...to hurt you. To go after you."

Natalie blinked. She visibly shuddered.

"We kept our eyes on you," Heyst said to Natalie, then swung his attention over to Arthur. "You too."

A question surged in Arthur. As much as he didn't want to ask it because he really didn't want to know the answer, he couldn't hold it back.

"Camille Rhodes," Arthur said. "Was she...intentional? Was..." He almost added, "Was she murdered because I visited Holden?" but refrained.

A loopy smile spread across Heyst's lips. "You mean the artist girl?" he said. "That wasn't me. That was Bob." He gestured with the rifle at Neil. "None of our cleansing woulda been possible without Mr. Valentine right here. He redeemed himself. Through sin and corruption the willing can find paths to purify themselves once more."

Arthur could see in Heyst very little of the intelligence, or perverse charisma, he'd observed in Benjamin Holden, so he understood why Holden had been the leader. While the world had undone both men, Holden demonstrated a certain philosophical grounding that Arthur found noticeably lacking in the man now standing before them. Heyst, a perfect disciple, was more like a piece of wind-battered debris Holden had managed to snatch and dispatch for his own purposes. Released back to the elements after Benjamin Holden's capture, Heyst had sought the only person he knew he could trust to conceal him: Holden's financial resource, the go-to man.

Heyst leaned his rifle against the wall and pulled an automatic pistol from his coat pocket. He trained it on Arthur and Natalie. Arthur's throat closed. His bowels trembled.

"You two, stand," Heyst ordered.

Arthur and Natalie rose. They glanced briefly at each other, exchanging looks that carried a mix of apprehension and confusion.

"Empty your pockets," Heyst said. "Toss it all on the floor here."

They obeyed, pulling out wallets and keys and clipped bills and piling them on the carpet. Heyst retrieved a roll of twine from a black duffel bag and handed it to Natalie.

"Tie his hands behind his back."

Slowly, Arthur laced his fingers together at the small of his back. His breathing grew both shallower and more rapid, keeping pace with the thunderous hammering of his heart. Natalie wrapped the twine around his hands until it bit into his wrist. Heyst then seized her by the arm. She yelped as he spun her around and bound her hands as well.

"Alright, let's go," Heyst said, waving them toward the screen door. Once again he rooted around in the duffel bag. Arthur couldn't see what he'd retrieved until Heyst turned back toward them, revealing the silencer he now screwed onto the nose of the pistol. He headed toward the door; then, as if reminded of some lingering undone chore, he swiveled and shot Neil twice through the chest.

Natalie screamed. Arthur went numb. Neil recoiled into the cushions, his expression unchanged as his body stiffened and fell limp. Blood spread across his chest in a growing stain.

Arthur and Natalie filed from the trailer. Heyst followed right behind them. Arthur scanned the woods for anyone else but saw no one. He heard only indifferent cries and caws from the trees. Heyst ushered them toward the wide blue pickup parked by the side of the trailer, opened the backseat door and watched while they climbed in, shoving Arthur in after Natalie for good measure.

Arthur stared dumbly at his knees. He would wake up anytime, yes. Anytime the projector would cut off, dissolving this three-dimensional movie that had somehow ensnared him.

Next to him, Natalie sobbed.

Heyst settled into the driver's seat and the truck roared to life. It lurched forward and then swung back around toward the road. Arthur's mind considered and dismissed a host of options, the best of them impossible and the worst downright absurd.

The truck rumbled along, swaying and crunching over increasingly rugged earth, then made a sharp left. When Arthur looked up after the turn he realized he had no idea how much time had passed or where they were.

The woods closed in tight on either side.

Heyst rolled to a slow stop, cut the engine and sighed. After what seemed a moment's thought, he disembarked and opened the backseat door. Pistol outstretched, he ordered Arthur and Natalie out of the truck. Natalie stumbled to her knees while exiting and Heyst dragged her, none too gently, back to her feet.

He motioned for them to start walking into the forest.

Arthur heard the wind rustling through the pines and felt the thread of spring beneath the gray chill.

You won't see spring.

Jim, I'm so sorry.

Pine shadows deepened.

—not happening not happening not happening—

How long would it be before anyone found them? After the roaches and rats and ravens and maybe even bears had had their fill of them? Would anyone find them?

It doesn't matter, said a voice.

Nothing matters.

"Here," said Heyst, businesslike.

In a small clearing Heyst forced them to their knees.

Arthur felt a fiery ache in his legs. He looked around—neither the road nor the truck was visible from here. He would die right here, in nature, Natalie alongside him. The thought was strangely comforting.

Natalie cried louder and her tears became torrential. Arthur's breath quickened. He felt the world spinning as Heyst positioned himself behind them. Cold metal suddenly pressed against the back of Arthur's skull.

Arthur felt an unexpected calmness begin to arise within him. It seeped into his heart and mind, softening the sharpened teeth of fear.

You've done this before.

He closed his eyes and remembered that he was endless.

NATALIE SCREAMED as the shot rang out. The ground trembled as the weight of the body dropped like a weighty sack. Something heavy struck her sharply across the ankles.

Kill me now. Just kill me now. Fucking end it.

"Natalie."

Still sobbing, she reluctantly opened her eyes. By some miracle Arthur remained on his knees beside her, strangely alive and—even more strangely—eerily calm and peaceful.

She twisted with stunned surprise and spotted Alex Heyst's lifeless body sprawled behind her in the dry grass, left arm flung carelessly across her ankles. A ragged opening split the bone in his temple, exposing brain matter. Rivulets of blood streaked his face. It looked to Natalie as though a crimson hand had come out from the clouds, grabbed Heyst by the scalp and tossed him down to the ground.

Is this what happens when you die? You think everyone else just dies instead?

She turned back to Arthur, who was surveying the surrounding woods intently.

"Up here."

A voice wafted down from a nearby tree. Looking up they saw a young boy, about fourteen or fifteen, squatting on a large branch of a gnarled oak. He wore camouflage gear and had a blanket of loose threaded leaves draped about him. His .22 rifle remained pointed toward Heyst's still body. His whitened face revealed both strength and terror.

"He was…gonna shoot you all, wasn't he?" said the kid.

Slowly, Natalie nodded.

"Ain't never killed someone before," said the kid, sounding dazed. "But he was gonna shoot you for sure."

For a serrated moment stillness reigned. The songs of nature played on as if nothing had happened.

His 'street uncle,' Natalie thought bitterly, her mind slowly snapping back to what had almost occurred. The Judges of God. *Neil fucking funded the Judges of God.*

"Thank you," Arthur shouted up to the kid. "Thank you." A breeze-whistling pause. "What were you doing there?"

"Hunting," he said. "Waitin' for deer. First time by myself. Pop wanted me out here more 'n' I wanted to come. I been sittin' out here for a couple hours but nothin's come by." The kid lowered his gun, his face tight as though suppressing nausea. "Till you and them come along."

"Christ," Arthur muttered.

"Thank you," called Natalie, feeling a warm wave of gratitude flood through her.

The kid removed his layer of leaves and made his way down from the oak tree.

"Don't mention it," he said, voice still tremulous. "The hell was goin' on anyway?"

"Good question," Arthur said.

Natalie sniffed. Heyst's body was terribly still. Gingerly she shifted her ankles to release them from the now-dead weight of his arm. The winter shadows grew darker, as if eager to conceal the brutal scene.

"Let's get outta here," said the kid.

"We need to call the police," Arthur said.

"Yeah," said the kid, his face blanched, mouth hung limp. "I guess so. Am I gonna be in trouble?"

"I promise you, you are not," Arthur reassured him.

As they made their way back toward the road, the kid turned and vomited behind a tree. Arthur eased up behind him, placed a comforting hand on his back and waited until the delayed effects of stress and fear and anxiety dissipated. Natalie watched from a short distance away, feeling like she might yet vomit herself.

VI

FEBRUARY'S END AND MOST OF MARCH were frigid, wet. On one occasion a raging snowstorm served up a final seasonal punch, as if nature had stumbled upon a back stock of winter and decided to use it before its expiration date. By mid-April, however, temperatures rose and warmer rains fell as the trees began to don fine new coats of green.

"It's very strange," Natalie said. She was sitting next to Arthur on his apartment balcony, basking in the spring sun that pooled over them. "I still don't think I've been *feeling* what happened as much as I should. Part of me seems numb to it. And then every once in a while I'll have these paralyzing and despairing moments of 'Oh shit, that was *real*. That really happened.'"

While meditation, love, company and commiseration all helped, Natalie of course knew that her true salvation—the only hope of reconciling herself to the incident in Pennsylvania—would be time; and she was grateful, now more than ever, that she had much of it. She found it particularly difficult to reconcile the part of the world that included her everyday affairs with the part that allowed someone like Alex Heyst to cause such destruction. In her mind they rubbed abrasively against one another, with her caught right in the middle.

And yet, she considered, perhaps it was not as difficult as it might have been without the recent tragedies leading up to it—the fire, their physical injuries, Camille's death. Maybe she was simply being initiated into another phase of life, graduating as a higher spirit toward some yet-grander resurrection.

She would think these things, yes, and then she would recall those last moments of seeing Neil Valentine in this lifetime, and she would try as best as she could not to either succumb to the despair or try and suppress it, but to meet it eye to eye—to allow it in so that it might run its course.

She craved a cigarette, even though she'd once again recently quit.

"Lunar moved up the release date on my book," Natalie told Arthur, "probably to ride the PR wave."

Arthur said nothing. He just kept glancing from her to the vista before them, and then back again to her.

"I still kind of want to just hide," Natalie said.

"Clear out the cerebral coliseum?" he suggested.

"Maybe. But I know me. That wouldn't last."

"We can't hide forever," Arthur said plainly.

"Says you."

"Says me."

"By the way," Natalie said. "Should you decide to come out of the woodwork, I think you should talk to *Soulful*. The magazine."

"They did an interview with you a short while back, right?"

"They did, yes. They're maybe more on the woo-woo side, but they're—"

"Levelheaded?"

"No. Well, yes, a little," Natalie chuckled darkly. "They've got a good head on their shoulders. They don't judge too much or tip too far either way. But their core intention is to help bridge science and spirit."

"I see," Arthur pointed at her. "By the way, you mentioned your new book. I think we should have the release party at my housewarming party, once the house is totally finished."

"Combined celebration. That sounds good," Natalie said. "It'll be about the same time, right?"

Arthur nodded. "Another few weeks, they estimate."

He reached over and took her lithe hands in his. "Also… there's something I haven't told you. About the incident."

"Yes?"

"The boy in the tree."

"What about him?"

"I'd seen him before," Arthur said. "But I don't know where. He was very familiar to me."

Moments passed. She waited.

"I know that Neil's situation, what he became..." Arthur began, staring ahead at the ponderous clouds. "His whole fall from grace, frightened and confused you."

Natalie remained quiet.

"By any chance, though," Arthur persisted, "have you considered if the whole thing was a way for him to smell the peanut butter again?"

"Huh?"

"What you told me, remember? Your analogy for leaving paradise and coming back and appreciating it even more," Arthur took a breath. "Maybe he was too mired in the whole spiritual business. He couldn't see the forest for the trees. So at some level he wanted to regress, to feel lost so that he might replenish and remake himself to feel that sense of...I don't know. Help me out here."

"Enlightenment?" Natalie said. "Spiritual renewal?"

"Something like that."

She looked at him, loving but dubious. "Sounds like wishful thinking," she said. "Though I like your thinking."

"The ideal would be to turn your thinking off."

"Don't say that," she said, lightly slapping his knee. "You know it's served you well."

"More or less," he said.

David returned home with bags full of groceries hanging from both his shoulders. He stacked the items on the kitchen counter and began putting them away.

"Sorry I've taken over the table here," Jim said, still hunched over his sketchbook. Charcoal and pastel and colored-pencil drawings littered the table surface, a crowded populace of light figure studies and hard-rendered pieces and doodles.

David moved closer and slid his arms around Jim's shoulders, then kissed him lightly on the top of his head. Jim squeezed David's arm in return.

"Never apologize," David said. "They're all versions of you. I don't mind more versions of you around here."

"I would."

"Shush."

"That interview with your dad came out."

"Oh?"

"Yeah." David hopped over to the counter and picked up a thin, saddle-stitched magazine and placed it in front of Jim. Soulful, it said, in an elaborately serifed font. The upper left-hand corner promised an "exclusive interview" with Dr. Arthur Moore.

"Picked it up on campus," David said. Idly he began scratching the back of Jim's head until Jim began to feel sleepy. "Been keeping an eye out for it."

Jim fingered the magazine. "Thanks."

"Yeah. Might be short enough for even me to get through."

"I got something as well," Jim said. He reached into his attaché case on the adjacent seat and brought out a slick paperback, the cover of which featured a yin-yang symbol made of two figures, black and white and androgynous and wrapped in coitus. The title declared: *Sexpirit: Unleashing the Sensual in the Spirit and Vice Versa.*

"Oh shit!" David said, gingerly taking it.

"Got the advance copy today."

David flipped it over, where on the back Natalie beamed an inviting smile. He flipped through pages, slowing or stopping at Jim's illustrations. "I remember these," he said. "Funny to see them actually printed. So awesome, though. Wait..." He closed the book and gestured at the front cover.

"This is you too, right?"

"Mm-hmm," Jim said.

"I thought the publisher was going with their own cover artist, or something," David said. "You wowed them that much, I guess?"

"Well, Natalie asked me to come up with something if I wanted to. Thought I'd give it a shot. It was more work, and not guaranteed, but it's the damn cover, after all. They ended up liking it." Jim hesitated. "I was lucky. I think Natalie has a lot of sway with them."

David leaned down and kissed him. "No luck involved, if you ask me."

"No, *too* much luck involved," Jim said, gazing toward the issue of *Soulful* on the table.

David chuckled. "I've got to hit the books."

His partner adjourned to the bedroom and Jim sat alone once more. He picked up the magazine and turned to his father's interview. They'd used a stock photo of Arthur, one usually featured on the jacket of his books.

He began to read.

INTERVIEWER: You've been away for quite a while.

MOORE: I have.

INTERVIEWER: Much has happened to you lately, it seems.

MOORE: I certainly can't argue with that.

INTERVIEWER: We're glad to have you with us. And I don't just mean here.

MOORE: Thank you.

INTERVIEWER: Dare we use the term "resurrection"?

MOORE [smiles]: You can use any term you'd like.

INTERVIEWER: Is there any particular reason you agreed to be with us today?

MOORE: It's as good a time as any. Well—[interrupted]

INTERVIEWER: I'm sorry, I cut you off.

MOORE: I was going to say that now might be a better time than any other.

INTERVIEWER: And why is that?

MOORE: It's the present. Present's the best and only time to do anything.

INTERVIEWER: I see. May we discuss the house fire?

MOORE: Sure.

INTERVIEWER: In September of last year, your house burned to the ground. You nearly died. You were hospitalized with serious brain trauma—I believe in a coma for a little while, correct?

MOORE: Yes, I was.

INTERVIEWER: I also believe, at one point, you were clinically dead?

MOORE: I was.

INTERVIEWER: Something happened to you, then.

MOORE: Yes. [pauses] I underwent what can only be classified as a near-death experience.

INTERVIEWER: What do you remember about it?

MOORE: Plainly, I was detached from my body. The feeling was rather like dropping the luggage that you've been carrying for too long, except in this case it'd been so long that I wasn't even aware I carried luggage. I was me, but lighter. And details were clarified. I almost felt

I could adjust my sight to the micro or macro level, take in everything of the hospital or zoom in on the sweaty pores of my surgeon's face. I noted all the hardware registering my death. My flatlining. I could not so much "float" but blink to places, snap one way or another. I began to perceive others that could perceive me, and I began to realize they may be undergoing the same thing I was. No one else, none of the staff, my son in the lobby, other patients, saw me. The world was gilded edged, almost like a door closed to a well-lit room, light pulsing behind the construct. This light seemed to grow brighter, washing out all else. So the light wasn't much of a tunnel, more a small glow that eventually bled through everything and engulfed me.

INTERVIEWER: Incredible.

MOORE: Some people have a life review. I didn't really have one, not that I recall. It was very individual. But hardly lonesome, because I felt like I grew. I came to understand, strangely intuitively, that I contained everything. As an individual, I had contained all thoughts and feelings and experiences of my past, present, even future. Then, I moved—or graduated, maybe—to some bigger space, where filling me was the whole of the human species, all its thoughts and feelings and experiences, readily digested—all ongoing—within me. Then, and this was the most fleeting...I touched another level, a sphere even greater, where I was the universe, the cosmic container, all things past and present and future that had happened anytime, anywhere, and I mean anywhere, running through my blood.

INTERVIEWER: A godly realm?

MOORE: Perhaps. But yeah, there was a light. And again it wasn't a tunnel, it was universal—as if, for a few moments, the universe was like a toy in my hand. Through all this I could see swirling spiral galaxies. I saw the Horsehead nebula. They were my body. No doubt, however, there was another presence there. All-encompassing. It wasn't in front of me and it wasn't behind me. There was no location here, no "here" and "there" and no sense of time. Everything bobbed in high knowing, as if the air itself crackled with consciousness.

INTERVIEWER: Did this "other presence" communicate?

MOORE: To a certain degree. Not verbally, though. I felt attached to this presence; I knew I was an inextricable part of it. Not a mere participant, mind you, but part. We are not crumbs on the cosmic cloth, as we tend to assume. We're stitches in the cloth, of the cloth. In this realm, before this presence, I would think thoughts and these thoughts were reflected back at me. That's how this presence communicated. As if I would send out junked-up thoughts that would boomerang back to me stripped of the junk, pure and clean in their perfect essence. I was speaking to some universal extension of me, the way a lake might, through a river, speak to the ocean. Different forms, but all water and all one essence.

INTERVIEWER: I can only imagine. What was it like returning to your body?

MOORE: Rather like a ball must feel striking pavement. It was a wallop, and immediately I knew I'd lost some of what I'd known and experienced in the....how do I say, file conversion process, I suppose?

INTERVIEWER: But clearly you've retained much of the experience.

MOORE: I hope I have. One of the things I remember most

about the presence, of my universal body, or mind, or whatever it was, was its sense of humor. Nothing bothered it, and as a result nothing bothered me. It was infinite calm and just…joy, I guess.

INTERVIEWER: A sense of humor, you say?

MOORE: [nods] Yes. And in the moments I'm able to reflect broadly and, as well as I can, objectively, on the whole thing, I can sympathize with the humor. In a way, the universe is a great brushstroke of irony. Much of what we think is meaningful is meaningless. I don't mean that in the crass way it sounds. Nor do I intend to diminish the immense suffering on this planet when I say that a part of me now suspects this is all some ironic experiment, or joke. But actually not a malicious joke, because no one is playing it on us. We're doing it to ourselves. The only thing truly meaningful, I feel, is the very act of making meaning. But the meanings we do attach to things, to people, to phenomena, are fleeting and our own—like notes on a chalkboard. You sense that, despite the enormity of misery here, everyone and everything is okay and will be okay. You sense… you sense that any alternative "perfect world," or theorized utopia, only sacrifices yet more perfection of the world we have before us. And I'm not being a Pangloss. I just mean that all things are possible here, all parameters set, and things will work out as they will. Though it's often difficult to see it as such, the chaos itself is a perfect utopia. If we extracted a utopia from it, we'd remove so many other possibilities and experiences the chaos once offered. If that makes any sense.

INTERVIEWER: What would you say to someone who might criticize, as you have done, that a near-death experience is only a drug-induced dream or the hallucination of a failing brain?

MOORE: I would say they'd need to have the subjective experience themselves before drawing such a conclusion. And I say that in full cognizance of my prior words on the topic.

INTERVIEWER: How has this particular experience influenced your view of death?

MOORE: [pauses] I no longer believe death to be absolute. And, quite honestly, I find myself not as affected when reading about certain tragedies in the news. That's not to say I wouldn't share grief or sadness, but more that I appreciate that we can feel grief and sadness. Making meanings out of meaninglessness, remember. Consider a dramatic movie—it affects you emotionally, possibly makes you cry if a character dies at the end, and while you know it's not real, that that very actor is still walking red carpets and giving interviews, it doesn't mean you shouldn't feel what the story's made you feel. And you love it because it's elicited such a reaction from you.

INTERVIEWER: If you will, I'd like to discuss the other, more recent occurrence in Pennsylvania.

MOORE: Okay.

INTERVIEWER: In what must have been extraordinary and harrowing situation, you bore witness to the death of Neil Valentine, author of the bestselling Divine Dialogues, at the hands of Alexander Heyst, revealed as the last member of the terrorist group the Judges of God.

MOORE: [pauses] I did.

INTERVIEWER: I'm very sorry.

MOORE: [nods slowly]

INTERVIEWER: I'm assuming you're familiar with Mr.

Valentine's legacy and work?

MOORE: I am.

INTERVIEWER: How do you see him now, if I might ask, in light of the revelation that he was involved, at least financially, with a terrorist group like the Judges of God?

MOORE: He's also a stitch in the great cloth. So are Benjamin Holden and Robert Gray and Alexander Heyst. And Hitler. And the smallpox virus. That's how I see him. That's how I see—or try to see—them all.

INTERVIEWER: Is it safe to say you believe in God now?

MOORE: As I said, it's safe to say I now believe that we will be okay.

Twice that afternoon Arthur strolled through the house, breathing in the vague, lingering aromas of fresh paint and sawdust. He dallied in the expanded library, pausing by the new window that welcomed daylight to new corners and crevices, and that brightened what were once somber, musty quarters.

Teacup in hand, he drifted back out to the larger kitchen, where he ran his fingers along the green granite countertops. He strode upstairs into Jim's old room, now a small art studio, taking in the details the way one might when exploring a new lover. All around him the minutes settled crisp and unruffled, awaiting the scuff of new life, the wear and tear of memories to come.

He returned downstairs to the living room, where on the mantel stood a large foam-board blowup of Jim's front cover for Natalie's book, *Sexpirit*. On the nearby coffee table

Arthur had already arranged several dozen paperback copies in a series of inviting semicircles.

Natalie appeared in the doorway. "You're not dressed," she scolded.

"We've got time," he said, sliding his arms around the small of her back. "Making sure things look good."

"Have you thought any more about the center?" Natalie asked, gazing up at him

Arthur exhaled. "Yeah. I think we ought to go for it. "

"I've looked into plots of land that could be good. Some are really beautiful. Bit pricey though, of course."

"It'll be pricey no matter what," Arthur said. "But hopefully worth it."

"It will be." Natalie leaned in and kissed him. "We can talk about it later. I'm going to finish getting ready. People are coming at five, right?"

"Five, yes."

Arthur watched her go, then meandered over to the large living room window and gazed at the shadows of clouds passing over the grassy mounds of the Kingsmill golf course. The morning light filtered through the windows, keeping out the weather, leaving him enveloped only by the warmth of the sun.

Drawn by sudden movement in the pond, he sipped his tea and watched the widening ripples and small splashes toward the center. A gray fin broke the surface. *Moby.*

Arthur chuckled. The sight of the big catfish filled him with a giddy sense of rightness and permanence. For a moment the fish frolicked along the surface before sinking back into the dark water. The ripples smoothed into nothingness, once more becoming the pond.

ACKNOWLEDGMENTS

Of all manuscripts to date, *The Atheist* has inspired from family, friends and colleagues the most fervent feedback and debate. Whether they felt it in urgent need, or something of the book's inherent spirit energized their opinions, I can't be sure. Maybe a combination of both. Either way, I am extraordinarily indebted to all who read, reread, noted on, emailed about, and discussed with me the evolving organism that came to be the book you now hold.

First, I must acknowledge my grandfather, Jay Robinson, who, in addition to always being so supportive of my creative pursuits (a form of paying it forward, I imagine, as he himself is a life-long artist), also had the misfortune of indirectly inspiring the central event of this book when lightning struck his home in Williamsburg, VA, and left him temporarily homeless. As of this writing, he's 100 years old, still painting and has since enjoyed years living in his reconstructed house.

Thank you to Dr. Bridget Reynolds, much the spiritual stimulant of the initial composition who also popped the book's cherry as its first reader. Every page of that first rough draft still bears her immaculate handwritten notes. She passed it to her mother, Mary, whose readership I am also grateful for.

A big thank you goes to my own mother, Dianne, the only non-editor who read *The Atheist* more than twice, and who, unlike the unconditional ego-stroker many writing seminars warn about, never bites her tongue when she doesn't like something. If a book or story of mine doesn't jibe with her, she has no qualms in quickly forgetting it. She never forgot *The Atheist,* her favorite, and the one she most promotes.

Thank you to Pamela Vescera, a colleague and friend who offered great advice; Sheri Norris, longtime friend and reader with an actively insightful pen; Gene Wilkie, for the ever-enthusiastic support; Kathryn Farren, close friend and fellow writer whose characteristically sage feedback and passion for the story carried me far; Jon Berke, another longtime friend of unfailing support and honesty; Ryan Rowen, friend since kindergarten and always reliable for a stimulating and broad-minded conversation about all things cosmic or cultural; my father, Tom, for the constant support and readership even though my stuff isn't exactly in his wheelhouse; Lani Furr, who despite having not yet met me in person, still gave me wonderful and enthusiastic feedback. Gratitude must also extend to fellow scribe Leslie Ann Moore for pointing me toward Muse Harbor.

The enormous and penultimate thank you must go to Dave Workman, my editor at Muse Harbor Publishing whose tireless championing and challenging pushed me and the book beyond prior boundaries, and who over many digital dialogues —and, eventually, in-person, Scotch-lubed conversations and dog-walks to the beach—offered invaluable insights and ideas. Much gratitude must also extend to Eileen Workman, my assiduous line editor and a very profound mind.

AUTHOR'S BIO

An avid writer since age 7, award-winning author Mike Robinson began selling professionally at 19, placing various speculative fiction stories in magazines, anthologies, e-zines and podcasts. He is the author of the novels *Skunk Ape Semester*, *The Prince of Earth*, the short story collection *Too Much Dark Matter, Too Little Gray* and the non-linear trilogy "The Enigma of Twilight Falls", which includes the novels *The Green-Eyed Monster*, *Negative Space* and *Waking Gods*.

A native of Los Angeles, Mike is also a screenwriter and producer, and edits the online magazine *Literary Landscapes*, the official publication of GLAWS, The Greater Los Angeles Writers Society. His official website is:

www.mikerobinson-author.com